Pure & Simple

Cyndy Beckhardt

*"Never give up.
Your dreams are always
worth reaching for."*

Acknowledgements

Creativity, writing and a good imagination have always been a part of me, since I was a little girl. I was reminded of these characteristics when my mother passed away a couple years ago. Tucked in the bottom drawer of my father's dresser was a handmade book that I had made for him when I was in elementary school. I had taken a piece of cardboard and cut it into two rectangles. I lined the inside of them with a piece of kitchen wallpaper. You know, the old yellow and orange kitchen colors from the '60s and '70s.

Drawing paper, which is now a tarnished yellow, was used to create the front and back cover. These pages were cut to size and bound to the cardboard using royal blue duct tape. The story itself is a rendition of Charles Schulz's "Happiness is a … Warm Puppy." I created my own ideas of happiness and drew a picture to represent each one.

The first page reads: "To My dad for Father's Day" in pale green marker. The pages, six of them, were stapled together in sets of three and then taped together using masking tape, before being taped inside the cardboard covers. I must say my crafting skills were pretty good considering the book is still in excellent condition for being about fifty years old. The last page reads, "Happinss is a flower to smell" written in cursive with a red marker, and yes the 'e' is missing in happiness.

I was surprised and pleased that my father was proud of the little book and kept it all his life, and that my mother kept it for the rest of her life. Somewhere in this story is the message that we should never give up on something that we were passionate about when we were younger. Even if it takes you half your life to circle around to that talent or gift, take a chance and step out of your comfort zone. Believe in yourself.

This book would not have been possible without the assistance of many people. A heartfelt thank you to my editor, Frances Archer, who is the first one to read my stories from beginning to end. You have taught me a great deal about writing and I appreciate your patience and candid comments that push me to be a better writer.

A sincere thank you to Robin Surface, my publisher and owner of Fideli Publishing. You were my first contact on my journey as an author. You have empowered me to achieve something I thought I wasn't capable of accomplishing.

As the editing takes place, Kelly Maher, my illustrator, is busy crafting the cover for the book. Part way through the cover design, I changed gears. After pitching the new idea to Kelly, she crafted a few pencil sketches before diving into the original. I thank you Kelly for all your insight, time, patience, and hard work. You are a very talented young lady and it's a privilege to work with you.

In addition to thanking my friends and family, who are always putting up with my ramblings, I need to thank a few other special people. First, I'd like to thank Heather Miller, one of my co-workers, for her insight when it came to writing the hot air balloon scene in my story. Your description of the ride was perfect and has propelled me to take my own hot air balloon ride in the fall.

A special thank you to my friend, Dana and my niece, Katy. Both of you took the time to read my story in its unfinished state and provide me with useful feedback.

Last, but never least, I must thank my husband, Charlie, for his baseball knowledge. Your years spent coaching our son's youth baseball games along with your thirty-five plus years of experience announcing play-by-play on our local radio station for high school sports teams, allowed me to create realistic dialogue within the pages of my story. Your support, as I delve into a journey that unfolded in a way I never dreamed possible, is deeply appreciated.

Chapter One

Matt tossed off the covers, showered and dressed before collecting his belongings and heading to his Jeep. He pulled out of the hotel parking lot, his last overnight stop, before reaching his cabin in the hills of West Virginia. He was done with work. Done with women. And done with his current lifestyle, at least for the next few months, if he had it his way. He left LA five days ago longing to escape his high-paced acting career and immerse himself into the pure and simple life he grew up with. As he rolled down Main Street, he spotted a little café and pulled alongside the curb. He didn't remember seeing the place when he traveled home three years ago. Sitting in his Jeep, he contemplated if he could dart inside to grab a snack without being recognized.

He had his fill of interactions with people to last him a lifetime and needed to break free from a lifestyle that was consuming his essence, and allow himself to breathe again. The only place that felt like home was the cabin in the mountains of West Virginia. His parents had purchased the vacation home when he was a young boy. Little did he know, it would turn into a haven where he could relax without anyone having any preconceptions that he was different from everyone else.

Taking a chance, Matt stepped into the café. After purchasing a coffee and peach Danish, he headed for the door. Just by chance he looked up and glanced towards one of the tables in the far corner behind the door. She was sitting with her head buried in a book, and casually looked up and smiled at him. He slowed his stride as he opened the door and had to sidestep as a couple entered the café. Turning to leave he felt compelled to take another look at the woman. As if she could predict his actions, her head came up and she pleasantly smiled again.

Walking to his Jeep he mumbled, "Don't even think about it, Matt? ... You know what your first long-term relationship got you ... Besides, you can't even get past first base. So just get in your Jeep and drive, before you decide to do something dumb and impulsive."

Matt couldn't get to the cabin fast enough. Peace and quiet was what he needed, with no one around to converse with. He had enough of the nonstop work hours on his last television season and needed time to fully unwind. He was pushed to the limits and he pushed himself. The cabin was just the place to recharge. Everyone who lived nearby knew him before he turned into a heartthrob television star. He was just Matt to the locals, and he loved it.

As he approached the ramp to the expressway he accelerated, but the engine only revved and slowed to a crawl. "Unbelievable!" he grumbled, slamming his hands onto the steering wheel, as he drifted over to the shoulder of the road. "Who in the world is going to come out this far and pick *me* up?" he said, lowering his head onto his hands.

He was about fifty miles from the cabin in the Briery Mountains and didn't feel right asking one of his older neighbors to make the trip down to get him. He considered flagging someone down, but given his popularity he nixed that idea in a heartbeat. He was about two miles from the café and since there was enough daylight, he decided to walk back. After placing a shirt in the window to keep his Jeep from getting towed, he locked it and left his belongings in the back seat figuring whoever gave him a lift would have to come back along the same route. As he walked down the shoulder of the road, the woman in the café drifted into the forefront of his mind.

* * *

"Well, that was interesting," Megan said.

"What was interesting?" asked Kayla as she walked up and sat across from her sister.

"Did you see that guy who walked out of here a few minutes ago? I swear I've seen him somewhere, but I just can't put my finger on where."

"Was he cute?" inquired Kayla.

"Not sure. But his eyes were lovely and mesmerized me for about three seconds. And don't go getting any ideas, Kayla," said Megan, seeing a grin emerge on her sister's face.

"So, how's the studying coming along?" asked Kayla quickly changing the topic.

"Not too good. I just can't seem to find a quiet spot to concentrate on all this anatomy. I need to pass this pre-med class. Every time I turn around someone wants my help fixing something or carrying something. I hate to tell people no, but ..."

"Look, Meg, you do too much for everyone here in Fairmont, it's about time you focus on doing something for yourself. When is your exam?"

"You know I enjoy helping others, it's in my blood. And my first exam is the second Thursday of September and my midterm is on Tuesday, the fifth of October. I'm making myself a bunch of notecards to help me memorize the different parts of the ears, nose and throat. It's really very fascinating!"

"Maybe anatomy is fascinating for you," quipped Kayla, "but it looks like a lot of hard work to me. I know you care about everyone, but you'll be able to care for them in a different way when you have your medical degree. And isn't that what you want?"

Megan nodded.

"I have a suggestion that might help you with your studies," Kayla said with a grin.

"And what would that be, sister of mine?" asked Megan curiously.

"Remember Aunt Linda and Uncle Paul?" asked Kayla.

"Of course," replied Megan, rolling her eyes. "You're acting like we haven't seen them in years. We just spent two weekends with them this past month. Get to the point, Kayla. I've got too much studying to do for you to drag out whatever it is you've conjured up. And if I know you, and I do, you've already set something in motion."

"You always could detect one of my plans even before I get the enjoyment of executing it. Anyway, since Aunt Linda and Uncle Paul always head down to Florida in September to get away from the cold ... I gave them a call a couple days ago to see if they would be willing to let you stay at their place this semester."

"You did what?"

"Look, you hardly ask for anything. I just thought it was time I did something for *you*. I know how hard you've worked to get to this point, not to mention all the odd jobs you took to supplement my own education. Aunt Linda and Uncle Paul are more than happy to help out. So go pack a couple bags," Kayla said with a smile.

"Kayla!" exclaimed Megan reaching across the table to squeeze her sister's hands. "Thank you," said Megan, but her smile quickly turned into a look of concern. "But I can't push Aunt Linda and Uncle Paul out of their house before they're ready."

"No worries," said Kayla with a grin. "They decided to meet up with some friends for a couple of weeks this year and said it would work out perfectly. There's only one condition. Well ... two," said Kayla grimacing and peering up into her sister's face.

"And what might they be?" asked Megan.

"You have to take care of Bosley for a week because Uncle Ryan, who usually watches him, is out of town and won't be able to swing by to pick him up until the end of next week."

"I love Bosley! He's such a friendly dog and smart, too. And two?"

"Aunt Linda and Uncle Paul need a lift to the airport Saturday afternoon."

"I think I can handle that," said Megan. "Wow, Sis! How can I ever repay you?"

"Passing your classes will be good enough," said Kayla. "Mom and Dad would have been proud of you. You've worked so hard for your college degree. And now that I'm married, you'll be able to start your medical degree as a full-time student next year. So go pack a few bags. I'll keep an eye on your apartment and collect your mail while you're away."

Megan got up and walked around the table to give her sister a warm hug and kiss. As she collected her belongings, she glanced up just in time to see the man she saw earlier re-enter the café.

He rubbed his hands on his pants as he strolled up to the counter and began a conversation with Dan, the co-owner of the shop and her brother-in-law. Dan's shoulders were broad and his dirty blond hair was secured to his head with a blue bandana, as Megan watched him lean his forearm onto the counter. After several minutes he glanced their way and waved Kayla over to join him. Within minutes Kayla was walking back towards her with a smile plastered on her face.

"I know what *that* look means," smirked Megan. "What favor do you need now?"

"I don't, but it seems that the gentleman by the counter needs a ride up to Briery Mountains. His Jeep just broke down near the entrance to the highway and since it's after five, Nate's garage isn't going to be open until tomorrow morning. He gave Dan the address and, coincidentally, he lives across the street from Aunt Linda and Uncle Paul. Do you have any objections to a driving companion?" asked Kayla. "He's pretty good-looking, too," she tossed in.

Megan rolled her eyes, hoping she hadn't given away her own inward fascination with the man. Apparently it worked, because Kayla didn't make the connection with this guy and the one she mentioned earlier. Megan watched him stiffen up, as she walked toward the counter, and briefly wondered what caused the reaction.

"Hi, I'm Megan Barnes. I've been recruited to give you a ride," said Megan stretching out her hand.

"Hi, I'm Matt Wilson. It's nice to meet you. I hope I'm not putting you out," said Matt as he shook her hand.

Megan felt self-confidence in his firm grip, despite his tense looking shoulders, which relaxed when she dropped his hand. "No problem. I'm heading that way, thanks to my little sister here."

"You're welcome!" chimed in Kayla.

"Can you give me about an hour?" asked Megan. "I need to collect several things from my apartment.

"Sure," replied Matt, "after all, you're the one doing me the favor."

"Kayla, do Aunt Linda and Uncle Paul know I'm coming?"

"I talked to them on Tuesday and told them I'd call when I had a chance to talk to you. They figured you'd agree, since they know how much you love the mountain air, and said they would get your usual room ready. I'll give them a call, while you're packing."

With her head in the clouds, Megan collected her class book and bookbag from the back table. Despite having to drive almost fifty miles from Fairmont to Briery Mountains, Megan couldn't resist the promise of peace and quiet. She needed time to complete her classes and prepare for her MCAT, because she was hoping to get into West Virginia Medical School, where her father had completed his studies. Kayla was right, she needed to devote her time to something she wanted, so she could give back to her community in a different way. Her final goal was to become an otolaryngologist, which was hard to find in a small town. Currently, Dr. Rhodes was the only specialty doctor in Fairmont. He had known Megan since she was a young teenager and was excited to learn of her career path. He even offered her the extra office space in his practice once she gets her license. Of course, he's more than willing to provide any clinical hours she might need for her education, too.

Chapter Two

Megan walked out of the café, turned left and briskly walked the block to her one-bedroom apartment. Her Uncle Paul, a retired CPA, who helped manage her and Kayla's finances following their parents' deaths, had found the renovated apartment eleven years ago. Megan insisted they live close to their high school so she and Kayla could finish school with their current friends and didn't have to deal with yet another change in their lives. With their family's help, the courts allowed Megan to be a foster parent for her sister, although her aunts and uncles were available whenever they needed assistance. Their inheritance had been set up in a trust fund, according to their parent's will, which limited the amount of funds they received every month, until Megan turned thirty. Determined to make it on their own, Megan worked to supplement their income, until Kayla was married. When Megan started college, Kayla and Dan opened up their café close by, and as luck would have it Megan was able to focus on her studies and earn some extra income whenever she needed to.

Megan stepped inside her apartment and scanned the room. It was small, but adequate. The kitchen was open and positioned against the far wall with an island in the middle of the floor. The remaining space was big enough to create a comfortable living room, eating and study area. Forcing herself to focus, she went around and pulled the plugs on all the appliances, and adjusted the thermostat. She then made a beeline for the linen closet in the short hallway that led to the bathroom and her bedroom, and retrieved two duffle bags.

She placed the bags on her bed and selected several pants, tops and jogging gear to take with her. Opening the closet, she chose two sweatshirts because she knew the weather would be turning cool in the evenings as her semester drew on. She placed several pairs of shoes and undergarments in the other bag and sat them near the front door. Toiletries were not a concern, because she kept a bin at her aunt and uncle's place under the bathroom sink, due to her frequent visits.

Two books for her anatomy class and several leaflets were strewn out on the coffee table. She collected everything and fit all of it into her book bag, except her fat anatomy book. After retrieving her music folder from the stand, she squeezed it in her book bag before folding up the stand and packing up her oboe. Once everything was by the door, she headed back down the hallway to turn down the temperature on the water heater in the utility closet. Making her way back to the front door she quickly scanned the room before loading up her pick-up truck.

Megan hadn't given any thought to her initial eye contact with Matt until she climbed behind the wheel and was heading back to the café. She was drawn to his deep-set eyes, which up-close appeared to be a mixture of hazel and blue. He had about four inches on her five-eight stature and solid body. He was slightly broad across the shoulders, but his muscles were clearly defined in his upper arms. She had a brief déjà vu moment when she let go of his hand by the counter, but her mind was unwilling to place the familiarity she saw in his face. A single crease formed between his eyes when he shook her hand which made her wonder what thoughts were rolling through his head when she introduced herself. His face was clean shaven and his thin lips rose into a pleasant smile, revealing round cheeks that projected a pure sense of sincerity and enhanced the warmth of his eyes. His straight light brown hair, which was layered and parted on his left, brushed the collar of his shirt. Shaking the thought of him from her mind she focused on topics of conversation for the hour-long drive into the mountains, then decided it would have to unfold naturally. Besides, she was usually a good conversationalist.

Pulling in front of the café, she took a calming breath before hopping out of her truck and strolling through the door to collect her passenger.

"Hi! Sorry, it took me a bit longer than I thought it would," apologized Megan. "I wasn't prepared to spend the next couple of months at my aunt and uncle's place. If I forgot anything I can pick it up after class one day."

"No worries," said Matt. "Dan and I were discussing baseball and who's in the running for the wildcard spot."

"Yeah, did you know that . . ." Dan started, but Kayla quickly elbowed him in the ribs.

"That's enough, Dan. I'm sure Matt would like to get up to his place, and our aunt and uncle are expecting Megan before the sun sets, so they need to be on their way," said Kayla, turning to face her sister.

Dan glanced at Kayla, who gave him one of those "keep your mouth shut" looks. Megan sensed there was something her sister didn't want her to know, but she didn't have time to corner her and draw it out. After eyeing Kayla suspiciously, Megan turned her attention to Matt.

"You ready to go?" she asked.

"I am, indeed," Matt replied.

"Send me a text when you get there," said Kayla. "I'll worry if I don't hear from you."

"You got it, Sis. Thanks again."

* * *

Matt followed Megan out the door and was surprised to find her walking toward a nice-looking beige truck. As he got in, he noticed an anatomy book on the seat behind her. He had wondered what book her head had been buried in when he first saw her, but his assumption that she was studying to be a lawyer now seemed unlikely. After buckling up, he glanced towards her with an inquisitive gaze.

"What?" said Megan, catching his look.

"Nothing," he said. "It just amuses me that you drive a truck."

"Women can drive trucks, too," she replied as she started the engine. "If you knew me, it would make perfect sense."

"Care to elaborate?" he asked.

"Not really," she responded, displaying a bit of irritation with his stereotyping.

He watched her shake her head before pulling out of the parking spot. After a few moments of strained silence she asked, "So how long have you had the cabin in the hills?"

"My parents bought it about twenty-five years ago," he replied, relieved by the calmness in her voice. "It's quiet and allows me to rest and relax, which is what I'm craving right now."

She relaxed her grip on the steering wheel and was quiet for a stretch, as if she needed a moment to process what he just told her.

"Well, there's no better place than the hills of West Virginia," she finally said with a smile.

Abruptly changing the topic, Matt said, "I left my bags in my Jeep. If you don't mind, could you pull up behind it so I can retrieve my things?"

"No problem. Just let me know when we're getting close," said Megan.

They rode in awkward silence for the next mile until Matt said, "There it is, up there on the right. It won't take me but a few moments to grab my things. Is there enough room in the back seat, or should I put my bags in the truck bed?" inquired Matt.

"There might be room for one bag in the back seat, but your other gear will have to go in the truck bed."

Matt returned carrying a guitar case and three duffle bags. He placed the guitar in the back seat and the bags in the truck bed. As he climbed back inside, he said, "Thanks, that's everything. Dan mentioned a shop I can call in the morning to pick up my Jeep?"

"Yup, I'll give you the number for Nate's when we get to your place. He's excellent and reasonably priced for repairs," said Megan.

"Thanks again. I'm sorry for any inconvenience and I'm willing to fill up your truck the next time you need gas."

"I appreciate that, but I was heading up to my aunt and uncle's place anyway. So, how long are you planning to stay?"

"Through January, if I have any say in the matter," Matt replied, as he briefly tapped his fingers on the car door.

Looking out of the corner of his eye, he studied the woman seated next to him. Her hair was a smooth cinnamon red, and curled slightly under as it brushed the tops of her shoulders. She had an endearing, slightly round face with a nicely shaped nose and hazel eyes that sparkled when she smiled, reminding him of his mother. She was fairly trim and her upper arms looked firm. He wouldn't say she was beautiful, but definitely very pretty and appealing. At the café he thought she looked young, but her mannerisms at the counter demonstrated self-assurance and a mature attitude. And the ease with which she handled the truck made him wonder again why she drove one. He shook his head to stop his wandering mind, then slowly leaned back in the seat and closed his eyes. Within minutes he dozed off.

* * *

Megan's thoughts drifted to wanting to know more about the man beside her. His answer about his family owning the cabin across the street from her aunt and uncle for twenty-five years stirred her curiosity. Glancing his way she thought, *so much for having an alert companion on the drive up.* She decided to let him be in spite of her curiosity. However, she made a mental note to study his face again when she pulled off the expressway. With her companion sound asleep, Megan turned the radio on softly and slipped in a Kenny Loggins CD for the rest of the drive.

Matt was still asleep when Megan pulled off the highway fifty minutes later. She drifted towards a stoplight and was disappointed when it changed green. After turning down Willow Street she paused at the stop sign, and took a few moments to discreetly observe the man next to her. She knew she had seen him before, but her mind still wouldn't allow her to figure it out. *How could it with all the anatomy rolling around in it?* she asked herself. As he started to stir, Megan set the truck in motion.

As she wound her way up the side of the mountain, her thoughts drifted back to how Matt's family had come to own the cabin across the street from her aunt and uncle. She never remembered seeing him during their numerous visits and he didn't seem like he was *that* much older than herself.

As Megan crested the hill into Briery Mountain, Matt woke up. The road leveled off revealing a mature and nicely developed neighborhood. The community consisted of thirty houses spread out on each side of the road. They were all designed as Cape Cods, but with varying attributes that made each one slightly different. They didn't sit on top of each other like traditional neighborhoods, but were laid out with about half an acre to each lot. Not too small and not too big for some of the older residents to handle. *Well, almost,* thought Megan, remembering some previous visits.

"Wow!" exclaimed Matt, "the tips of the trees are starting to change."

His comment made Megan reassess her first impression of him. Maybe he wasn't as judgmental as their initial interaction led her to believe.

"Yes, they are," Megan whispered under her breath. She smiled with the realization that she was going to be around to witness the full effect of the fall colors this year.

As they rolled under the stone and iron archway with the development name Briery Mountain spanning the arch, Matt said, "Look at those elm trees. They've really grown. I helped plant them three years ago, when I came home. They must be twelve feet taller."

"They do grow fast. I remember when the old tree on the right fell across the road damaging the tree on the left side," said Megan, intrigued by his knowledge of the event.

The development was unique with each house built catty corner from the house across the street, allowing each owner some privacy. Dan was correct in accessing Matt's house number. Aunt Linda and Uncle Paul's place was on the right side of the road coming up through the mountain and Matt's place was slightly before it on the left side. Despite this design, everybody was well acquainted with each other and helped one another whenever the need arose, which was quite frequently, from Megan's perspective. Going down the backside of the hill was the town's one and only shopping center. It had everything the folks needed from groceries to hardware, which is another reason everybody knew each other.

As Megan pulled into the mouth of Matt's driveway, she noticed a bunch of tree limbs scattered on the ground. After putting the truck into park, Matt jumped down and started clearing a path in his driveway. Megan killed the engine and joined him. Working silently they piled the branches and twigs at the head of the driveway. Megan felt his eyes glance her way several times, and for the second time wished she knew what he was thinking.

When the driveway was cleared, Matt unloaded his things and thanked her. She backed out of his driveway, drove across the street to her aunt and uncle's place and parked her truck. As she unloaded one of her bags, Matt surprised her by stepping up behind her and taking it out of her hand.

"Thanks, but you don't need to do that," responded Megan.

"It's the least I can do after giving me a lift up here."

Megan relinquished her hold and opened the gate to her aunt and uncle's walkway. Matt sidestepped around her then followed her onto the front porch. As she reached the landing, Linda and Paul opened the door. For being in their sixties they were fairly trim, partially due to the help they always provided their older neighbors.

"Meg, my dear, it's good to see you," greeted Linda as she gave Megan a hug and a kiss. Uncle Paul squeezed her so hard all she could do was squeak out a small hello.

"Oh, my lands! Look who's back in town! Why, Matt, you sure are a sight for sore eyes. What's it been, two, three years since you've been back up here in these hills?" exclaimed Linda.

"Three years, this time," said Matt. "It's good to be home."

Megan watched intently as her aunt embraced Matt like old friends. Tilting her head Megan asked, "You know Matt?"

"We sure do," said Paul, giving Matt a pat on the back. "His family used to spend time here over the summers."

Megan was puzzled even more. "Then how come I don't remember him? Kayla and I have been coming up here since we were little and I don't remember seeing Matt."

With the mention of Kayla, Meg remembered she needed to text her sister to let her know they arrived safely. As she texted, her aunt replied, "I guess you just missed each other or his family could have been traveling. I don't know, Meg. Well, anyways, let's not stand out here on the porch. The sun is going down and it's starting to get a little chilly."

As Linda led them down the hallway to the kitchen, Megan made a mental note to ask Kayla if she remembered seeing Matt before. As soon as they entered the kitchen, Megan heard loud barking coming from the back deck. When her uncle opened the door Bosley bounded inside and ran straight to Megan. She squatted on the floor to greet the tan colored mutt, and received a face full of kisses before tumbling backwards and landing on the floor in front of Matt's feet. As he leaned over to help her up, Bosley took the opportunity to pounce on him and plant several kisses on his face, too. Laughing they helped each other off the floor and managed to climb into the chairs at the table.

"Looks like Bosley has missed both of you," said Linda with a laugh. "I've kept some soup warm and there's just enough for the two of you," she added as she ladled some out into bowls. "Now eat up, you both look hungry and tired."

"Thanks," said Matt. "I am a little bit hungry and I know some of your homemade soup will hit the spot. What kind did you make?"

"Gnocchi soup," said Linda.

"Is that the one with the little potato dumplings in it?" asked Matt.

"Yes, and if I recall, it's your favorite," said Linda.

Megan's mouth dropped wide open. "You've fed him before, too?"

"Of course, dear. He *is* our neighbor," Linda answered in a flippant manner, which was highly unlike her.

"And contrary to what others might think, we do have a life up here in these hills. We don't sit around in our cabins all day and read," piped in Paul, after getting Bosley settled down.

Megan turned her head to face Matt and he looked up just in time to see her brow furrow and glare at him.

"What?" asked Matt, turning his palms up and shrugging his shoulders.

"I feel like I've missed something," said Megan.

For the first time in a long time, it hit Megan how much she had missed out on life, and the day-to-day events that had transpired around her and some, apparently, right under her nose. *How could I have missed seeing this man every time my sister and I came up to the cabin to spend time with my aunt and uncle?* Megan turned her attention to the bowl of soup in front of her, and without speaking or looking up, she consumed the whole thing.

When Matt finished he glanced at her briefly before walking his empty bowl over to the sink. On the way out, he stuck his head into the living room and thanked Linda for the soup and said he would see them later. As Linda walked him to the door she asked, "How long are you going to be in town this time?"

This time, wondered Megan. *How often has he come to town?*

"I'm aiming for the end of January," said Matt.

Megan walked over to lean on the wall near the entrance to the kitchen and looked down the hallway as her uncle stepped into the foyer.

"Thanks for the ride, Meg," Matt said, staring directly into her eyes.

She didn't care for his use of her nickname. Aunt Linda and Uncle Paul were the only ones who called her Meg. Well, almost. He had some nerve speaking so casually, when they had only met a few hours ago.

"You're welcome," replied Megan, barely moving her lips.

It was too complicated to explain the hurt she was feeling inside. Her aunt and uncle knew Matt and she didn't, intensifying her feelings about missing out on life. She suddenly resented Matt and decided she might not like him.

After Matt left, Paul turned to face Megan. "Did he do something to offend you? You weren't very friendly."

"It was nothing."

"There must have been something, Meg," stated her uncle.

It wasn't her fault her parents had died before she and Kayla had finished high school. And the fact that she focused her efforts on getting Kayla through college first and had to wait so long to pursue her own degrees, made her wonder how many *other* things she was missing.

"Don't you remember ..." but before her uncle could finish his sentence Aunt Linda elbowed him in the ribs.

"What was that for?" Megan asked, staring at her aunt.

"Never mind, dear, you were going to say something ..." prompted Linda.

"It's too complicated to explain right now, besides I'm tired and my brain feels like it's on overload. Do you mind if I just call it a night and head to bed?"

"Of course not, Meg," said Linda. Walking over she put her arm around her niece's shoulders and ushered her up the stairs while her uncle followed quietly with her bags.

Chapter Three

Waking in the early morning hours, Matt felt unsettled. He had a restless night as his thoughts constantly drifted back to Megan. Despite his desire to hide from the public's view, he wasn't used to women treating him like he was unpopular. She was definitely different from the women he had dated in LA. When she got out of the truck to help him clear away the branches in his driveway, he wondered if she had a natural tendency to help out, or was she just trying to show off, which is what most women did upon meeting him. Sitting on the edge of the bed, he tried to sort out his thoughts. Finally, he got up and fixed a cup of coffee before grabbing a blanket and his cell phone. Stepping onto the back deck he inhaled the crisp morning air. After cleaning off one of the lounge chairs, he wrapped himself in the blanket, and eventually dozed off into a deep sleep.

At eight o'clock Matt's cell phone went off and he just about leaped out of his chair. Irritated, he picked it up and was about to give it a heave-ho off the deck, when he noticed it was Paul and Linda's number.

"Hello," he answered, trying not to sound too aggravated.

"Oh, my. I'm so sorry to wake you, Matt," said Linda.

"That's okay, Ms. Linda," he answered, stifling a yawn.

"Dan called because Nate, the mechanic, stopped by the café late last night and Dan told him about your Jeep. Nate picked it up early this morning and is working on it right now. Evidently the fuse for the gas pedal blew. He had to order the part from the dealer down the street, which should be delivered by noon. So, your Jeep should be ready to pick up sometime this afternoon."

"That's great," Matt replied as a shiver hit him, forcing him to collect the blanket and mug and head back into the kitchen.

Linda continued, "Meg has to drive us into town this afternoon so we can catch our flight to Florida. We thought you might like to ride in with us."

"I'd appreciate that, if Meg doesn't mind," said Matt, wondering if she was still miffed by the fact that he knew her aunt and uncle. "What time are you leaving?"

"Our flight is at three-thirty this afternoon, but I'd like to leave here around twelve-thirty if that'll work for you."

"That's fine. It'll give me enough time to shower and eat something," said Matt. "I'll head over when I'm done."

Matt hung up and realized how much he missed the ordinary activities that were practically non-existent in LA. *Too many people trying to tell me what to do with my free time, instead of letting the day unfold naturally,* he thought. If he was being honest with himself, he didn't know how much longer he'd be able to keep up with his current lifestyle. The money was great and he had invested wisely, thanks to Megan's Uncle Paul, who helped him navigate the world of finance — and for Matt it was high finance. With Paul's guidance he had socked away most of his money, allowing him to do whatever he wanted when he decided to retire from his current line of work. And in his mind, it was getting closer.

In the shower, his thoughts traveled back to Megan again. He had been racking his brain trying to remember if he had seen her in the yard across the street years ago. The closest he came was an image of two girls running around the yard chasing a barking dog the summer before he went off to college, which meant Megan had probably been in middle school. But that fuzzy image was years ago and he was now thirty-three, making her around twenty-nine. The fact that she didn't recognize him intrigued him, more than he cared to admit.

* * *

Driving Matt back into town wasn't Megan's idea, but he would probably need her help to pick up his Jeep at some point, and doing it on the way back from the airport would result in fewer interruptions with her studies.

Not wanting to get into any schoolwork before driving to the airport, Megan decided to go for a jog to help wake her up and release some tension. After changing into jogging clothes, she poked her head into her aunt and uncle's bedroom, and said, "I'll be back in about twenty-five minutes. I'm going for a quick jog."

"Okay, dear. Enjoy the fresh air," said Linda.

Stepping onto the porch Megan did a few stretches before pushing in her earbuds and setting her workout music on her phone. She started out at a slow pace, but gradually increased her speed as she headed to the right then down the street. Taking in a few deep breaths she tried to clear her head, but despite her efforts Matt kept entering her thoughts. She couldn't stop wondering about her uncle's unfinished remark. *Why does it seem like everyone knows who Matt is but me?* she wondered. She had fourteen weeks left in the semester and she was determined not to let anything, or for that matter, anyone, stand in her way. Her curiosity was just going to have to wait.

* * *

With a fresh cup of coffee in hand, Matt stepped out onto his front porch. He caught sight of Megan in black leggings and a purple top. As she ran up the street, her ponytail swayed in rhythm with her steps. The tautness of her legs as she sprinted the last several feet and bounded up the porch steps by twos impressed him. She entered the cabin and reappeared shortly with a bottle of water. While pacing across the front yard she took an occasional sip, as she fiddled with her phone. Taking a deep breath Matt backed away from the railing and forced himself to go inside to scrape together something for lunch.

Sitting at the kitchen table he quickly became aware of the solitude he had been missing. The privacy and calmness offered him time to examine his life. As he ate he considered the path his life had taken. His career as a baseball player was cut short when he suffered an elbow injury his second year in the major leagues. He had pitched two games and was off to a great second season. It took him several months of physical therapy following surgery, before the doctors gave him their final, but devastating report.

The acting opportunity fell in his lap when a producer noticed him in a couple baseball commercials he had done after he was brought up to the major leagues. He was surprised, but quickly accepted the producers offer as the lead in a TV series. *It's not that I hate my current career, but it's the lack of breaks that don't allow me time to do a few things I want to do, that upsets me ... and that's something I need to talk to Kyle about. If he can't reduce the load, then maybe I need to look for a new agent.*

As he placed his dirty plate in the sink his thoughts rolled around to the women he had dated and his lack of intimacy. Ever since his first girlfriend, Matt constantly struggled when it came to advancing any relationship on an intimate level. *It's not like the women aren't attractive,* he thought, *but they're always forcing themselves onto me and wanting me to spend my money on materialistic things. It's the hollowness of the relationship, the fact that the women want me around for my looks and kisses, which in my book isn't the basis for a long-term relationship. The chances of finding a woman that would truly care about my personal and physical scars just doesn't seem to exist.*

The one woman he decided to trust years ago caused his intimacy issues and put him in a plight he never wanted to experience again. Ever since, his trust level for any woman has been slim to none, leaving him and the woman wholly frustrated and unsatisfied. However, the risks far outweighed his need for satisfaction. So, the number of cold showers he endured just about equaled the number of failed relationships he had suffered, largely due to his trust level and lack of sexual prowess. Considering his age, it was quite embarrassing.

After slipping on his shoes, he walked across the street just as Megan stepped out onto the front porch carrying a large suitcase with both hands. As she was maneuvering the suitcase down the steps, Matt reached up and plucked it out of her hands.

His quick movement caught her by surprise, but she immediately recovered and thanked him. "I don't know *what* my aunt put in there, but it feels like a ton of bricks," she said laughing.

Matt chuckled at her remark as he placed the suitcase in the bed of her truck. When he turned around, he saw Megan coming out of the cabin with another suitcase. "Hang on, I'll ..." he started to say, but before he could grab the handle, Bosley came bounding out the door, leaped down the steps and headed straight for him. He tried to reach for the railing to brace himself for impact, but the dog was faster. Bosley planted his front paws right in the middle of Matt's chest, sending him flat on his back.

Megan dropped the suitcase and hurried down the steps to pull Bosley off Matt. Once she got hold of Bosley's collar, she leaned down and asked Matt if he was okay. He started to laugh until he touched the back of his head.

"Wow, I wasn't expecting that," he said as he gently moved his fingers through his hair.

"Here, give me your hand," said Megan. She grasped his hand and slowly pulled him up into a sitting position.

"Let me take a look," she said, holding onto Bosley's collar with one hand and kneeling behind him.

"Ouch!" said Matt as she touched his head.

"Sorry. I want to see if you're bleeding. I'll try to be gentle," said Megan.

When Megan found the spot, Matt said, "That's it, right where your fingertips just landed."

"Well, I'm happy to say you're not bleeding, but you've got a lump forming on the back of your head. Stay put while I get some ice."

Before Megan made it into the house, her aunt and uncle emerged. "Matt, what happened?" exclaimed Linda heading down the porch steps.

"Bosley just got a little excited when he saw me," said Matt.

"A little. How about a lot. He jumped on Matt and knocked him down to the ground," explained Megan. "I think he needs another training class," she added, turning Bosley over to her aunt.

"His excitement gets the best of him sometimes and he forgets not to jump on people. I'm sorry, Matt," Linda said as she headed inside with Bosley.

"Can I get you some ice?" asked Paul.

"I was just headed inside to get some," said Megan.

Matt watched Megan step past her uncle and into the cabin. She reappeared with a plastic bag full of ice and a kitchen towel. She wrapped the towel around the ice then sat on the ground next to Matt and placed it on his head. She held it there for several minutes before turning the job over to him.

"You got it?" Megan asked softly, leaning into his shoulder.

"Yeah, thanks for the ice. This is not how I envisioned starting off my vacation. You sure I'm not bleeding?" asked Matt.

Megan gently touched his arm to remove the ice pack and slid her fingers through his hair, starting at the nape of his neck, causing him to shiver at her touch. She made no comment about his reaction and said, "Happy to report, still no signs of blood, but you *are* going to have one heck of a bump. I want you to keep that ice on for the next twenty minutes. Do you still feel up to going to the airport?" questioned Megan.

"Yeah, I'm kind of stranded here without my Jeep. Just help me up and let me walk around for a couple minutes to get my bearings," he said.

Matt struggled to shake off the chill that ran through his body. It had been a long time since he spontaneously felt anything when a woman touched him and the feeling made him anxious. Holding the ice on his head, Matt made his way over to the passenger side of Megan's truck and got in. Once everyone else was settled in the truck, Megan reached over and patted Matt's arm to make sure he was ready to go. His arm jerked at her touch, but he pushed through his reaction and patted the back of her hand. "Let's get this show on the road," he said.

* * *

As she drove Megan recalled the look on her Aunt Linda's face as she tended to Matt's injury. She knew it well. It was the same kind of look her mother used to give her, as if she knew something was going to develop but wasn't willing to reveal her inkling until after it happened. She also caught the smile on her aunt's face as it widened, and was momentarily annoyed. *What was there to smile about?* wondered Megan.

On the way to Morgantown Municipal Airport, her Aunt Linda and Uncle Paul had lots of reminders about her stay.

"There are some frozen meals in the freezer," said Linda. "And enough to share with Matt," she tacked on.

"Thanks," said Megan, wondering why she felt inclined to suggest feeding Matt, too. The whole reason she came up to the cabin was to get away from everyone to focus on her classes.

"We had our mail forwarded to Florida and the newspaper delivery was stopped," said Paul, preventing her from dwelling on her aunt's suggestion. "Bosley's gear is all packed and ready to go when your Uncle Ryan is back in town. He'll call you when he can swing by to pick him up."

Once they arrived at the airport and were headed to security Linda glanced at the two of them and smiled again. "Now please keep an eye on each other," she said. "Give us a call if you have trouble with anything and don't study too hard," she added, giving Megan a gentle hug and kiss. "Take time to do a few other things, too."

"Same goes for you, Matt," said Paul. "Take some time to relax and enjoy the nice fall days ahead. The warm days and cool crisp nights should make the foliage magnificent this year. And Megan here knows just where to go to enjoy it, provided she remembers," he teased.

"Thanks, Uncle Paul," Megan replied, rolling her eyes, "but I came up here to study, remember?"

"Surely, you can take a little time for yourself," he countered. "Get into a routine and stick to it and that doesn't mean studying all day."

"Okay, okay," Megan answered, shaking her head and putting both hands in the air. If they didn't stop talking, they were going to end up missing their flight.

"You two have a good time," chimed in Matt. "And we'll keep an eye on each other. Promise," he said, glancing at Megan.

She felt like socking him in the arm, but remembered the bruise on his head. "Speaking of keeping an eye on each other, have a seat on the bench over there and let me take a look at that bump on your head."

"I'm good," Matt said, walking past the bench.

Megan shrugged her shoulders and followed Matt back down the hallway towards the main lobby. As they stepped out onto the sidewalk, a woman ran up to Matt and asked for his autograph and a picture, catching him off-guard. Megan was practically shoved off the sidewalk when a few other people noticed him and forced their way over to Matt, too. He glanced up to make sure she was okay before taking the outbursts and excitement in a calm, orderly manner. Megan was taken aback and walked across the drop-off area to wait under a tree, brushing invisible lint off her shirt, until he was done.

Patiently waiting she glanced up occasionally and watched as he dealt with everyone politely before he hustled over and firmly gripped her right elbow. With a purposeful stride, he led her back to her truck. She could tell he wasn't too happy about the encounter.

Once in her truck Megan asked, "Would you care to explain all that?"

"No, I would not," he answered leaning his head back into the head-rest with a little more force than he meant to. "Ouch!" he yelled, jerking his head forward.

Without saying a word Megan reached over and gently rubbed the back of his head before reaching for the half-melted bag of ice in the console. Looking at her he saw the genuine concern in her eyes.

"Sorry, I didn't mean to take that out on you," said Matt reaching up and taking the ice in his own hand.

"That's okay. When you're ready to talk, I'll be happy to listen," she told him.

"Thanks. I think I'd just like to pick up my Jeep and head back home."

"You okay to drive?"

"I think so, but I'd appreciate it if you'd follow me. If you don't mind?" he added.

"No problem. I know where you live," she said with a slight laugh and grin.

Megan drove him to the garage and waited while he paid Nate for the repairs. By the time they were on the road again it was almost two-thirty. As Megan followed him, her mind drifted back to the commotion at the airport. She wasn't dumb. She knew that if strangers recognized him, then he had to be some sort of celebrity, but it hadn't been a priority to look up his name online. Then she thought, *but he didn't act like he wanted me to know back at the airport, so I'll just leave it up to him to tell me.* Although, she had to admit the incident made him more intriguing.

* * *

Matt was still frustrated as he drove down the road, but he couldn't drive like a maniac with Megan close behind. She would surely think the injury to his head had caused more than a bump. *I feel horrible for grabbing her arm like that. But what are the odds of running into fans at such a small airport? Extremely rare,* thought Matt.

It was bound to happen one day when his guard was down, but he just wished it hadn't been today and, for some reason, with Megan. His anger eventually subsided as he drove and allowed himself to reminisce about the touch of her hand against his head. He was still worried about the sensations she ignited throughout his body when her fingers slid through his hair. *But how could such a small reaction cause such mayhem inside of me? What is it about her that makes my body react so differently from the other women I've dated?* he contemplated. She had no idea what her touch did to him, and he wasn't interested in revealing his reaction any time soon. He was done with women.

They pulled into their designated driveways at quarter to four, and Matt watched Megan get out of her truck, through his rearview mirror, and walk around to her backyard. She reappeared shortly trailing behind Bosley, on his leash, as he pulled her towards the front of the cabin. He then leaned forward and placed his head on the steering wheel. Within a few seconds, he heard a tapping sound on the window.

"You okay?" asked Megan.

Matt opened the door and knew she could see the irritation in his eyes.

"Yeah," he breathed out with a sigh. "This first day didn't go exactly as I hoped it would."

Before she could respond, Bosley tried to pull her back across the street. Matt spontaneously reached down and grabbed for the leash, catching her hand instead. He pulled back with her hand in his, and spoke to Bosley in a firm voice. "Sit."

"How'd you do that?" asked Megan.

Matt just shrugged his shoulders.

"I'm sorry today didn't unfold the way you planned. Would it help if we just start things over?"

"What?" he asked, drawing his eyes together.

"Hi, I'm Megan Amelia Barnes," she said, formally extending her other hand. "It's nice to meet you."

"Hi, Megan, I'm Matthew Wilson," he returned. "It's nice to meet you too."

"And this unruly long-haired mutt is Bosley, my aunt and uncle's unpredictable dog," she said with a laugh and broad smile on her face. And as if on cue, Bosley caught sight of a squirrel and yanked her down the driveway. "Are you going to be in town for long?" ask Megan as their hands separated.

"For several months," he said, as Bosley continued to pull her halfway across the street.

Before she was dragged into her own yard, he couldn't help but shake his head before smiling and letting out a slight laugh. She sure was good natured, despite Bosley's antics.

As she reached the top of the steps she hollered back. "That's nice. Then I'll see you around," she responded as if the conversation had continued on, uninterrupted. "I'm thinking Bosley is hun ... gry. Oh, Bosley. Sit, boy!" she commanded. And he did.

Matt made his way up the steps to his porch before Megan hollered over again.

"What are you doing Monday morning?"

Startled by the question Matt responded with a tentative, "Why?" He figured she found out what he did for a living and wanted to pump him for more information about his life.

"I like to go running in the morning. Would you like to join me? It usually helps to clear my head and I thought, from the looks of the muscles in your arms and legs that you do some type of exercising."

"That's pretty presumptuous of you. Have you been studying my muscles for long?" he teased.

Matt could only imagine the color rising in her checks from embarrassment. But he didn't leave her hanging long before answering, "Sure. What time?"

"Is six too early for you?" she asked.

"Nope, that'll work," said Matt. Then added, "And Meg?"

"Yeah?"

"I'm sorry for grabbing your arm roughly at the airport."

"It's okay. Like you said, today didn't turn out the way you planned." After a brief pause Megan yelled, "Hey!"

"Yes?"

"Feel free to bring along your phone if you like to listen to music while you run, because I do."

"Okay."

"And Matt?"

"Yesss ...?" he replied slower this time.

"It was nice to meet you. Have a good rest of your day," she said in a cheery voice, waving her hand.

"You too, Meg. See you Monday morning," Matt responded before entering his cabin and closing the door.

It took Matt only a few minutes to realize what she had done. She had kept him engaged in idle conversation to keep him from dwelling on the past few hours, and on top of that she made no comment about the way he looked when he got out of his Jeep. He didn't feel upset or overwhelmed any longer; he was just plain hungry and tired. *Nice, Meg. Thanks.*

After dinner, Matt stood on his front porch with a mug of coffee and could hear Megan call Bosley inside. Shortly after, he saw the lights go out and figured she had gone to bed. Knowing she was safe he headed inside, stripped down to his underwear, crawled into bed and set the alarm.

She was growing on him rather quickly and he really wasn't interested in testing the waters again, but he did promise Paul and Linda he would keep an eye on her while she was up here. His last short-term relationship ended several months ago when he caught his so-called girlfriend, Rachel, sitting on another guy's lap during a mid-season party. Shaking the uncomfortable memory from his head, he fell asleep with a picture of Megan being pulled across the street by Bosley.

* * *

Megan spent the rest of her day getting her belongings organized. When dinnertime rolled around she fed Bosley, then fixed herself a bowl of soup. It had been a long day and she was tired. As she ate, she decided a schedule would help with her studies, like her Uncle Paul suggested. And going for a run in the morning would be a good start. She could take care of any chores afterwards and study just about every afternoon until class or dinnertime.

Her pre-medical anatomy class was going to be the one to make or break her from advancing in her field. Studying for more than five hours a day would just overwhelm her, along with writing definitions onto index cards to help her study. Using the cards made it easier for her to memorize the terminology and she could add more cards following each class. With a mental schedule in place, Megan crawled into bed around ten o'clock and turned off the lights.

Chapter Four

Waking early Monday morning, Megan changed into gray leggings and a mint green exercise top before letting Bosley outside to do his business. When she hit the foyer, she glanced out the screen door and noticed Matt standing on his porch in a pale blue top and dark shorts, with a mug in his hands. She pivoted and headed toward the kitchen to fix herself a glass of orange juice. Eating something was out of the question, but she needed the sugars to give her a little bit of fuel. When she finished her juice, she grabbed her shoes and headed outside to lace them up on the porch steps. Pausing to stretch her calves and thighs, she looked up and watched Matt make his way across the street.

"Mornin'! I want to let you know that I'm not much of a talker in the morning, but I'm not trying to be rude. Okay?" said Megan.

"Okay, neither am I," said Matt.

"If I'm moving too slow or too fast for you, please don't feel obligated to keep my pace," she added.

"Alright."

Megan plugged in her ears, turned her music on and started out at a casual pace, but after five minutes she stepped it up a notch. She barely talked except to say or point out which direction she was heading. By the time they returned home they had run four miles.

"How about some breakfast? I'm fixing," said Megan as he passed her gate. When he turned around she noticed the crease in between his eyebrows. "What?" she asked.

"I just didn't expect you to offer to do something like that," said Matt.

"Don't you think I eat?" she asked with a slight laugh.

"Well, of course I'd expect you to eat. I'm not that delusional to think you survive on air," he replied, shaking his head. "But I'm afraid I'm going to have to pass. I want to get the branches cleared off the lawn and to the dump this morning."

"Okay," she answered before turning and heading up the porch steps.

"Do you want to go out again tomorrow morning? Same time?" he asked quickly.

"That would be nice. By the way, I enjoyed running with you this morning."

"Me too," he called back. "Especially, since I haven't been out in ages. You have a nice running pace."

Megan waved before disappearing inside. He was right about the pace; it felt good to run with someone who didn't move two steps behind or in front of her.

After eating she headed outside and dragged the lawn mower out of the little shed in the backyard. She knew her aunt and uncle's weekly routine and didn't mind handling the regular chores, besides it was the least she could do for allowing her to stay at their place while they were gone. After six pulls, she finally got the mower running. When she finished the backyard she made her way around to the front. As she was walking back and forth through the grass, she noticed Matt had taken the top off his Jeep and was loading the fallen branches into the back. He moved across the yard, bending over every few seconds, to pick up more. She watched him for a bit, then focused on her own lawn.

As she turned to finish the final row of grass, she looked up and was startled to find Matt standing on the other side of the fence staring at her. His arms were casually crossed and he was leaning with his weight on one foot. She hadn't noticed his approach, but finished cutting the last strip before making her way over to him and turning the power off on the mower.

"Hi, sorry if I startled you. I was wondering if you needed anything from town. I'm heading to the dump with all the branches and need to stop at the grocery store," he said, "and thought I'd ask before I leave ... unless you'd like to go along."

"I was going to pick up some tulip bulbs to plant along the edge of the flower beds to thank my aunt and uncle for letting me stay here. And I could use a few things from the grocery store too ... now that you mention it. Do you mind giving me a few minutes to clean up? If you're sure you're okay with me tagging along," she asked.

"I wouldn't have asked if I wasn't," said Matt, curious as to why she felt the need to confirm his offer.

"See you in about fifteen minutes?"

"Works for me. Come on over when you're ready," he said as he headed back across the street.

While running through the shower, Megan wondered why she agreed to such a thing. She wanted to pick up some bulbs, but could have gotten them on her own next week. *I don't know what's causing me to be so impulsive when he comes around. However, his deep set hazel-blue eyes are nice to look at,* she thought with a smile.

Despite her inward fascination regarding her neighbor, she really wasn't interested in starting a relationship, she needed to focus on her schooling. Her last relationship ended several years ago, when her ex-boyfriend told her he would work and she could stay home and care for the house and children. That idea caused her to end the relationship. She'd spent enough time mothering her sister and wasn't interested in just staying home and raising children. Not that a family wasn't something she wanted, but she needed time to put her ambitions at the top of the list, for a change.

* * *

Matt wasn't sure what possessed him to ask Megan to go into town. *Although she has done quite a bit for me over the past two days,* he thought. But it wasn't even that, it was the fact that she treated him like he wasn't famous. *She probably thinks I'm antisocial after my reaction to her breakfast offer ... so until she figures out who I am, I need to relax and enjoy my time here like Paul and Linda encouraged.*

When Matt saw her heading over, he met her at the passenger door of his Jeep. Reaching for the handle their hands met, prompting them to lock eyes for what felt like several minutes. Megan recovered first and let go so he could open the door. Grabbing hold of his senses, Matt made his way around the back of the Jeep and rechecked the straps around the branches; he didn't want to lose any on the way down the hill to the dump. Climbing in next to Megan, he glanced in her direction before starting the engine.

As he drove, Matt subtly studied her. She was resting her elbow on the door and held her hand in the air feeling the breeze flow through her fingers as he coasted down the hill. Her head was tilted back as if absorbing the moment, as several loose ends of her hair flew around her face in a carefree way. Pulling into the entrance of the dump, they had to wait in line to get to the yard waste area. Looking towards her, he asked, "What cha' thinkin'?"

"Nothin' much. Just enjoying the ride. I've never ridden in a car without a top before," she told him.

"What do you think?" he inquired.

"I like it. It's very relaxing. I think I might even be able to focus on studying this afternoon. Thanks for asking me to come along."

"You're welcome. When are your classes this semester, if you don't mind me asking?"

"I don't mind. I have anatomy on Tuesday and Thursday evenings from six to nine and a music class on Wednesdays from two until four o'clock in the afternoon. I need the music class to fulfill a fine arts requirement that was missed my previous semester, preventing me from earning my bachelor's degree, and the anatomy class is a pre-medical class, which will transfer to medical school," she informed him.

"How did you miss a fine arts class?"

"Well, when you have three different advisors something is bound to go wrong. I wasn't very happy, but the college allowed me to walk across the stage for my undergraduate degree this past spring provided I took the fine arts class this fall. Since I played the oboe in high school, I figured it would be an easy class compared to anatomy. I was allowed to take the pre-medical class to help keep me from falling too far behind in medical school."

"Wow, I'm glad you were able to get things straightened out. What happens after this semester?" asked Matt.

"I'm hoping to get into West Virginia University Medical School. I'm also preparing for my Medical College Admission Test and Dr. Rhodes, the town's current ENT, is willing to help me fulfill my clinical hours. I'm sorry, I'm probably giving you more information than you wanted to hear," she said, glancing out the open window.

"I think it's very impressive to pursue something you've always wanted to do. What took you so long to get to this point? Did you need to work after high school to save for college?" he inquired.

She sat quietly for a stretch and wouldn't face him. After a few minutes she said, "Yes, but, …" then reached up and swiped her index fingers under the edge of each eye.

"Meg, look at me," he replied softly.

When she turned, Matt saw the moisture on her face along with a few strands of hair that had gotten stuck to her cheeks. He didn't realize the impact that simple question would have on her. Reaching over, he gingerly dislodged the strands of hair on her left cheek and tucked them behind her ear. As he reached over and touched her other cheek, she closed her eyes until his fingertips slid behind her other ear.

"What happened, Meg?" he asked consolingly, contemplating what compelled him to touch her like that.

Taking a breath, Megan said, "When Kayla was a sophomore and I was a senior in high school, our parents were killed when a truck driver crossed over the median and crashed into my parent's van. They were both killed instantly. The driver fell asleep behind the wheel," she choked out quietly. "Our families have been wonderful, but it wasn't easy. Kayla is a terrific sister, but our lives changed in a way I never imagined."

The traffic started to move and Matt made his way to the yard waste area. He truly didn't know what to say and the thought of telling her he knew how she felt wasn't right, even though he could partially commiserate with her. A sense of déjà vu hit him as he backed up to the dumping area, but before he could grab hold of the memory Megan surprised him by getting out and helping. Matt's thought dissipated as they worked silently clearing out all the branches.

When they climbed back in, Matt reached over and dislodged another piece of hair from her cheek. Placing his hand along the side of her face, he forced Megan to look into his eyes. "Sorry," Matt whispered. "I truly am sorry."

"Thanks," was all she could manage to say as he removed his hand from her face.

* * *

Megan never thought their conversation would cause so many emotions to surface. But the way he touched her face and the sincerity in his voice caught her off guard. There was something about the way he told her he was sorry that seemed familiar. She hadn't allowed herself to drift back to the days following her parents' deaths in a long time. She cut off any further thoughts as they headed to the local nursery, where Megan picked out some lovely purple and red tulip bulbs. When they pulled into the grocery store, Megan watched Matt grab his hat and sunglasses of the back seat again before they each took a shopping cart and maneuvered through the aisles separately. Meeting at his Jeep, they loaded their bags and headed home.

Very few words were spoken as they drove back up the hill. He pulled into her driveway and helped carry her bags inside.

"Thanks for taking me," said Megan as she followed him back to the front door. "I enjoyed riding in your Jeep."

"You're welcome," said Matt. As she started to close the door he added, "I didn't mean to upset you earlier. I had no idea about your parents."

"It's okay. Most people just assume I had to work to save for college. That's only partially true. My friends have all moved on with their careers and I'm in the midst of working towards mine, which makes having any type of social life difficult. I'll get there eventually. I'm just thrilled to have a quiet place to study without all the interruptions," she told him.

"Well, if you need anything, let me know," said Matt. "I promised your aunt and uncle I'd keep an eye on you."

"I appreciate it," said Megan, "but I'm good. I'll see you in the morning for our jog, okay?"

"See you then," said Matt as she slowly closed the door.

Once her groceries were put away and she had lunch, Megan focused on her studies the rest of the afternoon. Her professor emailed everyone to tell them he planned on giving a quiz tomorrow on the muscles of the throat. She pulled out the index cards listing the suprahyoid and infrahyoid muscles, which assist with speech by causing the rise and fall of the larynx and with a person's ability to swallow. Pacing down the hallway she memorized the position of each muscle and their function. By the time she had them down pat, it was dinnertime. She didn't feel like anything fancy and settled on a grilled cheese and tomato soup, which she had just bought at the store. It was getting late, and as the sun dipped behind the trees, she heard a knock on the door. Megan headed down the hallway while drying the soup pot, to see who was rapping at this hour.

"Who is it?" she called.

"It's your neighbor, Marcus. Is that you, Megan?" he asked.

"It sure is, Mr. Marcus," replied Megan as she turned on the porch light and opened up the door. "What brings you over here at this late hour?"

"I'm so sorry to bother you, Megan, but the toilet in my hallway bathroom won't stop running and the plumber can't get here until tomorrow.

"Mr. Marcus, if I recall, my uncle told you this past summer to have a plumber come take a look at it."

"Yes, but after Paul worked on it, I haven't had any issues with it, until now."

Placing the dish towel and pot on the upstairs steps, Megan wrapped her arm around Marcus' shoulder and ushered him back to his place to take a look. He was a warm older Italian gentleman, with twinkling light brown eyes, and he trusted everyone until they gave him a reason not to. Megan took the lid off the toilet tank and discovered that debris had built up under the flapper, preventing it from totally sealing the opening inside the tank. As a result, the tank constantly refilled when the water level dropped below the fill line. Megan turned the water off and drained the tank, before removing the flapper and cleaning up the debris. After scrubbing off the flapper she reattaching it and turned the water back on. She was pleased she hadn't lost her touch when the tank filled and none of the water trickled into the bowl.

Marcus was thrilled and gave Megan a big hug and kiss. "I'm a gonna make some beef stew tomorrow and bring some over to ya for dinner," he said as she made her way down his front porch steps.

"Thank you, Mr. Marcus, but I have class tomorrow night and won't get home until a little after ten," Megan told him.

"Then I'll freeze some for you to have later. Yes?" he asked in a fatherly way.

She wasn't going to turn down Marcus. "That would be great!" she told him. "I'll pick it up Wednesday morning after jogging. Is that okay?"

"That would be wonderful," he agreed as Megan waved goodbye and headed across the yard.

Collecting the towel and pot, she finished drying the pot before fixing herself a mug of hot tea. Carrying her tea, she opened the door to the deck. Bosley, who had been itching to go outside for his evening romp, eagerly followed.

She reclined in one of her aunt's lounge chairs and allowed her mind to drift back to Matt. She wished she could figure out where she had seen him before, but she just couldn't place him. She had to admit he wasn't bad looking and revealed a tender side when he touched her cheek. She recalled how his collar-length hair blew softly in the air while he drove. As she reminisced, Megan got lost in her thoughts and had just started dozing off when her body jerked her awake, prompting her to call Bosley and head inside to bed.

* * *

After eating dinner, Matt fixed a mug of coffee and carried it out onto the porch. As he planted himself in one of the Adirondack-style chairs his father built many years ago, he thought he could hear Megan calling Bosley.

As he sipped his coffee, he reviewed what happened that morning. He had been skeptical about being able to listen to his music while they jogged. The tactics women used to entice him into joining them was something he had become accustomed to; only to be disappointed by their ulterior motives. But Megan surprised him by not interrogating him about Saturday's encounter with fans at the airport, either. He had no trouble keeping pace with her; in fact, she had a nice rhythm going which helped him re-establish his own. He used to jog every morning until work got more demanding.

He was, however, discovering that Megan was true to her word. She allowed him to enjoy the solitude the morning offered. Their conversations carried more depth and she didn't require the constant reminders about how lovely she looked, every ten minutes. She also wasn't inclined to reach out and touch him periodically as if to say to the world, he's mine.

Reflecting on his own actions, he hadn't meant to make her tear up, but how was he to know she lost both her parents in high school. It couldn't have been easy raising a younger sister and sending her off to college while putting her own dreams on hold. He admired her strength and determination to complete something she had to put off for so long. *But what caused me to reach out and touch her face. I'm the one who's fending off the women, not casually touching them.* It was a spontaneous reaction, something he hadn't done in a very long time and stopped himself from doing because women usually got the wrong impression. But now that he was back home in the mountains, his old caring self was starting to emerge. He had considered reaching over to squeeze her hand, but didn't want her to get the wrong idea, whatever that might be.

She was slowly causing him to reconsider his declaration to be done with women. Megan wasn't Rachel, by any means. And he had to admit, her medium-length cinnamon red hair and hazel eyes were appealing. She was muscular, but her waist, chest and hips were delicately curved. He suddenly wondered what it would be like to wrap his arms around her and bury his face in her hair as he held her close.

"What are you thinking, Matt!" he scolded himself out loud. "It's only going to take you down a road you can't handle. Rachel figured that out months ago. And there isn't any way I'm going to prevent Megan from earning her degrees."

She kept out of sight the rest of the day, but he took comfort knowing he would see her in the morning. He was upset he couldn't bring her out of her gloominess like she had done for him the day before. Having to keep his own guard up, fearful others would misinterpret his actions, had truly blunted his comforting skills. *I need to work on them,* thought

Matt. *Which shouldn't be hard with Meg, because she clearly isn't faking her feelings and emotions like some of the women I know.*

After draining his mug, Matt forced himself out of the chair and headed inside to clean up the dishes from dinner. However, before going to bed, he peeked out the window to see if Megan's lights were still on. They were, but as he stood there, he saw them go out which meant she was headed to bed, too. Knowing she was on the same schedule felt important to him, even if he didn't know why.

Chapter Five

Megan walked briskly back and forth from one end of the fence to the other to help warm up her legs. Within minutes, Matt came out to join her.

"Mornin'!" he greeted.

"Mornin'!" she replied with a slight tilt of her head.

"Something wrong?" asked Matt.

"Nope, you just look different this morning," she commented.

"Maybe it's because I'm looking forward to jogging with you this mornin'," he said with a smile.

"Could be, and thanks, but I think it's something else," she said.

"Well, while you're figuring it out, why don't we start jogging?" he said, motioning with his hand for her to take the lead.

Between trying to figure out what was different about him and working to avoid obstacles in the road, Megan lost stride several times. As she sprinted around the last bend towards home, she suddenly stopped in her tracks.

Matt realized she wasn't beside him anymore and turned around. He evidently recognized the look, that glary-eyed star-struck look, and crossed his arms. She could tell by the way he pressed his lips together and shook his head that he wasn't particularly happy with her discovery. He seemed like he wanted to run away, but didn't. Instead, he just stood twelve feet in front of her, with his legs spread and his feet anchored to the road, waiting to see what type of reaction he was going to get from her.

Making her feet move, Megan slowly jogged up to him and searched his hazel-blue eyes. *I didn't act like a giddy school girl when I met him, and I'm not going to react that way now,* she told herself.

Reaching up she placed her hands on his unshaven face, and said quietly, "I know why you look so familiar to me. Your beard gave you away this morning. You didn't have it when I saw you the first time."

"Yeah," he responded. "Who am I?"

Megan paused, but only for a moment before saying, "You're someone special to a lot of people, Matt. Now I understand why you need to get away from everyone and everything for a while," she continued, unconsciously stroking his cheeks with her thumbs. Realizing what she was doing, she slowly dropped her hands.

Matt reached out, clasped her wrists, and drew her near. He leaned close to her ear and whispered, "And I'd like to stay incognito while I'm here, Megan." And this time he didn't use her nickname.

"Fine by me," she replied casually, taking in the woodsy scent of cedar and mint as he leaned in close. "Now how about some breakfast?"

Releasing her, he raised one eyebrow and looked into her hazel eyes. She thought he looked hesitant, and who could blame him given his celebrity status. But there was still something about him that perplexed her, and it had nothing to do with his career. A vision that lingered behind her eyes, but the sketch was blurry.

"Okay, but I'm fixing?" he countered, surprising her and breaking up the image.

Megan briefly wondered if he was in a relationship. *But why would he offer to fix me breakfast if he has a girlfriend waiting for him in LA?* she reasoned. Ignoring the skepticism on his face, Megan shook off her reverie before asking, "So, how are your cooking skills?"

"I'd say fair to middlin'. How's your appetite?" asked Matt.

"Pretty good right now."

Turning her by the shoulders, he steered her towards his place, up the front steps and straight into the kitchen. Placing a bottle of water in front of her, he said, "Drink up."

As she leaned against the island, she watched him take out a frying pan, two eggs, cheese, ham and two muffins. "Any objections to an egg sandwich?" he asked.

"Not at all, I love them. Can I help?"

"If you want to cut the muffins in half and toast them, while I get the eggs started, that would be helpful."

After cutting the muffins in half she paused before placing them in the toaster. Glancing sideways over her shoulder, she stared at his profile while he cracked the eggs into the frying pan. She tried to recapture the blurry vision that crept into her head moments ago, but instead of grasping that image, her thoughts diverted to pictures of his former relationships depicted in the tabloids. *Stop it, Meg! You don't need the complication a relationship can bring right now. Especially with him,* she scolded herself.

"What would you like to drink, besides water?" asked Matt, disrupting her inward thoughts.

"Coffee would be good," she said, focusing her attention back to the muffins.

"Then you're in luck because I made a fresh pot this morning. Would you like to eat inside or out on the deck?" he asked.

"The deck would be nice."

They carried everything outside to a small square table. Once they were settled, Matt said, "Go ahead ... ask away."

"Ask away what?" she replied, looking at him curiously.

"There have got to be a few questions rolling around in your head that you're dying to ask me," he flat-out stated.

"Okay," Megan said. "Where did you learn to cook?"

An incredulous look appeared on his face with his muffin sandwich poised in mid-air. After taking a bite, he said, "As a matter of fact I took a cooking class in college. I wasn't half bad either. The teacher said I had a knack for knowing what seasonings compliment a dish."

"That's impressive. Do you get to do much cooking when you're in LA?"

"Not really. I'm too caught up in doing the shows for the season. Meals are usually ordered from a local restaurant."

"That's too bad. Sounds like you don't get enough time to yourself?"

"Not as much as I'd like," complained Matt.

Megan picked up on the frustration in his voice, but decided to let his answer disperse without commenting. She remembered hearing that same tone on the car ride up, and when he was talking to her aunt and uncle.

When they finished eating, Matt carried their plates into the kitchen, and she followed with their mugs. After placing them in the dishwasher, she found herself hesitating to leave. When he turned to face her, she looked into his eyes and again wondered what the women he had dated were like, and despite her desire to avoid a relationship, she was curious if he had any interest in her. She wasn't anyone special; she was just Megan, a country girl from West Virginia.

As he looked back into her eyes, Megan quickly became self-conscious and turned to look out the window over his kitchen sink. He could have let her stand there, confused by her own reaction, but instead, he stepped up behind her and placed his hands on her shoulders before turning her around. He surprised her by slowly drawing her in and holding her securely and deeply for a moment. His warmth and woodsy scent filled her senses before he tensed up. Then without a word, he let her go. Placing his hands back on her shoulders he guided her out the door and down the porch steps. Just as he was about to turn her loose, Megan's other neighbor, Naomi came hustling across the street towards them.

"Megan, Megan," she hollered, waving her hand in the air frantically.

Breaking free from Matt's touch, Megan rushed across the street to meet the usually quiet older woman. "What's the matter, Ms. Naomi?"

"Oh, Megan, there's a snake in my hallway bathroom!" said Naomi in a shaky voice.

Megan glanced over at Matt, who turned and jogged back inside. When he emerged moments later, he was carrying a canvas bag and a long pole with a loop on the end of it. Megan patted Naomi's hand and together they followed Matt to her cabin.

"Matthew, I didn't know you were back in town. When did you arrive?" asked Naomi.

"This past Friday," said Matt.

"Well, it's good to see you. You're looking well, but I like you better without the beard," said Naomi as they headed up the path to her porch.

"Thanks for letting me know," said Matt before looking over at Megan, who had placed her hand over her mouth to stifle a laugh.

Please be careful in there," said Naomi as Matt climbed the steps in front of her.

"I promise," replied Matt.

"Have you done this before?" asked Megan.

"Lots of times ... on set," he yelled back as he entered the cabin.

"Oh, great! Just great!" replied Megan under her breath. "Should we just call an exterminator to remove it?" she yelled, as she helped Naomi up her porch steps and into a blue rocking chair.

* * *

Shaking his head and grinning, mainly due to her sheer concern for his well-being, Matt crept slowly down the hallway. Naomi's cabin was flipped compared to his so the bathroom was on the opposite side, allowing him to find his way. He poked his head into the bathroom and spotted what he knew was an Eastern Garter snake curled up in the corner of the room behind the toilet. Even though it was a non-venomous snake, Matt remained outside the door and used the pole to encourage the snake to stick up its head so he could capture it in the noose. On the fifth try, he lassoed it.

"Meg," he shouted.

"Yeah?" she responded, her voice revealing her trepidation.

"I've got him in the noose, but I could use your help holding the bag so I can get him in it."

"And you think I'm the one who's going to help you do that?"

"Are there any other options?"

"Damn it!" he heard her say.

By the time she made it down the hallway and around the corner, Matt was laughing his head off. The look on her face was priceless.

"Keep it up, buster, and I won't be jogging with you anymore," she said. "What do you need me to do? And before you say anything, let me inform you that if any part of that snake touches my hand, I will be out of here faster than you can say my name."

As soon as Matt saw the color start to drain from her face, he stopped laughing. He quickly instructed her to take one side of the bag and told her to look away. It was one thing to get the snake in the bag, but a whole other issue if she passed out on him. He saw that she was putting an awful lot of trust in him, as she held the bag and squeezed her eyes shut. Matt swiftly raised the snake high in the air and landed it right in the center of the bag.

"Don't let go yet," he said. He removed the noose and tightly drew the strings at the top of the bag.

"Okay, we got it. You can let go and head back outside now."

Megan just leaned against the wall and sunk to the floor without a word.

"You, okay?" asked Matt with concern.

"I will be," she answered. "Just get that thing out of here."

Matt carried the bag outside and put it in the back of his Jeep. He planned to take the snake down the hill to the stream and release it, but needed to make sure Megan was okay first.

Making his way back to Naomi's cabin, he saw Megan walk out the front door and drop down on the porch steps. He thought she still looked pale.

He sat down next to her and leaned close. She accepted his support and rested her head onto his shoulder. They sat quietly for several minutes without moving or saying a word.

"Thank you both very much," said Naomi getting up out of her chair. "I truly am grateful."

"You're welcome, Ms. Naomi. No problem," replied Matt.

"It's good to see both of you home again. I'm going to clean up my bathroom, but you two feel free to sit here for a spell as long as you need to. Can I get you anything?"

"Thanks, Ms. Naomi," said Matt. "Some fruit and water would be good for Meg, if it's not too much trouble."

"No trouble at all," said Naomi.

Naomi returned a few minutes later with two bottles of water and an orange. Matt gave one of the bottles to Megan and then peeled the orange. Handing her a section, he said, "Eat. It'll make you feel better."

"Thanks," said Megan, taking the piece from him.

"You were very brave in there. Most women *would* have run the other way," he said.

"Well, I guess you've deduced that I'm not like most women," Megan informed him.

"That's becoming apparent," he admitted, leaning into her shoulder again. "Was this your first encounter with a live snake?"

"Actually, no," she said as she swayed and bumped his shoulder in return.

"Care to fill me in?" asked Matt.

"Well, ..." she started, then finished chewing the section of orange he had given her. "I used to cut the grass on a tractor at my parent's house when I was younger. One time I decided to cut down some of the taller grass in the backyard. As I rolled closer to the neighbor's woodpile, a black snake raised its head out of the tall grass and stared right at me."

Shaking her head and laughing, she continued, "You've never seen anyone put a tractor in reverse as fast as I did and hightail it back to the front of the house. I bolted inside and told my dad what I saw, then headed straight for my World Book Encyclopedia to find out if black snakes were poisonous. Luckily, they weren't or my dad would have been cutting the grass himself from that moment on."

"I think the snake was probably as scared of you as you were of him," Matt commented.

"You're probably right, but I wasn't going to stick around for *that* conversation," Megan assured him.

"Just so you know, if the snake in Ms. Naomi's bathroom had been venomous, I would have closed the door, stuffed a rug under it and called an exterminator."

"Glad to know you have a limit to your self-reliance. Do you mind if I ask you something?" she inquired.

Matt sighed thinking, *here it comes. Questions about the similarities between me and the character I play on TV.*

"How is it that you happen to have a canvas bag and noose on hand?"

Matt laughed, mainly because her question surprised him. "When my parents bought the cabin, we used to come here on vacation several weeks out of the year. Every so often we would find a snake somewhere in the house. My dad thought we better be prepared to get rid of them. When I heard my mom screaming at the top of her lungs, I knew there was a snake somewhere inside."

"Okay, then on set was not the total truth," Megan said.

"Not quite," said Matt.

"Now I'm starting to wonder if there are any snakes roaming around in my aunt and uncle's cabin."

"I'd be happy to take a walk through with you if it would make you feel any better," he offered.

"I might take you up on that, Matthew *Thomas* Wilson," she replied, overemphasizing his middle name with a gleam in her eyes, before stepping off the porch and walking down Naomi's quaint path leading to the street.

Grabbing his bottle of water Matt followed her up the street. He rubbed his hand over his facial hairs, berating himself for not shaving this morning. He caught up with Megan, just as she was about to open the gate to her place, and said, "Meg, I *will* take a look around for any snakes if you want me to," touching her arm briefly.

"If I can't sleep tonight, I'll have you come over right after jogging tomorrow morning," she began, "but I think having Bosley with me should help to keep any snakes away. Thanks, anyway. I'm going to head inside to study, eat some lunch and study some more before class tonight. I have a quiz on the muscles of the throat," she informed him.

"Sounds interesting," Matt remarked.

"Then why don't you come study all the muscles of the throat, and I'll go for a drive into town and do some window shopping," she laughed.

"On second thought, I think I'll get rid of our friend and see you in the morning," he responded quickly, before turning abruptly and walking the other way.

"Ain't no way that snake is *my* friend, but I *will* see you in the morning. Bye," she said, waving her hand and heading up the steps.

Walking back to his place Matt headed inside to collect his keys, then drove to a small stream in the woods close to the wildlife sanctuary. He untied the bag and let the snake find its way out, which took several minutes. On the drive home he contemplated how Megan reacted to the revelation that he was a well-known actor. The way she touched his face and told him point-blank she had figured out who he was felt oddly familiar. He was also impressed with her gumption as she helped with bagging the snake, despite the fact she was scared silly. *How many times have women egged me on only to reveal their true personalities after I've devoted a couple months to developing the relationship?* he asked himself.

Battling through the thoughts in his head he said out loud, "But Meg isn't like the women I've met." He briefly tried to convince himself that taking the risk was worth the potential disappointment. But given his experience, the negative outcomes far outweighed any positive pleasures he had yet to enjoy. *Then why did you hug her?... Just to see how she'd react?* he asked himself, unsure of any justifiable answer.

As Matt drove up Willow Street, he looked her way and noticed her pacing on the porch, talking out loud as she studied. He pulled in his driveway, collected the empty bag and noose, and headed for his front door. As he turned the knob, he decided to take another glimpse her way. Her senses were still uncanny, for she paused and looked up in his direction. He froze for a moment before she waved at him. Making his feet move, he entered his cabin contemplating her level of awareness whenever he was in her presence. After fixing lunch he decided to test his speculation and walked up to his screen door. It didn't take long for her to look his way and smile as if he had control of her, like a marionette. Backing away from the door he headed onto the deck to give her the privacy she needed. *Damn,* he thought, *I've never believed in intuition, but her ability to sense my presence is incredible. Maybe she is worth the risk, provided she's even interested.*

Chapter Six

A little before five o'clock, Megan packed up her laptop, book and study guide for her anatomy class. She then grabbed a pack of nuts from the pantry, along with a fruit cup and drink for the road. She couldn't eat before taking any quizzes or tests, but was usually famished afterwards. She tried to force Matt out of her head so she could stay focused on the material for her quiz, but that didn't stop her from wondering why he pulled her close and hugged her. Glancing over at his place as she packed her truck, she saw him sitting on his front porch toiling with his guitar. To her surprise, he looked up and smiled. Megan raised her hand in a partial wave as she got in her truck. *So much for keeping him out of my thoughts,* she chided herself.

Megan walked out of anatomy class with a smile on her face, along with her fellow classmates. They decided to go to a late-night bakery to celebrate because everyone got an 'A' on their multiple-choice quiz, and the professor was so impressed, he let them all go a half hour early. Megan was elated, not only with her grade, but because her social life was practically non-existent, and doing something with her classmates put a little bit of normalcy back into her own life. She ordered a choc-olate éclair, one of her favorites, and enjoyed learning about her classmates' ambitions as she ate. Before leaving the bakery, she purchased two more éclairs to share with Matt for breakfast.

Pulling into her driveway around eleven o'clock, she felt exhausted, but still exhilarated enough to leap up the porch steps. After letting Bosley outside, she changed into her nightgown and fixed a cup of hot tea. She carried it out back and leaned against the deck railing, taking in the cool air, while watching Bosley roam around the back yard. After several minutes a cool breeze rolled across the deck. Shaking off a chill, she called Bosley in, turned off the lights and headed to bed.

* * *

Matt had spent part of the evening fiddling around with his guitar, but most of the time he meandered around the cabin. He felt lost without her presence for a reason he couldn't understand. After eating a bowl of ice cream, he kept himself awake by completing a few chores until her return. He knew she was a good driver, but that didn't stop him from worrying about her. However, he forced himself not to hover like the women in LA who constantly wanted to hang onto him. But Megan didn't make him feel like he needed to linger in her every movement, either. *Maybe she's someone I can trust,* thought Matt. Which was a feeling he hadn't allowed himself to believe still existed.

Keeping his distance from the front door he periodically checked to see if her truck was in her driveway. By chance he caught her arriving home around eleven. He figured she must have had a good night by the way she took the steps in twos. Knowing she was home safely, he relaxed and turned in.

* * *

The morning came too quickly for Megan. She was still exhausted from her class and the bakery outing afterwards. Dragging her body out of bed in a comatose state, she forced herself to get ready for her morning run.

"Mornin'," Matt mumbled.

"Mornin'," replied Megan yawning. "Ready?" she asked, rubbing her eyes.

"I guess," he replied lethargically.

Megan plugged her ears and started jogging down the road with Matt right beside her. They barely spoke the whole run. When they hit the bend Megan started walking and stopped by her gate.

"Matt," she called, turning in his direction.

"Yeah?"

"Breakfast? My treat."

"What do you have in mind?"

"By any chance do you like chocolate éclairs?" she asked.

"For breakfast?"

"No, for dinner," she responded as she rolled her eyes and stared at him. "Yes, for breakfast," she continued with a chuckle.

"Sorry, I've never had one for breakfast."

"Well, there's always a first. Come on," she said, motioning for him to follow her. "Besides, how is it any different from having a chocolate-cream-filled donut?"

"Good point," Matt answered, following her down the hallway to the kitchen.

Megan got out two plates and plucked a bag out of the refrigerator. As she walked past the island toward the table, she swung the bag in front of him.

"You went to Holly's Bakery last night? I love that place! She has the best glazed donuts," Matt said. "How'd you end up there?"

As Megan took the éclairs out of the bag, she explained, "The professor let us go thirty minutes early because we all got perfect scores on the quiz last night. To celebrate, we all decided to go to Holly's to unwind." Megan fixed them each a cup of coffee and gestured for Matt to have a seat at the kitchen table near the window.

As Megan sat, she caught Matt staring off into space. "Matt." She called his name a couple times to bring him out of his reverie. "Everything okay?" she asked in a concerned voice.

"Me ... oh yeah ... I'm good," he answered.

Megan sensed he was still a little lost in his thoughts, but didn't pursue it. She picked up the éclair with her fingertips and rotated it side to side, trying to decide the best spot to begin. Biting into it carefully, she tried not to make a mess, but ended up getting chocolate and cream on her cheeks. Matt's lips curved up into a wide smile.

"What?" Megan asked, smiling back.

"You've got it on your cheeks," he said laughing.

"Yeah," she countered, watching his shoulders drop, "let's see if you can do any better."

"You're on," said Matt as he enthusiastically picked up his éclair and just dove in. The creamy filling dripped out the back end and chocolate laced his unshaven mustache.

Megan began to laugh and moistened a few paper towels at the sink. "We're going to need these when we're done."

They enjoyed watching each other maneuver their éclair, trying to make the least amount of mess possible. When Matt finished he grabbed one of the paper towels and proceeded to wipe off his hands and face. Megan did the same, then reached across the table to wipe off some icing still under Matt's nose. He quickly caught her wrist but gently took the towel from her hand, all the while staring into her eyes. After a moment, he released her hand.

Megan wasn't sure what provoked Matt's quick movement, but she figured something caused him to respond with such a knee-jerk reaction. It reminded her again of his quick release after hugging her the other day after breakfast. Not wanting to pry, she wiped off the table and inquired, "Am I to assume you enjoyed your breakfast, Mr. Wilson?"

"Very much, Ms. Barnes. Thank you for thinking of me. What's on your schedule for today?" asked Matt, acting like nothing had happened.

"Well, first I have to go next door to see Mr. Marcus," said Megan, letting the conversation move along.

"Is everything okay?"

"Yes. He fixed me some beef stew the other night to thank me for fixing his toilet Monday evening," she said.

"You did what?" he asked with mock disbelief.

"One of his toilets wouldn't stop running, so I fixed it. Do you have a problem with that, Mr. Wilson?" she asked.

"Not in the least. Is there anything you can't do? he asked.

"Yes. You won't find me catching snakes again any time soon."

"Touché."

"Yup, very. So, do you want to walk over to Mr. Marcus' house with me?" she asked.

"Sure. What else are you doing today?" he asked.

"What is this, the third degree?"

"No, I'm just curious," he replied.

"Well, if you recall from an earlier conversation, I have my music class this afternoon and need to practice. If you're ready, I'd like to go see Mr. Marcus so I can get to practicing."

Marcus was glad to see them and handed a container of stew to Megan. "I didn't know you were back in town, Matt," said Marcus.

"Yes, sir. I got here this past Friday," said Matt.

"Well, welcome home. It's good to see you. There should be enough stew for two if you feel like sharin'," he said with a wink towards Megan.

"Mr. Marcus, you're incorrigible, but I love you anyway," said Megan, giving him a kiss on the cheek. "Thank you!"

On the walk back to Megan's cabin, Matt said teasingly, "I *am* available for dinner."

"I bet you are. It's not enough that I feed you breakfast, now you're trying to mooch in on my beef stew," she said, protecting the container. She paused at her gate and said, "I'll make you a deal."

"And what would that be?" he said eyeing her suspiciously.

"If you can manage to make your way down to the store — incognito — and pick up some garlic bread, I might be willing to share my beef stew with you tonight," she offered. "But remember I won't be home until five-thirtyish."

"Are you sure?" he asked.

What an odd question, thought Megan. *First, he tells me he's available, then questions if I meant my offer. Although I kind of reacted the same way when he asked if I needed anything in town.* A picture of Matt's life was starting to form in her head like a jigsaw puzzle, but she was still missing several pieces.

"Yes, I'm sure," she responded firmly.

"Then I accept the challenge," he confirmed. "I can put the food on if you're okay with leaving your cabin unlocked. I'll run to the store now and stay home the rest of the day to keep an eye on things."

"I'm not sure I feel comfortable leaving the door unlocked, but I have an extra key. And you do seem like the trustworthy type," she said, looking him over from head to toe, then realized she enjoyed what she saw.

Especially since he started to smile more, which caused his cheeks to rise, revealing a warm personality that he seemed to guard very well.

"Well, that's comforting to know you think so," he responded in a cheeky tone.

"On your way back from the store stop by and I'll give you the key," Megan said as she walked through the gate with a smile on her face.

* * *

Matt wasn't sure whether he felt glad or jealous when Megan told him about her outing at Holly's Bakery. She had a right to do what she wanted and he had no grounds to tell her differently. Maybe it was the fact that she could come and go as she pleased without having to look over her shoulder every time she drove into town. For some reason this trip home was feeling different from previous years. The simpler lifestyle he couldn't wait to leave behind years ago, was now tugging at his core.

One thing he knew for certain, she was creeping into his life without much effort. Everything he was learning about her derailed his preconceived notions that all women were after the same thing. Her selflessness and willingness to get her hands dirty were characteristics he rarely encountered.

After retrieving his public disguise — sunglasses and hat — he headed to the grocery store. Ever since the incident at the airport, he didn't want to risk being recognized again. As he drove by her place, he heard her playing the oboe. He pulled over and listened intently for a moment. Whatever she was playing sounded beautiful. He wanted to keep listening, but had to be back before she left for school.

* * *

Megan enjoyed playing the oboe in high school and often wished she could have minored in music, but the death of her parents forced her to put aside many wishes and dreams.

In between practicing her piece, she thought about her feelings for Matt. *What possessed me to ask him to dinner? Famous people usually like to hang out with their own kind, at least that's what the tabloids show ... and I'm pretty sure there are plenty of women in LA who would die to go out with him ... but his need to confirm my dinner offer makes me wonder about his personal life ... maybe he isn't as comfortable in his own skin as he appears to be.*

At times he seems carefree, acting as though he could take on the world, then all of a sudden he acts suspicious, like when she removed the icing from the éclair off his upper lip. It was as though he thought she had an ulterior motive for her innocent gesture. Suddenly the memory of his face smeared with icing made her smile, but then she wondered if her casual touch had triggered something. His piercing hazel-blue eyes had revealed an intense effort to remain calm, causing her to consider what his life was like in LA.

Just as she was about to take a breath to play through the piece again, Megan heard someone rapping on her storm door. "Who is it?" she hollered as she placed her oboe on its stand.

"It's Marvin."

"Hello, Mr. Marvin, what can I do for you?" asked Megan as she opened the storm door.

Marvin and his wife, Sue, lived in the house next to Matt. They were in their late seventies and the patriarchs of the community. They were a lovely couple and Megan admired how deeply they cared for one another, but she thought they sometimes tried to take on more than they could handle.

"I'm so glad you're home. I can't get my car started and was wondering if I could borrow a pair of jumper cables, you and your car. Sue and I have dentist appointments this afternoon and we really don't want to reschedule them. Is there any way you could possibly help us out?" Marvin inquired.

"I'd be happy to, Mr. Marvin. Give me a few minutes and I'll be right over."

Megan was irritated about the interruption, but she wasn't going to let Marvin know that. She had about two hours before she had to leave for class and needed to practice her music so she didn't make a fool out of herself.

After collecting her keys, she drove over to Marvin's driveway. She retrieved the jumper cables from the hidden compartment in the bed of her truck and after removing the covers off his battery terminals, connected the red clamp to the positive terminal.

She was standing on the fender with her head inside the hood of her truck uncovering the terminals when she glanced up just in time to see Matt driving around the bend. As she connected the negative clamp to her battery, she heard Matt's voice.

"Can I be of any help?" he asked, walking towards Marvin's driveway.

Megan took her head out of her truck and gave him a "thank heavens you're here" look. Leaning towards Matt, Megan whispered, "I can do this, but I need to practice for my music class. Can you take over?"

"I'd be happy to. I've got this," he whispered.

She handed Matt the last clamp, and approached Marvin. "Matt's going to help you out from here, if that's okay? I need to get a few things done before class this afternoon."

"No problem, dear. I wasn't aware Matt was back in these neck of the woods. Welcome home, it's good to see you. We'll get it figured out, Megan. And thank you," replied Marvin.

"Welcome," said Megan as she handed her truck keys over to Matt. Tugging at his arm to move him out of earshot of Marvin, she said, "I think the battery is totally dead. The date on the battery is from four years ago. If you end up having to drive them into town for their dentist appointments and to get a new battery, go ahead and take my truck. There's a coupon in the glove compartment for the battery shop; please let them use it. And, thanks," she said, standing on her tiptoes and planting a kiss on Matt's cheek. "You're a lifesaver," she added.

As she walked briskly across the street, Megan felt Matt's eyes on her. She glanced over her shoulder and caught him touching his face, making her wonder what he was thinking. When she resumed practicing, she blew through the instrument in total frustration. She didn't mind being neighborly once in a while, but a call for assistance had occurred every day since she arrived. If the neighbors kept up this pace, she might have been better off staying at her apartment. Coming up to the cabin was supposed to allow her to focus on her classes without a lot of interruptions.

It was already a little after eleven and she was feeling anxious about having enough time to prepare adequately for her performance this afternoon. The speed wasn't as important as the accuracy of her notes. The more mistakes she made, the lower her grade for the evaluation.

After taking a few deep breaths, Megan focused her attention and played more calmly.

* * *

After several attempts to start the car, Matt realized Megan was right about the battery.

"Mr. Marvin, I'm afraid the battery is dead. It's not accepting the charge. We're going to have to drive into town for a new one," Matt informed him.

"Oh my! Do you have time to take us into town, Matt?" asked Marvin.

"As a matter of fact, I do. We're going to take Meg's truck, because the top's off on my Jeep."

"Okay. Thank you for helping us out. I'll go get Sue," said Marvin.

As Marvin and Sue made their way down the walkway to Megan's truck, Matt said, "I'll drop you both off at the dentist, pick up a new battery, and come back here to install it. That way I can give Meg back her truck before her class. But I'll need your keys so I can pick you up in your car when I'm done, if you don't mind. Of course, you'll have to bring me home."

"That's fine, Matt, and thanks again for all your help. How long are you home for this time?" asked Marvin.

"No problem, it's actually been nice being able to help out around here. The days are calmer compared to LA. And I'm hoping to be home through January," Matt said.

Matt placed the dead battery in the truck bed and helped Marvin and Sue into Megan's truck. Backing out of the driveway, he lowered his window and heard Megan playing her oboe, again. He couldn't identify the piece, but it sounded complicated. Turning his attention to the road, he drove into town.

After dropping his passengers off at the dentist, Matt purchased a new battery. As he rolled by the local bakery he decided to stop and pick up a couple coffees and two big chocolate chip cookies, one for himself and one for Megan. Matt devoured his cookie and coffee on the drive home to hopefully hold him over until dinner since he hadn't gotten the chance to eat lunch.

Once the new battery was hooked up in Marvin's car, Matt rolled the truck into Megan's driveway. As he climbed out, he watched Megan jog down the porch steps with her music and case in her hand.

"Your timing couldn't be more perfect," she said. "Though I have to admit I was starting to get a little worried."

"How'd your practice session go?" he inquired.

"Not as good as I'd like, but I think I'll pass," she responded.

Megan put out her hand and Matt dropped her keys in it. "Thank you again for helping them out. I really needed the time to practice."

"No problem," said Matt as he helped her climb behind the wheel before closing the door. "Good luck," he added as she backed out of the driveway before heading down the road.

Matt walked back to Marvin's car and drove into town to pick up his neighbors. He ended up running an errand with them and would have brought his disguise if he had known he was going to be joining them in public. As it turned out they didn't run into any visitors who recognized him.

By the time he rolled through his front door it was three o'clock. He then remembered he needed to start dinner at Megan's around five and wondered if she left the door unlocked. After dealing with Marvin's car battery, they both forgot about the house key. Matt quickly walked across the street and was pleased to find she had left the door unlocked. "Thank you, Meg," he said to himself, closing the door.

Before heading back to his place, he glanced around back to check on Bosley and found him curled up in his doghouse taking a nap. As he walked across the street, he decided to bide his time by power washing his deck. He had just finished one corner when he looked up and found Ethel, an older woman with curly gray hair who lived next to Marcus, standing by the side of his deck.

"I tried Megan's place but there wasn't any answer. Marvin was outside and told me you were back in town," said Ethel.

"Meg has a class at the university this afternoon. Can I help you, Ms. Ethel?"

"My smoke detector is beeping. I think it may need a new battery," replied Ethel.

"Let me put on my shoes and I'll meet you back at your place."

"Thank you, Matthew. At my age I just don't think it's safe to be climbing a tall ladder. By the way, it's good to see you home. You and Megan look like you're getting better acquainted and becoming good friends. I've watched you two jog down the road these past few mornings."

"I'll be over in a few minutes," Matt said politely, as he mulled over Ethel's remark.

Matt unplugged the power washer and headed inside to put on a pair of old slippers before heading across the street. *Better acquainted,* he contemplated, as he climbed Ethel's porch steps.

It only took him a few minutes to change the battery. Ethel was so grateful; she gave him a bowl of homemade applesauce.

"Thank you, Ms. Ethel. This will go great with the stew and garlic bread Meg and I are having for dinner tonight," Matt said.

"That sounds delicious. You two enjoy yourselves," Ethel said with a cheery smile.

When Matt got home he felt grimy and headed for a shower. He needed to start dinner at Megan's and decided to tackle the rest of the deck later.

Chapter Seven

Megan reached the end of Willow Drive on her way to class before noticing the cup and small bag sitting on the console between the seats. When she picked up the bag she spotted a small napkin underneath. The writing on it read: *For a very talented lady, Good Luck! Matt.*

Megan drove the rest of the way to class with a smile on her face. She picked up the coffee and took a whiff. "Mmmmm, caramel." Opening the bag, she found a chocolate chip cookie. She tucked the cookie inside the console for the drive home because she was too nervous to enjoy it right now. But she took a couple sips of coffee hoping it would calm her down.

By the time Megan pulled into her driveway she was exhausted and looking forward to a quiet evening. She had forgotten all about dinner with Matt, until she walked up the porch steps and opened the door to an energetic Bosley, who knocked her down on her backside and licked her face profusely.

Hearing the commotion, Matt came hustling down the hallway just in time to witness Megan trying to fend off Bosley's kisses and get him to settle down.

"Oh, come on, Bosley, you're acting like you haven't seen me in years," said Megan.

Matt walked over and helped steer Bosley into the cabin. He then extended a hand to help Megan onto her feet, and with the other collected her bag and oboe case, which had fallen onto the porch during Bosley's infectious attack.

Megan noticed a look of calmness that had settled over Matt and encircled his essence. He held onto her hand causing Megan's attention to be drawn to his face. Their eyes met, and her face relaxed into a smile. He recovered first, and still holding onto her hand, led her into the kitchen.

"Everything smells wonderful," she said, realizing how hungry she was, even after eating the cookie on the way home. She noticed he had set the table and lit one of her aunt's candles, which he placed near the window. No one had ever done anything like this for her and she was touched by the gesture.

As he carried their plates to the table, she said, "This is very nice, thank you so much."

"Well, I hope you're hungry."

"I'm famished," she answered. "By the way, thank you for the coffee, cookie and note. It was really a nice treat."

"You're welcome. I thought you could use it."

Lowering herself into a chair, Megan said, "I only made two minor mistakes in the run-through of my piece."

"Is that good?" asked Matt.

"Well, I still have a shot at getting an A. How was your afternoon?" asked Megan.

"You were right about the battery in Mr. Marvin's car, which I replaced. But I wasn't expecting them to want to run an errand after I picked them up at the dentist in their car. Luckily there weren't any visitors in town who recognized me."

"Why does it bother you when fans recognize you?" asked Megan.

"I generally don't mind a small group, but sometimes that can turn into a large group and then things can get out of hand quickly. I don't want anyone getting hurt because of me," he told her honestly.

"I thought you handled the fans at the airport rather well," said Megan.

"But did you notice how they pushed you away? It's like they lose all common courtesy just to get close to me," said Matt.

"I do remember feeling like I didn't matter for a few moments. I made it a point to step far enough away to avoid any contact," she told him.

"And I kept an eye on you to make sure you were okay," he revealed.

"Just one?" asked Megan, wondering what he would say in return.

"Actually, I kept both of them on you," he told her.

"I see," replied Megan, unsure of what that meant. "So, what else did you get done while I was gone besides dinner?" she continued, changing the topic.

"So glad you asked. Ms. Ethel stopped by because the battery in her smoke detector was beeping. She gave me the applesauce to thank me for helping her. I thought it would go well with dinner tonight," he said.

"I was wondering where that came from. That was very sweet of her," Megan said with a smile. "I'm sorry I got annoyed earlier with Mr. Marvin."

"No worries. I get it. You wouldn't have had time to practice if you stayed to help."

"Well, I usually don't get irritated like that, but I started to feel overwhelmed. They don't mean to make me feel that way, but I've worked too hard to get to where I am. I can't keep being the town handywoman and put my studies on the back burner. I'm beginning to think Uncle Paul said something about me being available to help while I'm staying here."

"How about this," chimed in Matt, "for the next several weeks if any of the neighbors show up on your doorstep, you send them over to see me. I don't mind helping them out. And if I come across a two-person job, I'll let you know and we can pick a time to handle it together. Do we have a deal?" he inquired.

Megan's eyes grew wide. "You'd do that for me?" she asked.

"Sure. I must admit sitting for hours at a time, is not one of my best hobbies. Besides it's putting some normalcy back into my life and I'm enjoying it," Matt said with a smile that made his eyes sparkle.

Sitting at the table Megan felt like they had known each other for years as they comfortably talked about their day. She was truly grateful for his willingness to help with the neighbors. After dinner she collected their plates and headed to the sink. Matt followed with their glasses. As they washed up the dishes, Megan eyed him curiously. She was slowly learning about the real Matt; in a way no television show could reveal.

She actually liked what she was learning, considering she hadn't even known him for a full week.

"Any interest in watching a movie?" she asked out of the blue.

Taken by surprise, Matt asked, "What kind of movie?"

"I don't know. Are there any particular genres you like to watch?" Megan asked.

"Do you have any adventure ones?" Matt inquired.

"I have Red with Bruce Willis. Have you seen that one?"

"I don't think so. But I must warn you, I'm running low on energy so if I doze off, please don't be offended. I will make it up to you later."

"As long as that applies both ways," Megan countered with a grin.

While Megan made a batch of popcorn, Matt turned on the TV and Blu-ray player and plopped in the disc she gave him. He was settled on one side of the plush beige sofa in the living room when she appeared with the popcorn and some ice water for both of them. She placed the popcorn bowl between them and settled into the other end of the sofa.

They munched away watching the opening scene, which was full of action, and ended up devouring all the popcorn within the first fifteen minutes of the movie. Megan placed the empty bowl on the coffee table as Matt stretched out his legs. Not wanting things to get too intimate Megan curled up in the oversized chair and leaned her head on the arm to watch. It didn't take long before her eyes drifted shut.

* * *

Matt reached for the blanket on the back of the chair and covered Megan up. She stirred briefly, placing her head further back on the arm, before her breathing became slow and heavy.

Without thinking Matt pushed her hair out of her face before sitting back down on the sofa. While stretching out his legs he grabbed the afghan off the top of the sofa and draped it across his legs. He struggled with his emotions as he surveyed her features. *What are you thinking Matt?* he asked himself. *You hardly know this woman. How many times have you gotten into a relationship only to discover they're only interested in you because of your television series? Once she finds out you're not the sophisticated man her imagination has conjured up, and you have issues getting close, she'll want to move on like all the others.*

Despite the conflict going on in his head, deep down Matt felt there was something different about Megan. *She hasn't forced herself onto me. Not once.* It had been a long time since he had experienced a gradual progression of closeness in a relationship.

His first long-term relationship was long ago and went *so* wrong, it's a wonder he even remembered what the good moments felt like. For some reason, that he couldn't identify, he felt comfortable being in the same room with Megan. It was like he had done it before; another bit of weird déjà vu. Then Ethel's comment about getting better acquainted traveled through his mind. Pulling his eyes off her face, he watched a few more scenes of the movie before he leaned his head back into the soft pillow and fell asleep.

They would have stayed asleep until daybreak, if Bosley hadn't started barking to go out. Matt was the first to stir and regain his bearings.

"Meg," he whispered, "Bosley needs to go out."

"Then someone needs to build him a doggy door," she replied, shifting her body to lean on the other arm of the chair, not realizing what she was saying and who she was saying it to.

Matt couldn't help but chuckle softly, knowing she wasn't fully awake. He picked up Megan's blanket from the floor and covered her back up before letting Bosley out the back door to do his business. He then made his way to the bathroom.

Returning to the living room, he found Bosley sitting in front of Megan's chair. She was sitting up and rubbing the dog's ears. After slowly stretching out her arms and legs she headed to the bathroom herself. Matt turned off the TV and Blu-ray player before he carried the empty popcorn bowl into the kitchen then leaned against the island with his hands stuffed in his pockets. He wasn't sure what to do or how to react and it made him anxious again.

Stepping out of the bathroom Megan was startled to find him in the kitchen. She walked up and casually slipped her hands in between his arms and wrapped them around his body before resting her cheek on his chest. His heart was beating wildly as she gently held him. Slowly, she nudged his hands out of his pockets and encouraged him to wrap his arms around her.

The scent of lavender and lemon filled his senses as he took a deep breath, before finally allowing himself to hold her in his arms for several minutes. He waited for her to make another move, but it never came and he couldn't bring himself to take it any further. *How can I explain my whole horrible love life to someone I've started to care about? Someone who allows me to outwardly be myself,* he wondered.

"I need to go back to my place, Meg," he finally told her as he methodically brushed his chin against the top of her head. He imagined what she could see in his eyes: a look of uncertainty, fear and slight frustration.

"Will I see you at our usual time to go jogging?" she asked, keeping an eye on his face.

"I wouldn't miss it for anything," he confided, gently rubbing her upper arms.

Turning her around, he guided them towards the door.

"See you in the morning, Matt," said Megan, stopping at the bottom of the steps.

"Night, Meg," he said, pulling the door closed on his way out.

Matt spent a fitful night trying to figure out his feelings. When his body finally relaxed, his anxiety jerked him awake. Thoughts of taking this relationship to the next level were really scaring him. Maybe it was because her reactions were so different from other women he had met. Or maybe it was because his feelings of affection were growing too quickly, along with the urge to deeply kiss her, which had started drifting into the forefront of his thoughts. But he was fearful of opening himself up to *any* woman.

He knew that whenever things started heating up, he abruptly pulled away, which quickly turned a pleasant moment into a very awkward one. Even though the moments with Megan were pleasant and she wasn't doing anything to pressure him, he couldn't help his reaction. Most women threw themselves at him and he never had time to decide how he felt about them before they were in his face and kissing him. His lack of interest caused most women to withdraw. In the past, when he pulled back, the woman often revealed her true personality and confirmed he had made the right choice by letting her go. But now he was wondering if Megan would elicit a different reaction, provided he ever reached that point.

He continued to toss and turn, as memories from his past invaded his rising feelings for Megan. Unable to sleep, he finally got up, ran through the shower and fixed a cup of coffee. He found comfort in the crisp morning air and headed onto the deck with a blankct, again. Within minutes he drifted off to sleep.

*   *   *

Megan stepped onto her front porch with a glass of orange juice and took a deep breath of the cool morning air. Glancing across the street her thoughts drifted to the frustrated look on Matt's face last night. She was confused and bothered by the mixed signals he was giving her. Dropping onto her front steps she watched Matt meandering over, almost as if her thoughts had summoned him. She thought he looked awful, but decided to hold off asking any questions until after their jog.

He was very quiet the whole run and seemed lost in his thoughts. She bumped shoulders with him once, but he moved further away instead of bumping her back, like he had the last few days. She didn't want to pry and could only hope he would be able to tell her what was on his mind. She was starting to care for him despite her determination to put her studies first. Her concern and feelings got the best of her as they came around the last bend.

"Hey, are you okay?" she asked softly, touching his arm as they slowed to a walk to cool down. She watched him run his hands through his hair and could tell the wheels were churning in his head. Without warning he drew her close and held her securely. Resting his jaw against her forehead, Megan felt him take a deep breath as if he was trying to absorb the scent of her into his memory.

She wrapped her arms securely around him and rubbed her hands up and down his back. He relaxed a little as the minutes crawled by. Holding him tightly, she gave as much comfort as she could.

He finally rubbed her upper arms and whispered, "Thanks for last night; I enjoyed spending the evening with you."

"I enjoyed it too. Not that I stayed awake for much of the movie."

"No, you didn't," he replied with a partial smile. "I think I deserve a rain check," he said.

"Oh ... and on what grounds do you deserve that?" asked Megan, taking note of the slight change in his demeanor.

"I'm not sure yet, but I'll think of something," he said with what appeared to be a slight gleam in his eye. "Do you have class tonight?"

"Yes, and I have to study the parts of the nose this afternoon."

"Do you need any help studying?" he asked, with a hopeful look on his face.

"No, I think I've got this part handled, but I might need your help with the neck and shoulders. There are more components with those body parts then the other ones, provided you're up to the challenge of pronouncing them," she said.

"I didn't do awful in college, I think I can handle it," he said as he released her arms.

"All right then, Mr. Wilson," she said, noticing his sudden need to stay close. "I'll let you know when I need your assistance. And are we jogging tomorrow morning?" she asked.

"Yes, please," replied Matt, almost as if his life depended on it.

After showering and eating breakfast, Megan turned to her studies. The muscles of the nose were more interesting to her than the throat, but also more complicated than she anticipated. They were so intertwined with each other it was hard to tell where one set ended and another set began. She found a picture of the nose in her anatomy book and took out a sketchbook and some colored pencils from one of the end tables in the living room, which had been there since forever, to draw the image. There were enough colors to designate a different one for each muscle group. She was in the middle of working on the drawing when someone rapped on the front door. She looked down the hallway and saw Marvin standing on the other side.

"Come on in," she called out.

"I'm sorry to disturb you my dear, but would you be able to help us unload a couple cases of water from our car? A nice young gentleman loaded them up for us at the store, but I'm afraid we just don't have the strength to carry them inside," he explained.

Even though she had a good amount of studying to do for tonight's class, she couldn't bring herself to turn down Marvin, again. It was such a small task it didn't seem worth the time to call Matt over to help out.

"Sure, can you give me about fifteen minutes? I'd like to finish what I'm working on."

"Absolutely. And thank you!" he said as he headed out the door.

Despite Megan's willingness to help, she started mumbling to herself as she tried to focus on her drawing. *This is just too much. I'm going to have to call Aunt Linda and Uncle Paul to see if they had anything to do with these constant interruptions.* Giving up on her drawing, Megan headed over to Marvin's cabin.

As she stepped off her porch, she saw Matt walking around the side of his cabin with his power washer in tow. She waved and headed across the street to Marvin's cabin and met him at the back of his car. As she carried a case of water towards the cabin, she saw Matt shake his head and head in her direction.

"Can I help you with something, Mr. Marvin?" asked Matt.

"Thank you, Matt, but Megan came over to help."

"I see that. I'll get that other case for you so Meg can get back to her school work."

As Megan stepped out of the cabin she whispered thanks to Matt.

"No problem," he whispered back, smiling at her. "You been studying?"

"Trying," she said, rolling her eyes and shaking her head.

"If anyone else asks you for help today, remember to come get me," he reminded her firmly.

* * *

Matt took it upon himself to tell Marvin that if anything else came up they were to come get him. He explained that Megan came here to study for her anatomy class, which took a lot of time and uninterrupted attention to master. Marvin said he understood and agreed to support her.

On his way home, Matt decided to stop by Megan's to give her his personal cell phone number. As he rapped and opened the door, Megan yelled down the hallway in a slightly irritated voice, "Come on in. Might as well, it's Grand Central Station here."

Stepping into the kitchen Matt found her working at the kitchen table. "I'm sorry to disturb you, but I thought if you had my cell phone number you could just send me a text instead of coming over to let me know if someone else in the neighborhood needs help."

He could tell by her expression she was not expecting it to be him. Then Bosley, who was chained out back by his dog house, started barking excitedly. Leaning her head back onto the chair, she said, "You might as well go see him or he won't stop barking. Take his rope toy. See if he's interested in playing tug-of-war with it."

Matt wandered out back to hang out with Bosley, but felt bad for interrupting her while she was trying to study. After playing fetch with Bosley for about twenty minutes, he went back inside, sweaty and thirsty. "Do you mind if I get something to drink," he asked hesitantly, fearful of her reaction to another interruption.

"There's some lemonade in the refrigerator, help yourself," she said, without looking up from her work.

Matt filled a glass for both of them and brought hers over to the table.

"Thanks," Megan said.

"How's it going?" he asked, looking down at all the note cards, pictures and open textbook spread across the table. "It looks a little daunting from my perspective."

"It is," she replied. "I decided to color code and label all the different muscles, it helps me remember them more quickly."

"I'm not sure I even know how to say half of these words," he said as he flipped through the stack of note cards on the table. "You sure you don't want some help?"

"Not right now. We're having another quiz tonight on placement and labeling of the muscles. Next week is function and what happens surgically if you cut one of these muscles. I'm sorry, I must be boring you. Did you say something about giving me your cell phone number?"

"Yes. Do you have your phone nearby?"

"No. I left it in my bedroom on purpose. Let me go get it," she said.

As she made her way back into the kitchen, she caught Matt trying to pronounce some of the muscles. She laughed as he butchered most of them.

"Not correct, huh?"

"Good try, but no!" she said, shaking her head and smiling.

"I guess anatomy isn't my thing. You ready for my number?" he asked so she could get back to her studies.

"Go ahead."

Meg texted him and he replied back. Sharing his number was a big step, but he felt he could trust her to keep it private. As he got up from the table he leaned over and squeezed her hand before placing his empty glass in the sink. "Keep working, you can do it," he encouraged. "I'll see myself out. See you tomorrow morning!"

"See you in the morning," she answered, absently waving her hand in the air before sinking back into her work.

Matt walked into his kitchen and poured himself a fresh cup of coffee. As he stared out the back door, he realized she dealt with his changing moods and current well-being without prying into his past; not even once. He was learning more about her life every day, but kept his bottled up. He was worried. Worried that if he revealed any part of his past, that whatever this was growing into would disappear. "I'm not sure what I want," he said out loud, "but Megan's the first woman I've felt comfortable around in a long time and she doesn't seem to have any expectations regarding my actions. And if she does, it's not apparent."

Chapter Eight

When Megan woke Friday morning, she called her Uncle Ryan. She was caught up on all her classwork and decided a little break would do her good, like Uncle Paul told her. She hadn't been out to the farm in years and could save her uncle the trip down to pick up Bosley. He's a lovely dog, but a little more wired than she remembered and required more of her time than she thought he would. It would also allow him the freedom to run around with the other dogs a little bit sooner, which she knew he enjoyed. Her call ended up going right to voicemail, so she left him a message to call her back.

Shortly after she and Matt headed out for their morning jog, her cell phone vibrated. She pulled it out of her pocket and smiled when her uncle's name appeared on the screen.

"Hi, Uncle Ryan," she said, breathing hard.

"How's my favorite niece?" he asked. "And what pray tell are you doing?"

"I'm out ... for my morning jog."

As she talked, she watched Matt take out one of his earbuds.

"I know you were ... planning to pick up Bosley tomorrow ... but I have a free weekend ... and thought I could bring him to you," said Megan, still breathing heavily.

"Well, my dear, how would you feel about this evening? That way you can spend the night and stay with us through Monday morning. We can have a cookout Sunday night. Maybe your sister and Dan would like to come, too, or you can bring someone yourself. Maybe a boy this time?" he asked.

Megan could picture him grinning on the other end of the phone. "Uncle Ryan, you're incorrigible. I'll ask him," she responded with a slight grin as a warm feeling traveled through her core. She hadn't thought of Matt as her guy, he was ... heck, she didn't know what to call Matt. Yet somehow, she was drawn to him like a butterfly to a flower filled with nectar, wanting just a little bit more.

"What time would you like us there?" she asked as they made their way around the bend in the road.

"How about four o'clock? I'm looking forward to the assistance of a couple of strong men."

"Four sounds great, and I will warn the guys," laughed Megan, gasping for air. "I'm looking forward to seeing you both. Love you!" she said.

"Sorry about that. I left my Uncle Ryan a message this morning about bringing Bosley up to him, and he was just calling me back."

"You don't need to be sorry. I must say I'm intrigued by your end of the conversation though. Especially the last part about warning the guys."

"Oh yeah," she said with a laugh. "Would you like to go with me to my aunt and uncle's farm to deliver Bosley this afternoon ... and stay the weekend? We'd be coming back Monday morning," she quickly added. "I must warn you my uncle will probably be putting you to work."

"Will there be any home-cooked meals?" asked Matt.

"Absolutely. We'll have to run *five* miles just to keep off the pounds," Megan told him. "Oh, and do you know how to ride a horse?"

"It's been a while, but I think I might remember," he answered.

"So ... are you game? If not, you're going to be jogging by yourself for the next three mornings," she said.

"I think I'd like that, on one condition though ..."

Here it comes, she thought, *he's going to make me promise not to tell my aunt and uncle who he is, and I'm not going to be able to promise that.*

"I'd like to drive and take my Jeep."

"Sure, that would be great! I think Bosley would like that, too, but we're going to have to leash him to something so he doesn't get too excited and try to jump out," she said laughing.

Reaching over, Matt took hold of Megan's arm and quickly drew her close. She fought to control her emotions, but her willpower was slipping away. As quickly as he drew her in, he let her go, then turning her around he gave her a gentle shove back across the street.

Megan glanced back, even more perplexed by his actions. One moment he was drawing her close to his body, and as soon as she relaxed in his arms, he abruptly let her go. It was the third time he'd reacted that way. Turning all the way around and walking backwards, Megan said, "Oh, the drive is about an hour and a half, so we need to leave around two-thirty to get there by four. Also ... do you own a pair of boots you won't mind getting dirty?"

"Two-thirty is fine and yes," he answered.

"Great! I'll meet you at your Jeep at two-thirty," she said, climbing up the steps to her porch.

After showering, Megan called her Aunt Linda and Uncle Paul.

"Hello," said Linda.

"Hi, Aunt Linda, it's Megan. Are you still visiting with your friends or have you made it to your place in Florida?" asked Megan.

"We're still visiting with friends. How are things going with Bosley?" asked Linda.

"He's behaving himself for the most part. However, I called Uncle Ryan and arranged to take him out to the farm this afternoon to save him the trip down. I'm caught up on my studies, and like Uncle Paul said, I should fit in a few breaks," said Megan.

"Good for you. I'm glad you're arranging some time for yourself," said Linda.

"I hope you're having a good time in Florida."

"We are having a lovely visit."

"Do you have a moment for me to ask you something?"

"Sure. What do you want to know?"

"Do you know if Uncle Paul told the neighbors I'd be here the next couple of months?"

"I know he said something to Marvin. Why?" asked Linda.

"Because someone has needed help just about every day since I've been here. If Matt weren't around to help me out, I'd probably be behind in my studies," Megan told her.

"Sorry about that, Meg. We didn't expect everyone to come to you for help while we're away. I'll let your uncle know so he can call Marvin." said Linda.

"On second thought," said Megan, "don't have him call just yet. Since Matt's agreed to help, let me see if things settle down. At least now I know why everyone's dropping by when they need help."

"Okay, Meg. Are you sure?"

"Yes. Besides, you know how hard it is for me to turn folks away. If the interruptions continue, then I'll have Uncle Paul call Mr. Marvin."

"All right, dear. So how are things going between you and Matt?"

"Fine. We've been jogging in the mornings and he's agreed to go out to the farm with me this weekend," said Megan.

"That's lovely, my dear," said Linda with a bit more enthusiasm in her voice than Megan expected.

"I also figured out who he is. No thanks to the two of you or Kayla and Dan."

"You did?" questioned Linda.

"Yeah, he came out jogging one morning and hadn't shaved. He didn't seem too happy when I figured out he was an actor. And for some reason I feel a déjà vu moment every now and then, like I've met him before. Have I, Aunt Linda?" asked Megan, suddenly remembering Naomi's comment about seeing her and Matt home again.

"The family was dealing with a lot when your parents passed away. And your cousin, James, was graduating from college when the accident happened with your parents," answered Linda.

"But that's when Kayla and I spent more time with you," said Megan, wondering why her aunt was avoiding her question.

"True, but we spent a lot of that time at your parents' house, helping you and Kayla move into your apartment and dealing with a very difficult situation. We'd come up to the cabin mainly on the weekends," said Linda.

"Yes, but we also spent a lot of our summers up here. I just find it odd that I wouldn't have met Matt." replied Megan, increasingly perplexed by her aunt's responses.

"Does it really matter whether you've met him before or not?" she asked.

"I guess not, but ... I just wish I had an answer for the unusual feelings that keep popping up," Megan told her.

"Do you remember the poem your mom used to recite when anyone felt out of sorts or had a choice to make?" asked Linda.

"Mom had a lot of poems. She loved sitting on the bay window seat, in the quiet of the morning, on a rainy day, or during a snowstorm, to write poetry. With all my studying I honestly haven't thought about any of her poems in a long time."

"Well, I'm sure you'll remember this one," said Linda, "because we all heard her say it at some point."

> *Your life is a journey*
> *A puzzle worth learning*
> *You'll find the right path*
> *Come slow or come fast*

Then Megan finished,

> *So take a deep breath*
> *You'll figure things out*
> *When it's time.*

"I'm sorry I can't be much help, Meg. Things happened so quickly when your parents died that I don't even remember fixing meals. And you know how much I love to cook. You'll figure it out, like your mom always believed," said Linda. "She and your dad gave comfort in a very special way, just like you."

"I feel like the answers to this part of my journey will be moving rather slowly," Megan said with a sigh, sensing the puzzle wasn't going to be solved any time soon.

"Focus on your studies, everything will unravel as it's supposed to. My sister's intuition was exceptional, along with her patience. By the way, thanks for taking care of the place while we're away," said Linda.

"No problem. Thanks again for letting me stay here to study," said Megan.

When she hung up the phone, the end of her mom's poem lingered in her thoughts. "You'll figure things out, when it's time," mumbled Megan. *Now I feel like I've not only missed out on life, but that part of my memory is eluding me, too.*

Shaking the conversation from her head, she called Kayla to tell her about their Aunt Helen and Uncle Ryan's invitation.

"That sounds great, but I'm afraid we'll only be able to stay until Sunday afternoon because we need to get back to the café to make some fresh pastries for the Monday morning crowd. So, how's it going up there?" continued Kayla. "We haven't heard from you since you arrived last Friday."

"Evidently, Uncle Paul told Mr. Marvin, I was staying here and you know how everyone talks up here. I think between Matt and myself, we've helped out the neighbors four to five times since we've been here. But now that Matt has agreed to deal with their constant requests, things should calm down for me," she told Kayla.

"Really?" Kayla asked with a chuckle. "Sounds like we need to have some girl time this weekend so you can fill me in," she added in a "don't think you're getting away without talking to me" tone.

"So have you figured out who he is?" Kayla asked.

"Yes, it took me a bit, but I figured out he's an actor when he came out of his cabin to jog one morning and hadn't shaved. But, like I told Aunt Linda, I keep having these moments when I feel like we've met before. Then she reminded me of the poem Mom always recited when anyone felt out of sorts."

"The one about figuring things out?" asked Kayla.

"Yeah, so you remember it, too," said Megan.

"It was the one she used to say when we had a choice to make, but felt unsettled about the options. She'd comfort and help guide us with a couple of sound choices, but then leave it to us to figure out our own path. It was our journey, not hers. Well, try not to stress out about your déjà vu moments. Like the poem says, you'll figure it out when it's time. In the meantime, enjoy your new *friend*," Kayla said. "And don't look at me for answers, I was younger than you when our life was turned upside down."

"I guess," said Megan as she secretly contemplated her last encounter with Matt. "He doesn't want anything to get out to the public about being here. If you want to tell Dan that's one thing, but it doesn't go any further than that. Am I making myself clear?"

"Yes, Meg, I understand. But Dan already knows who he is," Kayla replied disappointedly. "It would be cool to tell my friends I know someone famous," she added.

"I'm sorry, but Matt seemed a little upset that I figured it out so soon. I actually think he enjoyed not having a reputation to live up to. I'll see you later tonight, and thanks for understanding, Kayla."

Megan hung up and turned her attention to gathering clothes, which included her boots, a couple pairs of jeans, t-shirts and her favorite comfy sweatshirt. She hadn't been up to the farm, or more accurately the ranch, in about three years. She was looking forward to a change in scenery.

As she filled a duffle bag her thoughts drifted to Matt. The fact that he agreed to go with her created a slight flutter in her stomach that she hadn't felt for a long time. Their friendship was growing, from her perspective, but she wasn't sure if he wanted anything more. On the other hand, she wasn't sure what she wanted either, but she did like his company. Over the past couple of days, he had gone from relaxed to tense, when she figured out who he was. But his comfort level was growing, which meant he was starting to relax again.

* * *

Matt could tell something was brewing as they jogged, but decided to wait for Megan to fill him in. He had been debating over the past two days, whether he should move the relationship along by asking her out to dinner or just let it continue to unfold naturally. Deep down he didn't want to ruin the path they were traveling by throwing an unnatural occasion in the mix.

When she asked him if he wanted to go to her aunt and uncle's farm for the weekend, Matt agreed to go in a matter of seconds. For one reason, not seeing Megan's face in the morning for three days straight didn't sit well with him. His decision to let things unfold naturally was coming to fruition. Despite his leeriness, she was growing on him.

Unbeknownst to Megan, he knew what to pack because he grew up on a ranch. Somewhere in the house he had a well-worn pair of boots. Eventually he found them in a box in the basement, along with his favorite soft denim work shirt. *It's sure been a while,* he thought as he reminisced about his younger days, when things felt less complicated. Shaking his head, he went back upstairs to finish packing.

Walking out to the Jeep he caught sight of Megan shaking out a pair of boots over her front porch railing and called over to her. "Hey, Meg, can you help me put the top back on my Jeep?"

"Sure, give me a second," she said as she finished, then dumped her boots by the front door. She looked a little disappointed and didn't say much as she helped him adjust the top to line up with the latches.

Matt sensed the slight change in her mood. "We can take it off again once we get there. I just don't like traveling too far with it off in case a shower should pop up."

"Oh, okay. That would be nice," she replied as a smile filled her face.

Matt was amazed that all it took to make her smile was a simple gesture — he didn't have to buy her anything to see her face light up. After finishing his side, he walked around to help her with the last hook, which was always the hardest. As he stood beside her, he noticed a slight dimple on the right side of her face when she smiled. It was very charming, causing an insurmountable sensation to slice through him, tantalizing his heart the way a warm ocean breeze can stir the soul.

"Are you done packing?" he finally asked, glancing up into her eyes.

"Almost. I'll meet you back here in about ten minutes, okay?" she asked as she headed back home.

"Works for me," he said, making his way up the porch to collect his gear.

A few minutes later, he was taken aback when he saw Megan walking across the street, carrying a duffle bag over her shoulder. She was wearing a pair of blue jeans that fit her like a glove, a coral flannel shirt and a pair of well-worn boots. She nearly took his breath away. He hoped he had recovered before she caught him gawking at her like some highschooler. Her hair was pulled back and she had a nicely shaped brown cowboy hat resting on her head.

Matt had seen her plenty of times, but usually in a pair of sweatpants and comfy sweatshirt or leggings and an oversized top she wore when they went jogging. He hadn't remembered, since catching her jogging that first day, just how smooth her figure flowed from head to toe, until that very moment. He met her at the back of the Jeep and took her bag.

While he loaded everything, Meg walked back across the street towards the backyard. Bosley, who was prancing and barking excitedly, practically pulled her to his Jeep. When she opened the door, Bosley jumped into the passenger seat and sat down like he owned the spot. It took both of them to shove him into the back seat.

Megan climbed in, removed her hat and tossed it back with her things. Matt closed her door and stood with his hands resting across the window seam for a moment, trying to grasp that she was real and not someone he conjured up in his imagination.

Megan touched his hands and asked softly, "You okay?"

Taking a quick deep breath, he replied, "Yes, everything is perfect."

Matt felt a wave of contentment settle over him as he walked around to the driver's side. After climbing in, he studied Megan, as she stared out the window. He briefly contemplated how the weekend was going to go. However, given Megan's unpredictability, which he was beginning to appreciate and expect, his thoughts wouldn't allow him to settle on one outcome.

They left the windows down and the air swirled around, causing strands of Megan's hair to come loose from her hair clip. When Matt stopped at the end of the hill, he reached over, brushed a few strands from her cheek and tucked them behind her ear, like he had done before. For a fleeting moment, a similar picture lingered in his mind, but he wasn't able to grasp it before it sailed out of his head.

Without thinking, he reached for her hand and laced his fingers with hers. He was prepared for her to push him away, but was relieved and slightly surprised when she placed her other hand on top of his and squeezed it.

They rode peacefully holding hands the majority of the way, but every so often Megan had to reach for her cell phone to check the route. It had been a while since she last visited her aunt and uncle's farm, mainly due to her studies. To Matt's delight she reached over and collected his hand after each separation. No other woman made him feel like he could be himself. But that didn't mean he wouldn't feel extremely nervous and fragile if things got a little more intimate. Not that he could picture that day any time soon, no matter who the woman was.

After about an hour they pulled off the main road, and wound their way down a dirt road for several miles until they reached a property sign that read Pleasant Valley Ranch. Bosley, who had been quiet and calm, was now up on all fours and wagging his tail like crazy, as they got closer to the ranch. Matt retracted his hand from Megan's lap and leaned back against his door.

"I thought you said this was a farm?"said Matt.

"Well, technically it is," she replied, shrugging her shoulders and rubbing her hands on her thighs.

"Are there any cattle?" he asked, glancing at Megan. He shook his head, not out of annoyance, but because the ranch was so unexpected. *This is going to feel more like home then she realizes, maybe too much*, he thought.

Megan slowly replied, "Yeah … about 275 head, if I remember correctly," she answered as she stared out the window.

"How many horses?" he asked next.

Megan cringed and replied, "About 30," still afraid to see the look on his face.

"And we came here to relax?" he asked, rubbing the back of his neck. "This is *only* one of the most notable ranches on the East Coast. I wasn't expecting this," he added.

"I didn't mean to deceive you. And, yes, my friend, we came here to relax," she replied, as Matt released the brake and drifted down the road.

If he felt he could function without her for the next three days, he might have dropped her off and headed back to his cabin. He knew all too well what he was in store for, and truthfully wasn't quite ready for the reminder. However, he reconsidered ever having the thought when he pulled around the next curve and got a bird's eye view of the ranch, and the huge log cabin house in front of him. For the second time that day his mouth hung open. As he came to a stop at the crest of the hill he took in the exceptional view and immaculate condition of the grounds. The love and care put into the place was unbelievable. There were dark brown fences on either side of the road with red and green maple trees alternating in color on each side providing ample shade for the horses.

Caught up in the moment, Matt picked up Megan's hand and kissed the back of it. "Thank you for asking me to come. I don't have the words to describe what I'm feeling right now. The best I can come up with is 'Wow!'"

They sat at the top of the hill for several minutes as he took in the whole scene. Looking over at him, Megan said, "I wasn't trying to be secretive about my connection with this ranch, but some people treat me differently when they realize it's part of my life. My Aunt Helen and Uncle Ryan, along with Aunt Linda and Uncle Paul, have helped Kayla and me since our parent's death. We worked hard to get where we are with sound support and guidance. So, I guess you could say I understand what it's like to want to get away from the limelight, and get to be yourself."

She didn't say another word as Matt studied her, digesting everything she told him. *Now I understand why she's never pried into my private life. We seem to have a lot more in common than I realized, but that doesn't mean I'll ever get comfortable enough to entrust her with my personal issues,* he concluded. Matt released the brake again and drifted down the hill towards the house. They rolled past the horses on the left and several cattle on the right.

As they got closer to the house Megan said, "That's my Uncle Ryan on horseback steering the cattle into the back field for the evening."

When she reached over and touched his forearm, Matt read her perfectly by slowing down so she could hop out. Bosley, who was pacing in the back seat, jumped down and squeezed himself under the fence and took off barking across the field, as soon as Megan opened her door. He was soon joined by two herding dogs and the frolicking began. Matt watched Megan run over and climb the lower rung of the fence before leaning over and whistling loudly through her fingers three times. He guessed it was a family signal because her uncle raised his head, and after securing the gate, galloped over to her.

* * *

"Hey, darlin'. Aunt Helen said you'd be here soon. How was the drive out?" asked Ryan sidling up to the fence.

"It was fine. That's Matt in the Jeep. I'll introduce you to him down by the house," she told him.

"'Bout time you took notice of some young man, Meg," her uncle chided.

"Uncle Ryan," she replied, turning as deep a red as her hair and hoping Matt hadn't heard him. "Please don't start that while he's here. He works very hard in LA and needs a break."

"Honey, I know just what that young man does for a living. According to Kayla, it took you a few days to figure it out."

Now she was really embarrassed, but at least her uncle had put it out there before she got down to the house. Here's hoping the rest of the family didn't feel inclined to point out the same fact in front of Matt.

"Want to ride in with me?" Uncle Ryan asked. He was never one to mince words, and Megan knew he needed to get that nudge about Matt off his chest. She loved him deeply, even if he was very direct.

"Yes," answered Megan without a second thought, waving Matt down to the house.

As Matt drifted down the road, Megan climbed to the other side of the fence, then swung onto the back of her uncle's beautiful deep burgundy stallion. While holding onto her hands with one of his gloved hands, her uncle set the horse to trotting down the fence toward the gate. Megan leaned her head onto her uncle's back and absorbed his smell and his strength. He had a strong back that could handle any burden. His deep hazel eyes reminded her of her father's and his heart cared about everyone and everything.

Megan watched as Matt rolled up next to the house and saw Kayla and Dan jog down the porch steps as they approached.

"Hi, Matt," Dan said, giving him a hearty handshake and pat on the back.

"She's in her glory here, Matt. You won't see this side of her any place else," informed Kayla as she joined Dan, and gave him a hug. "Welcome to Pleasant Valley Ranch!" she said, spreading her arms out and twirling around on her heels.

"I didn't expect all this," replied Matt.

"No one ever does, hon," chimed in Aunt Helen as she made her way off the front porch to join Kayla and Dan. Helen was a middle-aged woman with lovely blond hair and rich blue eyes. She was fairly tall, but solidly built with firm arms and legs. She carried her feelings on the outside and walking up to Matt held out her arms and welcomed him with her usual hug, whether he wanted one or not. Helen could feel him tense up and said, "Relax, son, we're all family here."

Megan could see he was surprised by her aunt's perceptiveness by the way he forced his shoulders to relax. He took a deep breath and, crossing his arms, leaned back against the tail end of his Jeep as Ryan walked the horse right up beside them. Megan slid her right leg over and wrapped her arms around her uncle as he lowered her to the ground.

"Let me put Stuart out to graze for a while, and I'll be right back for a more formal introduction. I sure hope you made enough stew, Helen, because Meg could use a little more meat on her bones," he informed his wife.

"Uncle Ryan!" scolded Megan, glaring at her uncle.

"I just tell it like it is, darlin'," said Ryan.

"I think you need to filter some things," said Megan.

"All right, you two! There's plenty to eat and I made homemade biscuits and apple sauce, too. Let's grab the bags from the Jeep and head up into the house," Helen said.

Everyone was seated at the dinner table as Ryan walked into the room rolling down his sleeves. Megan could smell the familiar woodsy and citrus scents of soap after his usual washing up in the mud room. As he made his way around the table to his seat, he stopped and placed his hands firmly on Matt's shoulders and said, "This must be Matt. Welcome to the ranch, son," he said. After squeezing Matt's shoulders, he continued, "We look forward to getting to know you."

Megan knew Matt could feel the strength and security through her uncle's touch, and hoped he felt as much comfort from it as she did. She had felt it many times, especially when the weight of the world was consuming her and she needed to step back and take a look from a different perspective. He wasn't tall for a man, but he could command the room if he wished to. His short reddish-brown hair matched the mustache he wore, making him appear older than he was.

"Please make yourself at home while you're here," he told Matt, kneading his shoulders slightly before letting go and making his way to his seat. "Have you had any experience on a ranch?" he tacked on.

"Wow, Uncle Ryan, why don't you give him ... what ... thirty minutes before you interrogate him," said Megan.

"It's okay, Meg. I've had a little, sir," Matt answered.

"Well, from the looks of your TV show you're not lacking in skills, and please, call me Ryan."

Megan just rolled her eyes, but she had to admit she was curious about Matt's career, too.

"Ryan, let up on the young man," said Helen. "Remember, he's taking a break from all that."

"Yeah, Uncle Ryan," chimed Kayla. "If I recall, you gave Dan at least an hour and a half to settle in before interrogating him."

"If you expect me to remember that fact after three years, you're crazy! Now, Matt, have you ever ridden a horse before? And I'm not talking about just on TV," he clarified.

"Yes, I have. It's been a while, but I believe I can handle myself in a saddle fairly well," answered Matt.

"See there, Helen, I believe I have two hired hands who can help me mend a few fences out in the north pasture tomorrow," confirmed Ryan.

"Ryan!" exclaimed Helen. "You ought to be ashamed of yourself. Well, before anyone agrees to anything, let's eat before the food gets cold," she said, giving her husband one of those "behave yourself" looks.

Ryan got the message as his eyes softened on the woman at the other end of the table.

Megan reached over and patted Matt's leg under the table, but as she removed her hand, he claimed it and gave it a slight squeeze, letting her know everything was okay, just as Helen had given her uncle a message with her eyes. *Maybe one day I'll find a man I can trust and form a connection like my aunt and uncle,* thought Megan. When she sighed, Matt let go of her hand.

After Matt's initiation interview, the conversation flowed easily. Kayla and Dan updated everyone on the new menu items they were going to try in the café and remarked that everything was running smoothly. They appreciated the chance to get away and unwind.

When the conversation finally made its way to Megan, she filled them in on her classes, and that she mixed up two of the muscles on her last quiz but still got a B. She also told them her music class was going well, but the piece she was given to perform, in front of the professor and classmates at the end of the semester, was intricate. Together she and Matt filled them in on all the neighbors who kept needing their help and how Matt was taking over so she could focus on her studies. Megan could tell her uncle was taking note of Matt's abilities and was impressed when Matt told everyone about the snake. As the meal ended and the conversation dwindled, everyone pitched in to clear off the table.

"That was delicious, ma'am. I can't say I've had anything taste that good in a long time," Matt told Helen.

"Thank you, Matt, and please call me Helen," she said.

* * *

While the ladies handled the dishes, Ryan led Dan and Matt out onto the back deck overlooking the ranch. "The girls will bring us coffee and dessert out here when they're done in the kitchen," he told them. "Have a seat and relax."

Matt crossed the deck and stood at the railing to explore the view. The peace and quiet felt powerful against the backdrop of mooing cattle and nickering horses. He missed this, more than he realized until that very moment. A desire to go back home for a few days to see his family crept into his head. It had been years since he felt this relaxed around people who weren't his family; a feeling he thought he had lost. And Megan was the one who allowed those feelings to seep back into his being.

Megan found him deep in thought and sidled up next to him before turning around and leaning her back against the railing to study his face in the moonlight.

"You seem more relaxed," said Megan.

"I do?" asked Matt, realizing it, but wondering how Megan knew. "How can you tell?"

"The furrow in your brow has subsided since we arrived. Your features have a gentler flow," she told him.

On an impulse, Matt reached over and drew her to his side before drawing her close to his chest. She gingerly placed her head on his shoulder and methodically rubbed the middle of his back. They were still standing that way, taking in the view of the land, when Helen came outside with some coffee and cheesecake topped with strawberries.

Before releasing her, Matt leaned down and placed two gentle kisses on the top of her head. He then slowly rode his hand down her arm and clasped her hand before walking over to sit with everyone else. He didn't know whether he was just caught up in the moment of being there, but he was enjoying the calmness that had settled into him and the comfort he felt just standing there holding her, without any pressure to offer more.

After dessert, Helen enlisted the girls to make up a few beds before everyone turned in. Ryan finished his coffee and as he headed off to bed suggested that everyone else do the same because there was much to do in the morning.

"What time does everyone get up around here?" asked Matt.

"Five-thirty for breakfast," Ryan told him.

"Are we going running tomorrow morning, Meg?" inquired Matt.

"I was thinking we'd better skip it because there's enough for us to do around here, and *you're* going to be exhausted by tomorrow evening," she told him before heading into the house to help her aunt.

When Megan returned to the deck, she found Matt sitting alone with his head back and his coffee mug firmly clasped between his fingers.

"Hey," Megan said softly as she walked around to join him. "Everything okay? I'm sorry about my Uncle Ryan at the dinner table. He can be overbearing sometimes."

"Everything is fine. Come sit with me for a few minutes?" he asked.

"Sure."

"I've been thinking I haven't been quite fair to you," he said as he lifted his left arm and gently pulled her back to his side.

"What do you mean?" asked Megan, taking a sideways glance into his face.

"Your uncle was secretly sending me a message tonight when he placed his hands on my shoulders at the dinner table. He was letting me know it's okay to open up about myself while I'm here and that I'm among friends, whether I realize it yet or not. I know you've been purposely avoiding prying into my personal life, which I have appreciated. But my perspective has changed and I'd like you to know a little more about me. I'm not going to lie, Meg, there are a few things that are going to take a while for me to discuss."

"Thank you for telling me, Matt. I appreciate it."

"So, is there something you'd like to ask me?" he inquired.

"I might have a few questions, but in due time," she answered, snuggling even closer. "But right now I'd like to sit here with your arms wrapped around me for about ten minutes before heading to bed, if that's okay?"

"I believe I can handle that," he said, reaching to put his empty mug on the coffee table. Sliding into the corner of the sofa, Matt pulled her back so he could fold his arms around her and rest them on her stomach. Leaning his head onto hers, he inhaled her scent before brushing the top of her head with his lips, knowing she didn't have any underlying expectations. *I just might be able to get used to this,* he thought.

Chapter Nine

In the morning, Ryan walked into the kitchen and found Dan and Matt already dressed in work clothes and boots, enjoying a cup of coffee. Matt took note of the broad smile on Ryan's face as he headed towards the coffee pot.

Helen appeared shortly and set about fixing eggs and pancakes in a timely fashion to get them on their way. While things were cooking, she made up some sandwiches and poured coffee into a thermos. Within thirty minutes they had finished eating, loaded the back of the pickup truck with supplies and headed down the back field.

* * *

Megan had spent most of the night wondering what type of women Matt had dealt with over the years. It bothered her to think that his life was anything but comfortable. Although she wasn't that naïve and knew the tabloids could fabricate a story through pure speculation.

It was eight o'clock when she finally rolled out of bed and made her way down the stairs and into the kitchen. Megan found her aunt sitting at the table flipping through an old recipe book. She recognized it immediately as her mother's and smiled.

"Mornin', Aunt Helen," greeted Megan with a yawn.

"Well, hello there, sleepyhead! Where is that sister of yours?"

"She still must be asleep. I think there's something in the air out here that makes me more tired than at home."

"Or it might just be anticipating all the work your uncle has left you in charge of. And it's a pretty extensive list … as usual," said Helen lifting her eyes toward the ceiling before sliding a piece of paper in front of Megan.

"Remind me why I came up here?" Megan said with a sigh as she picked up the note.

Helen laughed. "To get away from it all?"

"Exactly," replied Megan.

* * *

Ryan pulled up to one of the damaged fence posts, and before he had his gloves on, the boys were unloading the new lumber from the back of the truck like they had done the job all their lives.

"Well, I'll be damned! Maybe I should have slept in this morning and let you two handle this," said Ryan.

"Okay Matt, spill. Because I know you didn't pick up these skills on any TV show," said Ryan.

Matt grinned, knowing he was doing a job that was second nature to him. He hadn't given any thought to his actions and just dove right in.

"I grew up on a ranch in Michigan. My dad and I mended fences all the time. Although it's been a while since I've done this."

"How about that, Dan? We've learned something new about our hired hand that I bet he hasn't shared with too many folks. I had a good feeling about you, son."

Matt paused before looking up and smiling.

"How much does Meg know about you? After dinner last night I'm sensing it's not a lot. And I'm going to ask why? She's a good girl."

Matt wiped his brow with the back of his glove. He wasn't prepared to have someone read him as well as Ryan. It was true, he hadn't been forthcoming with any information about himself, but he also hadn't felt the need to fabricate any stories just to keep their conversations going. He tried to encourage her to ask him questions last night, but even though he had given her three other opportunities, she chose not to ask despite his prompting.

"Son, what did I tell you at the dinner table last night, which I meant? Dan will back me up on that, too."

"I'm among friends and can be myself."

That was going to be hard for him to get used to. That's why he needed the break up in the hills during the off season, so he *could* be himself and not have to live up to anyone's expectations.

"Well," encouraged Ryan as they worked to remove a second rotten post from the ground.

"To be honest ..."

"That's a good start, son."

"You're right. Meg *doesn't* know a whole lot about me," Matt continued. "When she realized who I was, she didn't drill me with a bunch of personal questions. Questions I truthfully wasn't ready to answer. She keeps surprising me with her actions and responses."

"That's Meg," replied Ryan.

"I got your message at dinner last night and gave her the opportunity to ask me whatever she wanted to. She told me she'd give it some thought, which confounded me yet again."

"She hides her feelings very well, too, Matt. And if I know Meg, she's purposefully trying not to get too close because she's worked so hard to get where she is and doesn't want anything to derail the goals she's trying to reach. She's always wanted to be a doctor and that goal has stayed with her through the years. She was determined to raise her sister, despite our willingness to make the journey easier. The drive to succeed is in her blood. And the fact that her father was a pediatrician makes it even more personal."

"I didn't know that. I mean the part about her father's occupation."

"So now you know a little more about her. Isn't it only fair that she knows more about you?" asked Ryan.

Matt had to admit, Ryan had a point. *Maybe I could start with a few things nobody else seems interested in knowing*, he thought.

"Well, ... so spill a little, son," prompted Ryan again, invading Matt's thoughts.

"It's been so long, I don't know where to start," laughed Matt.

"Growing up year's work for us... right, Dan?" inquired Ryan with a wink.

Matt told them what it was like growing up in Michigan and about his mom's passing. He told them he had an older brother, Brian, who lived on the ranch with his family and helped their dad. He talked about things most people in LA weren't interested in hearing about. But he also told them how he ended up becoming an actor and that he used to play professional baseball until he was twenty-six, which he had to give up due to a severe elbow injury. His life probably would have been totally different had he still played.

They continued working quietly, like a well-oiled machine, until Ryan asked, "So how are the women in LA, Matt?"

"Conniving, flirty, pushy, and I've had my fill …" he blurted out without filtering his thoughts.

Dan and Ryan looked at each other with their hammers in mid-air and simultaneously responded, "Tell us how you really feel," before they all laughed.

"Well, Uncle Ryan, I think you loosened his tongue up a little bit too much," said Dan shaking his head.

"How's it feel, Matt?" asked Ryan as he drove the last nail into the board.

"Not sure after that outburst, but I guess I'm more comfortable and relaxed."

"Good. Now let's get our tools packed up and have some lunch. I have one more section I'd like to tackle before heading home today. I left Meg a lengthy list of things to do with Kayla while we were gone," Ryan informed the boys.

"You did what?" asked Matt.

"Son, if I hadn't left her a list she would have been bored to tears all day. And if I know my niece, she's probably mucking out a horse stall right now."

* * *

Ryan was almost right. Megan was cleaning the hoofs on Blue and Cedar. Blue, Megan's favorite, was a gray Quarter Horse, with shimmers of blue reflected in his coat along with a black mane and tail. Cedar was also a Quarter Horse with a beautiful dun coat; his black mane and tail made him stand out in the field. When Megan finished with their hoofs she turned them loose in the field to graze.

She then turned her attention to cleaning out the two stalls before bathing and grooming them. Her uncle said he wanted them to get some exercise tomorrow. And knowing her uncle, Megan was sure he had something up his sleeve, but figured she better just roll with the punches for now.

Kayla did her part by helping to feed all the horses, goats and chickens, then she milked the goats before heading inside to help their aunt prepare dinner. They hadn't had a chance to talk most of the day, but planned on getting away to their favorite spot after dinner.

After Megan finished cleaning the two stalls and laid some fresh bedding, she whistled for the dogs to go round up Blue and Cedar. Bosley was having the time of his life, to the point she hardly saw him. He hadn't forgotten her, though, because he raced towards her from the fields along with the two border collies, Colt and Shadow. When she finally got them settled down she told them who to round up, and within five minutes they were ushering Blue and Cedar back to the side gate. Throwing a rope around their necks, she led the horses over to the water trough where she had lined up some grooming brushes. Pulling out her phone and ear buds, Megan plugged up her ears and turned on some country music before starting to wash off Blue.

* * *

That's where the boys found her as they drifted down the hill towards the house. Matt caught sight of Megan dancing and singing as she bathed the beautiful bluish gray horse. He had no idea she had such a lovely voice and was stunned to see her so relaxed, not to mention her uninhibited dancing. Her uncle inched the truck closer and stopped across from her.

After a few moments Ryan hollered out the window, "Looks like you're having more fun than working, young lady. But I must say I'm enjoying the singin' and dancin', and so are the boys."

Megan's face turned bright red as she rolled around on her heels and threw the sponge right through the truck window, hitting her uncle square in the chest.

"Serves you right," yelled Megan, "for creeping up on me like that."

Ryan tossed the sponge back in her direction. "Dinner's going to be ready soon. You might want to consider less dancin' and more scrubbin'." He was smiling from ear to ear as he drove the rest of the way to the house.

Matt got out and stared in Megan's direction for several minutes before Ryan came up beside him.

"Surprised you, didn't she?" he asked, but he already knew the answer. Placing his hand on Matt's shoulder Ryan steered him towards the house saying, "And I'm sure she'll find you more appealing after a long hot shower."

"Yes, sir," Matt answered, straining to keep his eyes on Megan.

* * *

While the boys and Megan were handling chores, Kayla and Helen had prepared breaded pork chops, stuffing, green beans and rolls for dinner. Everyone thought the meal was delicious and not a morsel was left over. After clearing the dishes off the table, they all strolled onto the deck to enjoy some coffee and a bit of relaxation.

Matt sat in one of the chairs leaving Megan to wonder if he didn't want her company. As she walked by, he reached out and leisurely caught her hand in his, steering her around to squeeze in next to him. She caught the reflection of the moon in his eyes before he placed his hands on her shoulders and encouraged her to lean back into his body. They all talked for a while, seated around the coffee table, until Megan and Kayla, along with their aunt, excused themselves to clean up the dishes.

Megan couldn't wait to escape with Kayla to their secret hideout in the barn, for a little bit of girl talk. Their aunt could tell something was brewing when they started giggling with each other as they dried the dishes.

"I think you girls need to get out of here and leave the rest to me," said Helen, who recognized their antics from years ago.

"Thanks, Aunt Helen. We'll surface in a couple hours in case the boys start asking for us," said Kayla.

Megan grabbed a bottle of wine off the rack in the kitchen and two glasses while Kayla collected some crackers and cheese. They headed out the front door and ducked back around one of the horse barns. Sliding the stable door open they made their way toward the far left corner. They climbed the ladder up to the loft and found their hideout miraculously untouched except for dust and a few cobwebs. After taking a broom to the webs, they settled down onto the hay bales and poured themselves a glass of wine.

"How long has it been since we wandered up here ... four years?" asked Kayla.

"Sounds about right. I don't know where we would be without our aunts and uncles. Our lives have been packed with a bunch of unexpected challenges. Although there have been a few pleasant memories tucked inside," said Megan.

"Got that right! Like my wedding. I never thought I'd be married and running my own café with Dan," said Kayla. "He's supported me through the years ... but I didn't come out here to talk about our past. Tell me how things are going with Matt. He seems pretty level-headed for someone who's usually in the spotlight, and apparently you two have been getting along."

"I guess we have," sighed Megan.

"What do you mean you guess?" asked Kayla. "You two seemed awfully chummy out on the deck."

"But I don't know a lot about him, Kayla. Although he's prompted me to ask him questions," said Megan.

"So what's keeping you from asking?"

"I don't want him to feel like I'm prying into his personal life. And part of me feels like he should be telling me, if he wants me to know."

"Well, he didn't seem to mind Uncle Ryan meddling a little bit last night at dinner. And you're one to talk. You have a way with people and getting them to open up. Your patience and ability to comfort others is one of your strengths ... just like Dad and Mom," Kayla reminded her. "But when was the last time you truly opened up about yourself? When are *you* going to let someone inside? I've seen the way he looks at you, Meg. He's hanging on the edge of falling head over heels for you. Any idea what's holding him back?"

"I haven't a clue. I see the hesitation in his eyes. He seems to make it a point to be outside on his front porch every day until he sees me and I acknowledge him. Every now and then he pulls me close for a hug, then just as quickly lets me go. I know I'm growing on him and he's ... he's ...,"

"It's okay, Meg. I can tell by the way you smile when he enters the room," said Kayla.

Megan dropped her shoulders and sighed. "His smile and those hazel-blue eyes just about melt me every time I see him. I can't seem to stop my thoughts from drifting to him, even while I'm studying. So, I guess I'm as guilty of wanting to see him every day, as much as he wants to see me. How am I going to get through this semester? I swore I'd never get involved with someone until I was done with my education."

"Talk to him on the way home, Meg. If he truly cares about you, he should understand and give you the space you need until the end of the semester," assured Kayla. "But I also think you need to reveal a little bit more about yourself."

"I would, but I'm worried we'll start to get closer and then he'll get called back to work. What if he's called back before my semester is over? Then what? I'm trying so hard not to let my feelings go any deeper while I'm in school."

"And the problem with that, Meg, is that love has a way of creeping into our hearts when we least expect it, but when we need it the most. Which, if you recall, is how it was for Dan and me. Things can be worked out, but you're going to need to talk it out."

"I can't see myself studying or working in LA, Kayla. And right now, I don't see a functioning solution for either one of us," she blurted out. "Provided there is an *us*."

"The way he kissed your head on the deck was endearing. Maybe he's leery about getting involved, just like you. Putting yourself out there is scary, because love's scary, Meg. It's based on a lot of trust, and that the person you're giving your heart away to will protect it for the rest of your living days. One of you is going to have to let go of your fears and be the first to start building that trust. The love will follow on its own accord," said Kayla.

"You know, for being my younger sister, you sure have become very wise," Megan said leaning forward to hug her. "Can I ask you something?" said Megan leaning back on the hay bale.

"Since when do you have to ask?" laughed Kayla.

"Do you have any recollection of Matt when we came up to Aunt Linda and Uncle Paul's place over the summers? I keep having these moments where he seems familiar. And I'm not talking about his acting career."

"I told you before that I don't recall seeing him. We hopped between the cabin, our house and up here so many times after Mom and Dad's death, it's a wonder I remember where we spent the holidays. And I was what? Fifteen? Everything seemed so blurry back then, like I was walking through a dream, Meg."

"Yeah, me, too. But I just can't shake this feeling about him," said Megan.

"I promise if something comes to mind, I'll let you know," said Kayla.

"Thanks."

"So, did you get everything done on Uncle Ryan's list today?"

"List? That was more like a summer to-do list instead of a help-out list. I know we haven't been here in a while, but I would have thought he'd have given me a break."

"Who? Uncle Ryan?" laughed Kayla. "I'm just grateful it's always directed more towards you than me, but you know I don't mind helping out."

"Well, he had me clean up Blue and Cedar today, which is his subtle way of telling me to take Matt horseback riding," said Megan. "So, I think I'll take Matt to Roger and Claire's stable in Maryland tomorrow morning. I don't want Uncle Ryan to think I've lost my ability to read between the lines."

"Got that right. He'll think he's lost his touch," said Kayla.

"Yup, and I don't want to deal with a more direct message."

"That's for sure. Although, I'd want to be around for that conversation," laughed Kayla before finishing the wine in her glass.

"Thanks for your support," smirked Megan, nudging her sister's shoulder before she drained her glass, too.

After collecting everything they made their way around to the back of the house and climbed the steps to the deck. They found Dan and Matt exactly where they left them, talking about baseball.

"Where have you two been?" asked Dan.

"Enjoying a little quality time together," answered Kayla, before placing a loud kiss on Dan's cheek and heading towards the sliding glass door.

"I think that's my cue. See you both in the morning," said Dan, following Kayla through the door.

"Did you two have a nice time catching up?" asked Matt.

"Yes, we did," said Megan with a yawn.

"Looks like someone else is tired," said Matt, patting the seat next to him.

"Matt, if I sit down, I'm not going to get back up," she said. As she walked by, she nonchalantly leaned over and kissed him on the cheek, just like Kayla had kissed Dan.

"Then I guess I'm going in, too," he said, catching the hand that carried the wine bottle as he stood. Drawing her close he held her for a while before kissing her softly on the cheek. He took the wine bottle and deposited it onto the kitchen island before they climbed the stairs.

"What time are we getting up tomorrow morning?" he asked.

"Well, Aunt Helen would like to have dinner for lunch tomorrow since Dan and Kayla need to leave here around four o'clock to get back to the café. And if you're up to it, I'd like to take you horseback riding in the morning. But we're going to need to hitch the trailer onto the back of Uncle Ryan's truck and haul the horses to Roger and Claire Stables, who also happen to be friends of ours, so I can show you something. Kayla and I used to ride there often when we were younger. I haven't been there in a little over three years. I'd like to leave here at seven o'clock ... okay?" asked Megan.

"That sounds nice. I'll see you at seven," said Matt as he opened her bedroom door. Placing his hand on the small of her back he nudged her inside. "Night, Meg!"

"Night, Matthew!" she responded in a sing-song voice.

*   *   *

Matt laughed as he made his way down the hallway to his room. As he stripped down to his underwear, he realized Megan was a little tipsy but coherent enough to carry on a conversation. And considering the wine bottle was still half full, she and Kayla's limit had to be very small.

I probably could have taken advantage of her right there on the deck, but I'm not that kind of man ... plus, I want all her faculties working when I….

"What are you thinking, Matt?" he whispered, chastising himself. *If anything is ever going to happen, I'm going to have to trust her, which isn't going to be easy for me ... I don't even know if I'll be able to allow myself to get closer ... or to relax enough to make it past the first kiss, let alone first base ... Although, I can't seem to deny myself the occasional hug and quick kiss, ... which I'm sure is leading her on in a direction I might not be able to handle. Besides, it would be a long distance relationship and those rarely work out ... Right?*

With those thoughts rolling around his head, Matt fell asleep and dreamed about Megan showing up on set during the filming of an episode, which scared and elated him.

Chapter Ten

egan's alarm went off at quarter to six Sunday morning. She used to be a morning person, but ever since college her morning routine had gotten all jumbled up. After silencing her alarm, she got dressed and moseyed out to the stables to feed the horses.

"Well, good mornin' darlin'," said Ryan, walking into the stall.

"Ah!" yelled Megan, causing Blue to rear his head up in the air and stomp his feet. "Next time could you make a little noise or something, Uncle Ryan. And you're out and about earlier than usual for a Sunday morning," she added.

"If you didn't have your thoughts on someone else, you would have heard me in the tack room when you walked by. I was just making sure you got my message," said Ryan.

Megan closed her eyes and shook her head slightly before saying, "Do you think you could have just suggested I take Matt horseback riding?"

"Now what fun would that be, besides you evidently didn't need me to. Having you clean Blue and Cedar was enough of a subliminal message," said Ryan with a grin.

"Any other reason you're out here at this hour?" Megan asked as she rubbed Blue's forehead to calm him down, then hung a bucket of food inside his stall.

"I just thought I'd give you a hand with hooking up the trailer this morning. Nice day for a ride, don't you think?" he inquired.

"Couldn't have asked for a better one," she replied with a sideways glance at her uncle before walking over to maneuver Cedar out of his stall. *There's more to it than that,* thought Megan. *But there's probably not enough time to flush it out of him before Matt shows up.*

"Let me give you a hand saddling up those horses, Meg. We want you back in time for the big luncheon Aunt Helen is preparing."

"Thanks," she said, eyeing him suspiciously as she walked past him with Cedar. Taking a chance, she turned and said, "Now would you care to tell me what's really on your mind, besides pretending that you're helping me out this morning? Because saddling the horses is something you usually let me handle."

"I could never fool you, Meg. You always could peg me down."

"Yeah, it's a family gift, but you still haven't told me anything. What gives?"

"The three of us had a nice long chat out in the fields yesterday," Ryan reminisced.

"And ...," said Megan.

"I'm just surmising here Meg, but you know I'm pretty good at reading a person by what they choose to reveal, as well as what they choose not to."

"That would be true," she agreed.

"Well, if I read that young man of yours correctly, I gather he's been in a bunch of surface relationships, but nothing as concrete as what he's started with you. It's embarrassing for a man of his notoriety and age to explain that to any woman, when their perception of him holds him to a higher level. He struggles with his emotions every time he sees you or comes close to you, if you've taken notice. And if you care for him, he's going to need you to stick with him and let him know you're there and not going anywhere. He seems like a good man, Meg. The more he grows to trust you, the closer he'll come to revealing his deepest fears. And you're going to have to decide if you're willing to care for his tormented heart as much as I believe he has fearfully started to care for yours. Only time will tell darlin.'"

"Thanks, Uncle Ryan, I appreciate every word," she told him honestly. Her head was now spinning as she tried to process everything her uncle told her. She didn't say anything as she led the horses into the trailer, for she knew there were several underlying messages woven into his words.

"Knew you would, darlin'. And here comes Matt now. Enjoy your ride today. I think you need it as much as he does. Relax a little," he said walking back into the stables to release the rest of the horses into the open field.

Matt walked up and surprised Megan by planting a good morning kiss on her cheek.

"Good mornin' to you, too! How'd you sleep?" she inquired.

"Pretty good. My arms are a little stiff from working yesterday, but nothing major," he said.

"Good. Then let's get goin' so we're back in time for lunch."

Megan got behind the wheel and started backing up when she heard her uncle whistle. He made his way up to the driver's side door and handed Megan a thermos and paper bag. "Almost forgot to give you these. There's a snack for you two and a couple apples for the horses. Keep an eye on each other while you're ridin', you hear?"

"We will, Uncle Ryan, and tell Aunt Helen thanks. See you in a few hours."

The drive to Roger and Claire Stables, in Oakland, Maryland, was quiet. But as the miles passed Megan sensed Matt was growing anxious by the way he bounced his foot, which was resting on top of his left knee. She thought he might be worried about getting on a horse again. As they got closer to the stables, she reached over and placed her hand on his bouncing ankle to help him relax. His brow was furrowed when he glanced her way.

"What?" asked Matt.

"You seem a bit anxious," said Megan.

"I'm okay. I'm looking forward to getting back on a horse," he said.

If that's true, he has a funny way of showing it, thought Megan. She figured there must be some other reason for the quiet ride. Looking inward, Megan had to admit she was apprehensive about the adventure herself. She didn't want Matt to think she had any hidden motives other than to do something relaxing, regardless of what her uncle revealed about him. She hadn't treated him as though he was different since she met him, and given her uncle's insight, it was a good thing she hadn't. This outing was to help them both relax, and that's exactly what Megan wanted. No pressure.

When they arrived, Megan jumped out of the truck and was greeted by Roger and Claire.

"Well, look who's a sight for sore eyes," declared Roger, before walking over and giving Megan a hug.

"How have you been, girl?" asked Claire, collecting Megan in her arms and briefly rubbing her back.

"I'm doing well. I'm working on completing my last semester of college before I start medical school," Megan told them. "Roger and Claire, this is my friend, Matt. His family owns the house across the street from Aunt Linda and Uncle Paul."

"Nice to meet you, Matt," Claire said, extending her hand to him. "Megan and her sister used to come here often. It's a beautiful countryside, with some fantastic views."

"Who are you riding today?" asked Roger after shaking Matt's hand.

"Uncle Ryan had me bring Blue and Cedar."

"Well, let's get them backed out of the trailer so you two can enjoy this nice day," said Roger.

Megan squeezed in next to Blue and talked to him as she made her way to the front of the trailer. He nickered and stomped his feet as she slowly coaxed him out. Once in the open he settled down and nuzzled her neck.

Roger worked to get Cedar out of the other stall, but it took Megan's voice to calm him down. She jumped up onto the side of the trailer and finding Cedar's eyes, talked to him as Roger moved him out. She inched her way down the length of the running board, until Cedar's head appeared. After jumping down, she turned to look at Matt, only to get nosed in between her shoulder blades by Cedar, sending her into Matt's arms.

Megan felt the redness rise in her cheeks as Matt stood her upright. She quickly whirled around and scolded Cedar. "There will be none of that or I might refuse to give you your treat at the end of our ride. And Aunt Helen gave me your favorite kind of apple," she said.

She turned and collected their snacks and thermos from the truck and placed them in her satchel on Blue.

Turning back to Matt she said, "Let me introduce you to Cedar. I would have introduced you at the ranch, but Uncle Ryan was up early and helped me load the horses into the trailer," said Megan apologetically.

"That's okay," said Matt as they walked to stand by Cedar.

"This is Cedar," said Megan. "Say hi to the nice young man, Cedar."

Matt reached out his hand and whispered gently into Cedar's ear as he caressed his forehead and neck before making his way back to the horse's left side. Taking the reins loosely in his left hand he placed his left foot in the stirrup and elegantly hoisted himself up into the saddle.

"Nicely done!" said Megan, with a broad smile on her face.

"Thanks. Guess I haven't forgotten everything."

Megan grabbed Blue's reins and just as effortlessly pulled herself up into the saddle. But as soon as she was up, she came sliding back down and ran to the truck. She reappeared with two cowboy hats in her hand. She handed Matt the black one and said, "Well, we need to look the part, too," as she placed her own brown cowboy hat on her head.

Matt grinned and slid the hat onto his head, while Megan climbed back into the saddle. "Good to go?" she asked, noticing the crease in between his eyebrows before admiring how tall and impressive he looked in the saddle.

Matt motioned forward with his hand.

Megan wove Blue through the woods, across a few streams and multiple open fields as they started working their way to the top of the mountain. The trail was so familiar to her, yet so different. When she and Kayla last visited the trees were all in bloom, now the ground was scattered with several leaves as fall started to shut down the forest for winter hibernation. As they reached the next open field, Matt galloped past her and she could tell he was enjoying every minute by his more relaxed form.

* * *

Slowing at the edge of the next section of woods, Matt turned and observed her as she trotted towards him. He forgot about his concerns regarding the progression of their relationship, which had been on his mind for the entire drive to the stables, as he watched her form. Her red hair reflected the sun's rays as it lifted and fell to the rhythm of the horse's gait.

"Well, you look more relaxed," commented Megan, noticing how quickly his body had settled into Cedar's rhythm.

Matt just nodded as he stared back over the field they had just traveled.

"Last section of woods before we reach the top. Shall we?" asked Megan.

"Lead the way," said Matt.

About fifteen minutes later, they came out of the last patch of woods. As Matt strode to her side, Megan turned to watch his appreciation of the view as he approached the top of the hill.

"Stretched out before you are the Appalachian Mountains in West Virginia," said Megan.

"Oh, my," said Matt as he looked off to his left and slowly scanned the mountains in front of him. "I don't think I've ever seen rolling hills like these before. Look at how the trees cover the whole mountain, not a bare spot to be seen."

"Nope. And the changing leaves are starting to color the tips of the treetops. Look at them glistening from the sun's rays. The trees will be at their peak coloration in a few weeks. By then the view will fill your senses, painting a surreal and vibrant display of color," said Megan.

"That was very poignant," said Matt as he watched her slide off Blue and walk over to stand closer to the edge of the hill. The wind was blowing gently as she stretched her hands out to soak up the moment.

Matt dismounted Cedar and stretched his legs before joining her. His emotions were building at the sight of her standing so carefree and lost in the tranquility of the moment. Stepping up behind her, he stretched out his arms and clasped his hands over her wrists before closing his eyes and letting the sun beat down on his face.

After several minutes, Megan removed her hat and looked back at Matt. "Isn't it lovely? I can just picture how colorful it will be in a few weeks."

He loved the way she appreciated the little things. The pure things that nature offers and you can't buy, even in a picture.

"Yes, it is," he answered, and he wasn't just interested in nature's picture, spread out in front of him. Overcome by the moment, Matt pushed his hat back, then swiftly pulled her close and greedily kissed her.

She broke away, taken aback by his abrupt and slightly forceful movements; he could see it in her eyes. Patting her hands on his chest, she peered into his face.

"What?" he asked, displaying the same anxious look that had settled on his face before they started up the mountain. He figured he knew what was coming next.

"I'm not going anywhere," she calmly told him, trying to help soothe the annoyance that sprung up in his eyes and voice. Reaching up Megan caressed his cheeks with her thumbs while looking into his hazel-blue eyes.

"Gentle and slow," she whispered, then watched him readjust his thoughts, as he fought to control a desire he didn't know how to handle.

Matt stared at her for several moments, trying to come to grips with the fact that he should never assume her reactions. Slowly she drew his mouth to her lips and sweetly kissed him. As he relaxed, their lips parted and he gradually discovered the taste of her, like no others before her. As she slid her fingers into the hair at the nape of his neck he wrapped his one arm around her shoulders and cradled her head with the other as the intensity grew. Drawing her slightly closer, he removed his hand from her head and wrapped it around her waist, resting it on the small of her back. Matt had never felt so many sensations coursing through his body as he stood there lost in her arms. He paused a moment to look into her face, making sure it was Megan standing in front of him, before gently devouring her lips again.

When he broke away, he pulled her head against his chest and held her securely for a long while staring across the mountains, wondering where to go from here. His interest in this energetic and passionate woman standing in front of him was growing. She may be several years younger, but her life experiences exposed a very mature young woman. After watching her with the horses yesterday he also sensed a playful side, which he hoped she'd reveal a little more frequently, provided he gave himself the chance to truly get to know her.

* * *

Slowly pulling away Megan watched him regain control of his emotions. She didn't have the words to express the pleasure and tingling sensations that traveled through her essence. The intensity of Matt's heartbeat was enough to prove that he was as overcome by emotions as she was. As the strumming of his heart settled down, he leaned her back in his arms to look down into her face again, before giving her another soft kiss on the lips.

Placing a hand on Matt's chest she took a step back and pulled out her phone. Matt looked at her inquisitively until he heard music and she put her hand out towards him.

"I have two left feet," said Matt.

"I don't care," she replied with a tilt of her head as she extended her hand to him again and wiggled her fingers to come closer. Matt couldn't refuse as the dimple appeared in her cheek, melting his defenses. Shaking his head, he took her hand and allowed her to teach him an easy two-step. Within minutes he was guiding her across the grass. Despite his two left feet, his rhythm was pretty good. As the song ended, he slid his fingers along the left side of her neck and caressed her check before slowly drawing her in and tasting her once more.

Megan drew back and kept an eye on him as she walked over to Blue and pulled out the snacks and thermos from her satchel. She walked over to one of the large rocks on the hill and sat before pouring some warm coffee. She then pulled out a large blueberry muffin her aunt had baked. As he walked over to join her, Megan said, "I have a question for you."

"Sure," said Matt.

"Why is it that a nice-looking man like yourself hasn't found a nice-looking woman and settled down?"

"Wow, I wasn't expecting such a personal question from you," he replied.

She watched as the crease in between his eyes returned as he considered his answer. She thought about brushing the question aside, but decided to give him a chance to respond.

After taking a swig of coffee he finally said, "Despite what people think, it's not easy when you're in the acting business to find someone who allows you to be yourself. Considering the women I've associated with, I'm not sure I *ever* see myself getting married and having a family."

"I see," replied Megan.

"Meg, I ..." he began, but she got up and walked back to Blue.

He watched her put the thermos away and give each of the horses their apple. Not knowing what else to say she turned around and asked calmly, "Ready to head back?"

"No, I'm not," he replied.

Megan watched him slowly stand and walk towards her. As he touched her shoulders, she could tell he noticed the tears brimming in her eyes. The concerned look on his face told her he was upset that he had caused them. His actions were truly causing her to wonder what direction their relationship was headed or was he just leading her on. Brushing his thumbs gently across her eyes, he tilted her face towards his and planted a gentle kiss on her cheek.

"I'm sorry, Meg. There's more to it than that. Please understand."

She watched a pleading look consume his face, and remembered what her uncle told her. She was going to have to open up her heart to him before he would be able to trust her with his innermost fears. And despite her inward declaration that she wasn't interested in building a relationship, her heart was telling her that life might have a different plan in mind.

He drew her close and this time she knew he wasn't about to let her go without some type of response. "Meg, ..." he prompted.

She could choose to make matters worse or tell him she understood. The problem was she *didn't* understand. But instead of lying she repeated herself, "Matt, I don't plan on going anywhere," which was the truth. With that he held her tighter and buried his face in her soft hair.

* * *

Matt knew she didn't understand. How could she? But he respected her for not fabricating a lie. He knew he was building a path of doubt surrounding his intentions. It's what he always did when it came to relationships and getting close. It was up to him to explain his comments and actions. He had never considered revealing his past to any woman, until now. But he didn't know how, even with Megan, which meant he still wasn't ready to divulge the turmoil that controlled his mannerisms.

Putting his hands on her upper arms he put her at arm's length before leaning over and kissing her cheek, again. He could only hope that the gesture told her he cared about her but he needed to work through some things. After helping her mount Blue, he climbed onto Cedar then leaned over and commandeered the reins on Blue. Maneuvering the horses around, he pulled out his phone and took a picture of the two of them with the mountains and early fall leaves in the background.

As they trekked down the mountain and across the fields, Megan led them to a natural spring watering hole so the horses could get a drink. As the horses got their fill, Matt remembered what Megan's uncle told him about opening up. Taking a deep breath he blurted out, ". . . So, did you know I have an older brother?"

Glancing his way, Matt could tell she was taken aback by this forthright bit of information.

"No, I didn't know that," Megan answered as they continued down the hill.

"His name is Brian and he's three years older than me. He's planning on visiting for a few days, so you might get to meet him, if you're not too bogged down with your studies."

"Do you have any sisters?"

"No, it's just Brian and me. We were both born in Cedar, Michigan, on a ranch, which is about ten hours from the Briery Mountains," he informed her.

He watched Megan stop dead in her tracks and shake her head as he passed her. Looking back, he saw her smirk before stopping to wait for her. Once she was close enough, she took off her hat and gave him a good swat on the shoulder.

"Grew up on a ranch, ... I should have known by the way you handled Cedar. And how ironic is that? The horse's name is the same as the town you were born in. Anything else you'd care to enlighten me on?" she said with a smirk.

"One. And I've wanted to tell you this for a while," he said.

"I'm listening," she said, keeping Blue as still as possible.

"When you told me about your parent's passing and I said I understood, it's because my mother passed away when my brother and I were in college. Granted we still have our dad, but I know what kind of adjustments have to be made to deal with that kind of loss."

"Thanks for telling me," said Megan as she reached her hand out to claim his. She gave it a slight squeeze before Blue shifted and pulled them apart. "We better get going so we don't miss out on lunch."

Matt followed her the rest of the way down the hill more relaxed and at peace with himself. Knowing he grew up on a ranch she had him coax Cedar into the trailer, while she secured Blue. They thanked Roger and Claire, who sent them on their way with some of their homemade honey to share with the family.

Matt volunteered to drive and climbed behind the wheel. He drove down the dirt driveway, but stopped at the end, causing Megan to glance over at him. Putting the truck in park he reached over, and gently slid a few strands of her hair behind her ear before taking her face in his hands. "I had a great time this morning. Thank you."

He methodically caressed her cheeks before leaning in and kissing her like he was replenishing his soul. As he plied her lips open, he tasted her, causing Megan to sigh under his control. He had never elicited or felt so overcome by someone else's reactions or feelings before. Her soft and gentle ways were causing him to lower his guard. He was entering dangerous waters, which could make or break whatever this was growing into. Breaking off the kiss, they sat with their foreheads together, breathing deeply.

"We better get going, Matt," she urged, sensing the sudden wave in his comfort level.

"Yeah," was all he could manage.

Putting the truck in gear he pulled onto the main road. Once he was settled behind the wheel Megan reached over and captured his hand. Putting the radio on, they rode in comfortable silence all the way back to the ranch.

* * *

They pulled onto the dirt road leading to Pleasant Valley Ranch around quarter to noon. As he drove down the hill towards the stables, Ryan came out to greet them with a wave of his hand. When Megan got out of the truck and her uncle caught a glimpse of her face, she knew he could tell it had been a meaningful outing.

"Don't you two look more relaxed," said Ryan disguising his true reading, by winking at Megan.

Megan's face turned beet red as she made her way around to the back of the trailer to unload Blue and Cedar. Matt met her at the back hitch and lowered the tailgate. They simultaneously worked their way past the horses. Cedar had grown to like Matt and nuzzled his neck as he talked to him and backed him smoothly out of the trailer.

Once Blue was out, they walked the horses over to the stables to remove their saddles while Ryan backed up the truck and unhitched the trailer. Her uncle left them alone to tend to the horses and Megan was sure he had a smile plastered on his face as he wandered up to the house, letting them find their way in their own time.

Once the horses were tended to, Matt couldn't resist capturing her for another kiss. He plucked Megan off the ground, and sat on one of the hay bales against the far wall. Tilting her head sideways he softly brushed his lips over hers, causing her to shiver. She skimmed her fingers around both of his ears and trailed them around to the back of his neck, pressing her torso into his while returning his kiss then tentatively ran the tip of her tongue over his lips. She tasted coffee and the warmth of his body as her yearnings for more increased. The ripples of desire intensified as their lips parted and her need to taste him, even more, started to break down his shield. It was at that moment Bosley came bounding into the stable and landed Megan on her bottom at Matt's feet.

After the initial startle Megan found herself laughing, much to Matt's relief, while Bosley lavished her face with kisses. Matt reached down to help her up and received his ample supply of licks too. After recovering from Bosley's untimely interruption, they walked hand in hand up to the house for lunch.

Megan truly couldn't fathom how someone like Matt would be remotely interested in her, but she was getting caught up emotionally as their friendship tipped towards something more concrete. She knew what he told her up on the mountain was true, but despite his declaration about marriage, he seemed determined to overcome whatever had consumed him over the years. And according to her uncle, she might be the one he was willing to trust. Of course, only time was going to tell.

Walking onto the deck they were caught off guard by the stares they received from everyone.

"What?" Megan finally asked as they made their way to the two empty chairs.

"What happened to the two of you?" asked Kayla pointing to her hair as casually as she could.

Reaching up and touching her head, Megan felt a few strands of hay sticking out. "Oh," she said, "Bosley decided to welcome us home by knocking us on the ground in the stable and licking our faces." As she answered she looked over at Matt who had a piece of hay stuck in his collar and another one in the back of his hair, which Megan removed.

"Sure, he did," said Ryan under his breath.

Chapter Eleven

The two weeks following their weekend at the ranch, Megan wasn't sure whether Matt was avoiding her or just letting her get on with her studies. The biggest surprise was when he told her he wanted a break from jogging, when they arrived home. She thought he enjoyed their morning runs followed by their quick breakfast afterwards as much as she did. However, he still smiled and waved at her whenever he saw her outside.

I'm just being paranoid, she told herself. *Maybe he wants to give me the space I need to get my work done. Besides, I'm really not interested in developing a relationship right now … or am I?* Occasionally peeking out the living room window, Megan would catch him carrying boxes out to his Jeep. He appeared to be keeping busy, but she missed his daily company and was beginning to feel left out again. Her studies were going well, thanks to Matt's help with their neighbors, but that only enhanced her awareness that she was sitting on the sidelines.

He finally dropped by the following week on Wednesday around noon, while she was packing up her oboe for her music class.

"Hey, I know you're getting ready for lunch and class, but I wanted to know if you'd like a jogging partner tomorrow morning?" asked Matt leaning against the living room archway.

"Sure. Everything okay?" asked Megan as casually as she could.

"Yes. Why do you ask?"

"Oh, no particular reason," she told him as she focused on securing the clasps on her oboe case.

"I just thought I'd give you a little space. How are classes going?"

"Thanks," she said as she stood and headed towards him to place her oboe by the front door. As she stepped around him she wasn't quite sure she believed his explanation for leaving her alone the past two-weeks. Turning around she said, "I had my first exam this past Thursday on everything we've covered so far."

"How'd you do?" he asked as he turned around.

"I got a ninety-seven percent, so I'm happy," said Megan without much enthusiasm as she contemplated if she had even wanted the space.

"That's great!"

"What have you been up to lately?" she asked, forcing her thoughts not to linger on a relationship she wasn't even sure she wanted.

"I've been working on a few repairs inside, nothing major. A few loose cabinet hinges, two tiles that fell off the wall in the shower, and a couple other small jobs. I've also been working on cleaning up the basement. I spent most of yesterday at Mr. Tom and Ms. Kathy's cabin."

"Oh, why?"

"Their hot water tank in the basement developed a leak in the bottom of the tank. Mr. Tom came over and asked if I had a wet vac he could borrow. I took it over and stayed to help."

"That's why the plumbing truck was parked outside their house yesterday. I noticed it when I came out onto the porch to study my next set of index cards for anatomy. Did they lose a lot of things?"

"A few books and old magazines. They have a couple damp rugs laying in their backyard to dry out. I went down to the store and picked up a few plastic bins because they had some items in cardboard boxes on the floor that got totally soaked on the bottom,"

"That was nice of you to do that for them," said Megan.

"I don't mind helping. In fact, I enjoy the everyday things that crop up during the day. Some are more involved than others, but I'm really enjoying helping out. In LA I rarely get the chance to help someone. As soon as they recognize me they start acting like I shouldn't be bending over to pick things up. It's really annoying," he said with a grimace and slight shake of his head. "Anyway, are we on for jogging in the morning? I've missed our morning runs."

"Yup, I'll see you at six?" asked Megan with a smile.

"Let's make it six-thirty," said Matt as he headed towards the door.

Evidently, you are paranoid, thought Megan as she stared at the back of the front door. She rubbed her hand over her forehead at her own irrational thoughts about their relationship, before walking into the kitchen.

* * *

Stepping into the road Thursday morning, Matt said, "I'd like to take you on a field trip this Saturday, if you don't have too much studying to do."

"Okay," said Megan as her lips curved into a smile. "I think that'll work. I'll get caught up on my note cards tomorrow morning. Then I can study for my MCAT in the afternoon and Saturday morning. By the afternoon I'll be ready for a break. Where are we going?" asked Megan.

"When was the last time you went to a baseball game?" he inquired.

"Not since Kayla and I were teenagers."

"Well, it's almost the end of the baseball season and I'd like to take you to a game if you'd like to go."

"I'd like that. I might have lots of questions about the rules, though."

"I think I can handle that. Have you been to any other sporting games before?" he asked.

"It's been years, but I used to go to my high school football and basketball games. This will be my first baseball game as an adult," said Megan. "Where and what time?" she asked.

"The Pittsburgh Pirates are hosting the Houston Astros at home. The game starts around seven o'clock. It'll take us about an hour and a half to get to PNC Park, so we should probably leave around four-thirty to deal with parking and get settled inside the park."

"Are we eating there?" asked Megan.

"Absolutely! They have some of the best food for baseball fans," Matt exclaimed.

"Nice."

"And, Meg ..."

"Yeah ..."

"It's my treat."

"You don't have to do that."

"I know. But I want to," said Matt.

*   *   *

They jogged the rest of the way in companionable silence. When they rolled back around the bend Matt stopped in front of her place. He had kept his distance, mainly because he wanted to allow her time to focus on her studies without any interruptions. But they had also seen each other just about every day since she drove him up to the cabin and he didn't want her to think he was monitoring her daily life. Keeping an eye on her was one thing, like he promised Paul and Linda, but checking in on her daily seemed a bit too much.

He was surprised she agreed to go with him to the baseball game. The majority of women he'd gone out with would crinkle up their noses at the mere mention of going to a sporting event. *This ought to be very interesting,* he thought.

"Matt, are you okay?" asked Megan, pulling him out of his own musings.

Without a word he touched her shoulders and pulled her close. Traveling his hands up to her face he kissed her like a delicate flower until her lips parted. He felt her body relax the moment his lips touched hers and knew she had missed their kisses as much as he had. He had mastered the art of kissing her and melting her insides in a heartbeat. Cradling her head in his arm, he placed his other hand low on her spine and drew her in closer. For the first time in years he allowed his own body to relax and felt the desire in him grow hard against her. Grabbing hold of her arms he took a step back, as his face turned red. Megan reached up and laced her fingers behind his neck before pulling his head down to touch hers.

"Remember, Matt, it's me. And I'm not going anywhere. It's okay. I'd be a little concerned if your body didn't react. Apparently, we've missed the closeness."

He smiled into her lovely face, kissed her on the forehead, then guarding against any further outward reaction, he turned and crossed the street.

"Wow!" he whispered under his breath in a bewildered state before walking up the steps to his front porch.

He walked straight to the coffee pot before plopping down on the deck to mull over his body's swift reaction; it caught him off guard. He tried to keep his emotions and heart out of the picture, but secretly he hoped his feelings would become physically obvious at some point. Until now, he hadn't allowed himself to lose his senses and fully absorb the sweetness of her kisses.

Ever since the trauma he suffered at the hands of his first girlfriend, he had to work to get his body to respond to a woman's touch. Evidently his desire to restrain his physical reaction wasn't fully under his control, at least not with Megan. By dropping his guard and relaxing, he allowed himself to share an intimate moment with her. It was significant because it happened spontaneously.

Sitting on the deck he tried to reason things out. *Why, Meg? It's not like I haven't gone out with several attractive women. Maybe it's because she hasn't thrown herself at me. Although I've never felt this comfortable with any other woman since college ... but that relationship blew up in my face in a heartbeat and I've been fighting those memories ever since. Perhaps I'm finally able to trust someone again. I feel like I know Meg better than anyone I've gone out with, but then she's the most natural and down-to-earth woman I've ever met. I guess I'm just going to have to see how I react the next time ... and my feelings for her have got to be growing to even consider a next time,* he reasoned.

* * *

Megan walked inside smiling from ear to ear after watching Matt stroll back to his place. All her thoughts about his lack of interest vanished with his touch and kiss. *He truly was giving me time to focus on my studies.* But she couldn't stop thinking about his response during their kissing interlude. "He's all man," was her first thought, but then she quickly thought about his reaction to his own body's physical response. *Give him time, Megan. If his heart is as tormented as Uncle Ryan suspects, his fear of starting a relationship could be deeper than my own reasons for not getting too close,* she surmised as she headed upstairs to take a shower.

* * *

Saturday afternoon, Matt texted Megan at four to make sure she was getting ready.

Megan:　I'll be ready! Do you want me to meet you at your Jeep?

Matt:　I'll pull up in front of your gate.

Megan:　Okay. Think I should take a jacket?

Matt:　Yes, it's getting cooler at night.

Megan:　Okay. See you in a bit.

Matt rolled over to her place at exactly four-thirty. When he saw her jog down the porch steps in jeans and a green flannel shirt, he noticed something different about her. Lost in his thoughts she climbed in before he had a chance to get out and open her door. As she tossed her baseball cap and jacket on the back seat next to his glove, he made a mental note to help her out when they got to the game.

"Good afternoon. All set?" he asked.

"Hello!" she replied leaning over to give him a quick kiss on the cheek. "I'm ready to go. I see you brought your baseball glove."

"Yes, I did. Always good to come prepared," said Matt.

As he drifted to the end of the street, he figured out why she looked different. Her hair was down and curled around her shoulders instead of in a ponytail or straight and wet. Suddenly a flashback of himself sitting on the front porch at the cabin drifted across his brow, then it was gone. Refocusing his eyes, he impulsively leaned over and returned the kiss.

"You look very pretty," said Matt.

"Thank you. You don't look bad yourself," she replied. "What did you do yesterday and this morning?" asked Megan, treating him like they were old friends.

"I cleaned and did some laundry," he replied. "And you?"

"I'm anticipating a quiz on Thursday, so I reorganized my note cards. Then I spent time cleaning, too. It was a lot easier without Bosley getting under foot. It was also nice not having any new notes from my anatomy class this weekend. I've been meaning to tell you; Dr. Rhodes called me this past week to discuss some days and times he would be available to help me obtain some clinical hours next year in med school. I think he's more excited about medical school than I am; I have to be accepted first. By then I should be back in my apartment, since Aunt Linda and Uncle Paul will be heading home sometime in March or April."

Out of the blue, it dawned on Matt that their budding relationship might not last, and he wasn't ready to think about their careers and figuring out if they could make things work. *So I might as well enjoy whatever this relationship is while it lasts, because I'll probably never be lucky enough to have another one like it.*

"I have no doubt you'll get into whatever medical school you want to. I know it's taken a lot to get to this point and you should be proud of yourself."

"Thanks." After a few minutes of silence, Megan said, "Anything new since Thursday?"

"Not really, to tell you the truth," he replied, collecting her hand in his and placing it on his thigh. She reached over and caressed his right arm causing him to let out a sigh. As her hand moved up and down his arm he silently confessed, *I'm not ready to give up on us yet. Not after the way she's slowly crept into my life, which has truly caught me by surprise.*

"If I forget to tell you, thank you for taking me to the game today," she said, interrupting his deep thoughts.

"You're welcome. Thanks for coming with me," he answered, squeezing her hand.

The seats were down in the front row along the third baseline, so Megan could see everything up close. As they made their way to their seats, one of the players warming up on the field recognized Matt and waved.

When another player started looking and pointing in their direction, Megan said, "Matt, why are some of the players looking at you? What aren't you telling me?"

Matt thought for a moment then leaned close to her ear and said, "I guess I told your uncle and brother-in-law when you weren't around. I used to play professional baseball."

"For how long?" she asked, looking up at the sky.

"I spent four years in the minor leagues and a little over one in the majors," he answered.

"What happened?"

"I had a comebacker nail me in the elbow when I was twenty-six. I had surgery, but it was never the same after they removed several bone fragments. If I continued playing and injured it again, I risked losing the function and feeling in my right arm. You would not have liked me back then; I was not happy about it or life, again."

* * *

Maybe that's why I've been having all the déjà vu moments, rationalized Megan. But before she could dig deeper into her memories, the players were introduced onto the field and the national anthem began. Matt's word, *again*, stirred up a few questions, too, but when the anthem ended and the players took the field, her thoughts faded as she turned her attention to the game.

By the third inning the score was three-to-one in favor of the Pirates. Megan had never seen Matt so excited; it was like watching a little boy hit his first homerun. Before the fourth inning started he went to get their food. He came back with a loaded hotdog, a chicken sandwich with fries and two sodas before the Pirates came up to bat at the bottom of the fourth. While they ate, one of the Pirates hit a ball that bounced off the top of the wall and landed back in the field.

Megan asked, "Isn't that a ground rule double?"

"Well, a ground rule double can only be awarded by the umpire. Otherwise, the ball is still fair when it lands back in the field. If it had gone over the wall, it would have been a homerun," Matt told her.

"So, when would a ground rule double ever happen?"

"Say, the ball lands in the warning track and then bounces over the wall, that would be considered an automatic double in every ballpark. Now, Wrigley Field has ivy growing on the outfield walls. Sometimes a ball lands among the ivy and the umpire can say it's a ground rule double, because that outcome is unique to that ballpark," said Matt. "Does that make sense?"

"Yup," said Megan.

Just as she was about to take another bite of her chicken sandwich a foul ball came flying their way. Megan watched Matt grab his glove off the ledge in front of him as his food flew off his lap. Using both of his hands Megan watched Matt open the glove before she scrunched up and turned her back towards the field.

"You, okay?" asked Matt, before checking out the ball securely tucked in his glove.

"I think so," said Megan. "I didn't expect it to sail that quickly down the line. I'll be better prepared next time."

Matt wasn't expecting that last part. He was prepared for her to complain and say, "I want to leave now," which never came. After helping her settle back into her seat he placed his hands on her face and kissed her gently on the lips.

"You sure you're, okay?" he asked again as he slowly caressed her cheeks.

"Yes, I'm good," said Megan.

As they dealt with all their spilled food, Megan looked up to find an usher standing next to Matt. Leaning down, he whispered something into Matt's ear.

"Meg, the announcers noticed me after that foul ball and would like me to come up to the booth for a few minutes. Are you okay with that?" he asked tentatively.

"Sure. I'll be okay. Leave me your glove, though," she said adamantly. "When do you think you'll be back?"

"I shouldn't be more than an inning," he told her, kissing her on the cheek. He watched her place the glove on her hand before following the usher.

* * *

Matt was escorted up to the broadcast booth and sat between Joe Evans and Ben Pullman, two well-known former baseball players. They gave him a headset and after a commercial break they introduced him to the listening audience.

"Set to begin the top of the fifth and the score is still three to one, we're honored to be joined by Matthew Thomas Wilson. As some of you might know, Matt was an up-and-coming baseball player several years ago who unfortunately had his career come to a halt when he suffered a severe elbow injury. Matt, we're truly sorry about that, but grateful for the contributions you make to the baseball youth programs across America."

"Thank you, Ben. The fact that I can't play professionally doesn't mean I can't help out those who love the sport as much as I do. I occasionally visit youth ballfields to give the kids a few pointers, when I have a break from filming."

"Cannale takes a strike on the outside corner and now here's a curveball that misses high, one and one," said Ben.

"I didn't know you were that involved," said Joe.

"Yes, it relaxes me and I do enjoy teaching the little ones," replied Matt.

"Sharply hit, but right at the short stop, and there's one down," said Ben.

"What brought you out here today, Matt?" asked Joe.

"Well, I just came out here with a dear friend of mine who hasn't been to a game in a really long time. Since this weekend is the last of the home games for the 2010 season, we decided to come to the game tonight," said Matt.

"Look out, that's high and tight to get the at-bat started for Peterson," said Ben. "We see you haven't lost *your* skill, Matt."

"Yeah, I'm a little bit surprised I reacted in time," said Matt.

"Well, it's a good thing you did," said Joe. "Those line drives have a way of getting your attention in a hurry."

"A foul pop will reach the seats and the count evens at one and one. So, how's your TV show doing? Will we see you for another season?" asked Ben.

"Yes, we're scheduled to start shooting the beginning of February," replied Matt, pausing as he watched the ball put into play.

Ben quickly interjected, "A cue shot up the first baseline and Peterson will be the second out."

Matt resumed, "So, I'm just enjoying some time off right now."

"Tavares swings at the first pitch and skies it to left for the third out," said Ben. "Well, we really enjoyed spending a few minutes with you and wish you all the best with the new season."

"Thank you, gentlemen, it was a pleasure," said Matt.

"Headed to the bottom of the fifth, the score is still Pirates three Astros nothing," said Ben.

After taking off his headset, Matt stood and shook both announcers' hands before he was escorted out of the broadcast booth. Turning on his heels he told the usher, "I've got it from here, thanks!"

"Hey," she said as he eased in next to her with a couple of fresh drinks and a bag of peanuts. "You made it back. They didn't score any more runs, but we didn't either. But you probably had a way better view than I did," she said with a laugh.

"We need to talk, Megan," Matt told her, forcing his attention away from the game.

"Sure, what's the matter?"

He pulled her down into her seat and leaning close to her ear said, "Everyone knows I'm here, now."

"And?" she said.

"Well, it might be tricky for us to get out of here without the press following us," he told her.

"Matt, the press is going to fabricate any story they want to, whether it's the truth or not. I know how to keep my mouth shut. So, just take my hand and guide me out of here like you would anyone else," she stated.

"Megan, I don't want you in the limelight. And the press has a way of finding people even when they don't want to be found."

"I understand, but I think we can dodge them, if they try to follow us home. Please don't worry about it. This was supposed to be a relaxing night for both of us and I don't want it to be anything different," she said, then kissed him on the cheek and turned her attention back to the game.

Pulling his attention back to the game, Matt realized that Megan's carefree attitude helped to reduce the stress from the interview and slowly allow it to slide off his shoulders. *She truly has a way of taking a stressful situation and turning it into something I never expected,* thought Matt.

When the last pitch was hit and caught by the center fielder, Matt claimed Megan's face and kissed her, and he didn't care who was watching.

"We won!" he shouted.

After the players congratulated each other, several of them walked over to shake Matt's hand before heading into the dugout. He congratulated them and wished them luck on the final games of the season before taking Megan's hand and strolling to his Jeep. The press followed, but at a distance.

Once inside his Jeep Matt claimed her hand and said, "Okay, how are we getting out of here?"

"Remember how to get back to the bottom of the hill before we turn onto Willow Street?" she asked.

"Yeah."

"Well, before we make the last turn to head up to Briery Mountains, there's a private driveway with a posted sign saying, Mr. Hampton's private drive, no trespassers. Mr. Hampton owns the ground behind the cabins on my aunt and uncle's side of the road. All the locals know there's a dirt road back there through the fields where he never plants any crops. It's a shortcut that winds up the side of the hill and comes out next to Mr. Marcus' house. I've only driven up it once, when there was an accident at the bottom of the mountain."

"I've always wondered where that little dirt road goes. That's ingenious," he cheered. "Where have you been my whole life?"

"Apparently, right here, waiting for you to stroll into it," she replied.

Before pulling out of the parking lot, Matt tugged her close and leisurely kissed her lips. When they broke away, Megan noticed that the heat they generated fogged up the windows. As he started the engine Megan began to giggle which quickly turned into uncontrollable laughter. Matt sat there staring at her until she snorted and tears rolled down her face.

She finally choked out, "those reporters are probably wondering what the hell's going on in here," before she lost it again.

Hearing Megan cuss caught Matt off guard and he laughed along with her. The way she said it prompted him to reach over and try to kiss some calmness into both of them. After several disruptive giggles, Matt gave up and rolled the window down a crack to let in some cool night air. Reaching behind the passenger seat he pulled a towel out of the pocket and wiped the windows clear.

"I'm sorry …," she said in between outbursts, "… that just hit me the wrong way."

Matt noticed how natural her reactions were, now that he knew her a little better. She was truly charming. Rolling out of the parking lot she exploded with little giggles every now and then. He shook his head, smiled, and chuckled softly to himself every time a ripple of laughter hit her, until she finally got herself under control. Besides his family, he never remembered anyone feeling so relaxed and carefree around him. She brought out a personal side in him he hadn't revealed to anyone in a very long time. In fact, he couldn't remember the last time he laughed that hard.

When they pulled onto Mr. Hampton's private road they discovered the press had decided not to follow. His Jeep was put to the test as he maneuvered through the fields.

"Hang on, Meg," he said, trying to avoid as many bumps and divots as his headlights revealed.

"No worries. This reminds me of the time … Uncle Ryan let me drive his … truck over the back field … when I was twelve," laughed Megan as the ride jostled her words.

Matt glanced at her quickly before turning his attention back on the road.

"And if you tell my sister that, … I'll deny ever telling you," she added.

As they rolled up past Marcus' house Matt stopped his Jeep before turning onto Willow Street. Leaning over he reached for Megan's face and after tilting his head back and forth several times, planted a loud kiss on her lips.

"What was that for?" laughed Megan, taken aback by his playfulness.

"You just amaze me," said Matt before letting her go and drifting onto Willow Street.

He pulled into his driveway and escorted Megan across the street.

"I had a great time. What a memorable game, especially that foul ball. You amazed me, too! I won't be forgetting that game any time soon," said Megan.

"Yeah, I'm just glad you didn't get hurt or I would have felt awful," said Matt. "Here, why don't you keep the foul ball," he said, pulling it from his jacket pocket and placing it in her hand.

"You sure you don't want to keep it? It *was* a great catch."

"I'm sure."

"Thanks."

"Are you up to going jogging in the morning?"

"I think I'm going to need to sleep in after tonight. How about Monday morning?" she asked.

"I can do that," said Matt as he pulled open her screen door.

"Great. I'll see you then. And thanks again," said Megan before leaning in and planting a soft kiss on his lips. It was the first time she had initiated a kiss on her own.

Matt watched her turn a lovely shade of red in the porch light before she stepped inside her cabin. "Night, Meg!" he said before smiling and closing the screen door gently behind her.

Chapter Twelve

The last two weeks of September rolled into October and their morning jogs became sparse due to the intensity of Megan's studies, which meant spending time sharing breakfast was sporadic, too. Matt had grown accustomed to their routine, which was fairly regular after the baseball game. However, he was starting to find it difficult to leave her alone, but forced himself not to disturb her. To distract himself he worked on cleaning out and straightening the rest of the basement, power washing the rest of the deck and the front porch, and repainting the shutters on the place.

He had planned his brother's visit to the Briery Mountains long before he left LA, but ever since spending the weekend at Ryan and Helen's ranch, Matt had a yearning to see his whole family. He had grown to enjoy helping the neighbors around him. In fact, he couldn't remember a more fulfilling and meaningful time at the cabin, and it was all because of Megan. How many times had he come up to the Briery Mountains, only to hide out in the cabin, because that's what he thought he needed. What he truly needed was a dose of the life he grew up with. The satisfaction of completing a task, for someone else or himself.

Reaching into his back pocket Matt pulled out his phone and decided to call his dad to arrange a long overdue trip home.

"Hi Dad, I'd like to come home for a visit," said Matt.

"Glad to hear it, son," said Matt's father, Thomas.

"Guess you're wondering why," said Matt.

"You really don't need a reason," said Thomas. "But if it will make you feel better, go ahead and tell me."

"Sometimes I think you know me better than I know myself."

"Let's just say, your words say one thing, but the way you say it, delivers a different meaning," said Thomas.

"I thought I've always needed to be left alone to unwind at the end of a season. Truth is, I want to be able to do things without everyone making a fuss over me," revealed Matt. "I need to sink back into the simple life I grew up with. The pure satisfaction of being able to start a task and finish it without someone else stepping in to do it for me.

"Sounds like something has changed," said Thomas.

"It has, but I'm not sure if I can move forward with the change," confided Matt.

"Well, we've got plenty of work here on the ranch and could surely use an extra hand before fall totally sets in. We can talk more when you get here. I'll have your sister-in-law, Molly, freshen the sheets in your old bedroom. When do you plan on arriving?" asked Thomas.

"I'd like to leave here this Saturday, the second. I plan on driving, so I'll probably arrive early in the evening on Sunday," Matt told him. "I'd like to stay until the ninth."

"Take your time, and you can stay as long as you want. I'm sure looking forward to seeing you."

"Me, too, Dad, me too," said Matt before hanging up.

Stepping into the road, the first Friday in October, Megan and Matt kept rhythm to the sound of crunching leaves under every step. As they rounded the bend toward home, Matt said, "I'm going to be heading home to Michigan tomorrow to spend time with my family and help out on the ranch."

"Okay," said Megan, slightly surprised by his declaration. "I'm going to miss you," she added.

"I'm going to miss you, too. I want you to stay focused on your studies while I'm gone, you hear me?"

"Yeah," she said. "My midterm is next Tuesday and I still have a few more muscles to learn."

"Well, breakfast is my treat this morning," he told her, seeing the downcast look on her face.

"Maybe I should just handle my own breakfast," she mumbled.

"Nope. Sounds like you need a break," he said, steering her to his place.

Matt fixed them his usual egg sandwich, which Megan devoured in about five minutes.

He watched her carry her plate to the sink and studied her back as she pressed her hands onto the edge of the counter and stared out the window. When he finished eating, he stepped behind her and placed his plate in the sink before wrapping his arms around her waist.

Matt heard her sigh before her head slowly tilted back to rest upon his upper shoulder. He had held her before, but the tranquility of the moment felt different. He felt different. A sense of calm settled into his body as he held her. There were no words. No requests. Five minutes turned into ten before he gently turned her around in his arms.

With his fingertips, Matt brushed her hair back behind her ears before tilting her head and touching his lips to hers. Her lips felt soft and warm as he sweetly kissed her. Leaning her back he caressed her cheeks with his thumbs, then stole two more kisses. As he collected her in his arms, she wrapped her arms around his torso before resting her cheek on his shoulder. Matt had never experienced such a peaceful and comforting moment with any woman.

After several minutes Megan leaned back and looked into his eyes. In a very quiet voice she said, "Thank you."

"For what?"

"For holding and kissing me without saying a word. It was exactly what I needed. Now I'm ready to get back to my studies," said Megan. "Walk me home?"

"Absolutely."

Matt collected her hand and walked her across the street. Once she was inside her door he leaned in and placed a soft kiss on her lips before closing the screen door.

As Matt strolled back across the street, he realized what he told his father was true, his feelings were changing. Never in his life had he felt so relaxed while kissing a woman. *Although no one has ever given me the chance to get comfortable enough to reveal that side of me. But then I haven't really allowed anyone to get that close to me, either.*

Matt tried to shake the thoughts about Megan from his head as he pulled two duffle bags out of the closet and focused on packing for his trip home. Despite his efforts he was struggling with his feelings about leaving Megan, and after their quiet kissing session, he was struggling even more. In the end, he thought it might be a good idea to put some distance between them, mainly to see if he felt the same way about her when he returned.

Matt got up early Saturday morning and stepping onto his porch, found Megan pacing back and forth on her own porch in a pale blue robe and fuzzy slippers. He would have called to get her attention, but was overcome with how warm the sight of her made him feel inside. Her hair wasn't combed, but sloppily pulled to the back of her head causing a few strands to hang down loosely on either side of her face. He thought she looked endearing.

He climbed into his Jeep and headed down the mountain to Dan and Kayla's café to pick up a few pastries for Megan while he was gone. When he entered the café it was already filled with customers stopping in for their morning pick-me-up. As he reached the countertop, Kayla had her head down and didn't acknowledge him at first.

"Hi, Kayla, how are you today?" asked Matt like they were old friends.

"Matt!" she practically screamed before clamping a hand over her mouth. She made her way around the counter to give him a hug. "It's good to see you again," she whispered.

"Good to see you, too."

"Hey, Dan, look who stopped by this morning," Kayla said yelling towards the back of the shop.

Dan made his way to the counter carrying a large tray of apple turnovers. "Well, look who it is. So, you decided to come out of the hills for a visit. Where's Meg?"

"Yes, and Meg's still at your Aunt Linda and Uncle Paul's place studying herself silly with her anatomy class. It stresses me out just watching her pace on the porch memorizing so many body parts," he informed them.

"What brings you down here so early in the morning, then?" asked Kayla.

"I wanted to stop by to let you know I'm heading home to Michigan for a week to visit my family and help out my dad and brother, Brian, on the ranch. And to ask you to keep tabs on Meg while I'm gone," said Matt.

"Sure thing. But you could have had Meg text us to let us know," said Kayla, "instead of driving all the way down here."

"Well, I also wanted to pick up some pastries for Meg. I've been fixing breakfast most mornings when she has time to jog, and thought having some pastries available would give her something quick to eat while I'm gone," Matt explained.

He watched Kayla look at Dan and smile before turning her attention back to him. He'd seen the look before when he first met Kayla and figured he'd find out sooner or later what the look meant.

"That's so sweet. What flavor of pastries would you like?" asked Kayla.

"I know she likes éclairs, but I don't know her favorite fruit. Can you help me with that?"

"No problem. Peach is her favorite, but since they're out of season right now the runner-up is always, and I mean always, apple. And it just so happens we have been baking apple turnovers, which Megan loves, all morning. How many do you want?"

"I'd like seven. If you think they'll last the week," said Matt.

"Meg knows to put a few in the freezer, so I'm sure they'll last."

"Okay, then seven it is, and two large cups of coffee, please."

Matt placed the pastries on the passenger seat and secured the coffee cups before heading back to the cabin. As he pulled into his driveway, he saw Megan outside forcefully digging holes in the ground along the front of her aunt and uncle's flower beds.

She had her ear buds in, the music turned up high enough for him to hear, and totally focused on the task. She didn't notice his return but kept moving down the line, and didn't realize he had walked into the yard until she bumped into him and fell on the ground at the end of the row.

"What the …" she sputtered.

"I thought you left already," she said in a not-so-pleasant voice, looking up into his face.

"Not without saying good-bye and bringing you this and these," he said, holding out the coffee and a square box in front of her.

Picking herself off the ground Megan took off her gardening gloves and accepted the coffee. After taking a sip she peeked inside the brown box. "Oh, yum. These are one of my favorite flavors."

"Yes, and there's one for every morning while I'm gone."

"Thank you," she responded a little sheepishly. "I should have known you wouldn't leave without saying good-bye."

"Is that why you're out here digging holes with a vengeance?" he laughed. "You thought I left without coming to see you this morning. You are a silly girl," he chided.

"I know. I saw you pull away and …" she started to say before the rest of her words became inaudible as she peered down at his feet.

Matt closed the gap between them, and taking a finger lifted her chin so he could look into her adorable face. "Never," was all he said before devouring her lips and the taste of coffee with it. He would have intensified the kiss even more, but it would only have made it harder for him to leave. He ended the brief interlude by touching his lips to her forehead, before wrapping his arms around her shoulders with the box of pastries still in his hand. As he started to pull away, she clutched onto the back of his shirt.

His body rocked forward, but he recovered quickly. He slid the pastry box onto the porch under the railing then placed her cup along the edge of the porch before engulfing her in a big bear hug.

He was caught off guard by the emotions she elicited, but held onto her with as much yearning and apprehension about his departure as she had. He took in the scent of her when he held her yesterday, but this time it felt more final because he wouldn't see her for a week. As she buried her face into his chest and neck, he slowly caressed her back, trying to sooth them both.

"Hey," he whispered, "I'm only going to be gone a week. I'll be back before you know it."

"I know," she choked out. "I'm just being silly again."

"I actually think it's kind of sweet," he told her, tilting her back to look into her face. Her eyes were misted over, but at least there were no tears rolling down her cheeks or he would have been a wreck. No girl had ever cried over him leaving before. "Look," he continued, "would you mind if I text you around dinner time every evening?"

Megan immediately brightened up with his suggestion. "I'd like that," she said with a smile.

"I can't guarantee it'll be the same time every night, but when we sit down to eat, I'll check in with you. Deal?"

"Deal," agreed Megan, before stealing one more kiss. "Could you also let me know when you get there?"

"I sure will. Now don't forget to put some of those pastries in the freezer so they last all week," he told her, leaning over to give her one last kiss on the forehead before heading back to his place.

After packing his Jeep, he got in and backed up far enough to wave to Megan before heading down the road. He was looking forward to seeing his family, but he didn't realize how hard leaving Megan was going to be. It wasn't like they had known each other for years, but her refreshing personal spirit was something he couldn't ignore. Putting on some music he turned his attention to the road. He hoped to knock out the first five hours of the journey today and complete the trip on Sunday. He would have flown, but he enjoyed having his Jeep so he could help out by running a few errands while he was home without tying up one of the trucks.

* * *

Megan knew she was acting childish, but she needed a few moments to absorb Matt's strength and the smell of him into her being, just like she had done with her uncle.

She finished planting the tulip bulbs then turned her attention back to her studies. Kayla called to check up on her later in the day and told her about Matt's visit to the café. Kayla thought it was sweet of Matt to care about her enough to provide breakfast for her while he was gone.

Megan agreed then quickly changed the subject, because the more he popped into her head, the less time she was able to focus on her studies.

It didn't take long for Matt's departure to make things seem a little quieter. She was grateful for the calm, but also sad about it. Although it allowed her to stay focused longer on her school work, it also gave her time to examine her feelings towards Matt. Feelings that were growing despite the fact she swore she'd never get involved in a relationship until her degrees were finished. But the fact she wasn't looking for a relationship didn't prevent one from creeping into her heart anyway, just like Kayla told her. *Although, he has encouraged me and I'm holding an A in both classes.*

Megan fell asleep early that night with her phone on her chest waiting for Matt to text her. When it rang at ten o'clock it jarred her awake.

"Hello," she answered groggily.

"Hi, Meg," he replied softly. "Sounds like you were sleeping, so I'm not going to keep you very long. I ran into a couple backups on the highway and I'm tired from driving, but I wanted to hear your voice. I'm about five hours away and staying in a hotel just inside the state of Michigan."

"Okay. Glad you're safe," she answered with a yawn. "Get some rest and I'll talk to you or text with you tomorrow."

"Okay. Night, Meg," he replied.

* * *

Matt hadn't needed to account for his whereabouts with anyone in a long time and figured he would find out how it made him feel this week. If the relationship was going to last into spring, they would have to deal with time apart from one another every now and then.

"What are you thinking, Matthew? You haven't even asked her out on a real dinner date yet, and a baseball game doesn't count," he chided himself before falling asleep with his cell phone clenched in his hand, pondering this facet of their relationship.

Matt left the hotel after lunch and pulled onto the dirt road leading to his father's ranch at six-thirty Sunday evening. He could barely make out the outline of the old wooden house with all the weeds that had grown around the front porch. He didn't know how much help his dad and brother needed until that very moment. The fences looked worn in spots, too, as he headed down the road. When he reached the side of the house, he tapped his horn a couple times.

His dad made his way down the side porch steps to greet him. Matt was glad to see him still looking so spry.

"Well, aren't you a sight for sore eyes, Matthew," said Thomas, giving him a bear hug and several pats on the back.

"You too, Dad!" he said, hugging him back.

"Where's Brian?" asked Matt.

"I'm here, I'm here." Matt saw his brother hustling down the steps and they gave each other a brotherly hug. Leaning back, he noticed a hint of gray creeping in around his brother's ears. But Brian still had a couple inches on him, and his arms were still solid from years of farming.

"Where's Molly?"

"She's back at our house settling the kids down. Said she'll see you in the morning. She's going to fix us breakfast. At least attempt to," Brain said with a laugh.

"Let's get you inside. Molly made up the bed for you today in your old room. We've all been anticipating your arrival," said Thomas.

"Looks like you could use a hand from what I saw driving up to the house," replied Matt.

"We had an unusually damp beginning to October and had to push back the corn harvesting until the ground firms up a bit. Hopefully it'll be a drier week while you're home," said Brian.

"Well, here's hoping? How many hired hands do you have right now?"

"Five and a possible sixth in the spring when the additional cattle arrive. We had nine calves born this past spring," Brian said.

"That's great. Got any coffee on?" asked Matt, patting his brother on the back.

"Yes," answered Brian as he grabbed one of his brother's bags and headed up the porch steps and into the house.

As Matt stepped over the threshold into the open living room, he was hit with all the woodsy smells of his childhood. He paused, taking it all in as he did every time he visited. But for the first time he stood there picturing Megan's reaction to this lovely old house, something he never envisioned with any woman. He must have been standing there longer than usual, because it took a nudge from his father to move him along.

"Sorry, Dad, I was just thinking … never mind. It's good to be home," he finished.

"It's good to have you home, son. Now let's go get that coffee and get you settled in. We've got a long day ahead of us tomorrow," said Thomas.

"And so it begins," said Matt walking toward the kitchen.

They chatted for a while before Matt said his good-nights, and made his way upstairs to his old bedroom. For some reason he'd never taken note of how small his twin bed was compared to a queen, until now. He barely had enough room to stretch out without hitting the baseboard with his feet. "Meg would get a laugh out of this," he thought, which reminded him to send her a text before he dozed off.

> Matt: Made it home okay. Busy day planned for tomorrow.
>
> Megan: Glad you made it the rest of the way okay. Enjoy yourself! Send me a pic of the place when you get a chance.
>
> Matt: I'll do that. Night, Meg.
>
> Megan: Night, Matt.

Matt slept like a rock until the crowing of the rooster woke him at dawn. He moaned, rolled over and slammed his foot into the footboard before stuffing his pillow over his head. He had forgotten about Walter. He knew it was him because his circadian rhythm had a break in it, like he needed to take a breath in the middle of his crowing. He had to be about eight years old, that ornery old bird. Matt had set his alarm for six but the dumb bird crowed at five-thirty. He started to doze off again when he heard a knock on his bedroom door.

"Who is it?" he asked curtly.

"It's Molly. May I come in?" she asked timidly.

"Give me a minute," said Matt. He crawled out of bed and threw on jeans and a clean t-shirt before opening the door.

"Hi, Matt, it's good to see you," said Molly. "I brought you a cup of coffee."

"Good to see you too, Molly," answered Matt, taking the cup from her hand. "Get over here and give me a hug and a kiss."

Molly was a sight for sore eyes. His brother was a lucky man to have found her. She was very sweet and her auburn hair framed her slightly round face before cascading down the sides and onto her shoulders. She had some height to her, and was shapely but solid. Her warm brown eyes and smile brightened up his morning.

"So how are young Thomas and Sally?" asked Matt.

"They're fine. Thomas is eight and Sally is six now. They are both full of energy. They're around here somewhere. They're up early to feed the chickens with their dad, before school starts."

"I forgot all about Walter. I can't believe he's still alive," said Matt.

"He's too full of himself to die," said Molly with a slight laugh. "It's good to have you home again. We missed seeing you last Christmas."

"Things have gotten a little out of hand with work, but I'll be working on that," said Matt with a bit of conviction in his voice.

As Molly reached out her arms to hug Matt, Thomas and Sally came running in behind their mother to greet him.

Molly couldn't do anything but laugh as they toppled their uncle to the ground, only to pile on top of him in a playful manner. Matt reached down and tickled them as he regained his stature before he plucked each one off the floor and gave them a hug and kiss before they ran off downstairs.

"Breakfast is ready," Molly told him followed by a quick hug and kiss.

"Give me a few minutes and I'll be down," replied Matt running his fingers through his hair. He hadn't shaved for two days and contemplated taking the time to do so this morning. In the end he tended to the necessities, threw a blue button-down flannel shirt over his t-shirt and headed downstairs.

The conversation was flying at the breakfast table as they discussed what job to tackle first. In the end they decided to pack up the pick-up truck and mend some of the fences along the driveway and deal with the hole on the side of the chicken house, and the broken barn door on Tuesday.

By the time Wednesday rolled around, Matt knew his family sensed a change in him by the way they kept studying him. He was more focused on the ranch in general and dug into cleaning up the flower beds in the morning. His mother would have been appalled had she seen how overgrown they had become. When he finished, he stepped back to take a picture of the front of the house with his cell phone and sent it to Megan, along with a text.

Matt: Hi, Meg. Sorry it's taken me so long to text you. I know I said I'd touch base in the evenings, but things got busy, rather quickly.

Megan: No worries. I understand. I was studying for my midterm and now I'm working on preparing for the MCAT.

Matt: Thanks for understanding. What does MCAT stand for again?

Megan: Medical College Admissions Test. I need to get a high score to get into the medical school I'm applying to.

Matt: When are you taking the MCAT?

Megan: I'm aiming for the end of March.

Matt: Okay, so not until you're done this semester.

Megan: Correct. Don't worry, I know my limit, but I need to start studying now.

Matt: Whew! Glad to hear it. Sent you a pic of the house. The flower beds were a mess — been weeding all morning.

Megan: It's lovely, Matt! The house looks like it's full of rustic charm.

Matt: It is, except for sleeping in my old twin bed. Didn't realize how much shorter it is compared to my queen. I've nailed the footboard several times with my feet.

> Megan: Ouch! Had my midterm in anatomy yesterday.
>
> Matt: And?
>
> Megan: It was six pages long, front and back.
>
> Matt: Yikes!!
>
> Megan: Got that right. It took me the whole two hours to complete it.

"Who are you texting, Matt?" asked Brian as he poked his head over his brother's shoulder. "One of those LA girls the tabloids show you hanging out with?"

"No, Brian, it isn't," said Matt, pushing past his brother to sit on one of the chairs on the front porch.

> Matt: How do you think you did?
>
> Megan: Fairly well, but I don't want to jinx myself. Let's just say I don't think I failed. That way, anything better will have to be good enough.

Brian reached around and snatched Matt's phone out of his hands. "Give it back, Brian!"

"Let's see … bed too small … midterm in anatomy … oh, Meg is it! … sounds like someone has found himself a young lady, Dad," called Brian towards the screen door. "What else have you been keeping from us?" Brain asked as he invaded Matt's privacy and read through the texts on Matt's phone.

"I said, give it back, Brian," growled Matt.

Matt resisted the urge to sock his brother in the stomach at that moment. But before he could react Molly appeared inside the screen door and said, "Some brother you are. You're behaving like a child, and a heartless uncaring fool, at best. If you wanted to know who Matt is texting, not that it's any of your business, why don't you just ask instead of yanking the phone out of his hand?"

Without a word, Brian handed the phone back to Matt and entered the house, letting the screen door slam closed behind him.

Making his way back to the chair, Matt sat down and finished his conversation with Megan. Molly walked over and sat in the chair next to him and asked, "What's her name, Matt?"

"Megan Barnes," he replied, wiping his hand across his face.

"Miss her?"

"Yes, Molly … I do miss her."

"Then give her a call and talk to her."

"I can't right now. I meant to text her earlier in the week, but things got busy really quick and I forgot. I'll text her later. She has a music class in about two hours and needs to practice."

"Do you have a picture of her?"

"Yes, I do, come to think of it." Matt found the picture of the two of them on horseback and showed it to Molly.

"She's lovely, Matt! How long have you known her?"

"Since the beginning of September. She's staying at her aunt and uncle's cabin across the street from our cabin. We go out jogging every now and then in the morning," he told her.

"Does she know who you are?"

"Yeah, she eventually figured it out on her own."

"What do you mean?"

"Let's just say that for about two days I wasn't an actor, but just Matt."

"And after she realized who you were?" asked Molly.

"She didn't change how she treated me."

Matt glanced back and found his father leaning on the door frame listening to them talk. He was the only one who knew of his love life or lack thereof and why. Walking over Thomas placed his hands on his son's shoulders and asked Molly if she would excuse them for a few moments. Molly got up and said, "She does sound lovely, Matt," before kissing him on the cheek and walking into the house.

"Thanks, Molly. She is."

Sitting down in the same seat Molly had occupied, Thomas stared off into the distance over the grounds. Matt waited in silence.

"Sounds like a very special lady, Matthew," said Thomas.

"She is Dad."

"And … you tell her yet?"

"No, I haven't."

"Going to?" Thomas inquired.

"Want to."

"Going to and wanting to are two different things, Matthew."

"I know."

"Sounds like you're in love with her, son. And if she cares about you, for who you are, then I suspect she's in love with you, too. Do you trust her, Matthew? You're going to have to when she goes to touch you where no other woman has lovingly touched you before."

"Dad, …" he began as blood flowed up to his face, reflecting the physical embarrassment he felt along with the emotional pain he carried.

"Matthew, allowing yourself to open up to a woman that you care about as much as it sounds like you care about Meg, should melt away any fears you still have. Then again, you might just have to do it afraid."

"I know, I know," said Matt softly as he closed his eyes and hung his head.

"May I see that picture you showed Molly?"

Matt brought up the picture of Megan and himself on horseback and gave the phone to his father. He watched the expression on his father's face and knew he was taken aback by her uncanny resemblance to his mother when she was that age.

Thomas handed the phone back and said, "If you don't reveal your innermost fears to that woman, then you're missing out on the possibilities life has to offer. She's lovely, Matthew, and looks like she has a good head on her shoulders."

"She does, Dad. She wants to be an ENT doctor and hopes to start medical school late in the summer next year."

"Then I wouldn't wait too long to show her that you trust her son. Women like that don't come around too often. I married one of them," said Thomas, patting his son on the shoulder, "and she gave me two handsome and caring young men, despite your brother's current behavior," he added before heading back into the house for lunch.

Matt sat for a long stretch pondering his father's words. Megan was the first woman he had ever seriously considered telling about his physical trauma. His father was right, he needed to tell her, but he didn't know how to even start *that* conversation. When he looked up, Molly was standing beside him holding a plate with his sandwich in her hands.

She handed it to him and started to leave when Matt reached out and caught her wrist.

She stood patiently and waited, because it was a trait of all three Wilson men to pause and give some serious thought to anything important they wanted to say.

"When you and Brian consummated your marriage, were you scared?"

Matt could tell she was startled by his question. As she formulated her answer, she walked around and sat down on the coffee table in front of him then said, "Yes, I was Matt. And I'm pretty sure Brian was, too. But I knew we were going down the same road together. When it's the right person and love is present along with trust, and the other person fully cares and respects your body as much as theirs, then there is no mockery." Placing her hands on his knees Molly added, "She looks like a good woman. Let go of your heart and you'll find out how much she has to offer you in return."

As Molly got up to go back inside, she said, "I could tell just by looking at the picture of her that she's trustworthy, Matt," as she patted him on the shoulder.

He sat for several more minutes digesting her words. He had built up so many years of distrust that he wasn't sure how or if he'd ever reach the level of trust his father and Brian had with their wives. *All I know is that I care for her deeply. And if anyone can show me the way, it's Meg.*

Matt spent his last two days helping to mend a few more fences and organize the supply sheds. In the evenings Molly and Brian had allowed Thomas and Sally to stay up an extra hour so he could spend a little bit of quality time with them, which he enjoyed immensely. As they were sitting down to dinner on Friday, Matt got a text from Megan.

> Megan: Aced my midterm!

Matt leaped out of his seat yelling, "Yes, yes!"

"What is it, Matt?" asked Brian.

"Meg aced her anatomy midterm."

Sitting back down at the table Matt texted back:

Matt: Fantastic! I'm so proud of you!

Megan: Seven more weeks to go — Ugh!

Matt: You can do it. I'm leaving tomorrow morning around ten-thirty.

Megan: Thanks and okay. I've missed you, Matt.

Matt: I've missed you, too.

Megan: Let me know how far you get on your way back. See you soon.

After playing two games of Trouble with Thomas and Sally, Matt made his way upstairs and stood in his bedroom doorway scanning the room, trying to ingrain a picture of it into his memory. His eyes drifted along the top shelf of his overflowing bookcase against the far wall. There were several items from his school days, and several baseball trophies. His eyes then came to rest on a navy blue box sitting on the right-hand corner that he didn't recognize. Furrowing his brow he collected the box and blew a layer of dust off the lid, causing him to cough several times. After fanning the dust out of his face he sat at his desk and gently lifted the lid off the box. Inside he found a stack of greeting cards wrapped with a rubber band that looked vaguely familiar.

As he picked up the stack the rubber band broke and the cards fell back into the box. Picking up the first card he read, get well soon. Reading through a few more cards he came across one with 1999 written in the top right corner. It was his senior year of college, the year his life changed. In addition to the physical healing he had to endure, his mental state prevented him and still prevents him from being able to prove the physical injury doesn't exist any longer. As he flipped through the rest of the cards, his dad appeared in the doorway.

"I don't remember half of these," said Matt, holding up one of the cards.

His dad walked into the room to get a closer look. "No wonder. You had a very rough stretch and were really depressed for a spell. That's why I took you to the cabin for five weeks over that summer, to allow you time to recover. Not until you found out you were drafted by a baseball team did you start pulling yourself together," said Thomas.

"You didn't tell everyone about ..." said Matt, trailing off the rest of his question.

"No. Everyone just knew you were injured, but I never said how," answered Thomas.

Breathing a sigh of relief, Matt stuck his hand to the bottom of the box and flipped through the rest of the cards. He came across one that was wider and different than all the others. Pulling it out of the stack, he noticed the card was handmade on a folded piece of paper.

On the front of the card, the message "Get well soon" was written at the top of the page. Below the words was drawn a forest of fall colored trees with two people sitting in adirondack chairs with their backs facing and holding hands, as if they were taking in the autumn scenery in front of them. A dog was placed in between the two chairs.

"As you can see, lots of people sent cards, and visited, too," said Thomas.

"You don't happen to remember, Meg, do you? She's Linda and Paul's niece. She evidently visited over the summer, but I don't remember ever seeing her," said Matt.

"I know Paul and Linda were over frequently. They have a son, but I think he graduated from college and found a job in another state. Linda fixed quite a few meals for us. I'll have to think about it. That was over ten years ago, son. Does it matter?"

"No, not really. I just find it odd that I don't remember seeing her at all," said Matt.

"You were in such a fog following your incident and to be honest, so was I. Your mother had only been gone for two years and the thought of possibly losing you was devastating," said Thomas.

"Sorry, I didn't mean to bring up difficult times right before leaving. I just noticed this box on top of the bookcase and didn't recognize it," said Matt.

"I don't know why I kept the cards. Probably because it's something your mother would have done," said Thomas.

"Do you care if I take them with me?"

"Nope. They *are* yours," said Thomas as he headed to his bedroom. "Night."

"Night. And thanks," said Matt.

Glancing at the handmade card in his hand he placed it on top of the stack of cards and closed the lid. After packing up the rest of his clothes, Matt curled up in bed on his side with his elbow under his head. He stared at the box he'd placed on the desk, trying hard to remember a past he worked so hard to forget.

In the morning, Matt said his good-byes and managed to get a group picture on his phone before he left, to show Megan. The drive home seemed shorter than the drive up, but it also could have been his anxiousness to see Megan. The mere thought of holding her close caused him to get uncomfortable in his seat. Smiling at his body's reaction, he shook his head and turned on the radio to distract his thoughts as he rolled through Ohio. After crossing the Pennsylvania border he pulled off for dinner and spent the night in a hotel. He texted Megan his progress and at that moment it dawned on him that she hadn't infringed upon his time away. *She allows me to do the things I want and encourages me. Just like I do for her.*

Matt woke with a headache Sunday morning and had to fall back to sleep for a while, which pushed back his whole day. By the time he got on the road it was four o'clock and he still had four hours to go. He finally pulled into his driveway at eight o'clock and was glad to be home. Reaching around to pull his duffle bags from the back seat he noticed the lights were still on at Megan's place. Making his way to his front door he unlocked it and placed his bags inside before crossing the street and climbing Megan's porch steps.

As he reached up to knock on the door, he caught sight of her curled up in her nightgown lying on the hammock with a mug clenched in her hand. He opened the front door, pried the cup out of her fingers, then gently scooped her up in his arms. Her face was cool as she leaned into the crook of his neck.

He carried her through the door and kicked it shut before taking her upstairs to her bedroom. He placed her on the bed and stood mesmerized by the wholesomeness of her face. *Just do it. Don't stand here analyzing every aspect of your emotions,* he told himself. Reaching out Matt touched her peaceful face and without further debate he walked around to the other side of the bed and removed his jacket, shirt, and jeans, then climbed into bed with her. Gently tugging her back up close to his body he tucked his right arm securely between her breasts.

"Matthew?" said Megan, straining to look back into his face in the moonlit room.

"Go back to sleep, Meg," he said as she enclosed his arm with her own before wrapping her hand around his.

"I've missed you," whispered Megan.

"I've missed you, too," he responded, slightly delirious. He hadn't felt the desire to sleep with a woman in years, but then he hadn't found one he was truly comfortable with to gradually let into his personal life. "I'm very tired sweetheart, go to sleep."

"You're staying here?"

"Yes, you're freezing. Go to sleep," he whispered into her soft red hair.

She pressed her body closer into his and let out a sigh followed by an unexpected sob. Matt became choked up by her reaction and a lump formed in the back of his throat. He freed his right hand and gently wiped away the moisture on her face. He never expected to be so overcome by her emotions. Swiftly he rolled her over into his arms and held her fiercely close.

"If I weren't so tired from driving home, you'd probably be in trouble right now," not fully realizing what he was suggesting. "And I sure hope those were happy tears."

"They were," she whispered.

"Good. Then go to sleep, Meg," he said endearingly, kissing the top of her head.

Chapter Thirteen

Megan woke early in the morning to Matt's soft snoring. She leaned over his face and briefly brushed his lips with hers. As she started to move away, he reached out and pulled her down to his warm torso. Rolling onto his side he tilted her head up and searched her eyes as he methodically brushed her hair out of her face and tucked it behind her ears. She watched as the tip of his tongue glided across his lips before he leaned forward and softly claimed her mouth. Within a heartbeat she felt his body stir as it had the week before his trip home. Instead of pulling away, he ground his desire into her thigh and quietly vocalized the sensations she stirred inside him. His hand caressed her side before he slid it around to her back and pulled her closer, causing a tingle to roll up her spine.

But as quickly as he started, Matt pulled back and searched her face as he toiled with the edge of the sheet. Drawing his head close to hers, Megan whispered, "What is it, Matt?" He didn't answer as she searched his face. The struggle going on behind his troubled eyes was real. Slowly Megan reached up and caressed his chest underneath his t-shirt. She could feel him tense up the further south her hand traveled. When she reached the top of his underwear, he swiftly grabbed hold of her wrist.

"Meg," he choked out, "I've ..." but his words were lost in the back of his throat. He suddenly let go of her wrist and rolled over taking the sheets with him. Megan rolled onto her back and laid next to him quietly. Her head was racing as she tried to process his reaction and words. He wanted the closeness. Needed it. She could sense it. But a look of terror consumed him. The grip he had on her wrist grew tighter the longer she lingered near his waistband.

Turning onto her side Megan slowly caressed Matt's back, then slid her hand around to his chest before snuggling close. Absorbing his warmth, she started to doze off when his hand enclosed hers and squeezed it close to his chest.

* * *

When Matt woke, Megan wasn't there. Placing his feet over the edge of the bed he sat quietly anticipating what questions Megan would have for him. Despite the lack of intimacy, he knew their relationship was changing. *I invited the situation by climbing into her bed,* he admitted to himself.

Making his way into the kitchen, Megan greeted him with her usual "mornin'" before handing him a cup of coffee. He leaned against the island feeling the need to explain, but lacked confidence to expound upon his actions. The absence of questions wasn't the norm under any scenario he conjured up as he watched her.

"Go ahead and sit Matt, I'll bring your plate over," she told him as if nothing had happened.

He watched her fix their plates and carry them to the table. When he hadn't moved, she walked over and nudged him over to his seat.

"Matt, is everything all right?" she asked.

"Yeah, everything is fine. In fact, it's *just* great," he answered.

She leaned over and kissed him on the cheek, then whispered, "Thanks for carrying me inside last night. I enjoyed snuggling up with you."

Matt just stared up into her face. No one had ever reacted to one of his withdrawals the way she had. It turned his assumptions about women upside down.

"I made special pancakes this morning to thank you," said Megan, glancing at his plate.

He peeled his eyes off hers and turned to focus on his plate. He noticed the pancake was in the shape of a heart.

"Thank you," she said again as she ran her fingers through the hair around his ear.

Matt stared at the pancake for what felt like an eternity before reaching out and pulling her down to his lap. Holding her close he whispered, "I've never been caressed like that before."

* * *

Megan gently touched his face and at that moment understood what he had tried to tell her earlier that morning. She remembered the first time her ex-boyfriend's hand traveled to her breast. Feelings of violation, wrong doing and curiosity about the unknown traveled through her head. Matt's reaction had resembled those feelings. Everything her uncle told her came flooding back into her head. He was struggling to fully trust her, and until he was able to, she was going to have to pay close attention to his responses.

"It's okay. You're okay. You've done nothing wrong," said Megan as she watched him take a deep breath and force his body to relax.

To ease his discomfort and draw him away from his inner thoughts Megan said, "Do you know how long it took me to get the pancakes into the shape of a heart? I crinkled up some aluminum foil into the shape of a heart and tried to flatten the foil on the bottom and insides. Now if I had Kayla's pancake mold, well, …"

"Matthew," she said softly as his glazed over eyes stared into hers, "As I told you before, I'm not going anywhere." She knew she was going to have to care for his mistreated heart very tightly, like her uncle predicted, especially when he worked up enough courage to tell her what was rolling through his head.

Coming out of his internal battle, he pulled her close and held her tight. "Please don't judge me by my actions this morning. I watched the gentleness in your eyes while you were touching me," he told her. "And I love the pancakes!" he added.

"I know you were watching me," she acknowledged staring at her lap.

"I'm starting to realize I shouldn't assume anything about you. At least compared to any women I've ever been around," said Matt honestly.

Concern for Matt's well-being and curiosity about his past were starting to surface in Megan's thoughts. *What's he so afraid of, besides the obvious, which we are all generally nervous about?*

Shaking the thought from her head she said, "I'd like a good morning kiss," making Matt smile.

He tilted her head and sweetly kissed her before sliding a hand into the hair at the nape of her neck. When she sighed he quickly released her and planted her on her feet next to him. The abruptness of his release caused her cheeks to redden. She was starting to feel embarrassed by her quickness to melt at his touch, which in turn was causing him to release her even faster.

There he goes again, thought Megan. *It's starting to really make me wonder what he's been through. It's like he starts to enjoy himself, like this morning, then realizes where things are headed and pulls back.* Then his comment on the mountain top, about there being more to his responses than what he was able to share, surfaced in her head.

When he finally noticed the redness in her cheeks, he said, "Lookin' cute," making it clear he liked her regardless of his actions, but he clearly wasn't ready to take their relationship any further.

Megan ended up reheating their breakfast and Matt followed suit by warming up their coffee. Once they were seated again, Megan asked excitedly, "So how was your trip home?" knowing a change in topic was needed.

* * *

"Well," Matt began after swallowing a bite of pancake, "I enjoyed my visit. I fixed a lot of food. Molly, Brian's wife, is still learning to cook, so I showed her how to make a few simple meals. She ends up burning quite a few dishes, according to Brian, but I think it's mostly due to my niece and nephew distracting her."

He told her about the whole week, then remembered the picture he took of everyone. Taking his phone out of his pocket he showed Megan his family. As she was taking in everyone's faces, it dawned on Matt he rarely shared this part of his life with anyone. He tried several times, but they'd start looking around at other things part way through his story, making him think it was boring. But watching Megan absorb and listen to all the stories he told her, melted a silent but different barrier within him. *She's genuinely interested in my family and where I came from*, he thought.

As they cleaned up the dishes, Matt told her about his niece and nephew and their schemes to sneak up and scare him. "They succeeded Tuesday morning," said Matt. "I fell out of bed and landed hard on my tailbone. After that, with Molly's help, we taught them a lesson. Young Thomas and Sally made their way into the kitchen Wednesday morning complaining they couldn't find Uncle Matt anywhere. Molly told them I'd probably gone out early with their grandpa and they would see me later after school. Then Molly asked them to get some fresh jam from the pantry. I surprised them when they turned on the light. You should have heard the screams and seen the way they tore back into the kitchen. The look on their faces was priceless. Needless to say, no one bothered me Thursday and Friday morning."

Megan laughed at his story, then asked. "How old are they, Matt?"

"Thomas is eight and Sally is six."

"Oh, I hope you didn't scare them too much?" said Megan.

"Well, they *were* a little gun shy around me Thursday morning, but we ran around outside in the evening. I threw a football around with Thomas, and pulled Sally across the yard in a wagon for a while."

"Sounds like you had a great time despite your injury and all the work you did."

"Yeah. Brian's heading down in two weeks. Like you and Kayla, we need a little time to talk and reconnect. You'll be able to meet him if you have some free time. Now, I'm going to head home to unpack and take a shower," he told her while wrapping the dish towel around the back of her neck and drawing her close. He kissed her leisurely on the lips several times then headed upstairs for his jacket.

"Maybe we can figure out something to do on the weekend before Brian gets here, if you want to," he said, still worried his withdrawal might have caused her to feel differently about him, despite the fact she made him heart-shaped pancakes for breakfast.

"I might be able to handle something on Saturday, but late afternoon or evening would probably be best. We're into the second half of the semester, which I think is going to be more intense than the first half because we'll be starting to apply our knowledge to case scenarios," she told him.

"That does sound difficult, but practical. Every patient's situation is unique and a basic issue could turn into something else," said Matt, knowing more than she realized.

"You're starting to sound like a doctor, Mr. Wilson. Maybe you should start studying my note cards and I'll go take acting lessons," said Megan with a laugh.

"I think I'll stick to acting for a little while longer," said Matt. "Are we jogging tomorrow morning?" he asked.

"Sure, but I'm afraid the rest of the week is out. I've got a research paper due on Thursday and I told Kayla I'd have lunch with her on Friday," she told him.

"That's okay. I can work on boxing up and labeling a few more things in my basement. I bought a couple of shelves earlier in the month that I need to assemble to store the boxes on," said Matt. "Plus I need to figure out something for us to do on Saturday."

"Let me know what you decide, 'cause my brain is quite fried."

"I don't know, maybe I'll just surprise you," said Matt with a smile as he walked out the door.

Matt couldn't stop smiling as he jumped into the shower. His dad was right, Megan cared about him a great deal. And despite his fears, which felt like they were going to consume him, he allowed her to caress him. If he thought about it, he briefly enjoyed her touch until she headed further down his chest. Then he slowly realized, *she didn't force herself on me or allow my reaction to make her break down and act like I didn't want her around. Her gentleness has allowed me to briefly envision the kind of relationship I've always dreamed about.*

As he pondered those dreams and how they would feel, he climbed out of the shower, dressed, and put a load of very dirty jeans in the wash.

* * *

By the time Saturday arrived Megan was exhausted. Her research paper, which focused on the veins and arteries of the arm and the complications that can result by severing each one, consumed her week. Not only did the assignment require a paper, but a handout and presentation to the class regarding her findings was also part of the grade. Thankfully her presentation was on Thursday, which freed her up for the weekend until the other half of the class presented their research assignments on Tuesday.

Megan dragged herself out of bed Saturday morning and pushed herself to clean the bathrooms, before changing her bedclothes. After lunch she put clean sheets on the bed and ended up flopping across it for a much-needed nap.

Around three o'clock Megan's cell phone went off and woke her from a deep sleep.

Matt: Heading over in thirty to pick you up for our outing.

Megan scrambled out of bed after reading Matt's text. With all the school work filling her every hour she had totally forgotten about their plans to do something today. *It was a good thing I took a nap or I wouldn't be able to enjoy whatever Matt's decided to do.*

Megan: I'll be ready. Where exactly are we going?

Matt: It's a surprise!

Megan: Has anyone told you I don't like surprises?

Matt: I think you'll like this one. Trust me.

Megan: In that case, should I wear anything in particular?

Matt: Something you'd wear on a cool fall day outdoors.

Megan: Now I'm intrigued.

Matt: Good. See you in thirty.

Megan rolled through the shower to wake herself up even further before throwing on a pair of jeans, rust-colored shirt and deep green button-down sweater. Popping into the kitchen she inhaled a yogurt and some nuts, then grabbed her low-cut boots and wandered out onto the porch to put them on. She then leaned back on her hands and stretched her legs out, letting the afternoon sun beat down on her face while she waited for Matt. She hadn't seen him all week and wondered how she'd feel when she saw him and even more curious about his reaction.

"You going to lounge there all day?" asked Matt as he crossed the street.

Tilting her head down Megan squinted out of the corner of her eye. "That depends," she replied.

"On what?"

"On whether our outing is as relaxing as sitting here and doing absolutely nothing," said Megan. "And after my week, doing nothing sounds wonderful."

"I think that's just a backhanded way of getting me to tell you what we're doing," Matt countered, opening the gate.

"I just think you're afraid I'm not going to like it," said Megan, heading down the steps and meeting him halfway along the walkway.

"Hi," said Matt as he reached up and brushed a strand of hair off her forehead.

"Hi, you ready to go?" she asked slowly.

"Nope."

"What do you mean, nope?" asked Megan, right before he commandeered her lips and slowly pulled her close and tasted her fully.

"Now I'm ready," he replied as he released her, then reached for her hand to guide her to his Jeep.

Megan couldn't get over how much she had missed Matt's closeness. He was getting more comfortable with her; she could tell by the way he didn't study her face before collecting her in his arms and kissing her. *Take it easy, Megan. You still have medical school to deal with before even thinking about making this relationship last,* she told herself. *And that's a long way off, provided he's even interested in keeping it going.*

Driving down the back of the development, they saw Marcus and Sue stepping out onto their front porch, and waved as they rolled by.

"So how long until we get there?" asked Megan.

"You just don't give up, do you. I can see the wheels churning in your head just by looking into your eyes. Sit back, relax and enjoy the ride," said Matt, shaking his head and smiling.

Within a half hour Matt pulled off the main road onto a gravel path lined with maple trees. Megan's mouth dropped open at the sight of the vibrant red leaves. But as they reached the end of the gravel road Matt turned right onto a little dirt road. As they crested the hill Megan's eyes widened. In the valley below was a purple, red and yellow striped hot air balloon.

Megan leaned forward in her seat and peered up through the window as Matt rolled closer and parked next to a pick-up truck with a trailer attached to the back.

"I-I ..." said Megan, unable to finish her thought. She had only dreamed of drifting across the sky in a hot air balloon, but never imagined she would ever get the chance to fly in one.

Turning around she placed her hands on Matt's face and mouthed, "Thank you" before wrapping her arms around his neck.

"I guess this means you like our outing?" asked Matt.

Megan took in a jagged breath as tears filled her eyes.

"Hey, what's all this for?" asked Matt. "This was supposed to make you happy."

"Oh, it makes me very happy," said Megan as a line of tears trailed a path down her cheeks. "After my parents died, I'd sit for hours on end dreaming of being carried away in a hot air balloon, just to get away from all the stress of being an adult before I had the chance to enjoy the rest of my teenage years. Thank you for this."

"You're welcome," said Matt as he reached up and wiped her eyes before pulling her close for a hug. "Now, shall we go enjoy the ride?"

"Yes, please," said Megan climbing out of the Jeep.

Matt made his way around to her, collected her hand, and led them over to the basket.

"Good afternoon, I'm Will. I'll be your pilot this afternoon. Looks like we're in for a lovely ride and a beautiful sunset," said Will.

"Hi, Will. I'm Matt and this is Meg," said Matt.

"Is this your first time riding in a hot air balloon?" asked Will.

"Yes," said Megan. "At least it's my first time," she said, glancing at Matt.

"I've been before, but it's been years," said Matt.

"Well, there's a step stool on the side of the basket. Take your time and climb in," said Will.

Megan watched Matt climb into the basket, then turned to help her in.

"What's that?" asked Megan pointing to one of the corners of the basket.

"That's the propane tank, which is used to fuel our flight," said Will. "Are you ready to go?"

"Yes," said Megan, grabbing hold of the basket.

Matt stood close and wrapped one arm around her back and placed his other hand on the basket. When Will pulled the lever and ignited the burners, Megan jumped. Despite the burners the air was cool as the balloon slowly lifted into the air. Her heart was racing as they ascended towards the sky.

"Oh, wow! I didn't expect it to be such a smooth ride. This is wonderful!" said Megan looking back into Matt's eyes.

"Yes, it is. So, surprises aren't all bad, are they?" asked Matt.

"Not this one," said Megan as she wrapped her arms around him. "Look at the trees, Matt. It looks like someone flicked a paintbrush and allowed all the colors to intermingle in a unique pattern all on their own. And look over there, see how the sun is splashing along that hillside as it's setting, it's creating an aura that appears right before the perfect rainbow. I can't believe you did this. Did Kayla say anything to you about hot air balloons?" asked Megan.

"Nope. This idea was all mine, unlike the apple turnovers," he said with a smile.

As they drifted along the treetops Megan got lost in his arms. It was peaceful and serene, just what she needed after a stressful week of school work. Reaching into her pants pocket she pulled out her cell phone.

"We need a picture of us," said Megan, holding her phone out to take the shot.

Once her phone was secure in her back pocket Matt tilted her head up and kissed her ever so sweetly. Never in her life had she felt so alive. Life wasn't passing her by this time. She was in the moment. Living it. Feeling it. Touching it. She was falling in love.

As they floated through the sky Megan took a few more pictures, for she never wanted to forget this moment. Will also took a few pictures of them as the sun set over their right shoulders. For the rest of the flight

Megan rested her head on Matt's shoulder. She sensed a change in him as they coasted across the sky. The same type of calmness that appeared when he held onto her in his kitchen after breakfast. He seemed more at ease with himself as he held onto her and buried his face in her hair. Comfortable in the moment, away from a world with expectations, for right now there were none.

"You're awfully quiet," said Megan.

"I'm just enjoying the calmness, too," said Matt. "It's nice not having to worry about where I am or who I am for that matter, if only for an hour."

As they made their descent Will said, "This might be a little bumpy, so hold onto the basket and brace yourselves."

Megan watched Will toss a drop line over the side of the basket to the men standing below. The basket skimmed the grass, bumped up and down twice, before coming to a stop. Matt climbed out first then helped Megan out.

"Thank you, Will," they both said together.

"That was the most wonderful adventure I've had in a long time," said Megan.

"You're welcome. Come fly with us again sometime," said Will.

Megan wrapped her arm around Matt's and leaned her head into his upper arm. "That was so wonderful," she reiterated.

"How about stopping for pizza, before heading home?" asked Matt.

"Sounds good to me, I'm starving," said Megan.

* * *

Making their way home, Matt pulled into his driveway then walked Megan across the street. He was elated that she liked the hot air balloon ride. She had worked herself silly this past week and he knew doing something relaxing and fun would help her get through the last several weeks of class.

However, that wasn't the only thing Matt was thinking about while drifting across the sky. His feelings were increasing towards Megan and he truly wasn't sure how he was going to confide in her what he was afraid to tell anyone. But it was something he wanted to do. Needed to do, like his father told him.

"Do you want to come in for a cup of coffee?" she asked.

"Sure," he replied, sliding his hands into his pockets, suddenly feeling self-conscious about being alone with her. They had a wonderful afternoon and his desire to turn it into a loving close evening caused his heart to race. *Just do it Matt. Get it over with.*

Walking into the kitchen Megan headed toward the coffee pot when he strolled up behind her and swiftly turned her around. He cradled her head in one hand, placed his left hand on her backside, then forcefully pulled her tight against his body. He was fully aroused, but the unsettled look in his eyes revealed a man who wasn't sure if he wanted to make a move or run away.

She widened her eyes then furrowed her brow telling him she was truly confused by his forcefulness and didn't know what brought about his sudden display of emotional instability. He wasn't relaxed any more as he assertively tried to make advances by capturing one of her breasts in his hand. He knew she didn't understand the change in his behavior. When he started to reach up inside her sweater she placed both hands on his chest and shoved him away with such force, it truly startled him.

"What the hell was that for?" he asked, raising his voice.

"I don't know what you're trying to prove right now, Matt, but I don't like your advances. You're acting like you want to advance our relationship, but you're forcing it in a very rough and agitated way. What happened to the relaxed Matt with the sweet kisses in the hot air balloon?"

"Maybe I've decided I'm ready for a little more action, Megan," he countered using her full name.

"That may be true, but it's not happening that way," she responded, raising her voice in return.

Matt just staried at her. No one had ever told *him* to back off before, and he wasn't prepared for that kind of response. "Then why don't you just show me how it *is* happening," he yelled back after several seconds.

"Well, it's not happening *that way* either. I don't know what's going on in that head of yours, and right now I'm not sure I want to, but treating me that way is not going to get you anywhere. Do I make myself clear?" she said.

"Perfectly," he said and headed down the hallway.

She swiftly ran around the island and caught hold of his arm. "Matt, what's going on with you?"

"It's just not going to work out, Meg," he said, closing his eyes and lowering his head.

Matt truly didn't know why he said that. His head was spinning and everything just started crashing down inside his mind. He wanted to experience more closeness; afraid that if he didn't try, he'd never get this close to someone again. By barreling into it, he'd have less time to think about the trauma he'd been through … or how he was ever going to reveal to her what he had been through when he was twenty-two … or his worst fear, that he couldn't perform. And Megan deserved someone who could love her and fill her up passionately and sexually. The turmoil just kept building up inside of him when her voice came slicing through his thoughts, trying to throw some rational element back into his head.

"How did we go from having a very wonderful evening to those words, Matthew? You threw the enjoyment of the evening down the drain in what … ten minutes," she said succinctly. "I don't know who you think you are, but this is not the Matt I've gotten to know over these last several weeks. Do you need to tell me something?"

Matt pushed open the screen door and put one foot over the threshold, because he didn't know how to undo what he had done.

"Matthew Wilson, what is wrong?" she yelled to his back as he proceeded to walk down the porch steps. "You can't just leave without … without … oh, what the hell, go ahead and leave. I don't need you or anyone else in my life right now!"

Matt stopped at the bottom of the steps and clenched his fists. Her words not only stung, but hit home. How many times did he want to be left alone, only to finally figure out he didn't want to be left alone at all? Suddenly he heard his father's words, *you might just have to do it afraid.* Matt was terrified at that very moment. Afraid he'd lose the one person who truly cared about him and allowed him to be himself. He slowly turned around at the bottom of the steps and for the first time in his life, ground out through clenched teeth, "I'm thirty-three years old and I've never made love before!"

"I get it, Matt, and doing it once myself, a long time ago, doesn't mean I really know what it feels like either!" she yelled back.

"Well, that doesn't compare to having some loony girl try to cut off your privates!" he yelled as he walked across the street and threw his arms up in the air. Within seconds his chest constricted and his eyesight became blurry. *There, I said it. It wasn't how I wanted to say it, but it's out in the open.*

"Wait!!!! What????" she yelled across the street. "Matthew, get back here!!" she pleaded.

But he couldn't. As soon as he made it to his front door his knees crumpled beneath him and he slowly slid to the ground.

* * *

"Good Lord!" yelled Megan, as she darted across the street. The comprehension of his response spun around in Megan's head and jolted her senses like a lightning bolt slicing through the sky. He was choked up and sobbing uncontrollably.

Sitting beside him, Megan turned him around by the shoulders and lowered him sideways into her lap. Cradling his head up against her chest, she felt him wrap his arms tightly around her as he fought to gain control of his body's outbursts.

Megan just sat there and cried with him, periodically wiping away both their tears while occasionally kissing him on the top of his head. She didn't prevent him from crying because she knew from experience that healing came from tears. Sitting there, she figured he must care about her a great deal to entrust her with such a secret. The emotions that traveled through his face, along with his despondent attitude in the early morning hours several days ago, all came flooding back in her mind. His reaction when she caressed his chest, followed by the way he grabbed her wrist and held onto it when her hand traveled closer to his waistband. She suddenly understood what caused him to pull her close, then quickly let her go.

After several long minutes his breathing settled down, as he regained control of his emotions. Megan leaned her head back against the door and closed her eyes as she tried to put the past several minutes into perspective. She knew something was causing Matt to treat her differently while standing in her kitchen moments ago, but she never, in any of her random thoughts, imagined what he had just dropped on her — it was unthinkable.

When he finally loosened his hold and pushed himself up, she could tell he was embarrassed by his breakdown, but she wasn't going to let his thoughts head in that direction. She pulled herself away from the door and edged up next to him until their shoulders touched. Turning towards him, she placed both hands on his face and forced him to look into her eyes.

He had no words for her, but she knew he saw the flash of fear in her eyes for what he had been through, followed by intense anger. Reaching her arms around him, Megan rubbed her hands up and down his back repeatedly to help remove the fear inside of him and in return ease all the pent-up anger that had formed inside her towards the person who committed such a violent act.

However, her hatred and anger didn't last before her love for him filled her eyes. After cradling her head in his arms, he lovingly kissed her the way she had wanted him to back at her place, before he was overcome by the need to prove something to himself. When he couldn't express the love he felt for her, the way he truly wanted to, he slowly released his grip and gently held her in his arms.

Breaking the silence Megan said, "You understand that you need to tell me what happened; but not tonight. When you're ready, I'll be here to listen. You know that, right?"

"Yes, I know," he answered in a quiet, gentler voice.

"Do you need me to come in with you?" she asked stroking his cheeks with her thumbs.

"I think I'm okay from here. Thank you," he told her softly.

After searching his eyes for reassurance, she kissed him sweetly before getting up and walking back to her place. Before she walked through the door she glanced back toward Matt's place, but he had already disappeared inside. Walking into the kitchen Megan made herself a cup of hot tea, before it registered in her head that every part of their private conversation had been yelled across the street. Praying nobody had been outside to hear them, she climbed the stairs and cried uncontrollably for what he had been through. As she changed into her nightgown, her mind was spinning with every scenario she could conjure up regarding Matt's injuries. In the end she slept on the sofa and tossed and turned all night as her head unraveled the physical trauma he had been through, then tried to imagine the circumstances that led to such a horrific experience.

Chapter Fourteen

Matt took a couple deep breaths as he walked into the kitchen and fixed himself a strong cup of coffee. He grabbed a blanket and crumpled into one of the recliners in the living room. The pain he felt and the years of healing physically, let alone emotionally, flooded his thoughts. The only other person who had seen him break down was his father, and that was a long time ago. His chest felt tight and he gripped the blanket in his fist for how he told her about his plight. He then lowered his chin and closed his eyes for treating Megan the way he had, in her kitchen, moments ago. When he finally let go of the blanket, he leaned forward and plucked his cell phone from his back pocket. He stared at it for the longest time before texting his brother.

> Matt: Hi, Brian, is Dad still up?

After waiting for what seemed like forever his phone lit up with an answer.

> Brian: Yes. Is everything okay?
>
> Matt: Yes. Well sort of. I need Dad to call me on my cell phone. It's important.
>
> Brian: Sure. Give me a minute.

After several moments Matt's cell phone rang.

"Hi, Dad," Matt answered.

"Hi, Matt. Go ahead and fill me in," said Thomas calmly.

Matt didn't know how his dad did it, but like Megan's Uncle Ryan, he had the ability to sense what was on his mind.

"I told Meg, or should I say I yelled it at her as I was walking across the street from her place to mine."

"I'm afraid to ask the details on that one," said Thomas.

"And I'm too embarrassed to tell you, so let's just leave that part lay," replied Matt.

"Go on," said Thomas.

"I collapsed on my front porch and cried like a baby in her arms," he blurted out, while rubbing his eyes with his thumb and index finger.

"And?"

"… and she let me," Matt said with a sigh. "She didn't stop me. She just let my emotions run their course."

"Sounds like she knew how to comfort you."

"Yeah. She seems to have a knack for doing that," said Matt, raking his hand through his hair. "Aw, Dad … who am I kidding … I think I'm falling in love with her."

"I know, son," he said softly.

"It hit me when I realized how much she cares about me. The real me."

"Then what's the problem, besides the obvious hurdle you still need to overcome? Look son," Thomas continued without waiting for an answer, "as your love grows, she will fill your senses in more ways than you can imagine, provided you give her the chance. I know you're scared, but I watched your reaction when Brian snatched your phone and flipped through your texts. This young lady is different from all the others, and it showed in your mannerisms. It's scary to open up your heart again, especially after what you've been through. But let your heart and senses guide you Matt, because even though it's scary, a life without love is even scarier. By trusting her with all of your being, you'll allow yourself a chance to experience what true love feels like."

"Thanks, Dad," said Matt, as he recollected the intimate moment with her the night he returned from Michigan, before he got scared. "She wants me to tell her what happened."

"You've dealt with your fears for eleven years, Matthew. Don't you think it's time to move on with your life? You're finally realizing that all women aren't out for the same thing, and that you don't have to settle for someone you truly don't have any feelings for," said Thomas.

"I know. You're right, Dad, but …"

Cutting his son off, Thomas continued, "How would you feel if she had suffered a similar experience?"

"I'd want to know what happened, so I could help her overcome her fears and show her that I wasn't like the person who harmed her," replied Matt, knowing his father was right.

"One more thing before I let you go," said Thomas.

"Yeah."

"You might want to consider telling your brother. He recalls the five months I left him in charge of the ranch, and despite his antics while you were home, he does care about you."

"One hurdle at a time, Dad. It's going to take me a bit to work up the courage to have the conversation with Meg. And she needs to hear it first."

"I agree. But don't wait too long," Thomas advised.

"I know. I'm going to have to figure out how to tell her without distracting her from her studies, which might be tricky. But then she's probably already distracted after tonight's events. Please tell Brian everything is okay for me, and I look forward to his visit next Sunday.

"You got it. Night, son!"

"Night, Dad and thank you," he replied before hanging up the phone.

Matt's thoughts were all over the place Sunday. He kept to himself and ventured out onto the back deck periodically to clear his head. He relived his injury multiple times and each time his memory couldn't visualize the actual incident and jumped right to his reaction.

After lunch he picked up the box of cards he had placed on the coffee table. He didn't remember receiving so many cards, but like his dad said, he was in a daze most of the time.

After taking the lid off the box, he picked up the homemade card he had placed on top back in Michigan. He stared at the drawing on the front. The chairs, people and dog were outlined in pencil then colored in. Opening the card, he read it and then studied the signature at the bottom. It was signed Peaches. Closing it he flipped it over wondering if there was a clue to who Peaches was on the back. All it said was, "made just for you by me." Sitting it aside he went through every card and took note who signed them. He knew most of them or at least recognized the name. But the only card he couldn't place was the handmade one.

He collected a magnet from a kitchen drawer and attached the card to his refrigerator before returning the rest of the cards to the box. *Maybe seeing it every morning might jog my memory and help me remember Peaches. It has to be a nickname,* thought Matt as he stepped back to look at it from a distance. He decided he liked the drawing, regardless of who made it. It was original compared to all the others, which made it special.

* * *

Megan didn't see much of Matt after their argument and his breakdown on the front porch. They managed to go jogging Monday and Friday morning, but the conversations were polite and he made sure to avoid any personal contact.

It bothered Megan that he had pulled back from her and apparently thrown away all the trust and closeness they had built up. She thought he knew her better than that, but she couldn't dwell on it now. She was swamped with studying the intricacies of the heart and her note card pile was growing bigger after each class. Her professor was also providing multiple scenarios to prepare them for any medical issues imaginable, during every class.

Maybe it's a good thing Matt's brother is coming to visit on Sunday, thought Megan. The possibility of Brian being able to straighten out Matt's belief that their relationship was over drifted into her head. Provided his rant about their relationship not working out was just yelled out of pure frustration and not Matt's true feelings. Although her comment about not needing or wanting anyone in her life was now incorrect, because she was discovering that the more time she spent without him, the more she truly missed having him around.

* * *

Matt finally stepped onto his porch the following Sunday afternoon and found Megan sitting on her hammock. He *was* intentionally avoiding her. Not because he stopped caring about her, but because he hadn't quite figured out how to tell her about his scars and the details as to how he got them. He rolled several scenarios through his mind, but none of them delivered the full impact of what he had gone through. Taking a deep breath, he headed down his porch steps to go talk to her. It had been long enough, and whether he was ready or not he needed to openly and honestly discuss what he had been through. As he took a step out into the street a blue pick-up truck rolled up beside him; it was his brother Brian.

Matt was startled, but elated to see him. He only wished he had been about an hour away. Brian got out of his truck and gave Matt a hug. As he did Megan stood up and glanced over at them. Matt picked up his hand and waved, which she returned ever so slightly before heading inside. Brain released him only to find him fixated on the house across the street.

"Meg, huh?" said Brian.

"Yeah, how'd you guess that?" asked Matt with an inquisitive look on his face.

"Remember … I've been down that road," he replied.

"Sorry, Brian."

"No need to apologize. Anytime you need to go see her, please don't let me hold you back," he told Matt.

"What did Dad tell you?" asked Matt so he knew where things stood.

"That you and Meg had an argument. Don't wait too long, Matt. I did that with Molly once, and I felt her wrath for a whole week. It's not worth being in that much heartache."

"I just might take you up on that, but right now let's get you settled in your old room," he said, helping Brian with his duffle bag.

Once Brian was settled in, he came downstairs and found Matt sitting at the kitchen table tracing his finger around the rim of his coffee mug.

"Wow, you've got it bad, bro," Brain said, taking a seat across from him.

Matt leaned his elbows on the table and buried his face in his hands. "That obvious, huh?"

"More than obvious. Go talk to her. You're not going to feel any better until you do," Brian said. "Anyway it'll give me a few quiet moments to relax on the back deck. I'm pretty drained after that long ride."

As Brian got up from the table, he tilted his head down the hallway toward the front door then glanced back at Matt.

"Do you hear that?" asked Brian. "Sounds like someone's calling your name."

"Matthew ... Matthew ... Matthew!" Each echo was louder than the last.

Just as Matt stood up, Megan flew into the kitchen. She looked extremely pale as she placed both hands against the island. Matt quickly stepped around his brother just in time to catch her before she passed out and collapsed onto the floor.

"Quick, Brian, get me a cool damp towel," said Matt.

After fetching the towel, he watched Matt place it on Megan's forehead, then ran it along the back of her neck. He cradled her head in his arms and talked to her softly.

"Hey, Meg ... sweetheart. You're okay. Wake up and tell me what happened," he pleaded, rocking her gently as he sat on the floor.

Megan's eyes flew open with a start and it was all Matt could do to keep her cradled in his arms so she didn't pass out again. "You're okay, sweetheart. Tell me what happened."

Megan's eyes got wide as she spit out three words, "Snake, kitchen, pantry."

Matt realized he should have recognized the look on Megan's face from the time she had almost passed out at Naomi's cabin when he asked her to help him bag that unwanted visitor. He immediately leaned over and kissed her on the temple. "I think we have a little job to do," he said to Brian.

Matt picked up Megan and carried her over to the sofa in his living room. He brought her a glass of water and a fruit cup to put some sugars into her system. Before collecting the bag and noose, he took her face in his hands and kissed her leisurely several times as he caressed her cheeks. The look in Matt's eyes told her he missed her terribly and it was time for them to talk, because he couldn't spend the rest of his vacation without her in his life.

Walking towards the door, Matt said to his brother, "You do remember how to do this, right?"

Brain shoved Matt out the door and followed him over to Megan's place. They found a black gardener snake stretched across the floor of the pantry. He had a lot of speed and it took them several minutes to finally corner the sucker across the hallway in the bathroom. Brian slipped the noose around its neck and Matt held the canvas bag.

As they made their way back across the street, Brian said, "I think you need to talk to her. I'll go release the snake down near the river. I'm sorry my timing getting here wasn't the greatest."

"You don't need to be sorry, Brian, and I appreciate your understanding. After I get done talking to Meg, we need to talk, too. I'm probably going to need about an hour with Meg, if that's okay."

"You take as much time as you need. She *is* lovely, Matt. She reminds me of Mom."

"Yeah, I figured out that much," he responded, bumping his brother in the shoulder as they climbed the porch steps. "Take my Jeep," said Matt, handing his keys to Brian.

Leaning into Matt's shoulder, Brian whispered, "Don't give up on her, Matt."

"I won't. Thanks." *Brian doesn't know the half of it*, reflected Matt.

Chapter Fifteen

Megan's body melted into the sofa as the smell of Matt seeped into her senses. Feeling safe, she relaxed and snoozed while the guys were gone. The snake had scared her down to her core. The fact that she hadn't eaten right or slept soundly over the past week had compounded her vulnerability.

When Megan heard the screen door bang, she knew Matt was back. Making his way into the living room he grabbed a pillow before sitting down next to her. She was curled up on her side but leaned her head back to peer up into his face. He placed the pillow on his lap and patted it, beaconing her to rest her head on it. Once she was settled, Matt started weaving his fingers through her soft hair. Looking back over her shoulder, she found him with his head back and his eyes closed.

When he finally opened his eyes, she saw the man she was falling in love with looking down into her face. An aura of contentment settled into her mind and body, telling her, *this is where I'm supposed to be and whom I'm supposed to be with.* Her mother's poem floated to the forefront of her mind. The path was before her and her journey was slowly unfolding. The feeling of déjà vu suddenly returned and tugged at her senses again. It lingered for only a moment before fading away.

"Hi," she uttered softly.

"Hi, sweetheart! We need to talk."

"I know. I've been waiting for you to come get me," she replied.

"And I'm sorry it's taken me so long. I've been struggling with how to relay what happened to me in a way that will allow you to understand its full impact on me," he answered truthfully.

"Why don't you start with how you got involved with the person who hurt you?" replied Megan.

"Well, we met in college. We were both business majors and had several classes together. I'm not going to lie, Meg, she was a nice-looking girl. We slowly advanced our relationship over the course of three years," he told her.

Megan listened intently, and made it a point to stay still, so she wouldn't disrupt his thoughts. He needed to tell her at his own pace, and it didn't matter how long it took.

Raking his fingers absentmindedly through her hair, he continued, "Thinking back, she never seemed ready and would get agitated when we talked about getting even closer. I just read it as being nervous, which is how I felt too. Anyway, we set a time and place when we were both free. We went out to dinner and back to her apartment because her roommate had other plans and wouldn't be home until later in the evening," he explained.

As he got closer to the incident, the strokes of his hand through her hair became a little firmer, as the anxiety was growing in his eyes. He finally stared across the room and she could see him struggle for the right words as she quietly waited for him to continue.

"She placed candles around her bedroom and proceeded to light them slowly. I remember them because they created a very relaxing atmosphere. She went to use the bathroom and changed into a little red camisole and panties. I kissed her when she came out, before I stepped into the bathroom. When I returned, she was sitting in the middle of her bed waiting for me. She held out her hand and beckoned me to join her. She started by removing my shirt over my head. After my clothes were off, I reached out to remove her camisole and…"

Megan felt him shiver, but didn't stop him. Holding tightly onto a bunch of her hair he said, "and … as I went … to remove her panties, she pulled out a small switchblade. Where she had it concealed, I have no idea. I can't clearly visualize how it all happened and within seconds she slashed me on the left and right side … of my privates."

"Oh, Meg!" he said, drawing her up to his chest. "Blood started pouring out of me like a fountain! When I saw what she had done, I slapped the blade out of her hand, sailing it across the room. Don't ask me how, but I grabbed my shirt off the floor and stuffed parts of it into my wounds before crawling to the phone and calling for help."

Matt's grip had gotten so tight in those seconds, that Megan had to rub his arms to get him to relax his grip. After a few moments he ground out, "She sat on the bed laughing, just laughing, at what she had just done. The only thought I could formulate in my head was, 'Why'?"

He was quiet for the longest time as he held her close. His breathing had become erratic, and she could tell the event was being relived in his mind. The terrified look on his face explained how this viral young man had succumbed to a life that forced him to retreat whenever a woman tempted him.

Sensing there was more to the story, Megan touched his cheek and whispered, "Why did she do it, Matt?" Looking down into Megan's sweet face he ground out, "Because her mother told her she was the product of a forced sexual encounter and all men were only after one thing … to satisfy their own personal needs. But I didn't find *that out* until we were in court, and she was standing in front of the judge."

Megan now understood why he had difficulty trusting women on an intimate level.

She started to pull herself out of Matt's hold, but he drew her back and absentmindedly kissed her temple. He took a deep jagged breath and continued, "After I called 911, I passed out. The next thing I remember was waking up in the hospital with my dad sitting at the end of my bed."

Megan knew what was coming, she knew her anatomy and how things were connected. Her thoughts started to formulate a vivid picture. Severing certain nerves and arteries could cause a man to lose … but she stopped her thoughts short, because she knew his regular body functions worked or he'd be carrying catheters with him. And considering their brief contact several weeks ago, she figured what he didn't know was his ability to perform intimately. And could he maintain … but she didn't want to think about that component right now.

Working herself free, she sat next to him for a few minutes before taking his right hand and placing it between her own. She could surmise what he had been through, but she knew he also needed to be the one to voice the physical and emotional injuries he had suffered.

"Go on, Matt, I'm listening. What happened in the hospital?"

Matt closed his eyes and leaned his head back into the cushion as tears slowly traced a path down his face. He reached up to brush them away and wipe his eyes. Megan curled her legs up onto the sofa and waited for him to continue. "I feared the worst as my dad filled me in. She had cut into both dorsal nerves which are crucial for normal sexual function and the blade had also punctured my internal pudendal artery, which provides blood supply to my … you know," he told her. "My dad said the artery which supplies the blood flow was repaired fully, which was a relief all on its own. But the dorsal nerves were almost completely severed and until I totally healed, they wouldn't know how much function I would have," he finished with a sigh.

And that was the rest of the story. All Megan wanted to do was curl him up in her lap and hold him like you hold a child that has been physically hurt, then proceed to tell them that everything was going to be okay. But Matt was no child and he had been through a horrifying experience, and on top of that, tortured himself for eleven years thinking no woman would understand enough to work through his fears without being degrading.

Taking both of her hands in his, Matt continued, "When I kissed you outside your gate after jogging a couple of months ago, you felt me become aroused. That was the first time, since my surgery, that it's happened instantaneously. I thought it might have been a fluke, until the morning I got back from Michigan and we kissed before you caressed my chest.

"But didn't they have you …" but she turned red even as the thought rolled through her head.

"Meg, that whole process was more embarrassing than I'd like to divulge. I had just turned twenty-two the month before," he confessed. "I'll tell you this … it took me two weeks for all the feeling to come back to my organ and another two to gain control of my normal bodily function.

The implication of his words caused Megan to tear up. "I'm sorry you had to go through all that. You know that I would never …" she began.

But he cut her off. "I know that, Meg. I know I can trust you, sweetheart," he said, reaching up and taking her face in his hands. He kissed her leisurely like she was the only one within a square mile of their location. She had missed the closeness that had developed between them and didn't want to feel the emptiness that had engulfed them over the past week. Leaning her down on the sofa, he stretched his full torso on top of her and brushing the sides of her breasts with his thumbs, made his way up to her face.

Megan reached up and laced her fingers along the back of his neck, and drawing him down kissed his cheeks before tasting his mouth, causing Matt to become aroused at her playfulness. He leaned his head back to look into her eyes and smiled. And this time she knew what that smile was for. Leaning down to her ear Matt whispered, "You're my girl, Meg, if you'll have me. I can't guarantee a smooth ride, but I can guarantee my faithfulness to you as we figure things out."

"I'd like that very much, Matt," she said as the tears started to roll down the sides of her face. He devoured her lips and ground himself into her, but stopped before he crossed his own personal boundary. Taking her hand he helped her sit up before sliding his fingers through her hair which had become unruly in their talking and intimate moment. She returned the favor before they both started laughing.

Matt pulled her to her feet then glanced at his cell phone. He was surprised to see that it was close to three-thirty in the afternoon. "Wow, where did the time go? Let's get you back to your place so you can get some studying done before dinner."

Taking her hand, Matt led her to the front door and out onto the porch. That's where they found Brian, sitting in one of the chairs with his ears plugged and sound asleep. Matt went back inside and grabbed a blanket to place over him before escorting Megan across the street.

As they stepped onto her porch he made her wait outside while he checked out all the rooms for any more unwanted little friends and around the perimeter of the cabin for any openings. Not finding any, he led her inside. Rubbing his hands up and down her upper arms he pulled her close and placed a couple kisses on her lips before leaving. Had he given her any more she wouldn't have wanted him to leave.

As he was about to walk down the porch Megan stepped back over the threshold and asked, "Jogging tomorrow morning?"

I'd like to skip tomorrow morning," Matt answered truthfully.

"Okay," she said, sounding disappointed.

"Brian and I are going fishing in the morning, but you're welcome to come over for dinner," he said, "provided we catch anything worth eating."

"I'd like that. Thanks," she said, stepping back inside.

"I'll send you a text later in the day tomorrow to let you know what time," he told her before heading back across the street.

Megan closed the door and sank all the way to the ground. Her emotions had been all revved up and she needed a few minutes to digest everything Matt had confided in her. She held her emotions in check as best she could to give him the chance to unload everything he had gone through. If she had broken down during his account, she never would have gotten to hear the details surrounding the whole unpleasant incident. And on top of all that, he wanted her to be his girlfriend. It was all those thoughts that brought her to tears. She cried for what he had been through, the years of frustration, and the trust he was slowly putting in her.

Despite Megan's determination not to get involved in a relationship before she finished school, her life was sure taking a detour, similar to the roundabout path she had to take when her mom and dad were suddenly killed. She knew Matt cared about her finishing her degrees, but whether they could handle being separated from each other when he was called back to work while she progressed with her studies, was unknown. She was scared, but her resilience would surely help them work out their careers and enable them to toss all their trepidations out the window. Plus, the only way she would even consider moving out to LA, was with a ring on her finger. But she wasn't even sure Matt could or would offer her that. "Only time will tell. One step at a time. I had a feeling this journey would move slowly," she said out loud as she collected herself off the floor and made her way upstairs to stand in a warm shower before fixing something to eat.

* * *

As Matt made his way back to his place, Brian shifted in his seat prompting Matt to walk over and tap him on the shoulder, "Come on inside. I'm on a roll and might as well tell you, too."

Brian got up and followed his brother back to the kitchen table. Before Matt opened his mouth, Brian said, "I'm going to make this easy on you, Matt. I caught the tail end of your conversation with Meg."

"Great!" replied Matt, exasperated that his brother had been listening.

"Look … I heard the part about removing her panties and then she pulled out a small switchblade … and I plugged my ears when you two started kissing … so don't get yourself too bent out of shape. I've been married long enough to know when to butt out."

"I know, I know," said Matt as he sat down and ran his hands across his face. "I asked you to come visit because I know you and I haven't been on the same page in years. Little did I know it would start out this way."

"I think that's the first thing we've been able to agree upon in a long time," said Brian as he sat across from his brother.

"Just so you understand, I haven't told anyone about my injuries. But then I really haven't had a reason to, until now. And I'm sorry it's taken me all these years to finally work up enough courage to talk about it with you."

"After overhearing what you told Meg, I feel like a real jerk right about now," said Brain.

"Well, that's on my shoulders, not yours. You couldn't understand what I didn't allow you to know. And don't blame Dad, I asked him not to share any of the specifics."

"I'm sorry for all the callus remarks I've made over the years, but you could have told me sooner. For Pete's sake, I *am* your brother, not some stranger."

"I'm sorry, Brian. I was twenty-two and it was just too embarrassing to talk about. And the longer I waited the harder it got. Just like you told me when you waited too long to talk to Molly when you disagreed," said Matt heading toward the coffee pot.

"I guess I understand that part, but jeez, Matt, had you told me sooner we could have talked about your fears and concerns. All this time I could have been helping you instead of acting like a callus older brother. But we can't go back and change all that," said Brian.

"No, but I'd like to move forward, if you're willing."

"Yes, I'd like to be a part of your everyday life, like we were before you went off to college."

"I'd like that, too. By the way, I'm pretty sure Molly's wondering what's going on after talking to her on the porch back home," said Matt as he set a cup of coffee in front of his brother. "I'd appreciate it if you'd give her the watered-down version. I know she suspects something, but I'm not comfortable enough to tell her."

"I can do that. I think she'd appreciate knowing," Brian told him. "She cares about your well-being, too, Matt."

"I know. You found a good one."

"Well, I think you've found a lovely lady in Meg, too. Have you told her you love her?"

"One step at a time. I just asked her to be my girlfriend this afternoon."

"How about wife?" inquired Brian smugly peering over his mug. "I don't think Meg will stand for anything less," he added quickly.

"I'm not sure I'm the marrying type. I'm already thirty-three years old and kind of set in my ways."

"Seems to me those ways are changing," challenged Brian. "And if that's your only excuse for not getting married, then you don't deserve to have Meg at your side, in any capacity. And the fact that … and I'm pretty sure of this … she's the only one you've even felt the desire to tell about the attack, after knowing her for only a couple months, when it has taken you eleven years to tell me, your own brother, says a lot. Which is a clear indication that she means more to you than you're willing to admit."

Matt sat across from his brother and briefly mulled over what he said. He knew Brian was right about one thing; Megan wouldn't stand for anything less than marriage. But despite confiding in her his deepest secrets, he wasn't sure he could set aside his physical fears and fully allow himself to give her the unrestrained love she deserved. She had proven both her patience and trust, but would she be willing to give him the additional time to get there. And in his mind, that would be the deciding factor.

* * *

Matt enjoyed spending the week with Brian and devoting time to rebuilding their relationship. He also noticed how effortlessly Megan fit into his family when he and Brian popped over to spend time with her in between her studies. To help her out, Matt, with Brian's help, cooked her dinner every night she had class. It was a good way to show Brian how to make a few more dishes he could share with Molly.

"I can't believe the week is almost over," said Brian as they prepared their last dinner together. "I must say it started out a little rough, but I'm glad about one thing."

"What's that?" inquired Matt.

"I'm glad you finally told me about your injuries. You truly seem more relaxed than I've seen you in a long time and I'm looking forward to more open conversations. We have a lot to catch up on; one week isn't enough."

"I guess I do feel a little more at ease. The memories are still very vivid and I would never have been able to reveal what happened without Meg."

"She seems like one special lady, just like Molly," he said with a broad smile on his face. "And if you even think about letting her go, I'll be back to kick your tail end all the way home to Michigan," said Brian.

Saturday morning, Brian found Matt sitting on the porch with a coffee cup in his hand.

"Got everything?" asked Matt.

"I think so. If not, you remember how to get to the ranch, right?" chided Brian. "And I'm sure Dad and Molly would love to meet Meg," he added.

"Yes, and I think they would like Meg," said Matt as Brian's cell phone went off.

Brian stepped back inside, but Matt overheard him talking to Molly.

"What? Really? When Molly? Did you know this before I left?" asked Brian.

Matt stepped off the porch and headed to the driveway to give his brother some privacy.

When Brian stepped back out onto the porch a few minutes later, Matt heard him say. "I thank you and I love you, sweetheart. I'll see you soon."

Matt waited by his Jeep for Brian to fill him in. He had a broad smile on his face as he jogged down the porch steps. "You're going to be an uncle again, Matt," he said, clapping his hands together.

"That's great, Brian! When?"

"The tenth of May."

"Please make sure you give Molly a hug and kiss for me when you get home."

"I sure will."

"Now let's get some breakfast in you, so you can get on the road and home to Molly and the children."

When breakfast was over Matt helped carry Brian's bag out to his truck. Megan must have been watching because she made her way across the street as soon as they stepped off the porch. Walking up to Brian, she kissed him on the cheek and handed him a tin can. "There are six pumpkin spice muffins in there. I got burned out from studying last night and decided to bake," she said, looking in Matt's direction for any sign of disapproval. "Please share them with your family when you get home. I also put in an extra one for you to eat tomorrow morning for breakfast." After handing him the tin she stretched her arms out for a hug and gave him another kiss on the cheek. "It was a pleasure meeting you, Brian. Please drive home safely and let Matt know when you get there. I worry about those kinds of things."

"Well, it was a pleasure meeting you too, Meg. I will certainly let Matt know when I'm home and thank you for the muffins," he told her.

Matt walked up to Brian and gave him a bear hug before heading over to stand next to Megan. He pulled her close to his side as Brian got into his truck and turned around in Matt's driveway. Stretching a hand out the window Brian waved as he slowly rolled down the hill. Matt leaned down and whispered in her ear, "Brian's going to be a father again."

Megan's face lit up like a Christmas tree. "That's wonderful, Matt! When is the baby due?"

"The tenth of May. Now Ms. Barnes, I believe you have some studying to do, instead of baking," he said playfully as he escorted her back to her front steps. "And I have some cleaning up to do. So, I will see you later," he informed her, teasing her with a kiss before gently steering her inside her front door.

Chapter Sixteen

Over the first three weeks of November, Megan noticed a change in Matt. He was keeping an extra close eye on her for starters. She couldn't say he was distracting her from her studies, although he would wander over occasionally to spend some time holding and kissing her. She was enjoying his new playful side and her resistance about getting involved with someone was being completely swept away downstream. He was winding his way into her daily life; showing up whenever she became overwhelmed with her studies and helping her figure things out. He even came up with a few tunes to help her memorize certain body functions, before her third exam, which just fascinated her.

* * *

Before Megan knew it Thanksgiving was almost upon them. Aunt Helen called on Monday to tell her she and Uncle Ryan would love to have her and Matt, along with Kayla and Dan, out to the ranch for the holiday and to spend a few days together. She quickly sent out a group text to Kayla, Dan and Matt.

> Megan: Hi, Everyone. Aunt Helen and Uncle Ryan would like to know if we can join them for Thanksgiving. My music professor canceled class on Wednesday because he's traveling. So, I have off from school

> Wednesday - Friday. Let me know if you're available to go and what days. I'll get back to Aunt Helen with our answers. Thanks!

The first response came from Matt.

> Matt: I'm good to go whenever you all are.
>
> Kayla: Dan & I decided we will close early on Wednesday but we have to be back sometime around noon on Friday to support the staff. We'll meet you and Matt there.
>
> Megan: Sounds good, Kayla. Matt, can we leave Wednesday morning?
>
> Matt: What time?
>
> Megan: 9:00 would be nice.
>
> Matt: I'll be ready.

By the time Wednesday came Megan was more than ready to get away to her aunt and uncle's ranch. Her professor had scheduled a challenging and lengthy quiz Tuesday night, which included six medical bios of patients she had to analyze and recommend a treatment for. She rolled in the door at ten-thirty in the evening and barely had enough energy to eat something before crashing on her bed.

She woke at eight o'clock the next morning and was frantically packing her duffle bag when she heard Matt calling her from the hallway downstairs. As she made her way down the steps in her fuzzy slippers, she slipped on the last two rungs and would have landed hard on her backside had Matt not reached out and grabbed her by the waist.

"Careful there," he said as he placed her feet firmly on the ground. He leaned her back and looked at her face with a quirky expression. "I'm afraid to ask, but what happened to you?" Looking down she took in her appearance. Her clothes were wrinkled and she could feel that her hair was completely messed up.

"Didn't you know," she said, placing her right hand on her hip and placing the other on the back of her head like a fashion model, "this is how I look every morning. It takes me three hours to put everything in order."

Matt couldn't help but laugh, but it didn't last long before concern filled his voice. "Okay, enough clowning around. What happened last night?"

"My professor decided to give us a *quiz* with six patient bios. I think he was afraid we'd forget everything we learned if he waited until after Thanksgiving break. By the time I got home I was so exhausted it took all my energy to eat a yogurt. I made it upstairs and before I knew it, I fell asleep sprawled out on my bed and woke up about fifteen minutes ago. I'd really like to run through the shower. Would you mind fixing each of us an egg sandwich?"

"Not at all," he answered, kissing her on the nose before dropping his duffle bag near the front door.

Megan turned and ran back upstairs. She gathered some clean clothes, and stepping into the bathroom, got a glance of her face in the mirror. "Oh, good heavens," she said with a partial laugh, "Well, if this is the worst I'll ever look, then so be it." Stepping into the warm water she closed her eyes and let it sooth her. When she stepped out, she could smell the toasted muffin and quickly dressed in blue jeans, a pale pink camisole, and rose-and-cream-colored flannel shirt. She combed her hair out and pulled it back loosely into a barrette on the left side of her head and took note that she needed a haircut. "Well, that'll have to wait for two more weeks," she mumbled.

After packing the rest of her clothes, she headed downstairs. When she came around into the kitchen, Matt was sitting at the table waiting for her.

* * *

Looking up from his phone Matt took her in. She looked clean, soft and warm and the thought of making love to her crept into his brain at that moment. It shook him to the core because his thoughts hadn't crossed over that line, since prior to his incident. Having opened up to Megan allowed his brain to contemplate desires he had forbidden himself to consider with another woman. A chill traveled down his body as he tried to dislodge the idea from his head. But when she leaned over to kiss him, he gently captured her face in his hands. In one fluid motion he tilting her head, and softly placed his lips on hers. With all the passion he was feeling inside, he lovingly kissed her. When he let her go, she slowly sank into the seat across from him and he knew she felt his changing feelings woven into the moment.

* * *

It took Megan several seconds to regroup before asking, "So, are you all packed and ready to go?" But he was apparently still swept away by the kiss as much as she was.

"Earth to Matthew," she said, touching his arm.

"Oh, sorry," he replied slowly coming out of his musings.

"Everything okay?"

"Yes, you look very pretty," he said, letting the words flow out of his mouth.

"Thanks. Well, I hope I'm prepared for anything my uncle throws my way this time," said Megan, attempting to divert them from heading into another intimate moment that could either turn into something beautiful or blow up in their faces.

Megan watched him struggle to stop his meandering thoughts before he asked, "You don't think your uncle's going to give you another list, do you?"

"Those are bettin' words, Matthew. Do you think my uncle won't have a list for me?" she countered, relieved she had finally moved their wandering thoughts forward.

"I think I just might have to bet you for the sheer fun of it," he replied with a broad smile. "But let's not bet on whether there's going to be a list, because having met your uncle, I'd be a fool to accept that one."

"Then what are you proposing, Matthew Wilson?" she asked as she took a sip of coffee and stared at him over the rim with a hint of curiosity in her eyes.

"I think we need to bet on what the tasks will be."

"Oooh, think you know my uncle now, do you?" Megan replied before popping the last piece of egg sandwich into her mouth. She then reached over and popped his last bite into his mouth, mainly to keep them moving along, so they could leave on time. "So, what type of jobs are you thinking?" she asked.

"I'm thinking along the lines of cutting firewood, mending fences and feeding the livestock."

"Okay, those aren't bad for starters, but I think you ought to consider cleaning the equipment, helping to wean the calves, and the one I like the best," she said leaning over to look into his lovely hazel-blue eyes, "giving pregnancy tests to the female cows."

Matt just sat there looking at her. "You give the cows pregnancy tests? Well, that's a new one for me. Why is that done?"

"We give them certain vaccinations to keep them healthy during the pregnancy," she told him matter-of-factly. "You sure you grew up on a ranch?" she added.

"Yes, but we just let Mother Nature take its course," he answered.

Changing the subject again, Megan said, "I'll be ready after I collect my bag and a quick trip to the bathroom. Do you need to go, too? Are we taking my truck this time, since you brought your bag with you? And do you want to drive?" she said, making her way back upstairs.

"Wouldn't hurt, yes, and I'll drive," he answered walking down the hallway towards the bathroom.

Once the kitchen was in order, they collected their duffle bags and headed out the door. Megan tossed him her keys and climbed in. After he started the engine, he captured her hand and headed down the back hill.

The drive was relaxing until they started bantering back and forth about what other chores her uncle was going to put on her list. Matt settled on firewood and Megan chose pregnancy testing. Then they decided that if neither of those tasks were on the list, their second options would be mending fences and cleaning the equipment, respectively. They decided to stop for a quick lunch along the way, because it dawned on Megan that her uncle would probably put them to work as soon as they got there, and working on a ranch with an empty stomach is never a good idea.

During lunch Megan said, "We haven't decided what the winner gets for our little bet. What would you like, if you win?"

"I'd like a bubble bath with a back rub," he replied, surprising her completely.

"Are you kidding me?" she asked, laughing and smiling from ear to ear.

"Nope. My mom used to give us a bubble bath once a month growing up, and I enjoyed the back rub that came with it," he reminisced. "What would you like if you win?"

"I think I'm going to have to give this one some thought," she told him.

"And I think I'm in trouble," he responded, laughing softly.

"Not necessarily," Megan said in an enticing tone.

* * *

Uncle Ryan was heading to the barn when they pulled up to the house. He paused when he saw Megan's truck and came to greet them.

"Well, look who's arrived. Grab your bags and get yourselves settled, there's still a lot of work to be done this afternoon," Uncle Ryan told them.

Matt peered over and caught the, told you so, look on Megan's face, which was priceless.

"Always getting to the point, aren't you, Uncle Ryan," she stated bluntly.

"Darn right. So, get a move on. Aunt Helen would like your help in the kitchen and I'm going to borrow this boyfriend of yours to help mend a fence."

Megan shook her head at her uncle's assessment of her progressing relationship with Matt. She had just agreed to be his girlfriend a little over four weeks ago, and hadn't told anyone yet. Rolling her eyes, she headed towards the front porch.

Matt followed with their bags and proceeded to carry them up to their rooms. When he stepped into the kitchen, Megan looked up from peeling apples and found him wearing a heavy flannel shirt, the black cowboy hat she gave him and a pair of heavy gloves in his hand. He walked over to Helen, removed his hat and placed a kiss on her cheek.

"Well, hello Matt. Glad you could make it back with Meg. I see Ryan has already pegged you for some assistance."

"Yes, ma'am, he has. And I'm better prepared this time."

"Well, dinner will be ready around six o'clock tonight. If you would let Ryan know, I'd appreciate it. I'm trying to get a few dishes done for Thanksgiving so tonight's dinner will be a little later than usual."

"I'll relay the message," he said walking up behind Megan and snitching two pieces of apple out of her bowl, before planting a very loud kiss on her cheek. Megan turned beet red before swatting at his arm. Then she tried to give him a shove on the backside with her barefoot, which he barely avoided. Peering back over his shoulder and smiling broadly, he retorted, "Not fast enough, Ms. Barnes," and placing his hat back on his head went out the front door.

"The day's not over yet, Mr. Wilson," she hollered after him with a smile.

Megan glanced at her aunt, who was mixing up the pumpkin pie filling.

"What was that, Aunt Helen?" asked Megan, noticing the broad smile on her aunt's face.

"Oh, nothin'. I'm just talking to myself about what dishes I want to fix for tomorrow's dinner," she replied. "Would you be willing to fix your stuffing, Meg? I've always liked how it tastes," asked Helen.

"Sure, I can do that," answered Megan, knowing there was an underlying message in her aunt's smile.

"What time did Kayla and Dan say they were coming?" asked Helen.

"I think they should be here sometime before six. They were going to close the café at noon, then head home to pack."

* * *

It was six o'clock by the time Ryan and Matt rolled back to the house. Cresting the hill from the back field, they saw Kayla and Dan coasting down to the house.

Kayla got out and jogged toward the truck while Dan collected their bags and joined Kayla as her uncle pulled up next to her.

"Hi, Uncle Ryan!" she said, jumping up on the running board to give him a sideways hug and kiss. "Hey, Matt! Good to see you, too! Did Uncle Ryan even give you five minutes before putting you to work?"

Matt laughed out loud and said, "I think it was three minutes. But that's okay, it always feels good to do something."

"Any more tasks before I go take a shower?" asked Matt.

"Just one. Ever change a shoe on a horse?" Ryan asked.

"Wow! Now you're taking me way back," said Matt. "I believe I watched my dad do it years ago when I was about ten, but no, not by myself."

"Well, if you can hold down Cedar and keep him calm for me, I'll replace the shoe," Ryan said.

"I can do that. I rode Cedar last time I was here, so he should remember me," Matt replied.

"We should be up at the house in about thirty minutes to clean up for dinner," said Ryan as Kayla jumped off the running board.

"Okay, see you in a few," said Kayla, as Ryan drifted toward the barn.

"Can I ask you something?" said Matt as they climbed out of the truck.

"Sure, son. Anything," said Ryan.

"What year did Meg and Kayla lose their parents?"

"Isn't that something you should be asking Meg?" countered Ryan as he opened the gate to Cedar's stall.

"I would, but I asked her why she started college late, the second day after we met and the question upset her so much she cried," said Matt.

"I see," said Ryan as they walked Cedar to the tack room. Ryan was quiet for a stretch before saying, "1999 was a very rough year for all of us. My brother, Phillip, and his wife, Annie, were wonderful people and parents."

"I'm sorry for your loss, Ryan," said Matt. "The same year I was injured," he whispered to himself as he stroked Cedar's neck.

"What was that?" asked Ryan.

"I can't imagine losing both my parents at once. I lost my mom to cancer two years prior to Meg losing hers," he told Ryan.

"It makes you grow up faster when you lose a parent at a young age. Sometimes I think Meg's missed out on a lot of things other children her age enjoyed. That's why we encouraged her to come out here as often as she could. It seemed to be the one place where she found solace and could fully relax. She used to come out here and talk to the horses in the morning," said Ryan.

"They are comforting," agreed Matt, stroking Cedar's neck.

"I'll never forget the time shortly after Meg's parents died when she took two chairs and dragged them across the field to the top of the back hill. She collected a tree stump and rolled it between the chairs, then came back to the house for two glasses of lemonade. She'd sit out there for a couple hours by herself. Then she'd return to the kitchen with two empty glasses," said Ryan as he raised Cedar's hoof.

"Did you ever ask her why?" asked Matt.

"Nope. It was between her and God or nature. She might have felt closer to heaven and had a conversation with one of her parents. But when she returned, both glasses were always empty and she seemed more at peace," said Ryan.

After a moment Ryan continued, "It seemed to be her way of dealing with a rough situation. She's always had the desire to help and comfort others. She lost it for a stretch, but eventually discovered it wasn't right not to do something that was so innate to her."

"How long did she go out and sit on top of the hill?" asked Matt.

"I'd say a little over two years. Then one day she brought the empty glasses in and went back to the hill and dragged the chairs back to the house," said Ryan.

"Did she ever say why?" asked Matt, slightly curious.

"Nope. But the stump is still out there. The last time she came out here was right before she started college. She took a glass of lemonade and walked out to sit for a spell," finished Ryan.

Matt's understanding of what Megan had been through and her struggle to pull herself out of an unfair situation, made him contemplate his own reactions to those who tried to comfort him years ago. *How many of those people who sent me cards to show their concern did I snub without realizing they just cared about my well-being? How many visits ended poorly because of my own attitude?* he thought. Shaking his regrets from his mind, Matt comforted Cedar as Ryan cleaned out his hoof and put on a new shoe.

Once Cedar was back in his stall, Matt and Ryan headed back to the house and wandered into the kitchen, only to be shooed away by Helen and Megan because they were filthy and smelled like horses. They both headed off to shower and joined the family at the table for a simple meal of sliced ham, noodles and broccoli.

After dinner, Kayla, Dan, Megan and Helen gathered in the kitchen to continue the preparations for Thanksgiving. Matt would have loved to help but he was exhausted after helping Ryan out in the fields. He ended up dozing in the chair near the fireplace and didn't stir until Megan placed her hands on his shoulders.

"Time for bed," she told him as she massaged his upper shoulders and neck. After several minutes he patted Megan's hand and pushed himself out of the chair. Taking her hand, she guided him upstairs.

When they reached her bedroom Matt pinned her against the door and leisurely kissed her before strolling down the hallway to his own room.

"Night, Matt. See you in the morning. Don't forget the Thanksgiving Day Parade is on at ten o'clock. Would you like to watch it with me?" she asked.

"Yes, I'd like that," he answered then walked into his room but before closing the door added, "Wake me if I'm still sleeping."

* * *

Thanksgiving was a perfect late fall day. Everyone sat around relaxing while the turkey baked in the oven for most of the day. When the bird was finished, Kayla put the stuffing in the oven to cook, while Megan sliced the cranberry mold and Helen put potatoes and green beans on the stove to cook. When Megan was done with the cranberries she lined up the rolls on a cookie sheet so they could be warmed in the oven when the stuffing came out. After the turkey had cooled Ryan was called into the kitchen to carve it.

After putting on a pair of oven mitts, Megan held the baking pan while her uncle poked a fork and carving knife into the ends of the turkey and hoisted it out of the liquid and onto the cutting board that Kayla had placed on the island. She removed the pan and started to pour the essence into an oil separator cup when Matt stepped into the kitchen.

"Here, let me hold that for you," said Matt.

"Thanks," said Megan as she poured the rest of the essence into the cup.

"That's an unusual measuring cup," said Matt.

"That's because it's used to separate the grease from the liquid. The strainer keeps the bigger solid pieces out and when the liquid settles down the grease rises to the top. The spout is down at the bottom so I can pour the liquid out, but I like to use a smaller holed strainer to get out even more of the solid pieces of skin that slip through the first strainer."

Matt watched her pour the clear essence into a sauce pan and prepare a mixture of flour, salt, pepper, thyme and water. He looked on as she rinsed out the strainer and poured the mixture into it while trying to stir the pot at the same time.

"Can I pour the mixture into the strainer, while you stir?" asked Matt.

"That would be great. Here," said Megan handing over the strainer and glass jar she used to prepare the flour mixture. When the gravy was a good consistency she turned down the burner to warm and walked over to watch her uncle carve the rest of the turkey. As he placed a slice of breast meat on the platter in front of him, Megan noticed the design on it.

"Oh, Aunt Helen …" started Megan as her eyes clouded over.

"What is it, Meg?" asked Matt after placing the strainer and jar in the sink.

"It's our mom's," said Megan, pointing back and forth between herself and Kayla.

"And it's yours whenever you are ready for it," said Helen, stepping away from the stove.

"Is there something special about it?" asked Matt.

"Meg's mom loved to write poetry," said Ryan. "She had this platter inscribed with a Thanksgiving poem she wrote."

"What's it say?" asked Matt.

Kayla and Megan said together:

> *Our thankfulness for this year,*
> *And the blessings we hold dear.*
> *Our memories we have of each other,*

And the care we show one another.
Our gratefulness for each day,
And the love we give away.
Remind us of the gifts we've been given,
And a life that is worthy of livin'.

When they finished, Megan walked around the island and embraced her sister, grateful they had each other to deal with their parents' deaths.

"That was really nice," said Matt as Megan made her way back around the island and into his arms.

"Well, I believe everything is ready for the table," said Helen as she gave the mashed potatoes one more swirl around the pan. "Pick something up and carry it to the table, please," she added as Ryan collected the turkey platter.

Once everything was on the table and they were seated, Ryan said, "I'd be grateful if everyone would take a moment and tell us what *they* are thankful for on this lovely Thanksgiving Day. Dan, would you start us off?"

"Sure, Uncle Ryan. As most of you know, this isn't my forte, but here goes," said Dan as he clasped Kayla's hand in his own.

"As always I'm thankful for my lovely wife, Kayla, who brings sunshine into my life every day. I'm also thankful for the support, guidance and love, all of you have given us as we fulfill our dreams," said Dan.

"Kayla, darlin'," said Ryan.

"Well, I'm thankful for Dan, the love of my life, who has encouraged and supported me. Especially as we experiment with new menu items in the café. I'm grateful for all of your support and wouldn't want to live this life without all of you in it. And a special thank you to Meg, who has always been by my side. I couldn't have gotten this far without you," said Kayla.

"Helen, your turn, my dear," said Ryan.

"I'm thankful for all of you and our family, near and far, on this Thanksgiving Day. I'm thankful for Ryan as we live out this life together and for all the adventures yet to come," shared Helen.

"Wouldn't miss it for the world, my love. Meg, you're next," said Ryan.

"I'm thankful for my family, who has supported me as I work towards my dream of being a doctor. And for Matt, who has encouraged me and given me a deeper appreciation for the simple things in life. Like egg sandwiches, apple turnovers, and a hot air balloon ride," she said with a smile.

"Matt, it's your turn," said Ryan.

"I'm thankful for Meg, who has allowed me to share a side of myself that I thought I'd never find again. She also enabled me to mend a relationship with my brother, Brian, that was broken for too many years. And I'm also thankful for all of you. You all have helped me to rediscover and appreciate the lifestyle I grew up with, allowing me to realign what is truly important to me, family and friends."

"I must say you all make me feel very blessed and I'm thankful for each of you present in this house today and for those who are with us in our own hearts. I'm also thankful for our children, Robert and Greg, who are healthy and celebrating with their spouses' families this year. I'm also thankful for my lovely wife, Helen, who has stuck with me and given me so many happy memories through the years. Now before everything gets cold, may we all be blessed with this wonderful meal," said Ryan.

Conversation during dinner was minimal as everyone enjoyed the meal set before them. When everyone had their fill, the women started working on storing leftovers and cleaning up the kitchen, while Ryan fixed the guys some coffee and ushered them into the family room to watch a little more football.

"So, what's new with you and Matt?" asked Helen, now that Kayla was present and the boys were in the other room.

"Nothing much … lately. I've been so busy with this anatomy class I barely have time to keep up with my wash," laughed Megan. "The hot air balloon ride we went on last month was lovely. And Matt took me to a baseball game back in September. I found out he used to be a pitcher until he injured his elbow."

"I didn't know that Matt was a ballplayer," said Kayla with piqued interest. "I wonder if Dan knows. Maybe they can go to a game sometime."

"If you didn't know he played baseball, why did you elbow Dan when you introduced me to Matt?" asked Megan.

"Oh, I knew he was an actor. I just thought it would be fun to see how long it took you to figure that out on your own," said Kayla with a grin.

"Thanks. But why did Aunt Linda and Uncle Paul feel the need to let me figure out who he was on my own, too? I don't understand why they didn't want to tell me.

"I don't know the answer to that one, Meg. Did you talk to Aunt Linda about it later?"

"Yeah, but like I told you the last time we were here, it was about remembering Matt being at his cabin when we visited, not about his career. His family has owned the cabin for twenty-five years and I find it odd that neither of us remembers seeing Matt. Aunt Helen, do you know anything about Matt living in the cabin across the street from Aunt Linda and Uncle Paul?"

"I'm afraid not, dear. But you have piqued my curiosity," said Helen.

"Anyway, some of the players knew who he was, and the announcers even invited him up to the broadcast booth during the game," said Megan.

Both Kayla and her aunt stopped what they were doing and looked over at Megan who was focused on drying the turkey platter. She looked up and caught both of them staring at her.

"What?"

"He's a former baseball player *and* an actor," Kayla remarked.

"Just where are you going with this, Kayla?" asked Megan.

"Do you have any idea what life will be like once the public gets a hold of your relationship with Matt?"

"And is that supposed to scare me?" countered Megan.

"No, but you do understand that life may not be all that private once the press and gossip columnists get a picture of the two of you," said Kayla.

"Okay, Kayla, that's enough. Why don't you get the pies out of the fridge and put them into the oven," said Helen.

Megan braced her hands against the countertop as Kayla's words started to sink in. Aunt Helen stepped up beside her and placing her arm around her shoulder said, "Do you feel like Matt knows how to deal with that part of his life?"

Megan briefly considered the question before remembering his concern as they left the baseball game. "Yes, Aunt Helen, I think he knows how to handle that."

"Then everything else that happens in the public's eye will be dealt with in turn by both of you. Just remember the impact and power of your words when you're out in public. You'll have to decide what to keep private and what to share," said Helen as she moved back to the sink.

As Megan finished drying the turkey platter, Matt walked into the kitchen and wrapped his arms around her waist before kissing the top of her head. She turned around quickly, wrapped her arms around him and grabbed hold of his shirt before resting her head in the middle of his chest. She held onto him for several minutes before loosening her hold, hoping he wouldn't read too much into her feelings.

"You okay, Meg?" he asked softly, into her hair.

"Yeah, I think so," she said. The last time she held onto him like this was before his trip home. She had a lot to contemplate, but then it dawned on her that if he was able to get away from everything up in the mountains, wouldn't it be possible for them to continue to do the same thing years from now. *What are you thinking, Meg? You don't even know if this will last once he goes back to work. But his kisses are becoming sweeter and causing my insides to ache. And after his admission about his traumatic injury, I'm finding it harder to control my own physical needs and desires. And my curiosity is starting to increase about his capabilities on an intimate level.*

"You sure?" Matt asked again as he rubbed his hands up and down her back.

Pulling herself out of her deep thoughts she answered more firmly, "Yes, I'm fine. The pies will be ready soon. We'll bring them into the family room when they're done heating up."

"Okay," Matt said as he tilted her face up and gingerly kissed her on the lips.

When the pies were ready, Megan helped carry them into the family room along with plates and forks. Soon after dessert, Dan and Kayla excused themselves since they needed to head back early in the morning to arrive at the café by noon. Minutes later her uncle yawned and forced himself out of his chair. As he walked toward the kitchen he reached in his shirt pocket and pulled out a piece of paper. Walking by the sofa he handed it to Megan. Her Aunt Helen quickly berated him as she got up from her own chair.

"Can't let my best hired girl feel like I wasn't thinking about her, especially since she has a strong partner to help her," said Ryan.

Megan laughed as she took the list from his hand and said, "You do realize we will be leaving after dinner tomorrow. I'm caught up with anatomy and need to spend time studying for my MCAT."

"Yes, I know. That's why it's a ... *short* list," he said, chuckling as he headed to the kitchen with his dessert plate. Aunt Helen followed after patting Megan on the shoulder.

"So, what's on the list, Meg?" asked Matt with a grin.

"I don't even want to look at it," sighed Megan as she leaned in close to Matt on the sofa and placed the list on his leg.

There was the usual mucking of the horse stalls, feeding the goats and chickens, and collecting eggs. About half way down Matt pointed to pregnancy tests for the cows followed by chopping firewood.

"Looks like we're tied 1-1 so far," Matt said.

"Did you read the last item on the list?" asked Meg. "Looks like I win with cleaning farm equipment."

Matt glanced at Megan sideways, "Yup. Have you decided what you want as part of our bet?"

"Not really. I'll let you know when I figure something out," she told him.

She started to get up when Matt reached up and caught his finger in the back pocket of her jeans and pulled her down onto his lap. Turning her sideways he slid his hands through her hair until all the loose ends hung down her back. Moving his hands to her face he caressed her cheeks with his thumbs before drawing her close and passionately taking possession of her mouth.

As her body started to ache for more than just his kisses, Megan broke away and patted her hands several times on his chest before saying, "I think it's time to head up to bed."

"Are you okay?" he asked, noticing how abruptly she cut off their kissing.

"I will be," she said, stretching her arms into the air and maneuvering out of his lap before offering him a hand.

They made their way upstairs where he kissed her lightly on the lips before she entered her bedroom. Megan changed into her nightgown and paced the bedroom floor trying to get her thoughts and body to calm down. She pulled back the covers, climbed in and sat with the light on for a while. Her thoughts were startled by a light tapping on her door. Walking over she opened it to find Matt standing in his underwear and t-shirt.

"Meg, ..." but stopped, unable to say anything more as the words hung in his throat.

* * *

She stood in front of him gripping onto the side of the door. Reaching up Matt placed his hand over hers and stepped inside. After quietly closing the door behind him he drew her close.

Bending down he picked her up and made his way over to the bed and sat down on the edge. The pleading look in his eyes lingered before he said, "Meg, I can't sleep."

"Neither can I," she replied quietly lowering her head so he wouldn't see the redness that had crept into her cheeks.

"Meg, I can't ..." he choked out, swiftly before burying his face in her neck and absorbing the smell of lavender and lemon. Until that very moment he hadn't fully considered the torment he was creating within her body. He wasn't used to being the one to initiate these moments. He felt selfish at that moment, thinking she could hold her own needs under complete control, while he struggled to express his own; a reaction he hadn't come close to dealing with in years.

She slowly lifted her eyes to his and he knew he never wanted a woman more than he wanted her, but the fear he felt was still real. Taking his hand, she placed it in the middle of her chest and waited for him to move it.

His body froze. Since the attack, he had never freely touched a woman without it being written in a script. And even then he blocked out his emotions. He wanted nothing more than to make love with her in a way he had always imagined. He suddenly became overwhelmed and immediately placed her by his side and wrapped an arm behind her back.

"I can't," he choked out again, before kissing her lovingly on the head.

"It's okay, Matt," she replied softly, urging him further onto the bed then snuggling up close to his side before laying her arm across his chest.

His desires were starting to take over and it scared him. He had grown to trust her in many ways, but he couldn't bring himself to trust her enough with his body and let himself become fully vulnerable with her. Although he knew she trusted him by letting her own guard down, he wasn't sure he wouldn't hurt her, since he'd never made love before. Nevertheless, the bond and comfort he felt when he was with her, was starting to make the moments without her emptier. He didn't know how much fuller his heart could get, but he was finding out. Closing his eyes, he found himself falling into a peaceful slumber holding a very special woman in his arms.

* * *

Megan hoped Matt would understand that she wasn't the type of woman who took their intimate moments lightly or would force him deeper into a situation he wasn't ready for. She truly wanted to tell him she loved him, but that sentiment needed to come from him first. The depth of his love for her needed to be revealed without her prompting him to say something he didn't feel. Closing her eyes, she held him and wondered if she'd ever get the chance to show him how much she truly loved him.

* * *

They were both exhausted as they drove home late Friday night. Ryan had worked them hard, but they enjoyed it nevertheless. Aunt Helen loaded them up with leftovers before letting them leave, and invited both of them to come back during Megan's Christmas break and promised that Uncle Ryan wouldn't create a to-do list for them. Matt said he hoped he could make it, but if not they would all be in his thoughts during the holiday.

It was the first time Megan heard him talk about not being around due to his job. She knew it was bound to happen, but she wasn't quite ready for it, especially after inching her way closer into his heart last night. The last time they had slept together was when he returned from Michigan. That moment was initiated by Matt before he had revealed his injury to her. But that was four weeks ago and the fact that he initiated their closeness this time was an indication, in her mind, that he was working towards a more intimate relationship. He was making progress, but she didn't realize how much she missed and enjoyed the comfort of his body next to hers. She only hoped she would finish her classes before he had to leave, so they could enjoy some uninterrupted quality time together.

When they arrived home, they parted ways following a lingering kiss by her truck. Her thoughts were focused on Matt and his career as she walked up the steps and entered her cabin. *How can our two lives ever mesh and allow us to keep this relationship going?* she wondered. But she couldn't mentally or emotionally deal with the repercussions of that type of decision until the semester was over. Dumping her duffle bag in the laundry room she blocked her thoughts from traveling in that direction, at least for the time being.

Chapter Seventeen

The last week of classes flew by and with finals week starting the following week, Megan's time with Matt came to a complete halt. She missed the closeness, but her feelings had to take a back seat to preparing for her final exams. He understood the importance of her goals and was at least trying to give her space. When he wandered over Monday to see how things were going, he didn't need to ask when he saw her kitchen table loaded with stacks of note cards.

"How are you doing, Meg?"

"My anatomy final is scheduled for tomorrow at four o'clock. I want to get through each pile of note cards at least three times between now and two-thirty tomorrow, before I have to leave for class."

"That sounds like a plan, but I asked how *you* were doing," he said, capturing her by the elbow and pulling her into his lap. He gave her a quick kiss then turned her back towards him. Reaching his hands under her sweatshirt he slowly kneaded her back and she knew he felt all the tension inside of her. Making his way up to her shoulder blades it only took about a minute until she finally gave into the relief he was offering and let her body relax.

Slowly leaning forward, Megan rested her arms on the table, followed by her head. She really didn't have the time, but couldn't believe how tense and strung out she had gotten. It had been a long time since she allowed anyone to get as close to her as Matt had gotten over the past three and a half months. She allowed him to knead her muscles for about twenty minutes before he pulled her back towards his chest and rested his hands on her stomach. She leaned her head back onto his shoulder and sighed, "Thank you. I believe I needed that."

"You're welcome. So, when is your music final?"

"Wednesday, afternoon. I'll be glad when this semester is done."

"Me, too. Just watching you has given me a different perspective on what it takes to get an advanced degree."

"Well, thank you for noticing, Mr. Wilson. And thank you for that heavenly back rub, I think I might be able to focus a little better now."

"No problem, they're free and you looked like you could use it. So, since your finals will be over on Wednesday, would you like to go out on a date with me Friday night?"

"You mean an actual date?" asked Megan.

"Yes ma'am, an actual date … in a nice restaurant … that requires you to get dressed up."

"I would love to," she replied before swiveling around on his lap and giving him a peck on the cheek.

"I'm afraid that kind of kiss won't do, especially if I need to leave you alone to study the rest of the day." Before she could object, Matt stood her up and turned her around to straddle his lap, then sliding his hands behind her ears and up into her hair, he drew her close. He teased her by playing with her lips before caressing her cheeks with his thumbs then passionately kissing her.

Megan could feel his passion grow and wanted nothing more than to press her body closer to his, but her head was spinning with all the terminology she still needed to review. Although, it wasn't just the classwork that was preventing her from fully enjoying the distraction. Breathing heavily, she put her hands on his chest and pulled away from his lips before leaning her forehead against his. Matt opened his mouth to say something, but she stopped him by placing her fingertips lightly on his lips.

"Matthew," she began and felt his body stiffened as his defenses emerged.

"Yes," he replied slowly, as an unexpected shiver rolled down her spine.

Megan wasn't sure why he tensed up and pondered how to express her thoughts without upsetting him, but she wasn't going to let him leave without trying.

"When I first came up to this cabin I had no idea what life had in store for me and to be honest I wasn't looking for anything or anyone to come into my life. And I'm pretty sure you were clearly not expecting things to unfold the way they have, either," she said, angling her head to search his face for some sign of a confirmation, which came in the form of a slight nod.

"So, here goes nothing," she said softly, letting her breath out. "You stir up feelings in me that I haven't felt in a long time," she explained as she absentmindedly combed the back of his head with her fingers. "I'm getting to the point that I want more from you then you're able to give me right now."

She had his attention now, because his eyes froze on her face.

"When you become aroused, you know I can feel it, but do you *fully* realize what you're doing to my insides at the same time?" she asked, lowering her head as her face became flushed.

"So, Matthew Wilson," she said looking lovingly into his eyes and patting his chest decisively with both hands. "Until my exams are over, which I'll remind you is in only three days, I'm requesting that you keep your distance or you may not know what hit you," she said with a wink and a youthful smile as she absentmindedly zig-zagged her fingertips down his chest.

* * *

Matt knew he needed to leave her alone until her final exams were done. However, *he* was usually telling the woman to back off, not the other way around. He knew her feelings were increasing after their last visit to her family's ranch, but he hadn't completely wrapped his head around the implications until now. Furthermore, it finally registered how hard it was for her to express her innermost feelings, too. He was so wrapped up in his own physical calamity that he lost focus on how their relationship was affecting her physically and emotionally. Her uncle told him that much at the ranch and he silently berated himself for forgetting.

"Let me tell you something, Meg," he replied in a soft, indisputable voice, pulling her even closer. "You constantly amaze me and I thank you for opening up with me. You are a remarkable young woman, and I am very fortunate to have you in my life. I treasure your drive to further your education and I will not stand in your way," he told her, rubbing her arms before willingly standing her on her feet and getting up from the chair. When he saw a frown appear on her face he tilted his head and looked into her eyes.

"I think I'm confused. Didn't you just get done telling me you need some space for the next three days?"

"Well, just because I'm trying to be practical doesn't mean I have to like it."

"Come here," he said with a gentle laugh in his voice. She walked into his outstretched arms and he rocked her back and forth then kissed her lovingly before turning her loose.

"I'll see you Thursday morning to go jogging," he told her as he strolled down the hallway and out the door.

"I'll be there," she hollered after him as she picked up a stack of note cards. "And with a clearer head, too!"

Heading back to his place Matt figured he could handle three days without seeing Megan. Besides, he wanted to get her a little something to show her how much she means to him and also look for a nice, upscale restaurant in the area. Walking across the street, it dawned on him that Megan had never asked him to buy her anything. Climbing his steps, he also acknowledged she was completely accurate about his physical and emotional state.

"Which only proves how much she has seeped into my life. I'm beginning to understand how much her open and honest friendship has empowered me to open up and recognize that everyone isn't out to control my life," he said out loud, grasping the implications of their increasing closeness.

Those implications scared him, but only lasted until Tuesday morning when he got up and went for a jog without Meg, then ate breakfast without Meg. "This was supposed to be easy," he said to himself.

He had gotten used to their morning routine despite the occasional disruptions, but now that he promised to leave her totally alone, he truly missed interacting with her. "I wonder if she felt the same way when I stopped jogging with her for a while? Well, off to the showers, Matt, you have an errand to run," he muttered, making himself move down the hallway to the bathroom.

As he showered, he pondered what to give Megan that wasn't gaudy but showed her how special she was to him. *I could ask Kayla, but then it wouldn't be a gift from me,* he reasoned. In the end he decided to go window shopping in town to see if anything grabbed his attention.

Walking down the porch steps to his Jeep, he glanced over and saw Megan pacing on her porch in her fuzzy slippers and robe with a stack of cards in her hands. Matt thought about waving, but a deal was a deal. He got in his Jeep and slowly pulled away towards town.

Matt enjoyed shopping, but he enjoyed it more when no one recognized him. Wearing his hat and glasses he tried a couple jewelry stores, but didn't find what he was looking for until he walked into Nelson Jewelers. They had pretty silver necklaces with a loop attached in the center that was designed to hold a few charms. It didn't take him long to decide which charms he wanted on the loop, and with a quick phone call to Kayla, who he swore to secrecy, he made his purchase and headed to the café.

Kayla was so excited she could hardly contain herself. "Meg is going to love it, Matt. That's very sweet of you."

"She's very special to me, in many ways. I'm lucky to have met her," he told Kayla who looked slightly perplexed at his comment.

Shrugging her shoulders Kayla asked, "What would you like today?"

"Two apple Danishes and two cups of coffee," he replied. "Meg is pacing on her front porch studying her note cards as we speak. It stresses me out just watching her, so I'm going to drop off a snack for her."

"Well, I'll let you in on a little secret. You think watching her now is stressful, you should have seen her when she started college. The notebooks she used were everywhere and no matter how much studying she did she couldn't get above a C. She finally went to the study hall for help and someone gave her the suggestion for making note cards. Well, you never saw a system click in her head as quickly as utilizing note cards.

Never mind getting B's, she jumped right to getting A's. So don't stress out over the note cards, Matt, it's her way and it works."

Matt was about to respond when his cell phone went off. "Excuse me, Kayla, I have to take this."

Matt walked outside and said, "Hello, Kyle."

"Hey, Matt. How has your break been? I've left you alone like you requested," said Kyle.

"Yes, you did. And I'm grateful for that. What's going on, because you wouldn't be calling me if something wasn't brewing," Matt said, pushing for a quick answer.

"The new season's script is out and they want you back to work and on location in Montana before the Christmas holiday."

A chill ran its course through Matt's body as he rubbed the back of his neck with the phone glued to his ear. He wasn't ready to leave the mountains, especially before Christmas.

"Matt, are you there?" asked Kyle.

"Yeah."

"That's not the sound of a man who's itching to get back to work. And if I know you it involves a girl. Well, bring her along, Matt. There's plenty for her to do out here while you're on set."

"It's not that easy, Kyle," Matt replied, rubbing his hand through his hair. "As my agent, is there any way you can hold them off until after Christmas?"

"I'm afraid not. They want to film these scenes in real snow before it gets too cold."

"What about the breaks?" asked Matt. "We talked about it after last season. You were supposed to make sure the breaks are adhered to, during this upcoming season. I can't keep up with the pace, Kyle. I end up having no personal life, which I would like to have. And that includes more than just a day for Christmas and Easter, Kyle."

"It's like this, Matt," Kyle began.

"No, Kyle, it's like this. Either you make sure there are at least two weekends off every month for me during this coming season or I'm going to be creating a few myself." And before Kyle could respond Matt hung up on him. If they needed him that badly, then there shouldn't be any reason why two weekends off a month couldn't be settled on.

Matt headed back into the café with a scowl on his face.

"Everything okay?" asked Dan as he brought some pastries out front.

"No," said Matt.

"Want to talk about it?"

"I'd love to, but I don't think there's anything you can do to help me."

"Then I'm going to take a stab by the tone of your voice. Am I off-base if I assume it's work related?" asked Dan.

"You couldn't be more accurate."

"Matt, remember not to give up on what you truly want out of life. It's your life and you're in control," Dan impressed upon him.

"Yeah, but I'm not sure where Meg fits into my life."

"You've gotten to know a lovely woman this fall, give her credit for who she is and let her know how you feel. She may have stated several months ago she didn't want a relationship until after she finishes her degrees, but things have a way of changing our original plans, causing us to rethink the direction of our lives. I'm not saying Meg will give up getting her medical degree, but where she ends up for that program and any further education could possibly be altered," Dan told him.

Matt hadn't considered the possibilities of changing where Megan went to medical school, only that it would be impossible for her to work in West Virginia while he worked in LA; at least he thought it would be impossible. Having a few things to consider, Matt completed his purchase and headed home.

Pulling into his driveway he noticed that Megan was no longer pacing on the front porch. He headed across the street and rapped on her door, instead of walking straight in.

* * *

When Megan opened the door, she frowned at him until he raised a cup of coffee and a little brown bag into view.

"Thought you could use a little fuel," he said with a smile.

"You're hopeless!" she said, opening up the screen door and laughing.

Stepping inside he wrapped his arms around her and hugged her briefly, taking in the scent of her hair before stepping back and handing her the Danish and coffee. He planted three kisses on her lips before turning and heading out the door.

"Go get 'em," he said, punching his fist in the air.

Megan was grateful for the warm coffee. She hadn't eaten anything and the timing of the delivery was perfect because she was heading to the shower. *Maybe this relationship could work after all,* she thought as she sank her teeth into the Danish.

After running through the shower Megan read over her note cards one last time before she got into her truck and headed down the hill to class. She was nervous, yet confident at the same time.

* * *

All Matt could do was wait while Megan finished studying and took her exam. *I think I'm more nervous than she is,* he said to himself. While he waited, he decided to check his calendar to see where he could slip in a few weekend breaks during filming this season. Once he had a handle on some dates, he called Kyle back to have a civilized conversation with him.

"Hi," said Matt when Kyle answered the phone. "We need to talk."

"Look Matt, I understand you wanting more time to yourself, I really do. But you have to be realistic about the things we don't have any control over. The weather conditions change the schedule when we're on location. Then there's periodic issues with the equipment. Both of those things set you back, which forces everyone to work longer hours or on the weekend," said Kyle.

"I understand all that, Kyle, but you end up cramming interviews and talk shows into most of my open weekends, which doesn't allow me to have any down time," said Matt.

"But we need to keep you in the public's eye, especially with the new season approaching."

"After six seasons I don't have any trouble with recognition," said Matt, remembering the incident at the airport with Megan and at the baseball game. "Look, I don't mind a couple interviews and talk shows every season, but I need more of a say regarding which ones I want to do and when."

"It's going to make a few people unhappy, but I can try," said Kyle.

"Trying isn't enough, Kyle. I need to see a change. Remember how long it took us to wrap up the last episode this past season?"

"Yeah, don't remind me. I had so many interviews to cancel or post-pone, it made my own head spin," said Kyle.

"And why do you think it took so long to finish?" asked Matt. But before Kyle could answer, Matt continued, "Because I was exhausted and couldn't stay focused. That's how it affected me, Kyle." After a pause he added, "Are you understanding anything I'm telling you?"

"Yeah, I get it. I get it," sighed Kyle.

"Good. Then from this point forward you are to contact me regarding any additional obligations before scheduling them. If people get mad, they'll have to get mad. If I don't have time to unwind and relax, I won't be a guest on anyone's show."

After hanging up, Matt felt better about getting Kyle to understand his point of view about having a personal life. Since the first several seasons were a big success, there wasn't any reason why he shouldn't be entitled to spend time with Megan and his family several weekends throughout the filming season.

Feeling a little better about his life and being able to make several visits over the spring and summer to see Megan allowed Matt to have a little more optimism about keeping their relationship afloat. *Of course, I have to talk everything over with Meg. I only hope we can figure out how to make this long distance relationship work,* he thought.

* * *

Four hours later, Megan pulled into her driveway and dragged herself out of her truck and into the cabin.

Making her way into the kitchen she texted Matt.

Megan: I'm home.

Matt: Everything okay?

Megan: Sheer exhaustion.

Matt: How long?

Megan: Twelve pages front and back which included six case studies. Ugh!

Matt: Wow! Have you eaten any dinner yet?

Megan: Having a can of soup and going to bed, that's if I
          can keep from falling asleep in my soup. LOL

Matt: Want a shoulder to lean on?

Megan: You are still hopeless, Matthew!

Matt: Can't blame a guy for tryin'.

Megan: You're making this hard on me, my dear.

Matt: I don't mean to, sorry.

Megan: Night Matt, hugs and kisses!

Matt: Night Meg, hugs and kisses back!

"One more day," said Megan as she pulled a saucepan out of the cabinet. "I just hope Matt can make it without stopping over," she mumbled with a slight chuckle.

Megan woke early Wednesday morning, feeling refreshed, and decided to go for a run. She changed into her warm jogging gear and against her better judgment headed across the street to Matt's place. *Well, it's clear he's having separation anxiety, so let's see if he wants a jogging partner this morning,* she told herself as she ran up the steps. She knocked on the door, and when she didn't get an answer, she opened it and called his name. She could hear voices coming from the living room and walked in to find him sound asleep on the sofa with the TV on. Shaking her head she covered him up and turned the TV off. She gave him a soft kiss on the forehead before quietly walking out the door.

As she came around the bend on her way home, Matt was standing on his front porch with his usual mug of coffee in his hands. Slightly startled to see her, he waved and to his surprise she made a beeline right towards him.

"You know, some people shouldn't leave their doors unlocked when they're passed out on the sofa," she chided, standing within inches of his handsome face.

Matt just stared at her incredulously for a few seconds taking in the sweaty smell of cucumber and lemon deodorant.

"So that's how the blanket got on me," he said smiling as his brain kicked into gear.

"And the kiss on your forehead too," she added with a grin.

"How would you like an egg sandwich, Ms. Barnes?" he inquired as he struggled to keep his hands off her.

"That would be great since I only have so much pucker left in my mouth at the moment to practice my music piece," she replied, following him into the cabin.

"So, how do you think you did on your exam last night?"

"Don't you remember? I hate taking a guess. There's that superstitious component that I don't like to tamper with. You're going to have to wait until the results are posted, which might be Friday," she said, longing to know sooner.

"Yes, you did tell me that. I forgot, sorry."

"That's okay. Now, let's get cooking, I'm starving," she said, patting him on the backside before heading to the fridge for some eggs.

Matt stood frozen and watched her take out two eggs, cheese and butter and place them on the island. The minute Megan glanced his way she knew what she had done, but with all his physical and emotional issues she had held back because she didn't know how he would respond. By the look on his face, she may or may not have succeeded in knocking down another small hurdle.

After several moments Matt placed his mug on the island, and taking her in his arms, dipped her, and with a wide flirtatious grin said, "so you want to flirt with me, huh?"

Megan let out a little yelp as he dipped her even further then playfully planted several loud and wet kisses on her face before putting her feet firmly back on the floor. "Oh, yuk!" she exclaimed, wiping her cheeks off on the sleeve of her shirt. "What have I started," she bellowed.

Matt laughed as he dipped her again to replace the kisses she had just wiped off with soft gentle ones before standing her upright and claiming her sweet lips as he slid her body up close to his.

She knew what she had started and secretly wanted their intimacy to advance, but forced her heart to remain separated from her head. Placing her hands on his face she broke away from his tantalizing kisses and whispered, "Matt, you need to stop please."

She knew Matt could hear the pleading in her voice which told him she couldn't take anymore right now. He was learning her limits. She knew he was feeling the strong emotional tug himself, but he still wasn't quite ready for the next step.

"Sorry. I seem to be rediscovering the physical boundaries of a relationship," he said, pulling her close and holding her tight as his body regained control.

"I think we need to turn our attention to breakfast so I can go home and practice for my music final. I'm beginning to think this wasn't such a good idea on my part."

"It was a fine idea, Meg. I'm the one who started the interlude."

"Correction, Matt. I'm the one who patted your backside, which, by the way, is very lovely and firm," she tacked on, shyly.

"I stand corrected," he concurred, leaning down to kiss her nose. "Now, let's get this breakfast under way."

After eating Megan headed home and made it a point not to call, text, or step out onto her front porch for the rest of the day to avoid any contact with Matt. She practiced her oboe piece in twenty-minute intervals all day long, hoping to further strengthen her ambusher and improve her technique. She had a high B in the class, and needed to get an A on the final to receive an A in the class, and she was determined to achieve her goal.

* * *

To occupy his time Matt made a reservation for dinner at a restaurant up in the mountains with a view of the countryside, which he knew Megan would love. He also decided to clean the house from top to bottom. He knew he would be heading back to LA and wanted everything to be in order until he was able to come back. Part of him missed his house in LA and the private oasis he had created in his backyard. The Norfolk Island pine trees around the perimeter of the backyard provided nature's privacy, and reminded him of home. He also had a yearning to show Megan the log cabin style house he had built there.

* * *

Megan was glad when Wednesday afternoon finally arrived. She had practiced as much as she could through the semester and liked how the piece sounded. Now all she had to do was play it smoothly in front of her professor. To help calm her nerves while driving to class, she tried to figure out what dress she wanted to wear for her dinner with Matt on Friday.

Walking into the auditorium Megan felt overwhelmed by the setup for her performance. When it was her turn, she placed her music on the stand and sat in a single chair that had been placed on the stage. The lights were shining on her face, preventing her from seeing the professor and anyone else who was sitting in the auditorium. After taking a few deep breaths, she began.

After all the practicing she had done, her piece was over in four minutes. When she finished, her teacher thanked her and immediately called the next student to the stage. She felt more strung out over this final than the anatomy exam and didn't like how the professor made her feel inferior. It felt more like an audition for a chair instead of a final grade for a music class. Before she left campus, she texted Matt.

Megan: Done my final. Don't ask. Need to run again. Can you be ready when I get home?

Matt: I'll be sitting on my front steps.

Megan: Thanks!

When Megan's feet hit the road, she began ranting to Matt about the cold atrocious attitude of the professor who taught the music program.

"It wasn't bad enough we were all stressed out about performing, but to make the room feel so frigid, like we were auditioning for a major orchestra, was uncalled for. My anatomy class was worth more credits than that music class, but it felt like the other way around." When they got home, Megan was still unloading her frustrations about the professor's inconsiderate attitude. "Who does he think he is, passing judgment like that?" she ranted.

So much for listening to music as they ran, Matt thought as they jogged. He had never seen her so incensed, but she had a good point and he interjected his two cents when he could.

As he prepared hamburgers for dinner, she continued spewing her injustices. "It makes me feel like writing a letter to the head of the music department describing how it felt to be put through such an ordeal."

He just let her vent until it was all out of her system. By the time dinner was ready she had simmered down enough for him to walk over and place his hands on her shoulders, kiss her and inquire, "Feel better?"

Taking a deep breath Megan said, "Yes … sorry. But when something bothers me …"

"It's okay, Meg. I do the same thing, so you've been warned," he told her as they ate dinner. After they cleaned up, Matt said, "Now before things get heated up over here, you need to head home. I'll see you in the morning to jog, if you want to run again."

"Okay and yes, but can we go around eight o'clock? It'll be a little warmer by then. I want some time in the morning to start cleaning, which I've pushed aside for too long. Are we still on for dinner Friday night and what time?"

"Eight o'clock is fine and dinner reservations are for six o'clock. We need to leave here at quarter after five," he told her.

"I take it you're not telling me where we're going, correct?"

"You are correct, Ms. Barnes, so don't ask," he said, smiling and steering her out the front door.

Chapter Eighteen

Megan was excited about her official date with Matt. It had been a long time since she had gone on an actual date. She settled on a dress that defined her curves, for the occasion.

While she was getting ready her cell phone went off. It was a notification from the university that her grades had been posted. Taking a deep breath, she hopped onto her laptop to access them. Slowly scrolling down the page, she peered out of one eye and saw her music grade followed by the one for anatomy.

"Yeah!" she cheered, tapping her feet on the ground and waving her hands in the air. As she was celebrating a text came in from Matt.

Matt: I will pick you up at your place.

Megan: Fantastic! I'll be ready. Guess what?

Matt: What?

Megan: My grades just came in.

Matt: And…

Megan: I passed both classes! Yeah!!!

Matt: I knew you would. That's great, congratulations!

Megan: I got an A- in music and an A+ in anatomy.

> Matt: That's wonderful news. See you in about 30 minutes?
>
> Megan: Absolutely!

Megan turned off her laptop and feeling on top of the world, headed into the bathroom to curl her hair before getting dressed. She then walked into her bedroom and put on her dress and a pair of high heels. Glancing in the full-length mirror in the corner of her room, she decided she liked what she saw. Stepping back into the bathroom, she applied a bit of makeup. As she was putting on some lipstick, she heard the doorbell ring. *Wow, this is official for him to be ringing the bell.*

"Come on in," she yelled down the stairs. "I'll be down in a minute."

Grabbing her sweater and a small purse, she headed down the stairs and got about halfway when she saw Matt standing at the bottom of the steps. He had his hands laced together in front of him and his look of self-confidence took her breath away. He was clean shaven and had on a dark gray suit, dark blue shirt and a gray-blue tie with specks of dark red, which made the blue in his eyes stand out.

* * *

Matt heard her steps before he caught sight of her. In all the time he spent with her, he wasn't prepared for how stunningly beautiful she would look all dressed up. She stood on the steps wearing a navy-blue dress with a delicate lace overlay through the bodice and skirt, with the delicate lace continuing above her bust line and down her arms to her elbows. Her high heels made her legs look long and shapely. When his eyes finally traveled up to her lips, she was smiling just enough for her dimple to make an appearance and make him wish he could sweep her off her feet and delay their dinner reservation by an hour or two. Traveling back to her face, he noticed the curls in her hair and how she had swooped a section back on the left side and secured it with a silver clip. The rest cascaded down in little ringlets. What he noticed and appreciated the most was her subtle use of makeup. It was just enough to make him notice a difference, but allowed her inner beauty to stand out. He appreciated that she was comfortable with her looks and didn't feel compelled to make herself up to entice a man. He got a lump in his throat just thinking how lucky he was to have her in his life, and that she agreed to be his girlfriend.

Without saying a word, Matt stretched out his hand and helped her down the rest of the stairs. Not knowing whether his vocal cords would resonate sufficiently he whispered in her ear huskily, "You look gorgeous, Meg!"

"You look pretty stunning yourself," she replied with twinkling eyes.

"I'd like to kiss you, but I'm afraid I'll mess up your lipstick," he said leaning into her ear as she made it down the last step to stand in front of him.

"Well, I'm not, Mr. Wilson," she said leaning closer. Tilting her head sideways she gently brushed her lips against his in a sweet kiss.

Matt's body was beginning to do things more spontaneously than ever before. The gentler and more sensual her touch, the quicker he seemed to react. Taking a controlled deep breath, he touched her elbow and asked, "Shall we go, Ms. Barnes?" before he decided to make a move that might cause the whole evening to fall apart.

"Yes, but I need my heavy coat," she said, placing her sweater and purse on the steps and heading to the closet. As she took it out, he stepped up and helped her put it on.

He was really having trouble digesting how beautiful she was as he stuck out his elbow and ushered her down the porch steps and out to his Jeep. For a moment he wished he had his sports car to ride in, but he brushed the thought from his head knowing Megan wouldn't want the glamor of the ride. He helped her into the Jeep before heading around to the driver side. Getting in, Matt looked at her again just to make sure she was actually sitting next to him, like he had done once before. After he started the engine, Megan reached over and casually collected his right hand and placed them both in her lap. "It's the same, Meg. My Meg," he said silently, letting the thought linger in his head.

Matt put the Jeep in motion and headed to a restaurant up in the hills of West Virginia that had a gorgeous view of the Cacapon Mountains. When he turned off the highway, Megan squeezed his hand tighter.

"What is it, Meg?" asked Matt. "Is something wrong?"

"No, just the opposite. I remember this road. I know where you're taking me. I can't believe you picked this place for dinner. My parents used to bring Kayla and I here on our birthdays. It's a very special place for me," said Megan.

Her eyes were glistening and he could tell she was a little choked up.

"I haven't been this way in a very long time," she mumbled, lost in the past.

When they reached the restaurant, Matt got out and came around to help her down from the Jeep. She collected her sweater and purse and without saying a word he presented his elbow. Slipping her arm through his, he led her up the ramp and inside. Much to Megan's delight, he had reserved a table on an enclosed deck overlooking a ravine. Matt watched her reminisce as he continued to take in the sight of her. She was lovely, and knowing the person inside made her even lovelier. After she put on her sweater and hung her purse over the back of the chair, Matt helped her into her seat.

Once their order was placed, Matt reached over and took Megan's hand. "So, you haven't said much. What are you thinking?" he asked as he caressed the back of her hand.

"It's perfect. I remember the ravine and the wooden beams inside. Thank you for bringing me here. I needed this," she said, staring into his deep-set hazel-blue eyes.

Megan finally continued, "My Aunt Linda called me earlier today. They won't be coming home until the twentieth of March. It's helped me a lot to be away from town and your help with the neighbors allowed me to focus on my studies. Speaking of neighbors, I haven't had anyone knock on my door in a long while. Has anyone else come to you for help?"

"Now that you mention it, I had to remove another snake from Ms. Naomi's cabin," said Matt as he watched Megan shiver. "I took the time to check the outside of her house for any open holes. I discovered that the foam caulking surrounding the electrical wire opening into her cabin for her outside air conditioner unit had dried up, cracked and fallen out. I bought a can of foam spray and filled the hole back up. Since then she hasn't had any more unwanted friends in her cabin."

"I'm glad you were around to help with that. I've had my share of snakes for a good while."

"So now that you're done this semester, what's next?" asked Matt, changing the subject.

"Now I need to continue studying for my MCAT exam, which I'd like to take in March. If I get accepted into West Virginia Medical School, which was my dad's alma mater, my classes will start the last week of July next year. I should have my medical degree in four years."

"That's great," he said, capturing her hand again and staring into her hazel eyes. Reaching into his pocket, Matt pulled out a little box wrapped in royal blue paper with a gold bow and sat it on the table to her left.

"What's this?" Megan asked, staring at the delicately wrapped box.

"You've been working so hard on your classes I wanted to get you something to show you how much I support you and your goals," he told her.

"Oh," she sighed.

Hearing the slight disappointment in her voice, he added, "It's not just for that, Meg." He felt foolish for not saying so from the start. "You crept into my life when I wasn't expecting it and have helped me regain a perspective I thought I lost. You've shown me that everyone isn't out to get something from me. That there are people out there that I can trust and that deep down inside my judgment and instincts are sound. You've helped me to be more confident and realize that what I want out of life is important. You're important to me, Meg. You've changed my life for the good and will always be a part of me."

Megan just sat there focused on the box in front of her. "What do you mean will always be a part of you?"

Matt took a deep breath because it didn't take her long to pick up on his subtle message, which was quicker then he anticipated. He should have known she would.

"I've been called back to work on location in Montana before the Christmas holiday. I'll be gone for about a month or two depending on how long it takes to film the scenes."

"That's not fair, Matthew," she responded softly looking down into her lap.

Her reaction didn't quite surprise him, but the way she said it hit him hard. "I know," he said, rubbing the back of her hand again. "I tried to get them to postpone until after the holidays but my agent couldn't get the producers to rearrange the schedule. I'm sorry, Meg. I didn't want to wait until the day before my departure to tell you. We both knew this was going to happen at some point," he said, trying to verbally reason it all out.

* * *

Megan lowered her head further and truly felt like crying but held it in for Matt's sake. It wasn't like he planned to leave just when she'd have a break over the holidays to spend some time with him.

"I appreciate you telling me sooner than later. When do you have to leave?" she asked, glancing up into his solemn and worried face.

"My plane leaves Sunday afternoon," he said without much joy in his voice, "and I'd like you to take me to the airport."

"I don't know if I can do that …" she answered, envisioning herself having to let him walk away followed by an emotional breakdown in the airport. Catching her thoughts before a vivid picture formed in her mind, she continued truthfully, "It was hard enough watching you go when you went home to Michigan."

She watched him toy with the stem of his wine glass, but stopped abruptly at her last remark. She knew he hadn't grasped how deep her feelings ran for him until that very moment. They had grown close, closer than he had gotten with any women since his incident. The vision of a knife coming out of nowhere repeatedly played out in her mind; an incident that turned his life upside down, destroying any level of trust when it came to women. Now she understood why he told her he couldn't envision himself ever getting married several weeks ago when they went horseback riding. He had never imagined he'd ever be given the opportunity to envision his life unfolding any differently. And frankly he had been too scared to find out. Not that he wasn't still scared. She knew he was. But she noticed that a glimmer of optimism had crept into his head, allowing him to ponder the possibilities.

"Matt … are you okay?" asked Megan, reaching over and caressing the back of his hand.

"I'm sorry, Meg … you were saying," he answered.

She watched his eyes change from concern to a hint of fear and knew his thoughts briefly drifted down the same path as hers.

"When the holidays are over, I'll be focusing on studying for my MCAT. You are coming back, aren't you, Matt?" she asked with a little bit of hope in her voice.

"I'm planning on coming back, Meg. But I honestly just don't know when that will be. I still want you to be my girlfriend. If you'll have me?" he asked in a soft pleading voice.

"I'd like nothing more, but I don't know how practical that will be given the circumstances. I have my career path to pursue and you have commitments to uphold. The odds of a long-distance relationship lasting aren't very good."

"I'd still like to try," he said with hopeful sincerity in his voice. "Please open the box," he requested as he squeezed and released her hand.

Megan slowly untied the gold ribbon and unwrapped the little box. Her hands trembled as she lifted the lid, anticipating what was inside. Nestled between two pieces of cotton was a silver chain with a small delicate loop on it containing three little charms. The middle one was a detailed silver horse and flanked on either side were two circular gems trimmed in silver. One was amethyst, which represented her birthstone for February and the other was garnet, which she figured, looking up through glistening eyes, was his.

"It's beautiful, Matt. Thank you!" she said clasping it in her hands and pressing it to her heart.

A single tear made a path down her face. As Matt leaned over he brushed it away, then kissed her gently on the lips.

"My birth month is January, which is garnet," he whispered, taking the necklace out of her hands and placing it around her neck.

* * *

Resting his hands on her shoulders Matt briefly prayed she would always be in his life. She was the one, the only one, who was slowly and with great care helping him to physically and emotionally remove barriers he had deliberately and unconsciously built up to protect himself from what someone else had taken away in a few quick movements. Letting go of her shoulders he sat down as their dinner arrived.

He watched her clasp the charms periodically in her right hand while she ate and wondered what she was thinking. When she finally let them hang she glanced up and he could see the pain reflecting back in her eyes. He placed his hand on the table again and she reached over and placed hers in it.

"Matt?"

"Yes, sweetheart?"

"I think I'd like to go home."

"I'd like to show you something first," he told her, calling the waiter over so he could pay the bill. "Is that okay?"

"Yes," Megan replied softly.

Before helping Megan out of her seat, he collected her purse and handed it to her. He then retrieved her coat, and helped her put it on before taking her by the hand and leading her out the door and around to the back of the restaurant. In the middle of the grounds was a blazing stone fire pit along with a wooden glider for two.

Megan glanced at his face before he helped her walk through the bumpy yard in her high-heeled shoes. He steered her down to the glider and helped her sit down before joining her and wrapping his arm around her. He drew her to his side and they took in the view of the mountains for several minutes before Megan noticed the fixings for s'mores sitting in front of the fire pit.

"Matt?" she questioned, glancing over her shoulder.

"I was wondering when you were going to notice," he said, squeezing her shoulder against his.

"Okay. I'm going to say this because I know all this didn't happen without some type of arrangement with the restaurant," she pointed out.

"Well, when you're ... famous," he said leaning down to whisper the word in her ear, "you find that people are willing to do things for a single autographed picture," he replied with a grin on his face.

"And that's also why we were the only ones on the enclosed deck," she pointed out, shaking her head slightly as she picked up the bag of marshmallows and stuffed some onto the skewers then handed one to Matt. "And that's also why no one has come up to you, ... but ..." she said, before turning around to look towards the restaurant. "Your fans are looking on from far away," she finished.

Matt glanced over his shoulder and shrugged. "Sometimes it's the only way to get a little bit of privacy."

"Well, I'm not really comfortable with it," she said, feeling uneasy about the tactics he had used to obtain their privacy. Then she mumbled, "There's got to be a better way," as she touched his arm.

Before Matt knew what hit him, Megan had taken off her shoes and quickly tiptoed back to the restaurant. She reappeared moments later with more skewers and six customers who joined them at the fire pit. Megan introduced them all to Matt. Within minutes he was comfortably answering questions and laughing with everyone as they ate s'mores together. Time flew, and after about an hour, Meg thanked all of them and excused herself and Matt, saying they had a bit of a drive to get home.

Matt hadn't been too happy about Megan turning a quiet moment for two into a camp fire of many. Although he had to admit she had a way with people and didn't fully understand the depth of her compassion until he helped her into the Jeep. Creating a comfortable environment for him, who tended to enjoy his privacy, was rare. It put the idea in his head that she might be able to handle living in LA after all. In addition, he could envision why she would make an excellent doctor; her ability to listen and her bedside manner topped the list. Those attributes, combined with her heartwarming personality, explained why the neighbors in Briery Mountains called on her when they needed help.

Climbing into the Jeep, Matt said, "You know something, Ms. Barnes. You're one amazing woman."

"Why, thank you, Mr. Wilson," she replied as a smile spread across her face.

"I must admit I was a little upset and very apprehensive about people joining us, but it turned out very pleasant. I don't know when I've had such a good time with a bunch of total strangers before in my life."

"Most people are good natured, Matt. They just want to talk to you and if you ask them a few questions, they start to feel more comfortable and in return you start to relax. And to be honest, I watched a few of your interviews," she said laughing, "and you don't seem to be able to sit still, especially when it comes to conversations about girls."

Matt tugged at the collar of his shirt. "I thought you didn't watch all that stuff?"

"Well, sometimes we all get a little curious, and having a little sister who entices you with tidbits of YouTube videos doesn't help." After a pause, Megan said seriously, "Matt, you know that I take those things with a grain of salt and I appreciate you for who you are, not by what some talk show host has prompted you to say."

Tears clouded her eyes and fell as she continued in a soft voice full of emotion, "I care deeply about the Matt that is sitting next to me … the one whose company I enjoy immensely … and the one I don't want to go away."

And there it was. Everything Matt had speculated about their relationship was summed up perfectly by this caring and lovely woman next to him. Her reason for inviting the crowd of people to their camp fire wasn't only for his benefit but for hers, too. He realized she couldn't handle sitting alone with him and allow her thoughts to fester on what little time they had together. "Oh, Meg, this isn't easy for me, either."

"I know … I'm sorry."

"You don't need to be sorry … ever."

He took her hand and kissing it tenderly before leaning over and kissing her softly on the lips. Keeping her hand tightly clasped in his he drove them home.

Matt walked Megan to her door and entered the foyer with her. After placing her purse on the steps, he helped her with her coat, then collected her in his arms. Planting his feet firmly on the ground he held onto her for the longest time, absorbing how their bodies molded seamlessly together, which was something he had never paid attention to before. At that moment, he was afraid to let her go. He took in the lavender and lemon scent of her cinnamon red hair and ingrained it in his brain before placing his hands on her upper arms and putting some distance between them. Before he could say anything, she voiced their thoughts.

"Well, we can do this the hard way or the hard way, because whatever way we decide it's going to be hard," she said, grabbing hold of the sides of his dress shirt under his suit jacket.

"So …" said Matt, "which is it going to be?"

Taking a deep breath she said, "We have a little under forty-eight hours, if my calculations are correct, and I don't want to be a fool and waste a single moment without you in it."

Matt held her as he mulled over her remark. She was right. It was going to be hard either way, but then watching her from afar for the next forty-eight hours would probably cause more anguish than either of them could willingly endure.

"What are you proposing?" he asked, biting his lower lip.

"I want to camp out at your place. That way we'll be together and you can get all your gear packed and I'll be there to take you to the airport early Sunday afternoon," she told him firmly.

Matt rolled her proposition around in his mind before asking, "And sleeping arrangements?"

She saw the discomfort settle in his eyes as he started to conjure up several uncomfortable situations. But within seconds Megan said, "Timing isn't good, if you get my drift. But I would definitely like some major kissing and hugging." With that fact, Matt's distress vanished immediately.

* * *

Over the next two days Matt and Megan were inseparable. They slept, worked, ate and, to Matt's delight, clowned around with each other like an old married couple until they headed to the airport. They were both subdued as he drove the Jeep into the parking lot. He unloaded three duffle bags and Megan collected one of them to carry through the airport check-in. As soon as the ticket attendant took his checked baggage, she looked up and excitedly said his name out loud, causing people to look his way. He smiled politely and shook several hands as he made his way to Megan, who had hung back in the hallway. He took his carry-on bag off her shoulder, which she had held for him while he checked in, and firmly locked his hand in hers as they headed toward the security area.

Without a care in the world, Matt scooped Megan up in his arms and kissed her like a man in love. Putting her back on the ground he placed his hands on her face and gave her three sweet kisses then whispered in her ear, "You're my girl, Meg, I'll see you soon. Go out to the ranch while I'm away, if you need to. Your studying will start up soon enough for your MCAT and I expect nothing but the best from you." Then Matt dropped his keys to the Jeep and cabin into her hand.

All Megan could do was nod, "Matthew, I …" but she couldn't say it. She kissed him on the cheek and after hugging him close to her body one last time, while taking in the woodsy cedar and mint smell of him, then let him go. It took all her willpower to keep from bursting out into tears and to keep her attention focused on Matt as he made his way through security and waved to her one last time as he walked outside to board the plane.

For the first time Megan was standing alone following an encounter with Matt's fans. Taking a breath she turned to face a few people who were standing near the enclosed security area and was grateful the airport was small. With a smile plastered on her face, she headed out of the airport and across the parking lot to Matt's Jeep. When she closed the door, she suddenly noticed the smell of him in the enclosed space. Keeping her emotions under control she drove back to his cabin. She walked through the door and headed straight to his bedroom and curled up in the middle of his bed. She knew it was bound to happen, but that still didn't prepare her for the full impact. She knew Matt was special and she cared for him more than anyone else who had entered her life.

She managed to make it through the rest of the day after snoozing deep within the confines of his bed. When her cell phone rang around ten o'clock, she answered without checking to see who it was.

"Hello!"

"Hi, sweetheart!" said Matt. "Where are you?"

"I'm hanging out at your place. I hope that's okay?"

"That is perfectly, okay. I miss you already."

"I miss you already too. How was your flight?" she asked.

"It was okay up in the air. The landing was a little rough."

"How's the hotel?"

"Not bad. I have a little sitting area and a huge king-size bed with too many pillows," he said laughing.

"Well, I'm glad you made it there okay. You left me a few curious onlookers at the airport."

"Ohhh … forgot about that. For once in my life I didn't care what other people would say, but I totally forgot about what it would be like on your end. You okay?"

"Yeah, no one followed me back to your Jeep. It was all good. I think dropping you off at a smaller airport helped."

"Well, I'm going to let you go 'cause I know it's late over there. I slept a little on the plane this afternoon to help with the time change. I'll give you a call or send you a text when I have a free moment, okay?"

"That would be great! Night, Matt."

"Night, sweetheart!"

Megan cried herself to sleep under the covers in the middle of Matt's bed and knew she was in love with him. He filled a hole in her life she hadn't known existed until he got on that plane. But there wasn't any way she was going to be responsible for not allowing him to hold up his end of his contract. She wasn't going to be selfish. He was a wonderful person and actor and needed to fulfill his agreement just like she needed to stay focused on passing her MCAT and getting into medical school.

Chapter Nineteen

When the sun peeked in through the window the next morning, Megan didn't feel like moving. She was surrounded by warmth as she clutched his pillow close to her chest. Reluctantly dragging herself out of bed she meandered around his place, collecting all her belongings. She cleaned up the rest of the dishes and washed a few loads of laundry from the past two days before locking up his place and making her way back to her cabin. She contemplated visiting her aunt and uncle's ranch, like Matt suggested, but decided to call and talk to her Uncle Ryan instead. Sitting down in the kitchen she placed her cell phone on the table and hit the dial button.

"Hello!" said Helen.

"Hi, Aunt Helen," Megan replied in a solemn voice.

"I know that tone. What's wrong, Meg?" asked Helen.

"They called Matt back to work; he took a plane out to Montana yesterday afternoon and I don't know when I'm going to see him again," she sobbed.

"Aw, Meg, I'm sorry."

"Thanks, Aunt Helen," she said as she absentmindedly collected the colored pencils on the table and wrapped them with a rubber band.

"Look sweetheart, I've got to get lunch together and it just so happens your Uncle Ryan has wrapped up for the morning. Hang on a moment."

"Well, isn't this a pleasant surprise! How's my Sweet Pea doing?" asked Ryan in a chipper voice.

"Not too good. Matt went back to work yesterday," Megan stated, noticing he hadn't called her by that name in years.

"But I thought you didn't want any distractions," he replied matter of factly.

"I don't … I didn't … but sometimes he was more help than a distraction," she confessed as she collected a stack of note cards and tapped them on the table to straighten them.

"Sounds like you need to figure out what's important to you," said Ryan.

"My medical degree is important," said Megan as she straightened another stack.

"Are you sure that's the only thing that's important to you or are you trying to convince yourself that it's the *only* thing important to you?"

Megan sighed before her uncle continued, "Meg, I saw how you two looked and interacted with each other while you were here for Thanksgiving. That man is in love with you Meg, but until he has pushed through all his fears, he won't be able to recognize what's right in front of his face. And even then, it might take him a while to realize it. The circumstances surrounding a person's life are sometimes altered and force changes we weren't anticipating. You've experienced that first hand when your parents were killed. Sometimes life has to take a detour. But if things are meant to end up a certain way, they'll work their way back around. What *you* have to decide, Sweet Pea, is if and how long you're willing to wait for him."

"That's kind of the meaning of my mom's favorite poem. She used to tell Kayla and I that our life is a journey and we'll find the right path or the way things are meant to be. I thought about asking him to take me along for the month or until after the holidays," she revealed.

"Your mother was an insightful woman, Meg. And I'm glad you didn't tag along because it won't help that man figure things out any faster. I think going off by himself will help him recognize what he wants and needs sooner," said Ryan succinctly.

"Yeah, I know you're right and I'm glad I didn't go either," Megan said as she rubbed her hand across her forehead.

"Do you love him?" Ryan asked point blank.

"Yes, I love him. And to be honest, he fills a gap in my life I didn't know needed to be filled. That's why this is so hard," she sobbed softly as the rubber band she picked up to wrap around a stack of cards busted and sailed across the room.

"I know, Sweet Pea. Have you told him how you feel?"

"No. I almost did before he went through security at the airport, but then I didn't want to put that kind of pressure on him. I feel like he needs to be the one to say it first, especially with everything he's been through," she answered.

"Do I dare ask what he's been through? Even though I know it's truly none of my business," Ryan asked respectfully.

"I'm not sure it's my place to tell you. What I will say is that it scarred him physically and emotionally as a man. And knowing your ability to read between the lines you'll figure it out," Megan divulged, willing to share no more.

"And has he overcome his fears?" asked Ryan.

"Working on it," replied Megan, her words trailing off as she realized what she had said as her face grew warm.

"It's okay, Sweet Pea, I was young once," he replied softly.

"The thing is, I don't know if he's willing to make a commitment," she whispered. "He told me he wasn't interested in marriage."

"And if I had to make a bet, he told you that when he was first getting to know you, didn't he?"

"Come to think of it, he did. He took me on a date Friday night at a restaurant I haven't been to in years and gave me a lovely silver necklace. It has a horse charm on it flanked by my birthstone and his," she said as a smile crept onto her face and she clasped the charms in her hand.

"I think that pretty much says it all, Meg," replied Ryan. "If Matt's been through such a traumatic experience, then I'm guessing he's trying to reverse all the years of uncertainty in stages."

"But how'd you …" Meg said with bewilderment in her voice.

"Remember, Matt's been out here a couple times and he does talk, once he feels comfortable with the company. He knew from the first time he was here that we're family, whenever and for whatever reason he needs us."

"Thank you for that. Tell Aunt Helen I appreciate everything, too."

"I'll do that. Now, if you need to get away for a week you know we would love to have you, even in your unsettled state. Your stump is still sitting on the top of the hill if you need to sit a spell. I can always use an extra set of hands and Aunt Helen would love to cook for more than us two old coots," he added with a laugh. Then he asked, "Have you given any thought to applying to medical school somewhere in LA?"

"No, and I wouldn't even know where to begin. Besides, Matt and I haven't even discussed that part of our relationship. And I really don't want to upset Dr. Rhodes by pulling out on him for my clinical hours. He's letting me shadow him for a few weeks at the beginning of next year."

"Nothing should keep us away from the ones we love and make us happy. You can apply anywhere for medical school, correct?"

"Yes, but I was also set on doing my residency at Dr. Rhodes' office during my third and fourth year of medical school.

"Remember, Meg, plans change for many reasons. Now this old man has to get some lunch in him so I can deal with the rest of the day," said Ryan.

"Thanks for giving me something to think about. I love you."

"And I love you, too, Sweet Pea," he replied.

Megan hung up and considered her uncle's insight. He was right, there wasn't anything keeping her here. Matthew owned the cabin across the street, which would allow them to visit whenever they wanted to. Taking a deep breath Megan decided to be more optimistic about her relationship with Matt. Maybe they could make it work.

Then her thoughts swung around to her uncle's comment about the stump on the hill and wondered what brought those days to the forefront of his mind. Her life had been filled with too many questions and decisions that overwhelmed her after her parents passed away. Sometimes she'd tuck a notebook under her arm and write a letter to her parents, other times she'd take a sketch pad and draw them a picture, and when things became too unbearable, she'd stuff a bunch of tissues in her pocket and have a good cry where no one could bombard her with questions she didn't feel like answering anyway.

Staring at the remaining cards on the table she stacked and labeled the rest of them. She had a bin in her apartment where she stored them, in case she needed to reference them for another class. After placing the cards in her backpack, she picked up the pencils and notepad and carried them to the end table. Squatting down she pulled the drawer open and noticed a drawing pad sticking out underneath another notepad of paper. Rocking forward onto her knees, she plopped down onto the floor and pulled out the drawing pad.

Flipping through the pages she found it empty except for the top page. Etched into the page was an almost invisible tracing of several trees. Running her fingers over the grooves, memories came flooding back of sitting on the hill at the ranch. There were times when the drawings she created started out with a gentle touch, but as her anger grew about the unfairness of her parents' deaths, she'd press the pencil so hard onto the page it would break the point. She tried to remember the last drawing she made, but that memory eluded her.

I wonder if Kayla remembers or has any of my drawings, thought Megan as her curiosity surfaced, now that her brain was more relaxed. Placing everything back in the drawer she got up and cleaned off the rest of the table.

* * *

Matt walked on set Monday morning and was greeted by the staff and crew. They all noticed a change in his demeanor as he sat down to look over the part of the script they were filming.

When he glanced up from the script, Kyle was headed in his direction. He clasped onto Matt's shoulder and giving him a slight shake said, "Look who's feeling much more relaxed. It looks good on you. Must be that hot little number you took to the baseball game last month? You two are all over social media," said Kyle with a broad smile.

"That 'hot little dish' as you just called her is Megan, and one day she will be Dr. Barnes. And let me make it clear," said Matt in a loud and defensive tone, "I don't ever want her referred to as that 'hot little dish' again, by you or anyone else on set."

"Sorry, Matt," Kyle replied. "I didn't know the depth of the relationship."

"Or anything about her. Which is why you need to stop believing everything on social media. You of all people *should* know more about me than anything posted on those sites."

"You're right. So, is it serious … the relationship?" asked Kyle.

"Would telling you she's my girlfriend give you enough of a hint?" Matt asked.

"That's great! It's about time, Matt."

"And that's where this conversation ends, when you start sounding like my brother," he responded, turning his attention to skimming over the script in his hands.

Matt read through the first scene which required him to ski down a slope to rescue a woman who had gotten caught in the fringe of an avalanche. After finding her, he takes her to a small shack where the rangers stay when they need to detonate charges to trigger a controlled avalanche. The woman turns out to be a former love interest. After making sure the woman has no life-threatening injuries a second avalanche occurs, trapping them in the shack and giving them time to get reacquainted.

* * *

The first week of filming went by slowly. There wasn't enough snow on the ground and more had to be carted in to encompass the shack. Matt texted Megan every other day, due to his schedule and the time difference, to see how she was and to find out what she was doing with all her free time. He was afraid to call and talk to her because of the love scene he was mentally preparing to act in; he truthfully didn't know how to handle Megan's reaction to him kissing another woman.

By the beginning of January the romance scene was scheduled to be shot. In the past Matt didn't mind kissing Veronica, one of the recurring leading ladies in the show, it was something he had done before. But how was he going to feel after solely kissing Megan for nearly three months, let alone anticipating how Megan might react when she watched the show on TV. However, he had to admit he was slightly curious how his body would react to Veronica's touch this time.

Right before the scene was shot, Veronica cornered him in the back of the shack.

"Hi, Matthew," she said, bumping her shoulder into his.

"Hi, Veronica," he responded, sounding disinterested.

"I'm going to be blunt, Matt," she started. "You've been pacing around this place like a skittish school boy. Care to unload? And remember who you're talking to," she added.

"It's that obvious, huh?"

"More than obvious, who is she?" asked Veronica smugly.

"Her name is Megan."

"And?"

"She's wonderful and I don't know how I'm going to make this scene look like I'm not forcing my emotions," he divulged in one breath.

"Look Matt, we've done these scenes lots of times and this isn't any different. Just pretend you're kissing, Megan. I won't be offended," she told him flippantly. "Well, maybe slightly," she confessed.

Matt turned his head and glanced at her, puzzled by her last remark, for he never thought of Veronica as anything but an acquaintance and good actress. "Thanks for the encouragement, but I'm afraid it's not that easy for me," he replied staring back towards the set. "Not easy at all," he added under his breath.

"Well, they're waving us over. Let's get this over with," she said brusquely. But before Matt walked away, Veronica grabbed his arm and pulled him into a kiss. As she walked away Matt slid the back of his hand over his mouth to wipe off any remnants of her lipstick and kiss. There was nothing appealing about her kiss, not that he thought there was ever any physical chemistry between them in the past. But her swift kiss enabled Matt to enter the scene with determination in his steps and as much charisma as he could muster and pretend he enjoyed kissing Veronica like it meant something.

It took five takes, too many in Matt's mind, until the director was satisfied with the kiss and only a second for Matt to decide where and who he wanted to share his kisses with. Matt's strong presence in the show would make or break him this season if he didn't start putting his foot down and insist another significant character be incorporated into the plot. He was also going to request that the number of romantic interludes be reduced for a while.

"Guess our little acting escapades are over," Veronica surmised as they moved off set.

Matt just stared at her. He wasn't sure where this conversation was going … but it wasn't going in a direction he cared for. "If you're trying to make a point, Veronica, please make it," Matt countered.

"You and I have known each other a long time. The women talk around here. You've gone out with a few and haven't allowed any of them to get close to you beyond the first couple of kissing sessions. Is there something we're all missing?" she asked curiously.

"No, and there never will be," Matt stated, knowing social media would have a field day if he decided to reveal his personal trauma.

"You can't keep dodging the issue, Matt, whatever it may be. And personally, I can't imagine you having any issues that would cause such turmoil inside you. If you can't resolve whatever it is holding you back, you're going to end up alone. And, Matt, you're too good looking of a man to live your life without a more permanent girl in your arms."

"Does Megan know you have trouble getting out of the starting gate? Hopefully, she won't give up on you because you're afraid to get close, spend your money, or make a long-term commitment. But whatever the hell you're afraid of, you best decide what you want, because your good looks aren't going to last forever," she berated him.

"Are you done yet?" he asked.

"Yeah, I guess I am, but I must have struck a chord for you to become miffed," she observed.

Taking a deep breath Matt spit out in frustration, "I love how everyone seems to know what's best for me when it comes to a relationship. Most of the women out here are more interested in making out by the third date because of the character I play instead of taking the time to get to know the personal side of me. And that includes you, Veronica, to some degree. You have no idea what I've been through in my life and for that matter you've never seemed interested enough to find out. As far as I'm concerned you will never know what that entails. On top of that, I don't want to have to settle for someone I don't have feelings for."

"What about this Megan woman?" she asked curiously. "Does she know who the real Matthew Wilson is?

"Yes, Veronica," Matt responded a little more forcefully than he intended. "But to answer your question and to solve the curiosity of everyone on set, she's a very important person in my life who has taught me a great deal about myself and others."

"Have you told her how you feel about her?" Veronica asked in a softer tone.

"Not in so many words," he replied, slightly remorseful.

"Well, if she's as nice as you say she is, then she's not going to stay single forever and without a ring on her finger she's under no obligation to stay faithful to you or for that matter you to her. So, I suggest you decide what you want before it's too late," she repeated before walking away.

Matt didn't need to be told twice. He knew there was some truth in what Veronica said. All of a sudden, the need to quell the fear inside of him started to build. Making love to Megan could and would be a sweet thing if he allowed himself to disengage his brain from the past and enjoy the moment he wanted so badly to experience. Not knowing what his full physical limitations might reveal Matt knew there was no one other than Megan he was willing to find out with. He had considered making love to her after their date, but didn't want to compound how difficult it was going to be to leave town. Besides, she had told him she was not in a position to do so.

Chapter Twenty

It took a little over four weeks to complete all the scenes in Montana. Despite the delays, filming wrapped up in the morning on Friday, January fourteenth, and to Kyle's dismay, Matt was ready and determined to head back to West Virginia for a couple of days before Megan was knee deep in studying for her MCAT exam. "What am I going to tell the talk show host that I lined up, since you're going back to West Virginia already?"

"Tell them I'll be available next weekend," Matt replied in frustration. "Look, Kyle, we discussed the breaks in between filming and not scheduling any talk shows or interviews without my consent. You are not going to fill up every open weekend this season. So, you can resign yourself to the fact that this is how it's going to be from here on out. You're my agent and I expect you to prevent me from becoming totally exhausted like last season."

"But Matt, …" said Kyle.

"Kyle, if you can't work with me to manage my personal and professional time better this season, then I'm sure there are several other agents out there who would be willing to accommodate my requests while making a decent commission. Do I make myself clear?"

"Yes. Very," he replied dejectedly.

"Good. Then book me a flight to Morgantown Municipal Airport in West Virginia for late tonight and reschedule anything that you added to my plate without asking me first. We will be discussing my schedule when I return. And, Kyle," Matt declared as he hurriedly collected the few things he had on set, "try to relax a little this weekend, too. I'll see you back in LA late Monday afternoon."

High-tailing it back to his hotel, Matt collected the rest of his belongings, grabbed a late lunch and headed to the airport. He didn't tell Megan he was coming because he wanted to surprise her and prayed she hadn't decided to visit her aunt and uncle over the weekend. His flight gave him plenty of time, maybe too much time, to think about his feelings for Megan. She never asked for more than what he was capable of giving her, but had shown him in so many ways how much patience she had by not questioning or berating him when his fears prevented him from advancing their relationship.

I'm not getting any younger. Time to find out if this body of mine has the ability to satisfy any woman. And the only one who has turned me on in a heartbeat is Meg, he told himself. He knew Megan was the one destined to guide him without casting judgment. "Being without her the past month has made me want her even more. And once the kissing starts, I'm sure I won't be able to restrain myself," he mumbled to himself. Knowing what he wanted and what he needed made him feel slightly uncomfortable in his seat, because making love to Megan scared him, yet aroused him at the same time. He just hoped she wanted him to make love to her because he would never force himself onto anyone, after what he'd been through.

Once the plane landed, he grabbed his luggage and made a beeline to the taxi cabs. He paid dearly for the drive up to his cabin, but he didn't care. Fortunately, he had an extra set of keys, since he had given his other ones to Megan. The drive to his cabin felt like it took longer than the plane ride. After paying the taxi driver, Matt dropped his bags in his living room then headed straight for Megan's cabin. His emotions peaked as he made his way up onto the porch in the early morning hours. His senses were charged as he reached for the doorknob, but he froze when he spotted her curled up beneath a heavy wool blanket lying on the hammock to his left. She was dozing peacefully, looking warm and inviting as the sun beat down on her face in the cool morning air.

Matt slowly let go of the doorknob and thought she looked heavenly laying there. He approached her, then leaned down and kissed her tenderly on the cheek. The warmth of her body drew him in, causing him to kiss her again before nuzzling his face into the side of her neck. She slowly stirred and rolled onto her back stretching her legs and arms before curling back up again. He watched as her eyelids opened ever so slightly. As recognition settled in, a slow smile turned her lips up as he crouched down in front of her. He returned the smile as her dimple presented itself before leaning closer and whispering, "Hi, sweetheart" into her ear. The meaning of those words raced through his core sending a shiver down his spine.

Her eyes revealed her disbelief that he was right in front of her. Before her brain was fully engaged, he scooped her up in his arms and claimed her lips with a passion that traveled through both their bodies. The taste of her was like a piece of heaven as she reached up and captured his face with her hands. Carrying her off the front porch and crossing the street to his place was something he only dreamed of doing. There was desire in his eyes mixed with fear, along with determination to fully and completely trust her with his being.

His stride was purposeful as he climbed the front steps to his porch, pulled open the screen door, crossed over the threshold, and closed the storm door behind him with his foot. The yearning inside of him was building to a climatic state as he reclaimed her mouth while carrying her down the hallway toward the kitchen. As he pivoted toward the bedroom his limbs started to shake just before he placed her down in the middle of his soft blue comforter.

Matt's senses were fully engaged at the implication of his actions as she locked eyes with him. The battle going on in his mind was visible as he stood by the side of the bed looking down at her, pining for the next step, but frozen by a past that could, if she left him standing there long enough, cripple him. But that wasn't all. He was dwelling on where this interlude could lead and fearful of disappointing her. She didn't have any expectations, but that didn't prevent him from worrying that he wouldn't live up to her passionate side, which came flowing out of her so gently and freely. The way she touched him, held his hand, caressed him when he truly needed it, wanted it, but couldn't ask for it.

Matt's emotions suddenly started running rampant with the repercussions from his first sexual encounter eleven years ago. He thought she could see the flashback playing in his eyes as she knelt in front of him. She had proven by her patience and gentle touch that he could trust her. All of their quiet moments molded together had propelled him along a healing pathway. She never pushed him in a direction he wasn't willing to take.

Softly her voice filtered in and disrupted his own thoughts. "I know you're scared, so am I. Sometimes we have to work through the fear, but only if you want to," she told him gently.

Sitting up on her knees, she stretched out her hand and watched him take a deep breath as he willingly placed his hand inside of hers. As she drew him onto the bed she whispered in his ear "You're safe with me," even though she knew he wouldn't be balancing on the edge of desire and fear in front of her if he didn't trust her. Tears suddenly sprang into her eyes as she watched him; for all the love scenes he had created in front of the camera he knelt next to her revealing his passionate delicate soul. Knowing words would only ruin the moment, Megan slowly unbuttoned his shirt. He shivered as she slid it down his muscular arms.

In Matt's mind the scene from so many years ago was repeating itself as he fought to keep his body from running away. Then, just like Megan, she reached up and slowly ran her fingers through every square inch of his chest, changing the path of his first sexual encounter. Traveling her fingers back up his chest she slid her hands down his arms and captured his hands in hers. Rubbing the palms of his hands with her thumbs, she slowly released the tension in them before guiding them to the bottom of her nightgown and together lifted it up and over her head. With loving hands, she stepped them through an intimate dance until they were poised on the edge of desire and had fully taken in the sight of each other's bodies. Glancing down slowly she clearly saw, in the morning light, the scars that injured him so deeply. He silently prayed she could replace the memory of his pain with a love so strong it dissolved the most vivid images from his mind forever.

Matt wasn't sure what his body was doing. The fear inside of him felt insurmountable because this was the point where he suffered the injuries that constantly made him withdraw from any relationship. His breathing became quick and his body tensed up causing the desire she had built up so easily within him to diminish as she slowly moved her fingers down his chest toward the scars no one else had touched before. He practically squeezed his eyes closed as her hands gently worked their way down his body.

He loved the touch of her hands despite the anxiety that was pouring out of him. She slid them towards his hips, avoiding his scars, before slowly drawing them across his backside and back around to the crevices of his firm thighs. When she moved them along the crease of his inner thighs his body slowly responded until her hands moved closer to his loins. He controlled the urge to grab her hands as she gently touched his partially aroused body. Gliding her hands back up to his chest she placed several kisses down the middle. Feeling her lips on his skin Matt opened his eyes and hung in the warmth and love he saw on her face, causing his desire to increase. As he took in a deep shuddering breath, he felt himself become fully aroused as he knelt before her.

Taking his hands, Megan placed them on either side of her breasts and told him in a soft whisper, "Caress me like you've always dreamed of caressing a woman."

Slowly and gingerly Matt ran his hands up and down her sides before allowing himself the pleasure of engulfing her breasts in the palms of his hands and stroking the tips with the pads of his thumbs. He watched as his touch quickly hardened the tips of each breast causing Megan to arch her back, presenting her aroused body closer to his before releasing a desirable sigh.

Matt had only witnessed and acted out the throes of passion in movies. But watching Megan's reaction in front of him presented his senses with something totally unexpected. She was a beautiful compassionate woman who slowly crept into his life and gradually showed him what his heart had been missing. As she freely expressed the pleasure his touch stirred within, Matt thought for a split second he had caused her pain and withdrew his hands only to have her lean forward and return them to her skin.

Having never made love to its fullest he felt embarrassed by not knowing the truly deep satisfying sounds a woman expresses as his fingertips caressed and explored her smooth taut body. Matt reveled in her carefree and uninhibited ability to share all of herself with him, knowing and trusting he would never hurt her. As she freely gave herself to him, Matt found himself slowly dropping his guard and eagerly began taking in the beauty and pleasure he elicited from her, and in turn allowed his own body to elicit its own uninhibited responses. The sensations she created within him began to arouse not only his emotional side, but his physical prowess. Leaning down to suckle one of her upturned breasts, he allowed himself to enjoy the act he denied himself for so long. He watched her arch her back again and sweetly moan out loud with every passing touch. Playing upon her body, it didn't take him long to soar closer to the precipice of his own self-control.

Leaning forward Megan saw the burning desire fill his eyes. He was painfully struggling with the need to satisfy her and to fulfill what he had denied his tormented body for years. His need to know the extent of his injuries was taking over his fears. Unable to bear the unknown any longer, Matt lowered her onto the bed. With her hands and arms she beckoned him to lower himself down to her. Capturing her lips, he kissed her with a passion he never knew he had. Without any reservations she guided him silently into the confines of her body and introduced him to the sensations that lay within. He restrained himself until Megan brushed his cheek with the back of her fingers and whispered gently, "I'm okay," bringing his focus back to her eyes and away from the fear of the unknown.

The sheer pleasure he felt as she set his hips in motion was like nothing he had ever felt in his life. Bracing his forearms on either side of her head he stared into her lovely face. Like water sailing down an ever-flowing stream, Matt became increasingly lost in this woman. What started out as fear and embarrassment, was slowly turning into something he would never forget.

Matt watched her face as he glided within her body, causing his elation to heighten. Using her hands, she helped him slow down and intensify his desire. All his senses peaked as he lost the battle over his ability to lengthen the sensations that gripped his body. Reaching up to caress his forehead and relax his brow, Megan whispered, "Enjoy the ride."

As those words faded from her lips, she slid her fingertips into the hair at the base of his neck causing him to close his eyes and sigh out loud, as the overwhelming sensations unleashed his essence and he shuddered inside her.

Rolling onto his back Matt laced his fingers through Megan's hand and stared at the ceiling. The fears he had created, along with all the personal barriers came falling down. He bared his whole being to her and in return she opened up and allowed him to discover a part of himself that had been sheltered to protect himself from any further damage. There were no more barriers, no more physical boulders to push through. He was free.

* * *

Megan lay next to him and couldn't believe how freely she expressed her own feelings. She revealed a vulnerable delicate side and allowed herself to be put in a place that required her to fully trust him with her own soul.

When Megan stirred a couple hours later, he was laying on his side watching her lovingly with his eyes. Resting his hand on her stomach, he felt the rise and fall of her breath as her body stirred. Rolling onto her side, Megan slowly played her fingertips down the middle of his chest before gingerly nudging Matt onto his back and straddling his waist. The wonder in his hazel-blue eyes made her own eyes sparkle with delight as she leaned down and kissed his slightly parted lips. She didn't remain there long for she yearned to make a path of succulent kisses down to his most intimate part.

The look of surprise plastered on Matt's face was endearing for she knew he wasn't quite sure how to respond to her quest. He finally took a breath and allowed her free rein of his body. The kisses started at his lips but soon traveled up and down the sides of his neck, stopping briefly to nibble each ear which caused him to shiver. She continued her journey along his collarbone and down his arm, but paused when she reached the scar from his elbow surgery. With the tip of her finger, she traced the faded line before trailing a line of kisses down its path. She then crisscrossed her way down his chest, traveling toward his stomach. The further downward she moved, the more aroused he became, until she knew he couldn't control the fever inside himself any longer. Sighing deeply, he maneuvered Megan's legs around, laid her down, and without over thinking his actions slid into her like fine wine flowing out of a bottle and into the glass.

Megan was completely caught off guard by how quickly her touch caused Matt's body to rekindle. But her startled expression soon turned to pure exhilaration as he took control and wove his way deeper into her heart. He was in complete control as he hovered near the opening of her femininity, tantalizing every square inch of her soul before plunging deep within, causing her to cry out in pure delight.

She had no idea what came over him. With every ounce of his body in control, he drove her higher and higher until she was floating, lost in the clouds. Gliding into her one last time, she felt the firmness of his masculinity before he cried out, "Ohhh, Meg. My Meg." Erupting inside her, he sent them both spiraling down a path they never knew existed. And at the end of the journey Megan was there to catch him, with her arms wide open when he landed.

She was speechless from sheer exhilaration and exhaustion. Never in her imagination had Megan ever conceived that two people could achieve such profound satisfaction pleasing each other's bodies. They laid wrapped in each other's arms as their pulse settled down. But before sleep overcame their weary bodies again, Matt felt moisture hit his shoulder.

Drawing her face level with his, Matt whispered gently, "Did I hurt you, Meg … because I would never …" he trailed off pulling her in closer.

"No, Matt, you did just the opposite … you filled me to the depth of my soul."

Letting out a sigh of relief, Matt pulled the sheet up over their limp bodies and held her in his arms as a state of euphoria filled their essence and enclosed them in a deep peaceful slumber.

Chapter Twenty-One

They slept until the sun crested past noon in the sky. Megan wasn't sure how Matt was going to greet her. Thoughts of shame, discomfort, and embarrassment filled her head for she hadn't fully understood the fear and conflict in this man until he bared the most delicate part of himself in the early morning light. She was the guiding force that drove them into sheer ecstasy and filled their souls. However, when she rolled over to greet him, he wasn't there.

Grabbing a blanket from the chair she wrapped it around her shoulders and padded down the hallway into the kitchen. It was empty, except for the sound of a fresh pot of coffee still brewing. She poured herself a cup and walked over to stand by the sliding glass door leading onto the deck. That's where she found him, silently sipping his coffee.

Opening the slider as quietly as she could, Megan stepped out onto the deck in her bare feet. Fearing the worst, she stiffened her back and slowly greeted Matt by casually placing her hand on his shoulder and whispering, "Hello!"

* * *

Matt wasn't startled, for he heard the door slide open. He was struggling with how to greet the lovely woman who revealed her desires and fulfilled his own without making him feel like a lost soul. Without saying a word, he took her hand in his and guided her around to sit on this lap.

Clasping onto his fingers, she told him quietly, "You were lovely." Matt kissed the top of her head as all the tension he had built up over the past hour rolled right out of his body. He should have expected nothing less. Leaning his chin on her head he whispered back, "Yes, you were. You are one special lady, Meg."

"And you're one very special man," she returned, stretching up to kiss his cheek.

"Sorry, it took me so long to get to this point," he said with his arms securely wrapped around her.

"You had to discover the right path and moment on your own, Matt. Forcing you to make love with me is something I would never do," she whispered into his arm.

"I thank you for that. How'd you get to be so wise?"

"Too much schooling," she chuckled softly, rocking her head from side to side.

Lifting her eyes to his, she was confronted with warmth and gratitude before lowering her head back down to rest on his shoulder. Matt felt her sigh and figured she had been worrying about the same thing.

In Matt's eyes, it was the man's place to guide the woman when it came to making love, but dealing with his physical and emotional intimacy scars over his lifetime and career had made it hard to trust anyone, until now. All the skepticism and fear he had built up over the years was behind him and Megan was the one he would always remember, for she was his first. The sweetness of her voice and her quiet guidance allowed him to learn about his own body's abilities and desires as well as hers. Matt was in love, but he had no idea how powerful a love like this could grow. Maybe one day he'd figure out how lucky he was.

* * *

After sitting in his lap for a long while enjoying the security she felt in his arms, Megan asked the ultimate question, "How long are you staying, Matt?"

"I'm here until late Monday morning."

"Then what would you like to do for the rest of the day?" asked Megan before taking a sip of her coffee.

"To be perfectly honest," he replied, "I'd like to just sit here and hold you."

Megan liked the sound of that, but she needed to run into college to pick up a couple copies of her transcripts. She had taken her uncle's advice and searched online for several programs in LA as well as close to home, but she also needed to talk with Dr. Rhodes about her possible change in plans. She decided not to tell Matt about her options until she finished her MCAT exam. Mainly to give them time to see where this long distance relationship was headed.

Pulling herself out of her thoughts, she said, "Well, as much as I'd like to have you do that, I need to stop at the college to pick up a couple copies of my transcripts for my medical school applications," she informed him.

"Rats!" was all Matt said tilting her head back and kissing her gently.

"Are you going with me?" she asked in between kisses.

"Nothing can stop me from tagging along. What time?" he asked, kissing her nose.

"I think we should eat something, shower and head out the door by two-thirty at the latest."

"Why don't you make that three," he replied with a mischievous look in his eye.

"Matthewww … I don't think I like the way you're looking at me! You seem to have acquired a new found freedom and I'm getting the feeling that I'm the guinea pig," she answered as she slowly set her coffee cup down on the table and tried to quickly get up from his lap.

"But I have," he replied slyly as he nabbed hold of her forearm with a little more force than he intended to.

"Ouch!" yelped Megan.

Matt got up quickly and kissed her arm where he had pinched her skin. "I didn't mean to do that, Meg," he replied looking sincerely into her eyes as he caressed the spot. Leaning down he picked her up and carried her over to the sliding door which she slid open and closed behind them. He carried her straight into the bathroom and placed her inside the shower. Hesitating slightly, he removed her blanket before turning the water on. Removing his robe he joined her and, pinning her against the shower wall, found her lips and drank her fully.

Megan stared at him, knowing what she wanted to do but uncertain about what Matt was willing to let her do in his playful state. He was still a little skittish, but she took a chance and leaning down she picked up the bar of soap and lathered him up.

She could tell Matt was enchanted by the direction she was guiding such an intimate act when she caught the partial grin on his face. She turned it into a moment of exploration, which allowed her to touch every square inch of his body. With his eyes glued on her, he even allowed her to soap up the scars and his loins before placing the bar in his hands.

He gazed at the bar half frozen before looking back into her eyes. Her smile was warm as she reached out and helped him create some suds. Placing the bar back she separated his hands and placed them at the top of her breasts before letting go.

"Did you enjoy what I did to you?" she asked looking back up into his eyes which had gone liquid as pearls.

"Very much! It just dawned on me what I've missed out on. I think I'm going to enjoy taking full advantage of some dearly missed activities," he said with a strange and seductive smile on his face.

She wanted to say, *only with me,* but refrained for fear of suggesting something he claimed he wasn't interested in committing to.

* * *

Matt took advantage of the moment and not only lathered her up, but proceeded to playfully rinse and inspect every inch of her body. He wasn't quite ready to enjoy her body again because his legs were uncharacteristically sore from their love making and the memory of it was still pleasantly floating inside his mind. However, as he rinsed her off, he periodically enjoyed kissing her charming wet lips several times. As he leaned down for another kiss, Megan slipped the hose from his fingers and proceeded to run the water down his back, removing all the soap from his body. Traveling her fingers downward, she worked her way to his toes. On her way back up she paused, startling him slightly, by gently placing her lips over one of his scars. The warmth of her lips miraculously washed away some of the pain he had endured through the years.

With the same care she enclosed her gentle warm lips over the other scar, repeating the process. Slowly rising to her feet, she made her way back up to his chest, rinsing the rest of the soap from his body before stealing a couple wet kisses.

Matt replaced the shower head when she was done and reached for a towel. He wrapped her up and rubbed her down before reaching for his own towel. Wrapping it around his middle, he stepped out of the shower. Megan looked so sweet standing there as she thoroughly dried her legs before rewrapping the towel around her body and disappearing into the bedroom. Matt followed suit after drying, but carried his robe and placed it on the bed before wandering over to his dresser to retrieve a pair of underwear.

It might have been a simple act, but the wide-eyed look on Megan's face in the mirror told him she could get used to his new uninhibited freedom. After getting dressed Matt offered to fix his famous egg sandwich, which they quickly prepared. As they ate, they refrained from discussing the inevitable: when would they see each other again.

* * *

Focusing on the day, they took time to stop by the café to see Kayla and Dan and to pick up breakfast for Sunday morning.

Kayla spotted them first and made her way around the countertop to give Matt a hug and a kiss. Matt still wasn't used to having friends greet him the way Kayla did, but he was slowly getting used to the friendlier greetings.

Dan waved at them from the kitchen and was busy pulling a batch of pastries out of the oven. The smell caught Megan full force and she knew they were one of her favorite flavors, apple.

"Look who's back in town! It's good to see you, Matt," greeted Kayla. "How long will you be here?" she asked.

"I have a flight back to LA late Monday morning," he answered solemnly.

Megan couldn't bear to think about Matt leaving and forced herself to focus on the smell of freshly baked apple turnovers. Making her way around the countertop and back into the kitchen she grabbed a napkin and snitched one off the tray. Juggling it between her fingertips, she walked back out front. She nibbled one corner and presented the other to Matt who took a small bite and ended up fanning his mouth to cool down the hot filling. Megan quickly ran to get a cup of ice water and handed it to him.

"Sorry, hon," said Megan. "I didn't think you'd get any filling on that corner."

Megan watched Matt's eyes widen before it registered what endearment had slipped out of her mouth. He looked a little choked up but proceeded to draw her to his side and kiss her head before saying, "I'll be fine."

When Dan surfaced from the kitchen, he struck up a conversation with Matt about the upcoming baseball season and before Megan could take a second bite of her turnover, Kayla ushered her into the back corner of the shop.

"So, when did Matt get back into town?" asked Kayla.

"Very early this morning, why?" asked Megan.

"Oh … no reason … I just wondered," she replied with a huge smile on her face.

Megan looked at her sideways and suddenly understood her sister's implication.

"Kayla Lorraine Barnes-Chase, what are you implying?" Megan asked.

"You know exactly what I'm implying Megan Amelia Barnes. Did you?"

"Maybe," was all she said, swaying into her sister's shoulder.

"Meg, you do know he's a catch out in LA, right? And to think my sister has taken him off the grid," Kayla said with a smile.

Megan touched her sister's arm and, leaning close, said, "Kayla, I need you to understand something and this has to stay just between you and me. You hear?"

"Sure, Meg. Is it that serious?"

"Matt has suffered some emotional and physical scars and I'd appreciate it if you wouldn't mention what you surmised to anyone. And that includes Dan. Maybe one day I can explain it all to you, but for now you have to trust me and I need your strictest confidence, little sister. Do I have it?"

"Absolutely, Meg," Kayla confirmed without questioning her sister. "Can you tell me if he's okay?"

"Yes, Kayla. He is beautifully okay," she answered, taking her sister's hands and squeezing them lovingly.

Matt walked over with Dan and Megan caught the concerned look on Matt's face.

Dan saw the look too and answered his unspoken question. "This is their usual corner for 'catch me up on your life.'" Matt looked toward Megan with even more concern in his eyes.

"I was filling Kayla in on my schedule for preparing for the MCAT exam starting next week, so she knows where I'll be if she needs me. We were also picking a date for her and Dan to come help me move back into my apartment before the twentieth of March. I can't get over how much stuff I relocated to Aunt Linda and Uncle Paul's over the last several months," she said to an incredulous look from Kayla and Dan. "Well, okay, maybe I can," she said laughing. "Anyway, I'm afraid I'm going to need an extra car."

To her relief the concern that was plastered on Matt's face was short-lived. Come hell or high water, there was no way she was going to break his confidence and trust in her. It was with those thoughts that it hit her, she not only loved him but she was in love with him, not just a little but with the force of a wind storm that just about blew her away. She wanted to hold him in her arms and not let go. Getting up from the table she walked over and slipped her arms around him.

Without giving it a thought, he wrapped his arms around her and kissed her temple, which he enjoyed doing when she came close. "I could get used to this," he whispered, snuggling her closer.

Megan's head spun at the possibilities that comment held, but squelched her feelings determined not to get her hopes up.

"Kayla, could we get four of those apple turnovers to take with us?" asked Matt.

"Sure, let me box them up for you. Do you both want a coffee for the road?"

"Yes, please," they answered in unison before laughing.

Matt paid the bill and they both headed toward the door. As they started to leave the shop a couple recognized Matt and introduced themselves as big fans of his. He paused long enough to say hello and thank them for watching his show. They caught sight of Megan standing at the door waiting for him and inquired about her. Looking at her Matt said, "She's a very dear friend of mine. Now we need to be on our way, but thank you again for watching." Matt joined Megan and placed his arm around her shoulder, as he ushered her out the door.

"Matt, why didn't you tell them I was your girlfriend?" Megan asked, a little dejected.

"With social media the way it is today, it would spread like wildfire, and your name would be everywhere. Your picture already hit social media after the foul ball I caught. I don't want that for you right now. You have to finish medical school and it would be very hard for you to get that done if the media were to find out where you live and constantly be in your face," he explained.

"I'm an adult, Matthew, and very capable of handling myself," said Megan.

"Meg, I've been dealing with the media for years and it's not easy. And I get it. I'm sure a part of you would like everyone to know who you are dating, now that you fully understand the kinds of things I deal with on a daily basis. I know what the tabloids say about me. But if it will make you feel any better, the cast and staff on set know you're my girlfriend."

"Really?"

"Yes, sweetheart."

"I'm sorry, Matt. The little green goblin just reared its ugly head and caused me to show my disappointment."

As Matt helped her into his Jeep, he laughed, "The little green what?"

"Goblin," she repeated.

"It's been years since I've heard that phrase. And if that's as bad as your disappointment gets, then I'm still one lucky guy," he said before climbing in and starting the engine.

* * *

Still lingering with the effects of their love making, Matt decided to pick up a movie from the store in the hopes of cuddling up with Megan on the sofa. Although he had never experienced spontaneity in a relationship before, he decided if something romantic developed, he was going to go with the flow, whatever that was. After running a few more errands they headed home to fix dinner.

About halfway through the movie Matt pounced on Megan, causing her defenses to kick in and knee him in the groin. Matt rolled off her cradling his privates cursing and moaning in pain. He knew Megan wasn't like other women and that apparently included her reactions. But then he had never been the one forcing himself upon the woman.

"What the hell was that for?" he asked, gasping for air, waiting for the pain to subside.

"What do you mean, what the hell was that for?" she replied partially annoyed. "I'm not a sack of potatoes, Matthew. And you still have a lot to learn about engaging a woman when you want to make love."

"Well, thanks for *that* lesson. It just can't start the same way all the time," he grumbled.

"I'm going to try my best to explain this to you, Matt," she said, helping him back to a seated position and slowly removing his hand to sooth his manhood in an apologetic way, which to her relief, he allowed her to do.

"Here it comes. The dos and don'ts of engaging a woman," he practically spit out before wishing he hadn't said anything at all. One of these days it might just sink in that Megan was not like any woman he ever met. This morning should have thoroughly ingrained that into his partially thick skull already.

Sighing at his words, Megan said, "Just like the world of social media is new to me, your newly acquired freedom to explore your desires are new to you. I'm not going anywhere, as far as I know, Matt. But you can't slam every aspect of making love into a long weekend. Once you learn what I enjoy the most and what turns me on will allow us to, for lack of a better word, have a 'quickie' that will drive both of us insane and satisfy our needs. I want to enjoy exploring your body and what turns you on too. But I want to enjoy the journey getting there."

Taking a deep breath Matt drew her close to his side and leaning his head against hers said, "I'm sorry." He felt foolish for thinking her explanation would be anything but accurate. "How do you manage to figure out my intentions like that?" he asked rhetorically.

"It's a gift!" she answered, wrapping her arms around him. "It's been a long day and I'm pretty tired. Can we just lay here and watch the movie? And if we fall asleep, I'm okay with that if you are?"

"I'm sorry," he repeated. "And I'd love to lay here with you and let whatever happens, happen."

"You're forgiven. And I'm sorry about nailing you in the privates. And for the record, both Kayla and I have taken self-defense classes at the request of Uncle Ryan, so sneaking up or pouncing on either one of us is not recommended.

"Now she tells me," he said, shaking his head and sighing.

"Now it's my turn to say, I'm sorry," she said, cringing.

Matt slid down to lay across the sofa and brought Megan with him along with the blanket. After kissing her he held her close. About half way through the rest of the movie he shut his eyes and dreamed about all the ways he wanted to make love to her.

Chapter Twenty-Two

Sunday morning Matt watched the sunlight angle through the sliding door, creating a warm glow around Megan's face. He slowly stirred her with the touch of his hand on her face and slid her body beneath him. He kissed her slowly and casually before traveling down her neck toward the V of her sweatshirt and back up the other side. Placing sweet kisses along her neck aroused his body into wanting more than just a little kissing session, especially when Megan started squirming and stretching beneath him.

He knew she could tell what he wanted in a heartbeat and she didn't deny his advances as he peeled off their clothes and slowly penetrated her body. He wasn't prepared for her acceptance of his desire and reveled in the sensations as they rippled through his body. He savored and controlled every movement until he couldn't hold back any longer and plunging deep within the confines of her body released his essence into her. She moaned and drove her fingers into his hair as her body savored every tantalizing movement, sailing her to the peak of ecstasy.

* * *

Megan couldn't get over how quickly he drove her over the edge and chastised herself for letting Matt stir and fill her desires so easily. She knew he was going back to LA and by granting him knowledge that he could jumpstart her engine, just by touching her, with minimal foreplay, was something Megan didn't want him to know so soon. But her body had other things in mind and betrayed her right to keep her secret, as he soared both of them into the clouds.

Megan loved him fiercely, but the thought of having to let him go again was something she wasn't sure she could handle. If she was ever to fully win his heart and love in return, she was going to have to let him go back to LA. Her Uncle Ryan was right, but it didn't mean it wasn't going to hurt; he needed to figure things out on his own. He was heading in the right direction, in her mind, but she didn't know how long it would take for him to realize she was right for him, if he figured it out at all.

He gradually maneuvered their bodies until she was lying on top of him. After brushing back her hair, he kissed her forehead, then wrapped his arms around her. "Oh, Meg, what am I going to do without you?" he said out loud before catching himself.

"That's a good question, Matt," she answered. "What am I going to do without *you*?" she countered.

"I can't think about it right now, Meg," he replied, rolling his head back and forth.

* * *

But Matt *had* been thinking about their future. It had crept into his brain on the plane ride to see her. Things seemed extremely complicated in his mind right now. He cared for Megan a great deal and following this weekend he truthfully wasn't sure if that bond was due to her capacity to remove all of his apprehensions and fears, regarding his body's ability to satisfy his needs as well as hers, or if he was truly in love with her. He needed time to figure it out. He toiled with the thought of marriage too, which was something that *never* seemed remotely possible before.

Megan slowly sat up and for the first time since Matt met her, he thought she looked lost. With a sigh she forced herself up, collected her discarded clothes, and padded down the hallway to the bathroom. Matt followed suit and together they meandered around the kitchen. Every now and then she would walk up, grab hold of his shirt, and bury her face in his chest. Each time he braced himself, and each time she broke away his heart ached more and more. Moving from one task to the next he found himself needing to steal an occasional kiss, something he never felt the desire to do with anyone else. The contentment he felt with her by his side was starting to consume him and make him wish for a simpler, less complicated life.

When dinner rolled around Matt fixed chicken on the grill and Megan made a zucchini casserole to go with it. They sat at his table in near silence, while their feet playfully interacted under the table.

Finally, Matt spoke, "You going to take me to the airport tomorrow?"

"As much as I'd like to, I don't think I can," said Megan.

"But if you do, we would have a little more time together."

She sat there staring into his deep-set eyes for the longest time, then said, "I understand. But letting you go this time is not the same, Matt," she confessed, dropping her eyes from his face and lowering them to her lap.

"I'll be back, Meg. I can make that promise," he replied.

"But how long do I have to wait for that promise, Matt?" she asked, looking fearful about the lack of emotion and depth in his answer.

"Before spring gets here, I hope. Look, Meg, what do you want from me?" he asked a little more forcefully than he intended because he didn't want to hear the answer.

"Matt, I've never lied to you and I'm not going to start. It was hard enough for me the first time you left. I know I have my MCAT exam and eventually medical school to keep me busy, but what happens when they're over? Do you just keep returning over the spring and fall for the next three or four years and expect me to wait for you?"

Matt hadn't thought far enough ahead to grasp the full ramifications of his request. Instead, he selfishly told her, "Yes." He was trying to arrange more weekends off, but it was hard enough getting away this time. Yet he sensed she wanted more from him, but he wasn't sure about his own future to know what he could truthfully give her. Heck, the only thing he really knew was that he wasn't ready to let her go.

* * *

"Matt, you can't just hold my heart whenever you feel like it. I can't keep ..." but Megan couldn't finish her thought. Her desire to provide him with the one component in his life that he had struggled so long to obtain, apparently made the depth of Matt's love making feel like it was sitting on the surface, instead of piercing his whole being. The pleasures that came along with the act were evidently more physical to Matt instead of the depth of love coursing through her own heart and soul. Remembering her uncle's words again, she knew she was going to have to let him go. She wanted to tell him how deeply she loved him, but she couldn't bring herself to say the words he wasn't ready to hear.

"I think it's best if you drive yourself to the airport. I can pick up your Jeep with Kayla later in the week.

"If you think that's best," he answered softly, reaching for her hand and caressing the back of it.

He's so confused, thought Megan. *Why would he choose to draw himself away after the most romantic weekend he's ever had. Although maybe he doesn't realize how romantic it was.*

"Aw, Meg." he said, pulling her to her feet and holding her tightly. "You will always be special to me. I will never forget you," he said, kissing her on the head.

Megan took a step back and just stared at him. *How could he say such a thing? It's like he's forgotten what he said moments ago, about wanting me to wait for him.* It just further proved, in Megan's mind, that he wasn't sure what he wanted. All of a sudden she felt violated for letting Matt satisfy his need to know his physical capability at the expense of her emotions.

"Meg, I didn't … that didn't come …" said Matt as he watched her place her hand over her mouth and back up even further. As he reached out to touch her arm she brushed his hand away before turning and darting out the door.

After walking through her front door she slammed it closed and sank to her knees before crumpling to the floor. *Where do my feelings fit into this relationship?* All of a sudden it dawned on her how his own emotions traveled like a pendulum, constantly in motion. One minute he was pulling her close and the next he was letting her go.

The tears came at the thought of preparing him for any woman who piqued his interest. *I enabled him to discover what other intimate plea-*

sures he's been missing. "How could you use me like that, Matt?" she yelled to the ceiling.

* * *

Matt was furious with his thoughtless remark and felt like a real insensitive fool. "How could I say such a thing … *never forget you?*" He berated himself as he paced the kitchen floor. "I made it sound like the relationship is over and I don't need her anymore. What a complete jerk I am." he said out loud, rubbing his hands forcefully through his hair. "My reaction wasn't any better than the women I've dated in LA. I finally met someone who allows me to be myself then treat her like her feelings don't matter. This isn't the way this weekend is going to end," he said heading towards the door.

Just as he reached for the handle his cell phone went off.

"What?" he practically yelled into the thing.

"Hey, Matt, just needed to let you know that I moved your flight up to ten o'clock tomorrow morning. They want to shoot the first scene at sunset Monday evening."

"Great! Terrific! Thanks!" he replied angrily.

"You, okay?" asked Kyle.

"What do you think?" responded Matt. "I've got to go, Kyle," he answered more calmly. "See you tomorrow."

Matt thought about texting Megan his flight change, but decided it would only complicate things even more. He knew he made her feel used and he felt awful about it. Turning around he headed to his bedroom, stuffed his clothes into his duffle bag and placed it by the front door. Feeling like too much time had passed to offer Megan any type of worthwhile apology, he walked into the living room and laid his head down on the sofa only to breathe in the scent of her. *What a mess you made, Matthew Thomas Wilson! A real mess!* he berated himself. He rubbed his eyes with his thumb and index finger near the bridge of his nose to stop the tears from forming until sleep consumed him.

* * *

Matt sat in the boarding gate area with his cell phone plastered in his hand regretting his decision not to text Megan about the change in his flight. She had given him so much and asked for very little in return. Driving down to the airport he kept replaying the question he aggressively asked Megan, *What do you want from me?*

He thought he knew how he felt about Megan, that she was the only one destined to guide him without passing judgment, at least that was the conclusion he reached on the plane ride to the cabin. And he was right. But having made love and proven that what he feared the most wasn't true, changed his perspective. He knew she wanted him to tell her how much he cared about her, that he might even love her. But he couldn't do it. He wasn't willing to give her false hope until he figured out his own feelings. His physical emotions were traveling high after making love. He needed to be sure his feelings for her were real, because he wasn't interested in leading her on. *Which is probably what she thinks I've already done,* he thought. Stuffing his phone into his pocket, Matt boarded the plane.

* * *

Megan woke up sprawled across her bed in the morning. Her thoughts were racing as she glanced at the clock on the nightstand to see what time it was. She knew Matt didn't mean what he said last night. They were both lacking the ability to comfort each other, because they were both inwardly struggling with their feelings and how their relationship could possibly work. They needed to talk, despite his hurtful words.

Throwing some clothes on, she made her way downstairs and started out the door. In the time it took her to get dressed, she decided she wanted to take Matt down to the airport, if he was still willing to let her. As she headed down the porch steps she glanced up to find his Jeep gone.

"No," she cried out, dropping down onto the steps. She sat there and cried for a man who truly didn't understand how much she cared for him. But then her doubts crept in and she started to think their whole relationship was superficial and lacking depth, despite all the time they had spent together. Deep down Megan swore there was more to their relationship, although fear has a way of causing people to be oblivious to what their heart already knows.

* * *

It took Megan till the middle of February to regain her focus. She had walked around every day with her phone by her side, in the hopes that Matt would at least send her a text. As the days turned into weeks, and without a single word from Matt since he left for LA back in January, she became despondent; lost in her own world. Kayla tried to get her to talk about him, but she wouldn't utter a word. If he didn't have the time to call or text, then neither did she.

As she regained her focus, she took full advantage of the peace and quiet at her aunt and uncle's cabin to study for her MCAT exam. She dove into studying with a determination that even Kayla hadn't seen her do before. If she wasn't studying, she was spending time shadowing Dr. Rhodes. And if she wasn't in Dr. Rhodes' office, she was in the library studying for her exam. She sat in on as many patients as Dr. Rhodes saw during the two days she was with him each week and absorbed as much as she could about the diagnosis and treatment of various ENT complications. On Fridays, she sat at the back table in the café working on note cards for all the subjects that were covered on the MCAT.

Her time spent shadowing Dr. Rhodes helped her to turn book knowledge into practical experiences in real world situations. He frequently presented Megan with different hypothetical patient scenarios and expressed his delight with her ability to diagnose and recommend the correct care.

"You'll make an excellent otolaryngologist one day, Megan. If that's what you still want to study after medical school," said Dr. Rhodes at lunch one day. "Your father would have been very proud of you," he added.

"Thank you, Dr. Rhodes," said Megan.

"So when are you taking the MCAT exam?" asked Dr. Rhodes.

"I'm scheduled to take it on March twenty-fifth."

"Might I suggest taking a weekend to breathe about two weeks out from your test date, then review your notes one more time. I found that tactic helped me to flush out the information I needed to study a bit more before taking the exam," said Dr. Rhodes.

"Thanks for the suggestion," said Megan.

"I have no doubt you will pass. Your knowledge is excellent and some of the hypothetical scenarios I gave you weren't easy. Now, I have enjoyed your company over the last six weeks, and my patients have been very gracious to allow you to shadow me, but I think you need to spend the next three weeks focusing on studying for your exam," finished Dr. Rhodes.

"Thank you, Dr. Rhodes, I appreciate you letting me spend time with you. I've learned a lot from you," said Megan with a smile before glancing down at her lap.

"What is it, Megan?" asked Dr. Rhodes, picking up on a change in her comfort level.

"Would you be upset if I changed my mind about fulfilling my clinical hours with you during my first two years of medical school?"

"Not at all. I think obtaining your clinical hours in a variety of locations is very wise. Every setting offers a different experience."

"Thank you. I might still want to come back here, but I wanted you to know I was thinking of other options, too," said Megan.

"My door is always open to you, Megan. Now get out of here and enjoy the rest of the day."

As Megan started to get up, her thoughts briefly drifted to Matt and she sat back down again. She really hadn't considered any other locations for her clinical hours since before Matt's departure back in January. She had worked so hard at pushing him out of her mind that when he crept back into it, she teared up.

"Everything okay?" asked Dr. Rhodes as she watched a look of concern settle onto his face.

"I'm sorry. I was just missing someone," she replied.

"Well, you must miss them dearly to tear up like that," said Dr. Rhodes, patting her clasped hands as they rested on the table before he stepped out of the lunch room.

The truth was, Megan missed him every day and feared she would never hear from him again. He needed to come to terms with his feelings, no matter how she felt. She knew what she wanted, and pressuring him into something he wasn't ready to give or didn't want, wasn't the answer, in her mind.

With the date of her MCAT exam fast approaching Megan turned her attention back to studying. She figured Matt had settled back into his life in LA and didn't need her anymore, since she hadn't heard anything from him for the past eight weeks. "Maybe I was right about him using me after all. Well, if he doesn't need me anymore, then I don't need him either," she said with as much conviction in her voice as a person jumping out of a plane for the first time. If she was being honest with herself, she needed and wanted him in her life.

*   *   *

Megan couldn't have been farther from the truth. If she could see Matt with her own two eyes, she would know how miserable he was. He had become curt and dissatisfied with his own acting ability, requiring more takes on a scene then he had ever needed, which frustrated everyone.

"What's gotten into you?" asked Kyle, sitting him down in his trailer. "I've never seen you like this."

"I know," he said, standing up to walk back and forth. "When will this *episode* be done, Kyle?" asked Matt.

"You've got two more weeks, but that could be until the very end of March if you can't get your act together. When was the last time you contacted Meg?" asked Kyle.

"I haven't talked to her or texted her since I left West Virginia!" yelled Matt.

"Why not?" asked Kyle, trying to cool Matt's jets.

"I made Meg think I was done with her and our relationship. And on top of that I left without telling her about my flight being changed or saying goodbye. So, as far she knows, our relationship ended," he told Kyle while raking his fingers through his hair.

"Then maybe we need to change things up and get you out in the field again with someone else," suggested Kyle.

"Were you even listening to me, Kyle?" asked Matt.

"Yes, I was. You made her believe the relationship is over. And if you haven't talked to her in two months, it probably *is* over in her eyes," said Kyle. "So get yourself out there again. You've done it before," concluded Kyle.

"Not that I agree with you, but who do you propose that someone should be?" asked Matt against his better judgment. Annoyed that Kyle seemed awfully quick to suggest dropping Megan off his radar and finding someone else to date.

"I talked to Veronica the other day and she said you went out with someone by the name of Rachel before you left LA. Well, apparently she's back in town and available."

"So …" said Matt shaking his head and rolling his eyes.

"We're planning a gathering on March twenty-fifth, to celebrate the halfway point this season and to give everyone a morale boost, provided you can get your act together," smirked Kyle. "It would be nice if you took a girl with you this time. So, let me know what you decide by next week and I'll text Veronica to invite Rachel," added Kyle.

Rachel was the last woman Matt dated before meeting Megan. She was very cute, but also a little bossy. She was a good actress and caught his attention early last year. They went out on a couple dates together, but when she wanted to get closer his shield went up. Then at the mid-season party last year he found her sitting on another guy's lap. That ended their relationship and he deleted her number from his cell phone.

After grumbling a bit, Matt said, "Fine." Only because Kyle was right about one thing; he could stand to relax and loosen up some. Besides, he was starting to come to the conclusion that Megan wasn't interested in seeing or hearing from him again, despite the fact that he was the one who left without saying a word or attempted to contact her in the last two months to apologize.

"What was that?" asked Kyle.

"I said fine, but I'll meet her at the party," spouted Matt. "Just make sure you tell her we're just going out as friends."

"Absolutely," replied Kyle, but Matt wasn't quite sure he was listening.

* * *

Matt truly didn't know what he was getting himself into when he agreed to meet Rachel at the party. As soon as she saw him, she tried to pick up their relationship where they had left off about a year ago. Kyle had apparently overlooked telling Rachel they were just going out as friends and nothing more. She was constantly kissing him and wrapping her arms around him, as though she owned him, any chance she got. He was continuously pulling himself free and walking over to talk to some of the guys at the party. When it finally got to the point he'd had enough, he told Rachel he was ready to leave. He ended up having to drive her home since she had come with Veronica, who had left thirty minutes earlier with one of the sound guys.

When Matt rolled up in front of Rachel's place, she practically pleaded with him to come in for a night cap. "What you really need is to let the past go and move on with your life, Matt. You can't keep getting a lady's hopes up, then walk away when things start to get intimate. How about spending the night with me?" she asked forthrightly as he walked her to the door with her arm looped around his.

Rachel rattled on as she searched for her keys. "Veronica feels that whatever happened to you couldn't have been that big of a deal. Put the past where it belongs."

Matt bristled as he listened to Veronica's flippant way of describing his personal life to Rachel. Veronica truly knew nothing about his past. *What right does she have to assume the trauma I've been through can be tossed aside so easily?*

When Rachel unlocked and opened her door, Matt followed her inside and closed it with his backside. He stood in place, trying to figure out why he even stepped inside Rachel's house, as he watched her place her purse on the sofa before returning to him and pressing her tall lean body up against his. Leaning in to kiss him, she raised her arms and laced her fingers together behind his neck before slowly driving her fingers into his hair. To Matt's amazement, her actions did nothing to arouse him. Sliding her hands down to his chest she slowly unbuttoned his shirt and slipped it down his muscular arms before flinging it onto the floor behind her.

Matt then closed his eyes and felt her hands travel up his chest before resuming their place around his neck, and in straightforward fashion she placed her lips onto his again. He hadn't spoken a word, but the more Rachel falsely rambled on about his past and tried to engage him into advancing the moment, the more Matt's head spun with growing confusion. When she started touching him where Megan had gently and lovingly ran her fingers several weeks ago, the act suddenly felt unclean. When she reached for his belt and started tugging to remove it, he caught her hands and drove them high into the air. The realization of how much

Megan meant to him, how much he trusted her and how deeply he loved her, hit him like a boulder rolling down a steep cliff at full speed.

"What a fool I've been," he said out loud to Rachel's face as he lowered her hands. "She never forced me to do anything I wasn't ready for, Rachel."

"What are you talking about, Matt?" she asked, sliding her hands up his chest again.

"You need to stop, Rachel," he told her, forcing her arms back into the air.

"I think you need to relax and open up," she responded, trying to wiggle her hands out of his grasp.

"I said no, Rachel!" he replied as he walked her backwards into her living room and slid her over the arm of a chair and into the cushion. Letting her go, Matt turned around, picked up his shirt and headed towards the door.

"You don't know what you're missing, Matthew!" she yelled after him as he started to close the door.

Sticking his head back inside he said succinctly, "The thing is, Rachel, I do know what I'm missing, and I know whom I'm missing it with." Matt closed the door gently and made his way down the walkway.

Once home, he walked inside, closed the door and leaned his body against it. "That, my friend, was the dumbest thing you've ever done. Well, second dumbest," he said out loud.

Peeling himself off the door he made his way upstairs to his bedroom, pulled out his duffle bags and started stuffing a few things in them for the weekend. He wasn't sure if Megan ever wanted to see him again after leaving her the way he had and without a single word for a little over two months, but he had to find out.

* * *

Megan was so caught up in studying that she hadn't noticed how quickly the days had gone by. The twentieth arrived quickly and with Dan & Kayla's help she moved all her belongings back to her apartment. She also heeded Dr. Rhode's advice and took a weekend off from studying to give her head a break and when she picked up her note cards, it revealed a few areas that she needed to focus on.

Megan woke early Friday morning, and packed her bookbag with a water bottle and several snacks. Her MCAT check-in was at eight o'clock in Morgantown at West Virginia Medical School. The test was to begin at eight-thirty sharp and estimated to last a little over seven hours, including a lunch break and two ten-minute breaks. Taking a deep breath, Megan walked into the building. *You've got this!* she told herself.

It was four o'clock in the afternoon when she stepped out into the afternoon sun. Pulling her phone out of her pocket she called Kayla.

"I'm done," said Megan.

"And?" asked Kayla.

"That was the longest test I 've ever taken," said Megan.

"Was it as hard as they say it is?"

"There were several questions I had to really think about, but I knew the terminology for the most part."

"That's great! When will you know your results?"

"I should know in one month, which is right before Easter," said Megan.

"So, what would you like to do to celebrate?" asked Kayla.

"I just want to go home and take a long hot bubble bath," said Megan. "Let's save the celebration until after my score is out."

"Whatever you'd like to do is fine," said Kayla. "Next step, medical school applications. Are you only applying to WV?"

"I'd rather not talk about all that right now, what I need is that hot bubble bath. We'll talk later, I promise," said Megan.

As she was about to place her phone in her pocket it rang. Turning it over she smiled before answering. "Well, isn't this a pleasant surprise?"

"How's it going, Meg?" asked James, her cousin.

"It's actually going great and your timing couldn't be more perfect. I finished my MCAT exam about a half hour ago. Where are you calling from?" asked Megan.

"I'm at my mom and dad's place at the cabin visiting for the rest of this week through the weekend and was wondering if we could meet and catch up with each other?" he asked.

"That would be wonderful! How about meeting me at Kayla and Dan's café tomorrow morning. It's my first day free from studying. Say around eleven o'clock?" Megan asked.

"That'll work out fine. I'll see you then. Do you want me to pick you up?" asked James.

"No, I'm within walking distance, so I'll meet you there," Megan replied.

"Sounds good. Bye," replied James.

"Bye," she said, hanging up the phone, grateful for the visit.

Chapter Twenty-Three

With her exam behind her, Megan's thoughts were free to wander. It had been a little over two months and she hadn't heard a thing from Matt. Even if he came back, she wasn't sure whether she'd want to continue their relationship, considering how he left her, along with his lack of contact. She never pressured him into anything and wouldn't despite how much her heart still yearned for not only his love, but having him in her life every day. He would have to come to terms with his feelings and what he wanted, what made him happy. And if she wasn't part of that equation, forcing him to believe the opposite wasn't an option. She just figured he'd be thoughtful enough to at least let her know.

* * *

Megan and James stepped into the café Saturday morning and claimed Megan's favorite seat in the back left corner. Once they were situated, Megan waved Kayla over to the table.

"Well, look who it is!" said Kayla walking over to greet James with a hug. "When did you get into town?" she asked, peering over his shoulder to glare at her sister.

"What?" asked Megan, not understanding what the look was for.

"I got into town this past weekend to visit my parents before starting my new job in Denver," said James.

Megan watched Kayla turn her attention back to James and say, "That's nice!"

"How about bringing over two spiced apple muffins? They smell wonderful," said Megan. "And maybe two chai teas, if that's alright with you, James?"

"Sounds great!" said James.

Kayla turned and gave her another odd look before walking back to the counter.

After their muffins and teas arrived, James thanked her for keeping his parent's place in shape while they were gone. He began filling her in on his new job when she looked up and spotted Matt walking through the door. Megan was startled, but smiled, then watched Matt's smile fade as he walked towards the table.

Taking a glance at James, Matt turned back to Megan and said, "Apparently, our time together truly didn't mean anything to you."

Before Megan could utter a word, Matt abruptly turned around and stormed out the screen door. The expression on Megan's face changed from elation to puzzlement, as she tried to process what had just happened. Getting up, she darted for the door, but was left standing on the front stoop as Matt pulled away at breakneck speed. Turning around she headed back inside letting the wooded screen door slam behind her. She furrowed her brow as she strolled back to the table.

"What's gotten into him? He didn't even give me a chance to introduce …" she spouted to James. "That's not like him," she fumed.

Kayla came running out of the kitchen when she heard Megan ranting and in time to witness her sister's pacing in front of James, as the other patrons watched.

"What happened, Meg?" asked Kayla as she tried to calm her down.

"Matt came home. He walked over to the table and out of nowhere, blew up at me, accusing me that our time together didn't mean anything to me," spewed Megan.

"What?" yelled Megan when she caught the smile that had taken over Kayla's face. "You remind me of Aunt Linda's expression as I tended to Matt after Bosley knocked him down. I didn't see anything worth smiling about then, and I don't see anything worth smiling about now."

"Meg!" hollered Kayla, grabbing her sister's attention before stepping close to her face. "He's jealous!" she whispered, leaning into her ear.

"Jealous! What the hell does he have to be jealous of, this is …" She paused then realized Matt had never met James. At first, Megan laughed, but that quickly turned back into frustration. "How dare he … he knows me better than that … he has some nerve assuming …" The words came pouring out of her mouth. "Well, he can just go on thinking the worst because he didn't even give me a chance to get two words out."

"Meg, I'm so sorry. I'm afraid this is partially my fault," Kayla confessed. "Matt called and told me he was coming back to town, but he made me promise not to tell you. I told him you've been eating lunch here on Saturday, but I had no idea James was in town and you were planning to have lunch with him. I'm sorry," said Kayla.

"So that's why you were acting so strange when you came over to say hello to James," said Megan. "What am I going to do now?" she said plopping down in her seat. "I know it's been over two months, and I've been working so hard to force him out of my head, but nothing is working," mumbled Megan as her eyes filled with tears. "Then he shows up out of the blue and … and …" she rambled as her tears started making a path down her cheeks.

Kayla placed her hands on Megan's back and tried to sooth her emotions. "I'm really sorry. Had I known you were coming with James, I'd have told Matt. I can't say I wasn't excited about Matt wanting to keep it a surprise." Sitting down and placing her head near Megan's, Kayla whispered, "He's in love, Meg."

James grabbed a bunch of napkins and handed them to Megan. "I feel awful, Meg."

"It's not your fault, James," blubbered Megan.

"I didn't know he'd see the two of you sitting at the table and react the way he did," said Kayla. Leaning over she collected her sister's hands and softly added, "Meg, he's finally figured out how much he loves you."

Megan just sat there unable to speak. Kayla picked her up by the shoulders and steered her outside and into James' car. She was so deep in thought that all she could do was wave to James after he dropped her off at her apartment.

* * *

When Matt walked into the café and found Megan sitting in her favorite back corner with some guy he didn't recognize, it tore his heart right out of his chest. His feelings went from being anxious, straight to disappointment then anger. Seeing her sitting in the café laughing with someone else, created an emotion he hadn't felt before.

Matt floored it all the way up to his cabin. *I know it's been two months, and I know it's my fault for leaving the way I did … but I thought she truly cared about me. I didn't think she'd find someone else so soon. I know I crossed the line myself by going out with Rachel … but that dumb decision made me figure out how much I truly love Meg. Brian was right, the good ones don't last for long. If only I could have realized sooner, what was right in front of my face,* he berated himself.

When he arrived at the cabin he tossed his bags in the foyer and paced the hallway trying to reason with his emotions. *Maybe what I saw wasn't what it appeared to be,* he thought. But that notion flew out of his head when he recollected watching her hand touching the other guy.

He rolled through the shower hoping it would cool down his emotions. Stepping into his bedroom, he took one glance at the bed and couldn't bring himself to rest in the same spot he had made love to Megan. Grabbing his pillow and blanket he tread heavily out to the living room and plopped down in one of the chairs. He tried to relax, but his mind proceeded to race all night long. After finally figuring out his true feelings, only to have them crushed, along with the thought of not having Megan in his life, made him want to withdraw from the public eye and hide. He wasn't getting any younger and the thought of having a family was quickly being washed down the drain.

After a restless night's sleep, Matt packed up his guitar and a few other items he had left behind when he flew out to LA. Having collected his Jeep from the airport's long-term parking lot, he decided he would drive back to LA. He could care less about Kyle's reaction.

Walking into the kitchen, Matt leaned against the island and stared off into the distance for a long while. *I don't know why I blew up like I did, it's not like me to react that way. But seeing Megan with another guy just set off a feeling I couldn't seem to control.* Not knowing how to deal with his emotions and rectify the situation, he quickly decided he wouldn't return to the cabin until next fall, if at all.

When he finally focused his eyes, he noticed that the handmade get-well card was missing from the fridge. The clip had slid diagonally across the door and was partially hanging off the edge. Matt tilted his head slightly and then repositioned the clip back into the middle of the door. As he opened and closed the door, for some orange juice, the clip slid back across the door.

He squatted, then slid his hand underneath the fridge and felt around for the card, but he came up empty handed. Glancing to the narrow gap between the counter and fridge he spotted the triangular tip of a piece of paper barely sticking out.

"I'll be damned," he said, trying to grab it with his fingertips, but the corner of the paper was too small to grasp and he couldn't reach into the narrow gap.

He stepped into the bathroom and returned with a pair of tweezers. After gently pinching the paper, he slowly pulled it forward and watched it unfurl as the front page slipped out before the back half. Brushing off the dust, Matt smoothed it out and returned it to the box on the coffee table. Knowing he wouldn't be heading back for a while, he packed up the box with his belongings and placed everything in the back of his Jeep.

Before leaving he decided to stop by Paul and Linda's to say goodbye and thank them for always keeping an eye on his place while he was gone. After knocking on the door frame, Matt was greeted by the same man he saw Megan sitting with at the cafe. Matt stared at him without saying a word until Paul stepped up behind him.

"Hello, Matt. I don't believe you've ever met our son, James. He's visiting us from Boston on his way out to Denver."

Matt stretched out his hand slowly and said, "Nice to meet you, I'm Matt Wilson. I think I owe you an apology."

James reached out and shook Matt's hand firmly and holding onto it said, "Thanks, but I think you owe Megan one more than me."

"I think you're right," replied Matt as he slowly let go of James' hand. "Well, I just stopped by to thank your parents for keeping an eye on my place when I'm not here. I'm heading back to LA and don't know when I'll be back."

"Linda ... Matt's leaving. Come and say good-bye," Paul yelled down the hallway.

"James told us you were back in town. I'm sorry to hear you're leaving so soon. The neighbors told us how helpful you and Meg were while we were away.

"Yeah, well, I enjoyed helping, but things have changed and I'm not sure how to fix them," said Matt truthfully.

"You'll figure it out. Sometimes the simplest gesture at the right time is all it takes," said Linda with a smile. "Anyway, be safe and I hope things change for the better and we see you soon," said Linda, giving him a hug.

"Thanks, Ms. Linda," he replied, thankful for her kind words.

Walking off the porch Matt chastised himself for assuming the worst when he saw Megan sitting with another guy. *Why didn't she just tell me ... because you didn't even give her a chance, you fool,* Matt said, answering his own question as he walked down the path to the little gate.

Glancing back at Linda and Paul's cabin, Matt thought about Linda's words. Pulling his cell phone out of his pocket he held it in front of his face for several minutes before doing something he should have done a long time ago: text Megan.

Matt could tell the message was delivered; at least she hadn't blocked his number. Not knowing what to do with himself he climbed into his Jeep and having no destination in mind, he drove around while he waited to see if Megan would respond.

Remembering what Ryan told him, that he was among friends and could visit any time, Matt drove all the way to Pleasant Valley Ranch. Sitting in the driveway, wishing his phone would ping, Matt was startled by a tapping on his Jeep window. When he looked up, Ryan was standing outside his car door.

"Made a mess of that one didn't you, son?" stated Ryan bluntly after opening the door.

"Wait, how'd you know ...?" he asked Ryan, completely taken aback.

"Remember, Meg has a sister," was all he said as Matt climbed out of his Jeep.

"It's okay, son," Ryan said, reaching for Matt and holding him in a bear tight hug. "Let's get this all unraveled. It's time for a nice hot cup of coffee on the back deck."

Matt walked out on the deck and placed his hands on the railing, before closing his eyes and breathing in the cool spring air. "Like Ryan said, I made a mess of things," he reiterated as he opened his eyes and scanned the treetops.

He berated himself for taking so long to realize he loved Megan. He knew she loved him by the way she occasionally held onto him, but she hadn't forced him to say what she was longing to hear. She never asked him to say he loved her. It had to be his discovery.

Matt jumped when Ryan's hand touched his shoulder.

"Easy, son," said Ryan, handing him a mug of coffee. "Have you figured out your feelings or do you need to go sit out on Meg's stump to think?" he asked, pointing to a mound that looked more like a rock hidden in the tall grass.

Matt squinted at the stump before his vision took in the whole scenery. "Will you excuse me for a moment?" asked Matt as he placed his mug on the railing.

"Sure, son," said Ryan.

Matt made his way out to his Jeep and returned carrying the box containing his get-well cards. After placing the box on the coffee table he pulled out the handmade card.

"By any chance does this look familiar to you?" asked Matt walking back over to the railing.

Ryan stretched out his hand and collected the card from him for a closer look. Matt picked up his coffee and watched Ryan open the card and read the words. He then stroked his chin with his thumb and index finger.

"This is a long shot, but the view from your deck reminded me of the drawing on this card," said Matt. "Any idea who Peaches is?" Matt asked, pointing out the name written on the card.

Ryan handed the card back to Matt and was quiet for a stretch. "There was a brief period of time after Meg's parents' deaths when she was inconsolable. She could have cared less about comforting others because she needed comforting herself. She needed time to work things out on her own. She finally started coming around after spending time sitting at the top of the hill."

"Are you telling me Peaches is Meg?" asked Matt. He watched Ryan swipe at the corners of his eyes, before gently squeezing Matt's forearm.

* * *

Megan walked into the café early Sunday morning and headed back to the kitchen. While she waited for her MCAT grade to be posted, Kayla asked her if she wanted to work in the café to keep busy. She didn't hesitate to take her up on the offer, since she needed to know her score before she could apply to medical school.

"Mornin', Meg," said Kayla, but she could see the puffiness under her sister's eyes as she wrapped an apron around her waist.

"You okay?" asked Kayla, stepping up behind her and squeezing her shoulders.

"I really don't know," said Megan. "Matt didn't try to call or text me last night. My head is so confused. Here I am, wondering if he's going to reach out or assume the worst and leave again without even talking to me. And if he leaves this time, …" she said, as her eyes filled.

"Aw … Meg. Do you want me to text him?" asked Kayla.

"No … no. He needs to do this on his own, Kayla," said Megan wiping her eyes on her shirt sleeve.

Grabbing a pair of oven mitts, Megan pulled a tray of strawberry turnovers out of the oven. As she placed them on the counter her cell phone went off.

Pulling the phone out of her pocket to take a peek, she was surprised to see a text from Matt.

"What is it, Meg?" asked Kayla.

"It's a text from Matt."

"What did he say?"

Megan paused and contemplated reading the message, but she wasn't sure she could deal with anything he had to tell her. So she stuffed it back in her pocket.

"What are you doing?" asked Kayla. "Aren't you going to read the message?"

"I can't. Not now," said Megan as she reached for a set of tongs to remove the turnovers from the tray.

After the morning breakfast crowd, Megan walked to the table in the back corner and stared out the window. Sticking her hand into her pocket she rubbed the back of her phone debating whether she was even interested in what Matt had to say. Taking a deep breath, she slowly pulled her phone out and opened Matt's text.

Matt: I'm sorry, for everything.

Megan's eyes filled as the screen dimmed. She rubbed it with her fingers and contemplated texting a response, but didn't know what to say to clearly tell him how he had made her feel. Instead, she stuffed the phone back in her pocket, wiped her eyes and refocused on the last few hours of work.

* * *

Without waiting for a response from Megan, and with Ryan and Helen's encouragement, Matt sent Megan another text.

Matt: If you can forgive me, meet me at Roger and Claire's
         stable tomorrow afternoon at three o'clock.

"Okay son, now let's get the horses groomed and the trailer hitched. Then I'm sure you have a few phone calls to make?"

"Yes, sir." replied Matt. But before he got up Helen stepped onto the deck carrying a small box in her hands.

"Matthew," she said softly, walking over to him and handing him the box. "Please open it."

Inside was a small silver ring with three small diamonds across the top.

"Megan doesn't know I have this, but it was her mother's engagement ring. It was left in her mother's will that Megan should be the one to have this when she found the love of her life. And I believe with all my heart that you are that man, Matthew," she said, placing her hand over her mouth to prevent herself from crying out loud as tears filled her eyes.

"It would be my pleasure and an honor, Helen," said Matthew standing to give her a hug and a kiss on the cheek.

Ryan walked over and rubbed Helen's back. "That was lovely, sweetheart," he whispered in her ear before kissing her on the lips. "Now let's see about grooming those horses for tomorrow, Matt."

Matt was up early Monday morning and had a difficult time sitting still. As of six o'clock in the morning Megan hadn't read his second text message. If she didn't at least read his message, he didn't know what he would do. He had kept his feelings for her at bay and now they were bubbling over and he needed to desperately tell her, regardless of how she felt. Putting on his jogging shorts and a long sleeve top he went running to help relieve the tension that was building inside of him.

He ran twenty minutes out before turning around to head back to the house. As he ran back along the dirt driveway he paused at the top of the hill which overlooked the house. The sun was casting a yellow glow over the fields to his right, reminding him of the homemade card, again. Taking a step to jog down towards the house the feeling of déjà vu returned. It swept through his head and created a vivid picture of a girl sitting on the steps to his cabin with her hair in a ponytail. He smiled as the memory surfaced, flooding his senses and connecting the past to the present.

Taking the porch steps by two he headed in to take a shower. Before stepping into the water he checked his phone once more and discovered the message was marked "read." His heart skipped a beat, and he was all at once hopeful for the future, but she still hadn't responded. "Well, at least she read it," he sighed before his hopefulness turned into doubt as to whether she'd show up.

Chapter Twenty-Four

Megan wasn't sure what to think or do. How many different ways did she need to show him she cared about him and he could trust her? And that the person he got to know was real. She thought she was done crying over a past she was sure would never happen. He'd left her causing her to wonder if he would ever figure out how his heart felt. But here she was again crying herself to sleep wondering if he was done testing her honesty. She couldn't keep having her heart ripped apart because of his indecisive feelings. *But if Kayla's right and he is truly in love with me, then all my wandering thoughts are unjustified.* She thought about calling Kayla or even Uncle Ryan to talk things out, but this decision had to be hers, not theirs.

Her thoughts drifted to her mother's poem, that Aunt Linda recited several weeks ago. Then she remembered a conversation with Uncle Ryan, who mentioned coming out to the stump and sitting a spell if she felt the need. *Both allowed me to find my own path. A poem to guide me and Mother Nature to help my grieving heart heal.* As those thoughts rolled through her head the feeling of déjà vu that stirred her memories weeks ago swifty touched her heart and drifted out again.

Not able to make sense of the feeling she turned her thoughts back to Matt's text. If she decided to meet him, it would be an admission that she was at least willing to consider forgiving him. Not just for his reaction at the café, but for not reaching out to talk to her over two months ago. She sat in her apartment in her pajamas, robe and fuzzy slippers all morning staring at her cell phone as if it had the answer, contemplating whether she should meet him. In the end she decided that if she didn't go, she'd regret her actions for the rest of her life.

With her stomach in knots she picked herself up and ran through the shower before getting dressed. She chose a pair of jeans, a white short-sleeved top and a pale green and white flannel shirt

It took her a little over two hours to reach Roger and Claire's place. She was greeted by Claire who ambled towards her with Blue trailing behind her. After Claire gave her a hug, she turned the reins over to Megan and said, "He's up on the mountain."

With a questioning look on her face, Megan slowly mounted Blue and headed the long way around to the mountaintop, where she had taken Matt several months ago. As she rounded the last bend, she caught sight of him. He was standing tall with his back towards her, peering over the edge of the mountain. He was wearing the black cowboy hat she had given him, and dressed in a pair of jeans and a dark green flannel shirt. The sight of him made her breath catch in her throat. He must have heard Blue knicker because he turned around and watched her sidle Blue up to the edge of the mountain top.

* * *

As she dismounted, Matt forced himself to stay grounded. His chest was pounding at the sight of her. He loved her more than anything and would have walked up within inches of her face if he didn't think she would mount Blue and trot away. She stood in front of him holding tightly onto the reins, which gave him the impression she was keeping her options open and would mount the horse and flee if she felt the need.

It took all his self-control to leisurely walk over and stop about two feet in front of her. Her eyes were slightly puffed and he could see the hurt he had caused was still lodged there. It was clear she wasn't going to talk first and make this easy on him.

"I'm sorry, Meg. I should have told you what I was feeling sooner and trusted you," said Matt.

"Yes, you should have," she stated, remnants of hurt and anger clearly audible in her voice.

"I got jealous and scared and thought I had lost you when I walked through the café door. I don't want to lose you, Meg," he said, taking a step closer and catching the scent of her hair on the breeze.

"You hurt me deeply. I've only felt hurt like that once before in my life, when my parents died."

Matt slowly turned and walked back to Cedar. Megan watched him pull out a piece of paper from the satchel bag. Making his way back to her, he held out what she could now see was a handmade card. Her eyes widened.

"Where did you get this?"

"My dad saved all the get-well cards I received when I had my misfortunate accident. I discovered them in a box on the top of my bookcase when I went home," said Matt.

Placing the card in her hands he guided them to open it and read the words inside.

When you're feeling blue
All you have to do
Is look at the trees
And take in the breeze
Nature will calm your soul
Keeping you in control
Making your life
Pure and simple.

Hope you're better soon,
Peaches

Matt watched Meg's eyes dart back and forth as her thoughts traveled back in time.

"It was *you*! You were the one who helped open my heart to caring again. You were sitting in one of the chairs on your front porch and I sat down on the steps. You were the first person I talked to after a very long bout of being angry after my parent's death. I can envision myself laying on the living room floor at the cabin and making this card. Ironically, with the pad of paper and colored pencils that are still in the lamp table drawer," said Megan. "I have this odd feeling that my Aunt Linda remembers something that she's just not willing to share," she added.

"That's right, Meg. And I believe my father and your Uncle Ryan know something too," said Matt, startling her with his response.

"What?" asked Meg. "But why didn't they want to tell me?"

"I think I can answer that, Meg. You were still a teenager and I had just suffered a severe injury. An injury that was demeaning, personal and devastating. I didn't want anyone to know, not even my own brother."

"You mean Brian didn't know …" started Megan.

"Until after I told *you*," finished Matt. "I think they saw that we had a chance at a relationship back then by how we comforted each other when we both needed a friend. But I wasn't ready for another relationship or willing to take a chance with anyone. It was too painful and embarrassing for me to tell anyone what really happened. However, I've come to realize that despite my request to keep my injury private, my father was distraught and needed someone to talk to, since my mother wasn't around," said Matt.

"But that still doesn't explain why they wouldn't tell me the truth," said Megan.

"Don't you see, Meg. If your aunt told you that we *had* met before, you would have started asking questions. Questions about my injury that I wasn't ready to answer and she didn't feel was her right to answer. I needed to be the one to tell you about my injury. When you walked back into my life, I think they thought it was fate that brought us together again. They left it in my hands to build up enough trust in you to reveal something that was devastating and life altering to me."

"Matt, as you already know, my mom used to write lovely insightful poetry. When I talked to Aunt Linda she reminded me of my mom's favorite poem. It talks about the journey of our life and that the decisions we make, along with the guidance of others, helps us find the right path when it's time. I'm glad you walked back into my life," said Megan.

"I'm glad you walked back into mine. But why did you sign the card Peaches? Why didn't you just sign your name?" asked Matt.

It was another missing piece to the puzzle. "I wonder how things would have unfolded if I *had* signed my real name?" said Megan. As tears formed in her eyes, she continued, "That's what my father called me. Whenever he caught me comforting someone he'd call me a Peach. It was you, along with my mother's insightful poetry and my father's constant caring examples that pushed me through my grief and allowed me to start comforting others again."

"Well, finding your homemade card was a stroke of pure luck. And the fact that my father kept it was serendipitous to say the least," said Matt.

"It's obvious I didn't inherit my mother's poetry skills," said Megan as she glanced at the words again.

"Well, the poem you wrote inside this card proves the complete opposite is true," said Matt. "It's like our lives were destined to come full circle at a time when we were both ready and needed each other, again. And I need you, Meg."

"I need you, too, Matt."

Taking a step closer, Matt reached for Megan's hands. As he caressed the tops of them with his thumbs he said, "You consoled me when you were a teenager, and have comforted me as a wonderful caring and loving woman."

After taking a breath he continued, "I was a fool, Meg … I was so fearful that my feelings for you were a result of my physical healing that I needed to be sure they were genuine. Those fears caused me to say something callous, which made you run away. Believe it or not, this foolish and fragile man standing in front of you is admitting that he's in love with you. My heart has been hurting terribly since I left, and I never want to feel that way again," he told her, squeezing her hands a little too hard, fearful she would slip out of them.

"Well, I wasn't going to force you into saying or doing anything you weren't ready for," said Megan, taking a step closer as the tears rolled down her cheeks. Reaching up she placed a gentle hand on Matt's cheek and added, "I've been waiting to hear those loving words from you for months. But you had to figure things out on your own, just like the meaning of my mom's favorite poem. And if you don't know it already, Matt, I'm in love with you."

Reaching up Matt placed his hands along the sides of her face, and after brushing away the moisture on her cheeks, he drew her close and sweetly placed his lips on hers. Standing on the highest peak in the hills of West Virginia, under a breezy spring sky, Matt cradled her head in his arm and passionately kissed her, dissolving all his doubts and fears which had consumed him and driven them apart. As he slowly released her, he ran his hands down her arms as he got down on one knee and peered up into her lovely face.

"Megan Amelia Barnes, would you do me the honor of being my wife? Will you marry me?" asked Matt, giving her hands a gentle shake.

Matt watched as fresh tears filled Megan's eyes before she looked up to the mountain tops and yelled, "Yes, yes, I will marry you Matthew Thomas Wilson!"

As she dropped the reins from her hands Matt reached into his pocket and pulled out the ring Helen had given him. Megan recognized it immediately, as he placed it on her finger. Glancing towards the sky again, she smiled and mouthed, thank you, for she knew her parents had been watching over them.

What they had been searching for was lost in a moment in time when their lives had been turned upside down. They only needed to step back into a life they had both worked so hard to push aside, to rediscover a connection that their inner hearts and heads already knew existed. Not until their lives crossed paths again, was Matt able to finally figure out what he was looking for all his life. A woman who would help him overcome the trauma of his past, build his trust in the present and guard his heart in the future.

"Meg, I came here thinking I needed to return to the simpler lifestyle I grew up with, but what I really needed was to find someone who had the patience to help me work through all my insecurities and fears. You captured my heart and touched my soul. What I needed was your love — pure and simple."

Collecting her in his arms Matt kissed her with a fervor that toppled them over into the sweet springtime grass. Lost in their passion for each other, Matt took complete possession of her. Savoring every square inch of her while she drove him to the point of no return. And for once, Matt revealed his longings and desires as they made unbridled love on top of that mountain, where he left his insecurities and discovered how powerful real love could be.

"I love you, Meg. With all my being," said Matt as he lay staring up at the sky.

Reaching over, he collected Megan up in his arms as she said, "I started falling in love with you when you first kissed me up here on this mountain top six months ago.

"Why didn't you tell me?" asked Matt, turning to look into her eyes.

"Because you weren't ready," said Megan truthfully.

"You're a very wise woman," he said, securely wrapping her up in his arms.

"So, where do we go from here?" asked Megan.

"What did your mom's favorite poem say, again?"

"That we'll figure things out when it's time."

"Right here, right now is the moment in time I don't ever want to forget," he said, kissing her forehead. "We'll figure the rest out in time, together."

About the Author

Cyndy lives with her husband in Carroll County, Maryland. Her love of books and reading began with many trips to the public library. When she was in elementary school, she would staple little pieces of paper together and create stories.Her love of reading continued to grow into high school, where she became a Library Aide.

Cyndy has a Bachelor's Degree in Communication Disorders and a Master's Degree in Audiology. She currently works in an elementary school library, where her love of books is shared with all the students and teachers who walk through the door. Her hobbies include scrapbooking, genealogy research, gardening and numerous crafts.

If you enjoyed this story,
keep your eyes out for Cyndy's next book,

Longing for Love

Rebecca Stevens wasn't looking for a relationship. Frankly, given her career as a 911 Dispatcher, she figured no one could handle her ever changing schedule, and that's exactly how her ex-fiancé, Jack, had made her feel, and that was nearly three decades ago. Rebecca loves her job and at her age, her life was settled; at least she thought it was, until she meets Holden. His empathetic ways stir Rebecca's emotions in a way she never imagined.

Holden Fields knew the likelihood of finding a woman who would give him a chance, given his past, was slim. That type of woman just didn't exist; he had never been that lucky. Then Rebecca walks through the door and the possibility of a loving relationship, one he has longed for, has a chance of becoming reality.

But when Holden's past starts to unravel in front of his face, will he find the courage to reveal his bumpy past — or will he end their relationship without allowing her the chance to decide for herself?